Praise for *The Unfortunate Englishman*

"Lawton gets the Cold War chill just right, leading to yet another tense exchange across a Berlin bridge, but unlike, say, the film *Bridge of Spies*, the principals here are not freighted with moral rectitude but, rather, exude a hard-won cynicism in conflict with dangerously human emotions. The result is a gripping, richly ambiguous spy drama featuring a band of not-quite-rogue agents that will find genre fans reaching for their old Ross Thomas paperbacks to find something comparable." —*Booklist* (starred review)

"Both series benefit from the excellence of Lawton's writing . . . All these adventures arrive gift-wrapped in writing variously rich, inventive, surprising, informed, bawdy, cynical, heartbreaking and hilarious." —Patrick Anderson, *Washington Post*

"Even reviewers have favourites and John Lawton is one of mine. Nobody is better at using historical facts as the framework of a really good story." —Jessica Mann, *Literary Review* (UK)

"Lawton [is] possibly one of the most under-appreciated British espionage writers . . . Nowhere as heroic as Le Carré or Deighton, Lawton confronts the absurdities and weaknesses of his highly fallible characters alongside the dangers of the Cold War. Endearing and all too human, as if Smiley was both morally flexible and at times a figure of fun!" —*Love Reading*

"John Lawton . . . manages to weave together all the elements of a le Carré-style Cold War thriller with the tough strands of good old-fashioned criminality. Joe Wilderness is every bit as brave, clever, devious—and anti-heroic—as the most famous black marketeer of all—Harry Lime himself." —*Crime Fiction Lover*

"Lawton's characters are so intriguing, they will undoubtedly send the reader looking for the first in the series, *Then We Take Berlin*. *The Unfortunate Englishman* is a spy novel in the best le Carré fashion . . . the chillingly realistic mind-games, intrigue, and political maneuvering of the Cold War era . . . Beautifully done and well written. Lawton deftly picks up the loose ends of the story and weaves them into a captivating narrative that keeps the reader hooked . . . An informative and entertaining read."

—*Killer Nashville* (Book of the Day)

"[A] stylish new espionage thriller . . . Joe is as smart, conflicted and cynical as any Raymond Chandler character . . . It's hard to find a more fascinating time and place than Cold War Berlin, but Lawton still uses his narrative skills to transform history into gripping fiction . . . Lawton is a master at weaving the historical facts into the threads of his fictional story and bringing both to vivid life."

—*Read Me Deadly*

"[A] stylish, richly textured espionage novel . . . With *The Unfortunate Englishman*, Lawton shows himself to be the master of colorful, unpredictable characters . . . His crowning achievement is Joe Wilderness [who is] loaded with personal charm and animal magnetism . . . Lawton brilliantly weaves real historical events into the narrative . . . His novel is a gripping, intense, inventive, audacious, wryly humorous, and thoroughly original thriller."

—*Open Letters Monthly*

"The tone of unsentimental realpolitik means *The Unfortunate Englishman* earns the right to that le Carré-esque title . . . A complex and beautifully detailed tale, a full-blooded cold-war spy thriller given an added dimension courtesy of Wilderness's quirky humour and his pragmatic take on morality and honour."

—*Irish Times*

"For those who want a bit of substance to their thriller reading . . . This is an atmospheric and convincing novel . . . The plotting is complex . . . [and] enjoyable, and few authors are as good as Lawton in framing their novels around interesting historical facts . . . Wilderness is a very engaging hero . . . The period detail is subtle and convincing and there are also some nice touches of humour and fascinating glimpses of real historical figures . . . A treat from beginning to end."

—*Sydney Morning Herald*

THE
UNFORTUNATE
ENGLISHMAN

Also by John Lawton

THE UNFORTUNATE ENGLISHMAN

A Joe Wilderness Novel

John Lawton

Grove Press
New York

First Grove Atlantic hardcover edition: March 2016
First Grove Atlantic paperback edition: March 2017

Published simultaneously in Canada
Printed in the United States of America

FIRST EDITION

ISBN 978-0-8021-2635-1
eISBN 978-0-8021-9067-3

Grove Press
an imprint of Grove Atlantic
154 West 14th Street
New York, NY 10011

Distributed by Publishers Group West

groveatlantic.com

17 18 19 20   10 9 8 7 6 5 4 3 2 1

for the blokes
whom chance encountered

Bruce Kennedy

Artigiano straordinario

Robert Etherington

L'Uomo in una mongolfiera

I

Wilderness

Why all this fuss about one of the oldest
and most useful professions in the world?

—Author unknown

Letter to the *Times*, May 1960

§1

He took Berlin.

Wilderness had done stupid things in his time. Stupid things. Unforgivable things. The only person who would not forgive him this time was Wilderness himself.

He took Berlin.

Why, after all this time, had he got involved with Frank Spoleto again? Was once not enough? Had he not learnt the lesson? You can lead a horse to water but you'll never make him trust anyone called Frank?

He took Berlin.

It was a ludicrous scheme from the start . . . to smuggle a nuclear physicist, a veteran of the Manhattan Project, out of East Berlin using the same tunnel they had used to smuggle coffee, sugar, and God-knew-what during the airlift in '48. Ludicrous? Crazy. Just asking to get caught.

He took Berlin . . . Berlin took him . . . Wilderness was in the Charlottenburg nick, on the Ku'damm. He'd denied everything. He wasn't at all sure how long he could keep this up.

Shooting Marte Mayerling had been a mistake. She'd slipped behind him dressed as a rubble lady, a *Trümmerfrau*, and he'd shot on instinct, shot on memory. For a moment, too long a moment, he and Nell Burkhardt had stood riveted to the spot, unbelieving, her hand wrapped around his. Then the mirror cracked and he had ripped up his shirt to stuff a finger in the dam wall and stanch the flow of blood. Nell had got rid of the gun. Surely she had? With any luck it was gone for good. He'd never see the gun again. He'd never see Nell again.

Berlin took him.

A squad car. An ambulance. A vanload of coppers. Then the slow crawl, hand on horn, honking a way through the surging crowds of Kennedy supporters back to the Ku'damm. A grey cell and black coffee.

As coppers went, this lot were civilised. No one had hit him, no one had so much as raised their voice to him. He had not asked for a lawyer; he had simply asked, repeatedly, that they charge him or let him go. For all his time in Berlin he still had no idea how long they could hold him. Only when the shift had changed and a day copper, a burly sergeant in his forties, had recognised him from the old days just after the war—"You used to sell me black-market NAAFI coffee. You *und* liddle Eddie. *Im* Tiergarten"—did it begin to seem inevitable that a chain of connection and causality would be set off that would lead him to this moment. The moment Burne-Jones walked in.

"You should have sent for me at once."

"I resigned two years ago. You surely haven't forgotten?"

"You know, Joe, when I have your balls in my fist, sarcasm is really rather ill advised."

"Alec, I would never have sent for you. It's all too . . ."

"Too what? Too bloody familiar?"

Wilderness could not deny that.

It wasn't just familiar; it was almost a carbon copy. Tempelhof, or thereabouts, that cold autumn of 1948, the height (or was it depths?) of the blockade. Lying in a makeshift, prefab hospital in the American Sector with a Russian bullet in his side. Rescued, promoted to a rank he'd never surpass, and thoroughly bollocked.

"Sign here."

"Eh?"

"Sign on the dotted, Joe, and all this will just go away."

Wilderness read the page in front of him.

"So . . . I'm re-enlisting?"

Burne-Jones said nothing. Just stared back at him, accepting no contradiction.

Wilderness turned the page around to show him.

"There's a typo. The date's wrong. You've typed 1961 instead of 1963."

"Just sign."

"If I sign this, it's as though I never left. It's dated the same day I resigned."

"Quite."

"Quite my arse. It means all the time I've been here I have technically been working for you."

"And how else do you think I could get you out? The West Berliners want your guts for garters. You were found with a half-dead woman clutching a smoking gun."

"No, Alec, that is not the case. There was no gun."

"Oh. Got rid of it did you?"

Wilderness said nothing.

"Well . . . it will put in a ghostly appearance when these dozy buggers get around to testing your clothes for powder residue, so I suggest we get out now. They won't like it; after all it's a stark reminder that they don't run their own city and that what we and the Americans say counts for a damn sight more than what the chief of the West Berlin Police says. Sign, and it, whatever it is, becomes an Intelligence matter. Sign and walk, or keep up this nonsensical surliness and get charged with attempted murder."

Wilderness signed.

The sense that once again Alec Burne-Jones had him by the balls was palpable. A tightening in the groin demanding all the flippancy he could muster.

As they stepped out into the summer sunshine on the Kurfürstendamm, Wilderness blinked, looked at Burne-Jones and said, "You owe me two years' back pay."

And Burne-Jones said, "Joe, how exactly did you get rid of the gun?"

§2

The zoo, West Berlin: June 26

Marte Mayerling might well die. Wilderness dropped the gun, threw off his jacket and tore at the tails of his shirt to stanch the flow of blood from the wound in her side.

Nell seemed frozen, standing over him in silent shock.

Marte Mayerling was far from silent.

"So, he shoots me . . ." over and over again, a mantra of delirium, the deathly high that is blood loss.

"Nell . . ."

"Joe?"

"Take the gun. Take my passport and go."

Nell snapped out of her trance and rummaged in his jacket for the passport.

Wilderness took his hands off Mayerling for a moment, the blood surging up again, slipped out of his shoulder holster and threw it to Nell.

"Get to the zoo station, call an ambulance and then disappear."

"Disappear?"

"Nell, vanish . . . you were never here."

He pressed down on the wound. Mayerling's insane chant grew softer and softer. She might die on him any minute and the only plus to that scenario would be her silence. She might die before the ambulance arrived. She might die just to spite him.

Time melted at his fingertips. He had no idea how long he leaned on her. His hands went numb. Fifteen minutes? An hour? It seemed to him an age since she had spoken. He heard the sound of sirens approaching, and Mayerling stirred again, one last croaking complaint of "He shoots me . . . so he shoots me . . . " Then they were there, a white-suited ambulance crew, a huge Daimler ambulance and seconds behind them West Berlin coppers in their tiny Opel, guns at the ready.

§3

West Berlin: June 28

"Not going to tell me, eh?"

They headed back along the Kurfürstendamm to the Kempinski Hotel. The summer light still striking Wilderness like pinpricks after a day and a half in windowless cells. He wanted out of the ill-fitting clothes the West Berlin Police had lent him when they'd stripped him of the remains of his blood-soaked suit. He wanted a bath and breakfast. Burne-Jones wanted answers he was never going to get.

"Alec, there was no gun when the cops got there; that is all you need to know."

"Fine, Joe. Just tell me they'll never find it. They're dredging the Landwehr. Tell me it's not there."

"It isn't. All coppers are thick. German coppers might be thicker than most. I'm not. Dump it in the canal? Not bloody likely."

Coffee never tasted so good. A delightful morning scorch. There was a time, an age ago, when Wilderness had smuggled so much coffee the smell clung to him, unscrubbable, and set dogs barking in the street. And for a while he found he could not bear to drink the stuff. He brought home exotic teas, stolen from the PX or the NAAFI . . . Jacksons of Piccadilly's "Finest Earl Grey." Nell had asked who Earl Grey was. He'd no idea, now or then.

The dining room at the Kempinski was almost empty. They caught the last shift of waiters serving breakfast, and over scrambled eggs and croissants he told Burne-Jones as little as he thought he could get away with.

Every so often Burne-Jones would put a hand to his forehead as though about to mutter "Jesus wept," but he never did. Wilderness did not mention the fifty thousand dollars Frank Spoleto had promised him, now floating off up the Swanee. He did not mention Nell, and in conclusion, dismissed his attempt to smuggle Marte Mayerling, nuclear physicist, from East Berlin to Israel as "a bit cockamamy."

At last Burne-Jones said, "Frank Spoleto cooked this up?"

"Frank . . . and the Company."

"It's not as cockamamy as you might think. Not that I could see our people approving, but it has a certain . . . *je ne sais quoi* . . . a certain 'balls' to it."

"Do our people need to know?"

Burne-Jones strung this one out. It seemed to Wilderness that he wanted to inflict some semblance of punishment on him—the price of rescue.

"Need to know? No. Do they know? That's a tricky one. The copper who recognised you went through channels to find me. Showed initiative, contacted 'our man in Berlin,' Dick Delves, whom I can assume you assiduously avoided . . ."

"Damn right I did."

"But I have no idea how many ears pricked up between here and London at the mention of your name and a dead German woman."

"She died? I thought you said 'half-dead'?"

"No . . . half dead is half alive after all. 'Dead' was just an assumption on someone's part. She pulled through. She's in the hospital on Kantstraße. You probably saved her life. I gather they pumped endless pints of blood into her and she's stable. Nobody knew her name, she had no papers on her, and you were saying nothing, but when she came to she told them she was Hannah Schneider, and I assume that was the cover name you or Spoleto assigned her. I wasn't wholly sure who she was until you just told me."

"Shocking, isn't it?"

"Quite. And I rather think I have to get you out of Berlin before honesty overtakes her and she tells the coppers who she really is."

Wilderness could not think why she hadn't told them already.

"I need a little time."

"You don't have any time."

"A day, two at the most. There are loose ends. You have been telling me for nearly twenty years now never to leave loose ends."

"Joe, go back to London. Go back to London and look to your marriage."

"To my marriage?"

"Why? Do you think I could conceal from my own daughter that you were in jail?"

"We've both of us a cellarful of secrets from our wives."

"Quite. But this could not be one of them. Go home and repair your marriage."

The inherent conflict between the roles of boss and father-in-law had almost never surfaced in the eight years Wilderness had been married to Judy Jones. It required juggling, and juggle they both did. But it sat like a stubborn knot in the old school tie between them now. Wilderness wondered which Burne-Jones he was appealing to as he said, "Tomorrow, I'll get myself back to London—tomorrow. I'll fix whatever needs to be fixed. But if you spirit me away today, it will come back to haunt us."

Burne-Jones abandoned the attempt to stare him down, got up from his chair all but sighing, and whispered a parting "My God, Joe. What have you done?"

And from where Wilderness sat that seemed all too familiar.

§4

He could have let her die. He could have let her die but the thought had not crossed his mind until now. He could have walked away and let her die, vanished into the crowds chanting "Ken-ne-dy!" and no one would be the wiser. But the thought had not crossed his mind until now.

He walked the half mile to the hospital, the litter from the Kennedy celebrations strewn everywhere, blowing in the wind, gathering in the gutters. He'd glanced at the front page of the *Tribune* in the bar at the Kempinski. JFK's rapturous reception, the made-for-TV tag line "*Ich bin ein Berliner*." And he could hear Nell's voice in that. Her habitual cry, her ethical position, her reason to come back to the ruins of Berlin summed up in four words. He could see the last of Nell, walking—no, running—away from him as he knelt over Marte Mayerling, nursing the wound he'd inflicted on her.

Now—looking down at Marte Mayerling. Still and silent, a drip in her right arm, an oxygen tube clipped to her nose. A nurse who had told him to keep it brief.

Her eyes flickered open, took in the man before her.

"Again, Mr. Johnson? Again? What could you possibly want with me?"

She spoke in English. Just as well. Wilderness wanted as few people as possible within earshot to understand what he or she might say.

"What can you possibly want from me?"

"Not much. Just to see with my own eyes that you were alive."

"So, you didn't mean to kill me?"

"I've only ever killed one man. And the only man I've ever wanted to kill killed himself before my eyes."

"Ah . . . I understand now. I am to receive your confession. I am to absolve you of your sin."

It took a moment or two before Wilderness realised that the wheezing cackle arising from her throat was laughter.

He turned to leave; there was nothing more to be said. Inwardly he kicked himself for the weakness that had led him there.

"Mr. Johnson."

Wilderness turned back. As much as she could, Mayerling had twisted her neck to see him more clearly.

"They tell me I will live. I may be here a week or more, and after that weeks more in recuperation."

It was at this point Wilderness thought she might be waiting on the words "I'm sorry," which he was never going to utter.

"I will have ample to time to reflect upon my folly and yours. No matter. I doubt I will change my mind. So I will give you the reassurance you seek but will not ask for. It was a scheme thought up by madmen. I was an idiot not to see it for what it was. You were an idiot not to see it for what it was. But it is over. I shall live and you shall face whatever fate awaits you, but it is over. No bomb, no Israel. *Genug.*

"I am an Austrian. Austria exists once more. I shall go home . . . not a word I ever thought I would use again . . . feel again. I shall go home. If you have a home, Mr. Johnson, go to it. Go to it and count yourself lucky."

Again Wilderness turned to leave. Again she called him back.

"Mr. Johnson? That is not your real name. Do you have papers in the name of Johnson?"

"Of course."

"Forgeries?"

"Only insofar as I'm not James Johnson."

She pondered this a second, and it seemed to Wilderness she had discerned his meaning.

"But you can obtain forgeries."

And he hers.

"What name would you like, Dr. Mayerling?"

"Hannah Schneider of course."

Of course. He and Frank Spoleto had renamed her.

"German?"

"Austrian. Born second of May 1913. My real birth date. Then I won't forget it. Can you do this?"

"Yes."

"And get it to me?"

"Someone can bring it to you, yes."

"Then . . . strange as it may seem, Mr. Johnson, I wish you well. Bon voyage."

§5

Everyone was telling him to go home.

He went instead to a building that had been home for nearly two years not long after the war, to Grünetümmlerstraße, where he and Nell Burkhardt had lived like squirrels in a sprawling room under the eaves, freezing in the fuel-starved winters of Berlin's broken years and sweltering in the summers. On the floor below them had lived, and still lived, Erno Schreiber.

Wilderness stood on the top floor in the empty room, looking at the scars of past lives, of the lives he and Nell had had together, mentally replacing every stick of furniture. He'd come to Berlin with no expectation of seeing Nell and none that she would want to see him. Seeing her at all just before the Hannah Schneider cock-up had been chance—pure chance and disaster.

Erno must have heard his feet on the bare boards and shuffled up the stairs, carpet slippers and cardigan, whatever the weather.

"Eh, Joe."

"What have you heard, Erno?"

"Come downstairs. I have a fire of nicely burning evidence. Come warm yourself at the flames of guilt."

Light scarcely penetrated Erno's room. The seasons never changed. Something always to be concealed from the sun, something always needing to be consumed by fire.

Erno stuck a mug of black coffee in Wilderness's hands, flicked open the stove door, raked through the "evidence." Eulenspiegel the cat wove his way between Wilderness's legs, motor running.

"I heard," Erno began. "That things did not go exactly as planned."

"Nell?"

"Yes. Nell. She came here before breakfast yesterday. I have your gun and your passport—the fake I made you in the name of Schellenberg."

"Keep 'em, Erno. Just in case hang on to them."

"Will anyone come looking?"

"Doubt it. Burne-Jones is here to bail me out. And Marte Mayerling wants to put it all behind her."

"Großer Gott. Why?"

"I don't know. What was it you said about masks? About Hannah Schneider being the assumption of innocence on her part?"

"Not quite. Are you saying she wants to stay as Hannah Schneider? To become Hannah Schneider?"

"Oh yes."

"And how do you know?"

"I went to see her in hospital, the one on Kantstraße."

"Oi, Joe."

"She wants a passport in her new name. Austrian, born second of May 1913. I'll pay. Can you do it? I don't have a photograph. You'll just have to bluff your way in there."

"Perhaps a bedside visit from her old 'Uncle Otto' and his trusty little Minox camera. But I shall have to bite my tongue to avoid asking her a thousand questions. It is most intriguing."

"You said it yourself . . . something like 'it is Freud's own mask.'"

"Joe, I say so many things."

"Don't piss on it, Erno. You know what I'm talking about. So why is she doing this? Why is she not screaming it all from the rooftops? Where is your man Freud in all this?"

Erno shrugged, stared into the fire for a moment.

"From middle age onwards, and you are not yet there my boy, life is perceived as a series of regrets. I know few middle-aged men who do not have a mental checklist of life's might-have-beens. I know men to whom you could sell second chances . . . like some goblin in a Grimms' tale . . . popping up to tell you that every mistake you have ever made can be undone . . . that the second chance is there for the taking. You maybe did not know it, and I am damn sure Frank Spoleto didn't, but when you dangled the prospect of freedom in front of Marte Mayerling you held up second chances the woman never knew she wanted. After all, regret is such a male notion. But, she is a woman in man's world . . . beating men at their own game. And on some other level of consciousness, I will not go so far as to say 'unconscious', the freedom she wanted was not to split more atoms, to make more bombs, it was to be Hannah Schneider. Frank chose the plainest of Jewish names and in so doing gave her exactly what she did not know she wanted."

"When she came out of the tunnel . . . I didn't recognise her . . . she was dressed as Hannah Schneider, a dowdy little Jewish hausfrau . . . she looked like . . . like . . ."

"Like Yuri Myshkin the night he shot you back in '48?"

"Yes."

"So you shot first?"

It didn't need an answer.

"Speaking of Major Myshkin, I also have . . ."

Erno reached to the mantelpiece above the stove. Handed Wilderness a rusty key.

Wilderness looked down at the key to the tunnel's entrance in the Soviet Sector nestling in the palm of his hand.

"Nell left it with the gun and the passport."

"She must have found it in my pocket. I wonder if she even knows what it is."

"Am I to keep this too?"

"Why not? A souvenir of human folly. As Dr. Mayerling said . . . it was a scheme dreamt up by madmen. I can't imagine I'll ever need this again."

"Who knows . . . folly is like regret . . . it knows no limits."

Wilderness turned the key over in his hand, said, "I need to see Nell. Can you tell me where she lives?"

"No, Joe, I cannot. She expressly told me not tell you. Joe, she doesn't want to see you again."

The biggest regret in Wilderness's life, the what-might-have-been, was Nell Burkhardt. Perhaps at thirty-five he was more middle-aged than Erno might ever imagine. To Erno he might seem impossibly young, too young to have regret, too young as yet to be haunted by the ghosts of the living.

He said nothing. He knew he could con, trick, or cajole Nell's address out of the old man, but he wouldn't. He could go round to the mayor's office in Schöneberg and catch Nell at her work. But he knew he wouldn't do that either. He would go home. "Home," a word for him that had so little of the resonance it now seemed to have for "Hannah Schneider."He stood up, took two hundred dollars from his wallet and put them under a candlestick on the mantelpiece. And noticing a large, square-headed nail protruding from the wall above the candlestick, he hung the key on it.

"Too many symbols for one day, Erno."

He'd go home now.

§6

London: July 1

Few women Wilderness had ever met could do rage like Judy Jones. Every year or so he'd make a trip to Petticoat Lane and restock the kitchen with cheap crockery to make up for plates thrown at him in the course of uxorial dispute. Every three months or so he'd slink off to one of the spare bedrooms and give her a fortnight's cooling off before the inevitable reconciliation, which would begin with "You're just being silly" or "Can't we talk about this like grown-ups?" to which Wilderness would reply "We can talk about anything when you stop throwing things."

She hugged him on the doorstep. Flung the door open before he could even take his key from the lock. Arms around his neck, head pressed to his chest. And was that a hint of tears in her eyes?

She drew back, and yes a tear was wiped away.

"I've been so worried. Dad said you were in prison."

"Jail not prison."

"And then he came back without you."

"I'm here now. Any chance I could come in?"

This made her smile.

"You'd better. I want to know everything, and I'd rather not broadcast it to the neighbours."

Wilderness hefted his bag and followed her upstairs to the living room, but she'd gone up another two flights. He shucked off his jacket, followed the train of discarded clothing, to their bedroom on the top floor.

Judy was in her bra and pants, pulling down the blind on the south-facing roof light.

Wilderness stood in the doorway while she flung her underwear at him and peeled back the sheets.

"I . . . I thought you wanted to know everything?"

"Later, Wilderness, later."

She turned, yanked on his tie, dog on a lead, and pulled him on top of her, whispered in his ear.

"Come on, togs off, you dozy bugger."

§7

Afterwards he was churlish enough to wonder, "What was that about?" and enough of a gentleman not to ask aloud.

Judy filled the gap, as though she had read his mind. He lay on his side, looking at the wall; she fitted herself spoon-like to the curve of his backside and said, "Never been with an old lag before."

"I told you, it was jail not prison."

"There's a difference?"

"Yes. And if I've suddenly become your bit of rough because I spent a couple of nights in the cells, then you're forgetting . . . I was in the glasshouse when your dad found me in 1946."

"Oh . . . that's just military prison. They can lock up who they like can't they? This was the real McCoy. Nicked for a . . . well for whatever it was you did. And you're not military any more."

Of course, Burne-Jones would ration what he told his daughter. Truth and lies were all the currency a spook needed. That he had told her he was in jail in Berlin spoke volumes. There was no necessity to tell her anything. He'd told Judy because he wanted her to know, wanted her to be the one to punish Wilderness. He'd be very surprised at the nature of the sentence. It would never occur to Burne-Jones that danger, jail, and whatever nonsense Judy was piling on to that would prove to be a turn-on, that, for as long as it lasted, Wilderness had entered Judy's fiction. Her bit of rough.

"Actually . . ."

"Yeeees? Actually what, my old lag?"

"I am military."

"Eh?"

"I signed up. It was Alec's condition for getting me out."

She rolled off him. He could hear her gathering steam. A 4-6-2 at King's Cross couldn't sound more pressurized. But then he noticed the calendar tacked to the wall just by her reading lamp, and the red rings around yesterday, today, and tomorrow, 30th, 1st and 2nd, and her explosion vanished into a vacuum. She was letting him have it, and he heard not a word. She stood by the bed, arms raised, breasts shaking, giving him the bollocking of a lifetime and all Wilderness could hear was the ticking of their biological clock.

He'd been had. She'd had him. All their discussions about family usurped in moment.

§8

He awoke, early he thought, but not so early that Judy had not already left for work—or left to avoid the row that was surely brewing.

He made coffee, went back to bed, flipped on the radio, listened to Jack de Manio on the BBC, waiting for the next dropped brick, verbal gaffe or total lapse of manners.

An hour or so later, no conclusion reached regarding wife and future family, he heard the crocodile snap of the letter box closing and the yowl the cat sent up to announce new post, which for some reason the animal confused with food—Wilderness had not named him Desperado for nothing.

It was a letter in a Connaught Hotel envelope on Connaught Hotel paper.

Sorry kid. No dame no game. Consider this payment in full. Frank.

Wilderness shook the envelope. A single green dollar bill floated down like the first fallen leaf of autumn, eddying to land in front of the cat, who sniffed in disgust and ran away.

"Exactly," thought Wilderness. "What I should have done."

The next time he saw Frank Spoleto coming he'd cross to the other side.

For now, he was down $49,999 . . . but he had a job again. A job he didn't much want, but then he had always regarded the world as one made up of wolves and doors.

II

Alleyn

For he might have been a Roosian,
A French, or Turk, or Proosian,
Or perhaps Itali-an!
But in spite of all temptations
To belong to other nations,
He remains an Englishman!

—W. S. Gilbert

H.M.S. Pinafore, 1878

§9

Germany: May 1945

They found Alleyn wandering—somewhere in Lower Saxony. His memory had left him, but the tatty remains of his RAF uniform and the dog tags strung around his neck were enough. They knew who Alleyn was before he did.

Two days later as bits of memory bobbed flotsam-like to the surface, he said, "Alleyn . . . Bernard Forbes Campbell Alleyn. Squadron leader," and rattled off his number. The squadron number and base proved more elusive. All the same they knew.

"Kelstern—625 Squadron. Welcome back, old man."

He had to admit, the cover was brilliant. Moscow had really delivered. Not for a moment, it seemed, did they—that is the English—doubt that he was who he appeared to be. Squadron Leader Bernard Forbes Campbell Alleyn, third generation Scots-Canadian from Perth, Ontario—sole survivor of half a dozen straying Lancasters blown from skies somewhere east of Dresden in February 1944.

Alleyn was still alive when the Red Army overran Stalag Luft VIII-B in Silesia on St. Patrick's Day 1945. Alive, but only just—badly burned and badly patched up, he had succumbed to pneumonia only a fortnight later . . . but by then Liubimov had sat at his bedside for seven days and nights, listened to his mortal ramblings and let the cloak of his identity float down upon him as Alleyn breathed his last.

The men who'd been interned with Alleyn would make their way home in nine months or a year—shipped back to Blighty via Odessa, the Dardanelles, the Med . . . and a bundle of excuses.

Those who'd known Alleyn well never would.

§10

Liubimov was a fair match. The same height as Alleyn, only a year or so younger, and a recent recipient of plastic surgery after the Riga Offensive. It was the last heroic piece of stupidity he would ever indulge in. He had had no need to be anywhere near the front line, and could have stayed in the rear, "mopping up" with the rest of the NKVD, but curiosity had almost killed him. This new adventure also might kill him, but at least no one was shooting at him. Indeed, some of the English officers who appeared regularly at his bedside didn't even seem to be carrying weapons.

"I'm a psychiatrist, old man. No need for a gun. The pen is mightier than the sword, and I rather think that applies to Webley and Smith and Wesson too."

"Ah. Do you think I'm mad?"

"Not at all old man, but you have been through hell."

"Haven't we all?"

"Not really. I've never picked up as much as a scratch these last five years . . . but you . . . the trauma . . . the burns . . . the surgery."

"I don't remember any of that. But I know, I remember, I flew Lancasters, so . . ."

Alleyn rubbed gently at the tight, shiny skin of his left cheek.

"So . . . I suppose, burning petrol?"

"That does seem the most likely explanation. The Jerries seem to have made pretty good job of patching you up."

"Ah. Do you have a mirror?"

"Nurse will bring you one later. Believe me you look fine. Positively handsome. But I'd rather like to shift the conversation back to my field of expertise."

"Ah. The mind."

"Yes, old man . . . your mind."

§11

The psychiatrist—his name was Hancock, but Alleyn found it convenient to pretend not to remember it from one session to the next—found very little wrong with Alleyn's mind, and recommended immediate discharge once he was pronounced physically fit.

"Chances are you'll remember everything in time," Hancock told him.

"I'd rather not," Alleyn had replied. "If my memory is a jigsaw puzzle and I have some pieces and not others, then I think I've seen enough to prefer forgetting."

"As though of hemlock I had drunk?"

"I have been half in love with easeful Death."

"Touché, Mr. Alleyn, touché."

It would, he realised, pay him to mug up his English literature. At least to mug up beyond the cardboard boundaries of the *Oxford Book of English Verse*, beyond the Dickens novels and the Kipling stories that had been his prep as a spy.

They put him in a hospital out in the country, six or seven miles from Hanover—insulated from the wreck that was the Thousand-Year Reich. He found himself in a schloss, barely grazed by British shells, mostly intact, big airy rooms, high ceilings, and walled gardens. It was rather un-German. More than a touch Russian. It felt as though he had his own dacha. Looking back, years later, it seemed to him to have been one of the happiest months of his life. For all the deception and the rehearsal of lies that would be his identity and his modus operandi for years to come, he had felt content, protected, perhaps delighted. A burgeoning Continental summer, long days relaxing in the tangled gardens, dressing gown and pyjamas, patchy neglected lawns, unpruned apple trees, bobbing clusters of marigolds and Michaelmas daisies, sweet milky tea and something called Dundee cake, hidden from his fellow recuperants behind the twin shields of amnesia and psychiatry. The very word "psychiatry" seemed to undermine the English sangfroid. All a bit too Viennese, all rippling with sexual innuendo. They couldn't even say it—instead they called it the trick-cyclist, as in, "Been under the trick-cyclist, old man, bloody bad luck, eh?"

He was to have just a weekly psychiatric session. To stimulate the mind and memory. He was to rest the body and recover, to build up the weight he had shed so rapidly in a month of self-imposed starvation, losing thirty-two pounds in a little under five weeks before they dropped him off the back of a Red Army truck just beyond the green border.

They'd given him a small piece of cordite to swallow.

"You'll look grey for while. As though you'd lived on boiled spuds and lacked all the right vitamins. Just like a POW."

It tasted of nothing. A mild nausea as his stomach wrestled with digesting it. It was the real reason he'd asked for a mirror, not to see his scars. He knew them as well as he knew the back of his hand. He'd shaved them every day for eight months. It was to see if he was still grey the best part of a week later. He wasn't. But nor did he look healthy and normal. He looked sick as a dog.

Three British officers hacked away at a lawn, created a flat if lumpy clearing and hammered wrought iron into croquet hoops. Broom handles nailed onto wooden blocks served as the mallets.

"Need a fourth, old man. Just like bridge. Feel up to it?"

He was clueless. He caused fits of laughter when he whacked the ball with enough force to send it fifty yards past the hoop into the long grass.

"Bloody funny place Canada," one of them opined. "Don't have Dundee cake, don't play croquet. What do you chaps do over there?"

"We sit in our igloos and freeze our bollocks off."

More laughter, hoots of laughter, backslapping, thigh-slapping laughter.

And he realised how ill prepared he was, how little the NKVD had been able to teach him and how quickly he would learn. He would learn to play the Englishman. He was certain of it now.

A month in the country and he'd regained about half the lost weight. He tipped the scales at ten stone exactly—which made him skinny at five foot eleven. And his skin, whilst not exactly rosy, had passed the pallor of death.

After Hanover, Hamburg. Billeted with a host of other officers at the Atlantic Hotel—awaiting a flight home. Lancasters, which his alter ego had flown—and with which he had not the faintest familiarity—which had pounded Germany's cities to dust, were now used as transports.

The first offer came in in a matter of days. A short hop to RAF Kelstern. Far too risky. Whilst most of the squadron were dead or missing, there was a chance the ground crew might recognise him—or, worse, would fail to recognise him. He faked a stomach ache and lost his place in the queue. It was three weeks before the adjutant out at Fuhlsbüttel found him a flight. Another stripped and impotent Lancaster—he could at least now describe one, if asked, but God forbid anyone should ask him to fly one. That moment came sooner than he thought. Low over the North Sea the pilot invited him into the cockpit to take the flight engineer's seat.

"You can take her in if you like, old man."

"It's been too long. Very kind of you, but far too long. One forgets."

He wondered about the "one"—his first dropped brick. Very English, scarcely Canadian. But the pilot seemed oblivious to pronouns.

"Whatever you say, old man. Personally I don't think I'll ever be able forget. I'll be flying a Lancaster in my dreams when I'm eighty."

Alleyn would have other dreams.

They touched down at RAF Wyton, only twenty miles from Cambridge.

Cambridge suited him to perfection. He would be officially demobbed the minute he set foot on English soil. Cambridge was where Moscow had set up his first contact. They had, the NKVD had told him, plenty of willing hands and willing minds in Cambridge, still.

"They're idiots of course. But well-meaning, Marx-reading, Moscow-loving idiots."

One of the well-meaning, Marx-reading, Moscow-loving idiots found Alleyn a job almost at once. He had landed, crossed the first bridge—he had an identity, a passport, a demob suit and a job . . . B.F.C. Alleyn BSc (Toronto) of the Physics Department, King's College, Cambridge. England looked strange to him. It was beginning to dawn on him that he did not look strange to England, that the red star riveted to his forehead was a figment of his very self-conscious imagination, that he was just another "bloke," another middling Englishman in a decent job and a cheap suit.

§12

Cambridge: May 1946

In May of 1946 Alleyn was walking home from King's, along the backs to his digs in Sidgwick Avenue, when he came across a damsel in distress. The chain had come off the rear sprocket on her Sturmey-Archer three-speed hub and she was crouched at the side of the path with a bicycle he had heard referred to as a sit-up-and-beg lying on its side. The young gentlemen of Cambridge passed her by with not a gentlemanly word.

"Can I help?"

"Oh, if you would. I know nothing about bikes. I just pump up the tyres every so often."

Alleyn had ridden his bike all over Moscow before the war. He had a British one. A Raleigh made in Nottingham. It was the proletarian Rolls-Royce. Identical to this but for the absence of a skirt-tangling crossbar.

He righted the bike.

"Much easier to keep it upright. Would you mind picking up a couple of twigs?"

She looked baffled but did as he asked, and while she held the handlebars Alleyn flicked the chain back on with the twigs. Then he held up his hands.

"See? No oil."

The girl held up one of hers, black with grease.

"I'm so sorry," Alleyn said and fished in his pocket for a clean hanky.

"Oh, I couldn't. It's Irish linen."

"It'll wash."

She took it.

"Then I'll wash it. And I'll return it to you. You've been so kind. You must let me buy you a coffee one day soon."

Alleyn got a good look at the girl. Twenty-ish, almost as tall as he was himself, a wide mouth, good un-English teeth, red hair tied up at the back of her neck and a smile flickering in green eyes.

"I'd love to. You're at Newnham?"

They were so close to Newnham College, one of only two colleges that admitted women, it seemed logical that they might be neighbours.

"No, Girton. So it really was rather important to get the bike fixed or I'd be pushing it for three miles. Look, my last exam is on Thursday morning. I'd like to buy you coffee. Do you know that little Italian place near King's? Practically opposite King Henry's statue?"

He knew it.

"Okeydokey. Shall we say half past twelve?"

§13

"Do I detect an accent?"

In the café L'Ombelico del Mondo—an affectation reduced simply to The Bellybutton by the students—the redhead had been waiting when Alleyn arrived. She had taken the elastic band from her hair and was shaking it free as he crossed the room.

"Canada. I would hope it's rather faint by now. I've been here since '38. Do I detect an accent?"

Now one hand brushed at the liberated mop of hair.

"Well, if you do you have very good ears. I'm from Hertfordshire. Home counties King's English. The voice of the BBC. A quite ordinary accent really . . . but my parents are Irish. Perhaps a hint of blarney?"

"More than a hint I think."

Another sweep of the hand.

"You know, we haven't introduced ourselves. I'm Kate Caladine, and I'm in my second year at Girton, reading English."

"And I'm Bernard Alleyn. I'm at King's. But I'm not a student. I'm a demonstrator in physics. I got my degree long ago. In Canada."

"Hmm . . . Cambridge seems full of chaps about your age. You know, finishing their degrees now because the war sort of got in the way."

"Oh the war certainly got in my way."

"How long?"

"Forty-two to forty-four in a Lancaster. Forty-four to forty-five in a Stalag Luft in Silesia."

He was, he realised, weaving quite a web. There was a limit to how much he knew about the real Alleyn simply because they had not had the time to learn or long enough with the man before he died. The first rule of impersonation was never deny a known fact and never invent a lie that can be easily contradicted by record. No one had been at all sure what the real Alleyn had been doing between the outbreak of war and volunteering for the RAF. It would have been easier had he arrived from Canada simply to volunteer in '41. It would have been a clean line. The past put safely behind him and hence behind Liubimov. But he hadn't, and that was a matter of record. No one was even sure he had a degree of any kind, but Liubimov was a physicist, so physics it had to be, and a diploma was mailed to him from the forgers at the London embassy, together with references from a Canadian academic who had conveniently died during the war. Alleyn—the real Alleyn—had muttered about living in Edinburgh in his dying and his rambling, and it would make sense never to go near Edinburgh. He hoped she wouldn't ask now. He hoped that ubiquitous phrase "before the war" would not be used. He had nothing prepared.

"Oh, you poor thing. Was it absolutely awful?"

This helped. It was the textbook response. As easy to handle as his phony birth date.

"Not entirely. I lost weight, I learnt some German . . . and I played a lot of table tennis."

She laughed. The big green, Irish eyes lit up. The tangle of hair shook.

"Physics?" she said, clearly tacking away from what she saw as a painful matter despite her laughter. "I thought all you chaps were at the Cavendish."

"Oh no, by no means all of us. They're the competition. Our cheeky younger brother."

She laughed at this too. Her laughter reminded him that he had been starved of laughter. Crossing Prussia with the Red Army had provided moments of laughter—black, vicious laughter, an all-pervading, self-congratulatory schadenfreude . . . you were alive, some other bugger wasn't. That was always worth laughing at. He hadn't heard a woman laugh in months. Even then it would only be the college cleaners' morning-after-the-night-before ribaldry—indifferent to his presence. Now, a good-looking woman was laughing at something he had said. Words would not describe the pleasure that rippled up his spine, down his arms, to bring his skin up in tingling goose bumps.

Just before she left, standing on the pavement in King's Parade, she stuck out a hand, rather stiff and manly. Surprised, Alleyn shook and found she had slipped his handkerchief back into his hand, and as she walked off in the direction of Caius with not a backward glance, he squeezed the linen and felt something firmer than cloth. It was a tightly folded piece of paper: a note.

7 o-clock, Saturday. Arts Theatre. Major Barbara. Meet me there. KC.

He felt a flutter in his chest, a rapid increase in his pulse rate, heard the sound of his own beating heart, and with it the roar of suspicion and the howl of fear. Who the hell was Major Barbara?

§14

At Christmas the same year Kate and Bernard engaged to marry. He'd met her parents at the end of the summer, out at a worse-for-wear Victorian rectory perched on what passed for a hill in Hertfordshire. Her mother talked too much to ask any question that might have foxed him, and her father, a Church of England vicar, preferred to bury himself in his study and his sermons rather than bother with most of the responsibilities of parenthood. They accepted him as who he pretended to be.

In the New Year of 1947, Bernard sat the Civil Service entrance exam and was accepted into the top (administrative) grade. At the interview he was told that the Service was delighted to receive applications from men with a scientific background.

"So much of it is technical these days. The War Office is crying out for chaps like you."

War Office? Pay dirt.

"Won't you be sad to leave Cambridge?" his future mother-in-law asked.

"A little. But the only future at King's would be to transfer to the teaching staff and to do that I would need to publish and quite possibly write a PhD. I think I have better prospects at the War Office."

Mrs. Caladine had smiled at this, not quite the beguiling smile of her daughter—he had used a word so telling when marrying into an English family: "prospects." Bernard Forbes Campbell Alleyn not only had an identity, he now had prospects. And had chosen the word after much careful thought.

§15

In March he moved up to London. Cold, damp digs in Charlotte Street. A couple of fleeting, chilly visits from Kate. A constraining single bed. Winceyette sheets. Then in May she had sat her last exam. Nothing more to do.

"You'll be staying on for the May Ball, though?"

The May Ball was always in June.

"Bernard, have you ever been to a May Ball?"

"No."

"Good. And we'll neither of us be going to this one. Bunch of bloody Hooray Henries in penguin suits. I'd rather be here. I'd rather be here with you."

"We can't stay here for ever,"

Indeed they couldn't. A senior Civil Service post proved highly mortgage-worthy and in an era of chronic housing shortage Alleyn considered himself extremely lucky to get a 972-year lease on a first-floor flat in Cholmondeley Road, Highgate. Mortgageable he might be, but he did not have the necessary two-hundred-pound deposit. The Rev. Caladine did and obliged. And in September 1947, newly wed, Mr. and Mrs. Bernard Alleyn moved into their new flat just in time for the coldest winter in God knows when, to huddle around a paraffin heater, hoping love might make them indifferent to temperatures in the low 20s.

In 1949, their first child, Beatrice Perdita, was born. And in 1951 their second, Cordelia Rosalind.

"I didn't study Shakespeare for nothing, now did I?"

"If you say so."

"I do say so. So there!"

By 1955 Alleyn held a senior position in the Directorate of Military Operations and Intelligence equivalent to that of an army colonel; he answered to the Minister for War, dealt daily with generals, with MPs, with the Cabinet Secretary, advised select committees, nipped in and out of Downing Street, had an office overlooking Whitehall and a salary well beyond the glass wall of the thousand-a-year-man. With the housing shortage easing, Britain tentatively recovering from a war that whilst over seemed nonetheless eternal, he managed to buy the lease of the ground floor flat and put the late-Victorian red-brick and stained-glass villa back together. A house once more. A home once more. A family home.

The day he took a sledgehammer to the jerry-built partition in the hallway that had framed the door to the upper flat he counted as one of the most pleasing days of his life. Life held many pleasing days. Days when he could put one of Virginia Woolf's ticks on the page of life. He had not imagined life could be this way. A round of simple and not-so-simple pleasures. Austerity be damned. Rationing be damned. Life was good. The girls' names were down for Godolphin and Latymer School. Kate gave up teaching, stayed home and reviewed fiction for the *Observer*. Life was too good to be true.

His home was his castle. The Englishman's God-given right, even if the Englishman was a complete fake.

And his contacts never called at the house. Everything he passed from the War Office to the Soviet Union was done by dead letter boxes or clandestine meetings in London parks. His home was his castle. It wasn't England and it certainly wasn't Russia. Russia was dour men barely glimpsed on meeting, grasping hands and muttered half-somethings. Russia was . . . a world away.

Life was too good to be true . . . and it wasn't.

§16

London: November 1959

Alleyn sat in his cell and waited. There seemed to be little else he could do. They'd confiscated his belt, his tie, and his cyanide capsule—not that he would have swallowed cyanide, and after this long was it even potent any more? Who knew? He didn't.

He'd asked for something to read and the day copper had brought him *Just William* by Richmal Crompton. He read it and counted it a gap in his training that he'd never read it before. All those Will Hay films he'd been force-fed, all those John Buchan novels and Rudyard Kipling short stories, and no one had thought that the preparation for the essential Englishman might include a grasp of the anarchy of a middle-class English childhood.

He'd asked to see his wife and had been told that would not be possible, yet.

He thought of the room as a cell—a door that was permanently locked, windows with the shutters nailed up and a permanent police presence just outside the door—but really it was the back bedroom of a Regency villa in Belsize Park used by MI5 as a safe house. At some point he was certain, he'd be taken to the cells, to Pentonville or Brixton, but not before they charged him and not before they'd finished interrogating him.

Retired Chief Superintendent Westcott was a patient man and once he'd posed a question listened carefully to the answer, occasionally jotting something down in his notebook and courteously sharing his cigarettes.

Alleyn answered as truthfully as he could, drawing the line at naming names.

"Forgive me, Mr. Westcott, but what ideology I believe in is irrelevant now. It's a matter of what I believe myself to be as a man."

Material was another matter. He told Westcott details, such as he could remember, of every document he'd passed to the Soviet Union, but after thirteen years the oldest memories were vague at best.

It was three days before he was charged, and Westcott no longer being a serving police officer, the Special Branch inspector who'd arrested him on Millbank between office and home, on his way to the Underground, was called in to read him his rights and formally make the charge.

Westcott was stuffing his pockets, gathering up his notebook, pencils . . . cigarettes.

Clutching the packet, he opened it and, finding only two of the twenty remaining, offered one to Alleyn saying, "We might as well split these."

He held out his lighter and flicked it.

As Alleyn took the first drag he said, "I know it will sound naïve, Mr. Westcott . . . but what will happen to me?"

"That's for the courts, but I think I should warn you that the death penalty still applies for treason."

His hand shook as he put the cigarette to his lips once more.

"Really, I . . . I had no idea . . ."

"Think of Lord Haw-Haw . . . think of young Amery."

"That was in wartime."

"Really, Mr. Alleyn, you think the Cold War isn't war?"

"No, I don't think it is."

"They were British subjects who betrayed their country. No different from you and what you have done."

For a few stretched moments they smoked in silence. Alleyn had known he might come to this bridge one day or the next and had no idea if he would ever cross it. But Westcott made it easier for him.

"Spit it out, man. There's something. I know there's something."

"I am not a traitor."

Westcott sighed.

"I am not a British subject."

"What?"

"I am not a traitor, I am a spy. My name is Leonid L'vovich Liubimov. A captain of the KGB, or at least I was the last time I checked."

Westcott turned to the policeman.

"Sorry to ask this of you, George, but would you mind nipping out for some more fags? Forty Capstan. And ask the lad downstairs to put on a pot of coffee."

Then he turned back to Alleyn, motioned him to sit with a hand patting the air.

"Shall we begin again, Mr. Alleyn?"

§17

"Lies, Bernard! Lies!"

Alleyn knew it would be like this and had dreaded it whilst hoping for it. It might just have been better in the safe house or in a room at Scotland Yard, where everything was not naked brick and two shades of mud, but his captors were offering him no favours and his first meeting with his wife since his arrest was in a visiting room at Brixton Prison, where he was on remand awaiting trial.

"I can only say I'm sorry."

"You have lied to me for over ten years, you lied to my family, you lied to your own children—"

"I don't suppose—?"

"Bernard don't you dare bloody ask! You fucker, you complete fucker. See the children? See the children? Don't you bloody dare ask me that!"

"I would like to . . . to have seen them."

"Really? And what do you think I should tell them? That daddy's in prison? That daddy isn't daddy—"

"I am still their father."

"That daddy isn't Bernard Forbes Campbell Alleyn, he's . . . whatever your fucking name is!"

"Liubimov," he said, not much above a whisper.

"And you expect two little girls to get their tongues round that?"

"Kate, I'm sorry."

"Stop fucking saying that!"

Her anger hit a gap, an empty space in her own rage that did nothing to diminish it. She hated him as much in silence as in noise—he could feel it like a fist across the table, punching him under the heart.

She fumbled in her handbag for her cigarettes. Did not offer him one. Lit up and exhaled at length, the plume of smoke hanging in the stillness of air between them.

"When will the trial be?"

"Before Christmas I'm told. It should be quick. I'm told they've been gathering evidence for weeks, and of course I'll plead guilty. That should speed things up."

"London?"

"The Old Bailey."

"So you'll be up there with . . . with . . . with Dr. Crippen and Neville Heath."

"I'm not a murderer, Kate."

"Really? You think so? Try talking to that ex-copper who came to see me. He seems to think you have blood on your hands. All the men you betrayed."

"All I did was pass on documents."

"And Westcott says that got people killed."

"He's wrong. They told me—"

"They?"

"The Russians."

"The Russians? Your people."

"Yes . . . my people . . . assured me no lives were at risk."

"And you believed them?"

He knew she was right, he knew Westcott was right, and there was nothing he could say to this.

"Oh God, you're so bloody naïve. You've always been a bit of a dreamer, a romantic. It was one of the reasons I was attracted to you . . . it was one of the reasons I loved you."

The past tense was telling.

"But what you don't seem to be able to grasp is that you have betrayed people, not pieces of paper, and the people you have betrayed most of all are your children. When Westcott came . . . came with three Special Branch coppers and turned the house over I had to pretend I'd lost one of my diamond earrings and the nice men had come to help me look for it. Do you have any idea how humiliating that was? Lying to my children to protect their shit of a father. And this was when we still thought you were Bernard Alleyn. There is no way I can ever tell them who you really are. There's no way I can ever tell them what you are."

She swept a lock of red hair out of her face. Another momentary silence that he could only fill with another apology, the sorry machine on autopilot, the refrain that would punctuate the rest of his life, and what was the point of that? He'd tell her he loved her but was certain this would simply drive her to rage.

"There's only one thing I can do," she said. "I must get them out of London before the trial. They must know nothing about it. I'll take them to my sister's in Wales. And . . . and I'll change our name."

"Really Kate . . ."

"Well we're not Alleyns are we? I mean, bloody hell, Bernard, we never were Alleyns . . . we were Lub . . . Lub . . ."

"Liubimov."

She stubbed out the cigarette and stood up. Turned her back on him.

"A name I cannot even fucking pronounce. Oh God, Bernard, what have you done?"

"Changing your name might be a good idea."

She only half looked at him. A glance over her shoulder, not enough to hide the tears.

"Well you have two, one that sounds like pure fucking gobbledegook and the other a complete liability. I can't go back to being Caladine. Or I'll take my mother's maiden name. Oscar Wilde's wife did something like that when he went to prison. That should lose the scent. The press won't find us."

"What? Howard?"

"It's as good as anything."

"You'll be Catherine Howard?"

"I can feel one of your tasteless jokes coming on, Bernard. Just don't say it. In fact don't ever say another fucking word to me."

"But . . . the children, my girls."

Now she turned fully, her face a ragged mask of red-raw skin and streaming tears.

"You'll never see them again. You have no children."

III

Masefield

It did not occur to him, an ordinary run-of-the-mill copper, that intelligence officers who work because of ideological motives and patriotism instead of for money are people of a special mold; people whose lives are dedicated to danger, to whom arrest is an everyday possibility, and who are prepared to accept severe punishment with equanimity as an inevitable occupational hazard.

—Gordon Lonsdale/Konon Molody

Spy, 1965

§18

London: 1960

Masefield resembled a grown-up version of the fifties cartoon character Nigel Molesworth—the plump, bespectacled prep-school duffer from the sketchbook of Ronald Searle. He'd even heard others call him this derogatory name in the invisible corridors of secrets that ran parallel to the corridors of power in St. James's.

Molesworth—fat and useless.

He'd grown a moustache for a host of reasons . . . to look more "distinguished" (whatever that meant—grey hair was distinguished, bald wasn't), to look "posher" (which meant growing the right kind of moustache—pencil-thin, all but drawn on with Marlene Dietrich's eyebrow pencil, was fine, a yard brush wasn't, a Hitler toothbrush wasn't), and lastly to look less like Nigel Molesworth. But who knew what Molesworth would grow up to look like? Masefield did. He was damn sure that any day now Searle would come up with an image of the mature Molesworth and he would be a dead ringer for Geoffrey Masefield.

The posh were not called Geoffrey. The posh were Neville and Nigel and Hugh. The posh were also called Alec . . . as in Alexander Burne-Jones . . . (a set of letters followed, indicative of Burne-Jones's wartime service, but the only one Masefield even recognised when he'd looked him up was OBE . . . and the old gag Other Buggers' Efforts). Oddly, Burne-Jones appeared to be his real name.

He'd met Burne-Jones in 1960 at Rawley's . . . a Mayfair club— gambling, to the limited extent the law allowed, in the back room and music, girls, and overpriced drinks in the front. It wasn't, he thought, a venue that suited Burne-Jones or left the man feeling at all comfortable. But it suited him. When Burne-Jones had said they could meet almost anywhere they would not be overheard, Masefield himself had suggested the notorious London club.

Everything about it pleased him. Banquettes were so much more sophisticated than tables. Banquettes in deep green Naughahyde, so "now," so "American" . . . nurturing images of Rock Hudson and Doris Day in some nameless New York nightclub, of Liz Taylor in *BUtterfield 8*, and the prospect of semi-accidental frottage with a woman's bottom as she squeezed past.

The music was not too modern. The standards of the interwar years given a slightly upbeat tempo, a touch more Dankworth, a touch less Joe Loss (although his personal preference was for Edmundo Ros—the girls in Ros's Regent Street club didn't strip), but none of that bebop nonsense that grated on the ear . . . and better still a sense that the "trad" revival had never happened . . . not a bowler hat, a washboard, or a banjo to be seen. It was "The Lady Is a Tramp" rendered as it should be . . . bare-breasted and devoid of irony by a young woman whose failings as a singer were more than compensated for by the length of her legs.

The young, well, youngish man, Burne-Jones had brought with him seemed more at his ease—a Mr. Brown, which Masefield thought but the slightest variation on Smith or Jones, and not at all (oddly enough) a nom de guerre (we were at war, weren't we?). But he wasn't posh—the undercurrent of cockney in his voice was not disguised. It was as though he had grown out of the accent rather than attempted to change it.

Unsurprisingly, what Burne-Jones wanted was never mentioned. He might have been chatting to anyone he'd met propping up a bar on a dull Tuesday night in the West End. They'd swapped war records as any two Englishmen would from 1945 till the last of them popped their clogs, and that wouldn't be until around 2025, and even then there'd be one or two grimly hanging on, chock-full of antibiotics and nostalgia. Burne-Jones had been of necessity more than a little coy about his "desk job" in Whitehall, and Masefield less so in describing his unexpected commission in the RAOC and the three and a half years he'd spent as a second lieutenant instructing erks in the structure and use of hand grenades while inwardly counting his blessings not to be an erk himself. He'd not seen a whiff of action. He'd never left England. He was embarrassed about this. It was the central experience for men of his generation, and his relation to it was oblique.

"A bit like coming last in the sack race," he opined, wanting and not wanting to seem apologetic.

Burne-Jones waved it aside.

"We all did our bit, Geoffrey."

All the same, the letters after Burne-Jones's name in *Who's Who* hinted at a war not entirely spent at the desk job.

Brown said nothing about his war, and Masefield readily concluded he was too young to have been in it. His bit, if such it be, had been at school.

Burne-Jones seemed quite interested in Masefield's school.

"Bemrose in Derby. Boys' grammar school. Only a couple of years old when I got there."

"Ah, nothing wrong with a good grammar school."

And he felt the first hint of the condescension that he had been expecting to set the tone for this meeting all along. But Burne-Jones moved rapidly on, not volunteering whether his had been Eton, Harrow, or Westminster . . . to university. Nottingham, the nearest university to home, which meant that he had been able to live cheaply, back with his mum—washing done, commuting on the train with a packed lunch and home again in time for a hot meal in the evening . . . Nottingham had held a place for him from his call-up in 1941 until his demob in '46. After Nottingham, Manchester Municipal College of Technology and the first sense of being able to spread his wings—a feeling even serving in the army had not been able to instill in him.

"Metallurgy," he said, the first word he had been able to utter with any pride. "BSc in '49, MSc in '51. I could have flipped a coin really. I was a bit of an all-rounder if I say so myself. Could have read arts or science, but I'd always been a bit of rockhound as a boy, so metallurgy seemed the next logical move. I kept languages as a hobby. I have good French and passably good Russian. Not that I've ever been there, of course."

Brown spoke—not for the first time, but making his first real contribution to the conversation.

"Мы тоже не были там, Джеффри. Все равно мы говорим свободно."

Neither have we, Geoffrey. And we're both fluent.

He was smiling as he said it. Burne-Jones laughed, and Masefield hesitantly joined in, forcing a smile to his lips and a boyish giggle to his mouth. And then he found he was laughing for real, laughing for real because at last the cat was out of the bag and they all three knew why they were there, and Masefield knew what would be asked of him, not now perhaps, but any day soon—and that they might make a dream come true.

It was also the cue for Burne-Jones's exit.

"I'm too old for this lark. Forgive me, gentlemen, but I will away to my wife and the rolling pin that surely waits for me. Joe, settle the bill. Only when you're good and ready of course. In fact, why don't you and Geoffrey take in the second house."

Masefield was only too happy to oblige. Brown had an air about him of being already bored, but Masefield knew that he'd just received orders and was hardly likely to buck them.

He had only to look at his empty glass and Brown's hand went up for the waiter and another bottle of Dom Pérignon '55.

"Thank you, Joe. Joe is your real name isn't it?"

"No, but I've answered to it for years."

"Will I ever know your real name?"

"No."

"Then why is Colonel Burne-Jones not Colonel Smith?"

"Because the Russians already know who he is."

Brown paused as though picking his next words carefully.

"So . . . if anything goes wrong . . ."

"Wrong?"

"Yes. Wrong. If anything goes wrong, you give 'em Burne-Jones, a name they already know, and Brown, a name which means nothing."

A pause, a turning of heads as the band started up again, a too-rapid rendition of "I Get a Kick out of You." Another bottle of champagne opened in front of them.

"Well . . . cheers, Mr. Brown."

"Cheers, Mr. Masefield. And before we either of us gets legless, and before the next tart onstage gets bra-less . . . Room 54 Imperial Hotel, Russell Square, Thursday at three. Got it?"

"Oh yes."

Brown's timing was impeccable. The girl onstage was unhooking her bra even as he spoke.

§19

The Imperial had seen better days. Wilderness had forgotten who had designed it, but had a dim recollection that the same bloke was responsible for the interior of the *Titanic*. It resembled a poor imitation of the Midland at St. Pancras. Red tile and turrets—a hideous piece of London Gothic with bits of Tudor revival and all dusted down with a thick coating of London grime. Perfect for a biscuit tin, hideous for a hotel. He could all but hear the swish of the wrecker's ball gathering speed behind him. The trick today would be to get out before it came hurtling through the window of room 54, or the hotel hit an iceberg. All the same he knew why Burne-Jones had chosen it. It exuded that quality so beloved of spymasters, "anonymity," which was spy-speak for "no one in their right mind would choose to be here."

"How did the two of you get on?"

It might have been phrased casually, but Wilderness knew Burne-Jones wanted a considered opinion. He might not act upon it but he wanted it all the same.

"Can I take it Mr. Masefield approached us?"

"Introduced would be the word."

"Reliable contact?"

"Oh yes. Now spit it out, whatever it is."

"I'd think twice before taking him on. And since you're asking me, I suppose you are thinking twice. I didn't need to be there last night after all, did I?"

More and more Wilderness was thinking he did not need to be anywhere.

"Always good to have the occasional night out with you, Joe."

Wilderness ignored this fiction.

"I can't deny he's keen. He's keen, but perhaps too keen. I often think your best people are the ones you have to whip in."

"Like you, you mean?"

"No . . . not of all us need to be given a choice between a prison sentence and serving Queen and Country."

"And?"

"He's a romantic. A romantic with a silly streak. He loves everything about this. You're offering to make his dreams come true."

"Aren't we all romantics? Isn't Queen and Country a romantic notion in itself?"

"No. It may be to you, but it's not to me. I'd have sat out the charge of the Light Brigade with a ham sandwich and a couple of bottles of pale ale. I didn't fall for a country or a cause. I fell for a woman. And speaking of women. After you left last night, Masefield downed that second bottle of fizz all but single-handed and then decided it would be a good idea if we went backstage and chatted up the girls."

"Well, we've all done that."

Wilderness's look told Burne-Jones that not everyone had done that.

"And . . . of course . . . you didn't let him?"

"Of course not. But he sees himself as a ladies' man. Never been wholly sure what that means, but perhaps he's one. I'm not saying he's a fool for any woman who jiggles her tits at him, but . . . "

"But . . . you are . . . ?"

"No harm done. He took the hint, big as it was. But whoever runs him in the field needs to know his weakness."

"You're not volunteering then?"

Wilderness ignored this too.

"Masefield has come to us at a very good time. We can't go on much longer just watching the trains go by."

Wilderness knew exactly what Burne-Jones meant by this. In the 1950s almost the sole resource of secret services was to look at the movement of men and materiel across the ambiguous zones of occupied Europe in the hope of anticipating a build-up of Soviet forces that might be the prelude to invasion. But all that had altered, however slow they had been to accommodate the change, with the independence— for independence read "guaranteed neutrality," for "guaranteed" read "enforced"—of Austria, for ten years the four powers' stomping ground of the less-than-secret services. Watching the trains go by was almost Victorian when both sides could stick a nuclear warhead on top of a missile that allowed only four minutes' warning.

One of the funniest lines in *Beyond the Fringe*, which had just taken the Edinburgh Festival by storm, was Peter Cook imitating the Prime

Minister and intoning, "I'll have you know, some people in this wonderful country of ours can run a mile in under four minutes." There were times when that one line seemed to sum up the British defence capability against the Soviet Union.

"We need people on the inside. I'm not saying Geoffrey Masefield is perfect, but he's got more going for him than anyone else I've been offered lately. The mining and metallurgy thing is kosher . . . he works for New Caledonian Ores, he's a member of all those professional bodies that scientific chaps have, Royal Society of This, National Institute of That . . . New Caledonian Ores is keen to expand, he's sold them on the idea of Russia as a vast reserve of raw materials . . . plenty of room for scientific visits, buying missions, trade delegations . . . all the cover we could ask for . . . and the beauty of it is he speaks Russian and the buggers won't even suspect that."

Wilderness concluded that the decision had been taken. He wasn't about to repeat his reservations. Masefield was not his problem, and once this meeting was over they need never meet again. Wilderness did not run agents in the field; he was the agent in the field. And the more he sat behind a desk preparing digests for Burne-Jones the more Burne-Jones relied on him and the less he liked it. To "run an agent" would be on par with working behind the counter at a Woolworth's . . . a Woolworth's in Scunthorpe.

"OK, let's get him in."

$20

"Of course, it would pay to be precise. Rather than just looking to buy anything the Russians want to sell, would it not make sense to have something specific in mind?"

Masefield was way ahead of Burne-Jones.

"I thought of that. Offering to buy all the pig iron they can produce might get me as far as a handful of shipping dockets and a trip to a marshalling yard in some industrial hole in the Ukraine. I think I should be looking for something a little out of the ordinary, something specific . . . well . . . something with the potential for travel. I was thinking of post-transition metals or rare earths, something like that."

Just when Wilderness thought Burne-Jones would ask what a rare earth was he asked instead,

"Anything in particular?"

"I was thinking of indium."

"Indium, eh? I see."

It may have been delayed in its appearance by a few seconds, but the look on Burne-Jones's face told Wilderness that he was all at sea now. He'd survived rare earth, only to hit the iceberg, and he was taking in water rapidly at indium.

For God's sake, Alec, just reach for the lifebelt.

"Do you know anything about indium, Joe?"

"Yep. Atomic number 49, atomic weight 114 point something. Umpteen isotopes, in fact more than any other element, all but one are radioactive. About as common as mercury, somewhat harder . . . solid at room temperature but still soft . . . and not as rare as you'd think. It's simply that it's hardly ever found as pure ore . . . more often than not found in zinc dust and refined from that. In fact silver's rarer. The only reason indium isn't as valuable as silver is no one's really found a use for it. I believe we coated aero-engine bearings with it during the war . . . and . . . er that's about it."

Burne-Jones blinked. Looked from Wilderness to Masefield. Had someone just said "radioactive"?

"Can't argue with that," Masefield said. "Pretty good summary. I think I should be looking for indium for two reasons . . . It has no application whatsoever in nuclear fission or fusion, so it won't set alarm bells ringing . . . indium-115 is radioactive and has a half-life that's practically infinite, but of course indium-113 is harmless, and that's what I'd be looking for, a perfectly stable element . . . and since there is no real use for it everyone wants to find a use for it . . . My people would be keen to get as much as they can to stockpile against future uses . . . so looking for it in a country with sizeable zinc production would seem pretty natural. Indeed, it won't be long before someone does find a use for it . . . it has a great propensity to covalent bonding with other elements via the electrons in the penultimate valence as well as the ultimate. Makes it very, shall I say, versatile?"

Burne-Jones blinked and said nothing. Wilderness knew he hadn't the faintest idea what an atomic valence was, ultimate or not, nor was he going to ask.

"And of course," Masefield concluded, "it's transparent. There aren't that many transparent metals after all."

He might just as well have said "luminous porridge."

"Transparent metal? Good Lord, whatever next?"

"It's transparent only as an indium tin oxide, of course."

"Of course."

"If you could get me in with all the right permits I'd have the perfect cover to go poking around in places like . . . like . . . well Chelyabinsk for example. Been a metallurgical plant there since the thirties and the five-year plans. The old T-34 tank was built there. And these days there's a lot of zinc processing in Chelyabinsk."

"Chelyabinsk? Where's that?"

Wilderness answered first. "East of Samara, north of Kazakhstan. Arse end of nowhere, but lots of zinc, as Geoffrey says."

"Good," said Burne-Jones warming to the idea. "Good, good."

"And a bloody great nuclear missile silo . . ."

Both heads turned.

"Whaaat?" Burne-Jones and Masefield said in unison.

At last, Wilderness thought, something Burne-Jones could understand. He'd have been at home with a poem in ancient Greek, but he'd been baffled by "isotopes," puzzled by "half-life," panicked by "radioactive," yet here was something he could grasp.

"Or so we think," he added.

§21

When Masefield had left, Wilderness said, "Why pretend you've never heard of Chelyabinsk?"

"Oh." Burne-Jones assumed an air of diffidence. "Just trying to draw him out, but you would leap in feet-first, wouldn't you? Showing off your knowledge, top of the form again. And why mention bloody missiles?"

"I suppose I just felt wicked. But, Chelyabinsk is the last place photographed by that U-2 the Russians shot down in May. If you check out its flight path across Kazakhstan, it was heading directly for Chelyabinsk. The Russians tried to shoot it down before it got there and failed. They took it out with a surface-to-air missile only minutes after it photographed Chelyabinsk. Do you really think they'll let Masefield get anywhere near Chelyabinsk? And another thing . . ."

"Yes. I thought there would be."

"Indium may not be a nuclear component, but plutonium is, and they process that as well as zinc at Chelyabinsk. There was some sort of accident there a few years back that the Russians have been keeping very quiet about. I might even suggest that zinc is just a cover."

"Bit like an old tin bath out in the backyard then?"

Wilderness ignored this.

"And . . . if you wanted to hide a missile silo what better place than a uranium enrichment plant?"

Burne-Jones was grinning now, his act as the silly-ass toff readily shuffled off.

"Perhaps you're right. Perhaps there are missiles at Chelyabinsk. There must be a half a dozen launch sites and we haven't positively identified one of them yet."

"Half a dozen . . . or Khrushchev's bluffing."

"When is the bugger not bluffing? Life with Stalin was a chess game . . . with Khrushchev it's poker. You never know what he'll do next. You never know what hand he'll slap down. One minute he's hobnobbing with the likes of Frank Sinatra and Shirley MacLaine, the next he's banging his shoe on his desk at the UN and telling us he'll 'show you Kuzka's Mother' . . . whatever that means."

Wilderness would never admit it, but he liked Khrushchev. Stalin was the silent tyrant. If you could discount mass murder, he was dull. Eisenhower was dull. All plaid pants and golf spikes. Macmillan had second billing in the music hall of international politics, but he was still just the warm-up act for the man with the star on his dressing room door—Nikita Sergeyevich Khrushchev.

"Кузькина мать. It means something like 'Kiss my arse.'"

"Really? Vulgar little man. Fact is, I don't know what will work. I think letting Masefield try is better than doing nothing. Just having someone on the inside is better than doing nothing. Anything's better than doing nothing. Finding out Mr. K is bluffing would be far, far better than doing nothing."

"You weren't really going to send him out without knowing what he was getting into?"

"No, probably not."

"And you'll run him how exactly?"

"Out of Berlin, I think. Assign him to Tom Radley . . . New Caledonian has an office there. Pretty well perfect cover. We'll let our Geoffrey look around and report back to Tom, that's all we can do."

"And if our Geoffrey finds out Mr. K is bluffing by just looking around?"

"Oh . . . the usual. The honours will be boundless. George Cross, life peerage and a night on the razzle with Princess Margaret. That sort of thing."

Wilderness was sure the jokes were meant to conceal rather than reveal, but reveal they did. It was all a bit half-arsed, and Burne-Jones knew it.

§22

Wilderness had, at Burne-Jones's request, one last meeting before Masefield set off for Berlin and from Berlin to an international trade mission—French, Belgians, Dutch, a couple of other Englishmen—bound for Moscow. A man on a mission, without a mission. A man who'd been told in the precision of Cold War spy-speak to "have a bit of a look around." They sat in a deserted, seedy coffee bar in Marylebone Lane one dark November afternoon—scratched Formica, rusting chrome chairs, sauce bottles ringed in darkening goo, the scorch marks of a thousand cigarettes. The natural home of beatniks—a fast-vanishing London breed. A bit of fifties flotsam washed up in a new decade that seemed too slow off the blocks.

Wilderness had felt a little foolish offering Masefield the standard speech. He didn't even believe it himself. "Regard every Russian you meet as a spy because that will be their attitude to you" and "Sex is a quagmire: blackmail is the KGB's strongest weapon and yours is discretion."

"Don't pick up any loose women, eh?"

Wilderness didn't blame him for smirking as he said it. It was but a fraction away from laughable at the best of times.

"I was thinking more of 'don't let any loose women pick you up.' Even more . . . 'don't let any loose men pick you up.'"

This embarrassed Masefield. For a moment or two he stared down into his frothy coffee.

When he looked up he said, "I'm not queer, you know. I may not be married, but I'm not queer."

Wilderness did know. All the same he said nothing, let the pause ramble on.

"I had . . . I had expected a bit more."

It seemed almost plaintive. Wilderness was not entirely sure what he was on about.

"You'll be paid what was agreed."

"Oh no. I meant . . . well, more in the way of briefing. Not just a bit of a warning about the tarts and queers."

"Such as?"

"Well . . . for example, I haven't got a gun."

Wilderness stared back at Masefield, hoping he felt like the fool Wilderness thought he was.

"Why would you need a gun?"

"I don't know. I just sort of assumed I'd have one."

"Geoffrey, let me put it another way. Why would a metallurgist on an invited trade mission have a gun?"

This shut him up for a while. He sipped at his fashionably frothy coffee. His head came up with a strand of white foam clinging to his moustache.

"I'm sorry. I suppose that was rather silly. But a camera?"

"Buy one and bring us the receipt. Anything you like, nothing too ostentatious. Berlin's a very good place to buy a camera. For that matter so's Moscow. Most tourists would pick up a Zenit or a Zorki simply because they're cheap."

"I meant . . . a miniature camera."

"What, hidden in your bow tie?"

"Now you're just making fun of me."

Who could resist? It would be harder to take the piss if he hadn't been wearing a bow tie in the first place. It had been Wilderness's contention all along that Masefield's vision of the job in hand was based on his innate romanticism, "gullibility" might be a better word, and a fondness for spy novels. In his heart of hearts Mr. Masefield wanted what he was never going to get—the armourer's scene with which Fleming had opened *Dr. No*, swapping a dainty Beretta .22 for a lethal Walther PPK 9mm. Wilderness almost felt sorry for him—almost, but not quite. He'd played that scene himself when he was still a teenager, taught how to shoot and kitted out with his first gun by Major Weatherill. He'd let him down as gently as possible.

"Geoffrey, it's in your own interests. If the Russians were to find a gun or a miniature camera your cover would be blown at once. I hope to God you never need a gun. In the meantime, for this mission you need a tourist camera. A simple, compact 35 mil SLR. Something up front that will arouse no suspicion, something you can afford to have confiscated if they do get suspicious. If you see anything of interest then you bury it in a mass of tourist snapshots. Snap the local totty if you like, shoot all the damn statues of Lenin, photograph the domes of St. Basil's. And if you should ever need a miniature camera, Tom Radley, our man in Berlin, will issue you with one."

"Tom Radley? Good man, is he?"

"One of the best," Wilderness lied, regretting the throwaway remark and making a mental note to tell Berlin never to issue a miniature camera to Masefield.

More coffee, more foaming moustache. Surely there were no more bits of spy-trivia the man could trawl up to quiz him with?

"Tell me, Mr. Brown. Have you ever . . . killed a man?"

It occurred to Wilderness to answer. It occurred to Wilderness not to answer. And while he made up his mind, Masefield was waiting, looking up at him in anticipation.

"Yes."

"May I ask why?"

"Why? Because he left me no choice."

That was another lie, but no amount of straining for sympathy with Masefield could convince Wilderness that the man was entitled to the truth.

§23

Moscow: December 1960

Philip Bowles, fat and brutal, had given Masefield a black eye—on three separate occasions.

Ronald Shaw, short and ugly, had kicked Masefield in the balls. So hard he was wincing with pain hours later and his mother had tripled any embarrassment by dragging him to the doctor.

Patrick Gratian, tall and mean, had broken his glasses by knocking them to the ground and stamping on them. Masefield had refused to wear glasses "ever again." He had blundered blearily around for years until common sense, NHS specs, and a newly nurtured moustache prevailed. Glasses branded you as a runt. Glasses and a moustache might hint at distinction.

These indignities had befallen him years ago, a war had come and gone in the years that passed, an empire—our empire—had wrapped its shining yards and departed in shame, but there was something in Masefield that nurtured "never forget," and at odd turning points in his life he would find himself remembering the school bullies of the thirties. Not in any sense of "I wonder where they are now"—they were every one of them in overalls at Rolls-Royce or British Railways, working at menial jobs for scrimp-and-scratch wages. He knew because his mother had kept up with the failures of all his school contemporaries via a network of over-the-garden-wall gossip, for as long as she had the wall, and reported to him with a neutrality that he never found quite credible. Masefield could not be neutral. He greeted every piece of bland gossip, every sacking, every divorce, every pennyweight of debt, with joy at the news—none of them had clawed their way out of the abyss. He remembered them with an inner voice saying "if they could see me now." At every advance in his own fortunes a silent Masefield gloated over his invisible opponents—"if they could see me now."

Fewer advances in fortune, fewer moments of self-regarding glory could equal landing at Sheremetyevo Airport, as a paid-up MI6 agent. All he lacked was a gun and a camera. He'd buy the camera as soon as he could as Brown had suggested. Part of him wished he could buy the gun—it would complete the dream, but Brown had been adamant about that—only part of him: dreams were dreams and he wasn't dreaming now.

The chap sitting next to him said, "What's so funny?"

"Was I laughing?" Masefield replied.

"No. But you were smiling like the cat that got the cream."

"Oh, just glad to be here I suppose."

And in his mind's eye he glimpsed the faces of his oppressors, three men condemned never to travel further than the Trent valley or earn more than fifteen pounds a week. Three men who'd live in the back-streets of Derby until the wrecking ball swung, in cold Derby houses, having cold Derby sex with their cold Derby wives.

"First time, eh?" said chap next to him. "Well I hope you brought enough woollen underwear. Moscow in December has all the warmth of the proverbial witch's tit."

§24

The Hotel Muromets was about as shabby and as chic as the Imperial back in London. It needed a makeover, but one preconception about the USSR that Masefield was certain would not be challenged was that the whole country would be in need of a makeover.

Their "watcher," ostensibly a guide and interpreter, who Brown had assured him would be a KGB agent, had met them, all seven of them, at the airport and in an overheated, and rather smelly, glass-roofed

ZiL minibus had ferried them to the Muromets, registered them, and as soon as they had dumped their bags had assembled them all in the lobby.

"Good afternoon, gentlemen. My name is Tanya Dmitrievna Tsitnikova, I will be your guide for the next five days. Please, call me Tanya . . ."

Masefield stopped listening. She was tiny, blonde and really rather beautiful in a Slavic sort of way—that is, broad at the cheekbones, with dark blue eyes and misshapen teeth. Nothing that could not be overlooked. He watched in a near-vacuum of half-heard murmurs as her bee-sting lips recited the predictable list of dos and don'ts, all of which he knew by heart. Yes, they were free to roam Moscow, she was a guide not a guard—Brown had been adamant about this too, that on his first trip they would dog him every step of the way, even to the point of following him into public lavatories—but leaving Moscow would require permission, although, of course special trips could be arranged, if there was anything they particularly desired to see. And as he surfaced, the last words she seemed to have on those kiss-me lips were "black market," and he realised he'd probably daydreamed through all her warnings about money-changers and prostitutes.

She urged them to get to know one another, passed out welcome packages in neat, shiny, white folders, said she would join them for dinner, and left.

Masefield found himself shaking hands with half a dozen blokes and managed to grasp two names—the chap who had sat next to him on the plane, neither thinking to introduce themselves any earlier, who said he was Arthur Proffitt and represented the English Sewing Cotton Company—and Terence Glendinning, who "travelled in ball bearings." Two blokes of roughly his age, both speaking rather posh and both striking him as pretentious fakers. The rest were a blur. Men in shapeless suits with shapeless faces. A jumble of grey wool, greying hair, and bad breath. Some sort of cross section of British and Continental manhood and industry, about which Masefield gave not a toss. They could stay a blur. They were simply his cover—a seven-man European trade delegation on an invited five-day mission to Moscow. If only they knew . . . if only they knew . . . if his friends could see him now. He could all but hear the zither playing—and it played for him.

As a man who'd been on two previous trade missions to Moscow, Proffitt held forth, assuming the utterly unnecessary role of leader. Masefield tuned him out, only to find Glendinning was tuning out too.

"You know what they say about Russian women?"

"Eh?" said Masefield.

"You know, old man . . . dumpy as a sack of spuds . . . all look like Khrushchev's wife . . . that sort of thing."

Of course he knew. It was a cliché.

"Weeeeell . . . I wouldn't mind giving our Tanya a good seeing-to while I'm here. Forget the teeth, her tits are pretty damned amazing."

Masefield had no idea what to say. To find the immediate content of his own id so readily regurgitated was neither pleasant nor enlightening.

"I suppose they are," he admitted, wishing silence had been an option.

"Race you, old man. First one to fuck her gets the other's forfeit . . . let's say loser picks up the bar bill on the last night."

Now, silence really was the only option. He found Glendinning disgusting, a coarse reflection of himself. He found himself wanting to rise above the situation, to restore some sort of moral margin between himself and this Mephisthophelean alter ego. Instead he found himself mentally undressing Tanya Dmitrievna.

§25

In the morning he went to meet the man from the ministry—the Ministry of Foreign Trade, a department subsumed under the Foreign Ministry, an organ of the state dominated by Andrei Gromyko, a man who had survived countless purges and the death of Stalin to become one of the more recognisable faces of the USSR. Masefield would not know Foreign Trade Minister Patolichev if he tripped over him. Besides, he knew very well he would not get within half a dozen bureaucratic layers of a full minister.

Outside the Muromets, about half the trade mission had gathered on the pavement, hands thrust deep in pockets, breath misting in air, morning dew freezing on eyelashes. Even in cold this savage Glendinning found the energy to flirt. Masefield could not hear what he was saying to her but the mixture of amusement and bafflement on Tanya Dmitrievna's face told him she knew she was being chatted up and had little or no idea what to make of it.

Then her pro mode kicked in. The French were going one way, the Belgians another, she would be escorting Glendinning to some factory or other in Konkovo, in the south of the city, and the ministry was sending a car for Masefield.

"OK? Yes?"

"Yes. OK."

He watched her as Glendinning played the gent, holding the car door open for her and walking round to the other door. Tanya Dmitrievna looked back at Masefield through the window, the amusement and bafflement in her expression now battling it out with apprehension.

The ministry car never came. He gave it five minutes, then ten, and then counted himself lucky. He could easily walk to the ministry and be on time—it looked to be scarcely more than a mile on the map. He would enjoy the streets of Moscow without a guide, interpreter, or minder.

This must have alarmed the bloke in the black mackintosh who had been hanging around in the lobby, chain-smoking and failing to feign indifference. As Masefield set off on foot, it must have dawned on his follower that he would not be spending the morning sitting in malodorous warmth on a set of broken springs in the back of a Moscow cab. Masefield found he could take a perverse delight in making the man earn his keep. He'd spent weeks studying the map of Moscow. He knew it as well as he knew the streets of Nottingham or Derby. It would be fun to lead the apparatchik around the houses, but probably not worth the effort. Instead he took the obvious route, along Teatralny Proyezd, down the Arbat to Smolenskaya Square, where the Foreign Ministry loomed up like a cinematic fantasy from the set of *Things to Come*, impossibly large, impossibly ugly—a monolithic, vulgar statement to a world that wasn't looking in the first place.

And then they kept him waiting.

Whisked to the thirteenth floor and parked in an outer office for an hour whilst waiting on Comrade Koritsev, undersecretary to the blah

blah blah. The view was amazing, out over the western suburbs, a clear midwinter's morning. Really, he didn't mind waiting. He'd waited half a lifetime to be sitting here, to be sitting anywhere in the USSR, anywhere that wasn't Nottingham or Derby.

If they could see me now.

Comrade Deputy Undersecretary-Minister Yevgeny Vasilievich Koritsev was aptly named. He was beige. So was his suit. The darkest thing about him was his moustache, which Masefield took to be the result of endless cups of black Russian tea.

He wasn't sure why he wasn't supposed to let on that he spoke Russian. He'd stick to the plan, but it was awkward. Koritsev greeted him effusively, welcomed him on behalf of the government, people, and Communist Party of the Soviet Union and had the interpreter not nipped in sharpish would doubtless have welcomed him on behalf of his children, parents, and dog. The hardest thing, he realised, was looking as though he didn't understand. And it was easier to listen to Koritsev than to the interpreter, whose accent was so strong that Masefield would not have known what the man was saying had he not heard the original Russian.

Koritsev pursed his lips at the word "indium," and uttered a "hmm" that required no translation.

"You're the first person ever to come to me with that request. Do you have any idea how little indium there is in this world?"

Masefield warmed to the philosophical ending of the remark. "This world." Here was a man who traded in commodities and who spoke like a scientist.

"No precise knowledge, no. No one has that. But I can tell you how much was produced last year. Less than fifty tons."

"And how much of that do you think we refined in Russia?"

"Oh, I'd say about forty per cent."

"Not bad. It was actually eighteen tons. You know your stuff, comrade." The interpreter stumbled over "stuff" and translated a colloquial phrase with an overprecise "you are in full knowledge of your possessions," and Masefield was glad he wasn't relying on him or he would have had no sense of Koritsev's inflection and quite possibly of his meaning too.

"How much would you like?"

"All of it," Masefield replied, and Koritsev roared with laughter, got up from behind his desk, slapped him on the back and rattled off a string of exclamations so quickly neither Masefield nor the interpreter could keep up. It was all rather . . . Khrushchev. He imagined that this was what meetings with Khrushchev must be like. The rush, the physicality. The hand on the back . . . the shoe on the table.

"Leave this with me. A day or two. You will appreciate, I rarely get orders so large. I shall have to go downstairs and look in the cellar."

Masefield waited for the translation before laughing.

"In the meantime you must enjoy Moscow. Is there anything I can do for you while we wait?"

"Well, comrade minister . . . Great Britain has no indium. It would be of great interest to me to see a zinc processing plant and the extraction of indium."

"Hmm . . . you have anywhere in mind?"

In for a penny.

"Chelyabinsk?"

Koritsev just shook his head and said "no"—no explanation, no pretence, no joke. A syllable entirely without qualification.

"But," he went on, "perhaps I can find you something nearer home. Andrei Semyonovich, see what we can do for Mr. Masefield."

Back in the outer office, Andrei Semyonovich told Masefield what he already knew and said, "I think this can be done. Here. In Moscow. I will arrange. I will leave word at your hotel."

Here? In Moscow? Bugger. The point was to travel.

§26

He found his way back into central Moscow with enough time to stare at the forbidding facade of the KGB offices in Dzerzhinsky Square—more than a bit like Buckingham Palace, he thought—and to linger in front of Lenin's tomb as he crossed Red Square. The tomb reminded him of nothing quite so much as a World War II air raid shelter, built, as they said in Derby, like a "brick shithouse."

Black Mackintosh trailed behind.

It was a time to go with the flow, to play the tourist. To be in awe of St. Basil's Cathedral and in search of the GUM store, a block from Red Square and next to the КПСС (Communist Party) HQ, banded in a lurid shade of green with every shade pulled down against the prying eye—and once GUM was found to be in awe of that too. He had heard it described as grim. He could see that "grim" might be one possible take on it, but there was no denying the other—it was beautiful . . . the outside was . . . St. Pancras without trains . . . the inside was . . . Kew without palm trees . . . Venice without canals, a network of slender iron bridges suspended in space . . . the arcades of Piccadilly recreated on an unimaginably large scale.

Brown had suggested buying a camera, had even suggested that MI6 would pay for it.

In a crystal cave of consumer desirables a young man showed him a Zorki 4. A brief explanation of what was what that told Masefield nothing he didn't already know, then the price and then the inevitable statement, "We accept only dollars or sterling."

Masefield looked around, at the flurry of hands and greenbacks, at the acquisitive exchange, and realised he had no wish to acquire. The camera was beautiful, better by far than anything he'd ever owned, at an affordable price—but this was buying for the sake of buying. It was no more than the Russian version of coming back from a summer trip to Spain with a straw donkey and a sombrero. He wanted something else to be his souvenir of Russia. He did not simply want to own a Zorki 4 because it was cheap. He did not want to own a Zorki 4 simply to be able to show it off back home as a bargain. He wanted something of Russia and this wasn't it.

He said sorry, the young man put the camera back on its shelf, and Masefield went back to the arcade to stare at the little Piranesi bridges and the vast, overarching glazed roof, to drift out into the street once more . . . just to drift.

§27

A couple of blocks from the Hotel Muromets he stopped by a pierogi stand at the kerb. The man in front of him in the queue handed over a few kopecks, and turned around, stuffing a dumpling into his mouth. It was Arthur Proffitt.

"Hullo old man. How's the People's Republic treating you?"

"Oh, I've had a pleasant enough day. Apart from feeling . . . sorry . . . knowing I'm being followed. He's just over there, been with me since I left the hotel."

"Par for the course, old man. Of course you're being followed. These buggers think we're all spies."

"Until proven otherwise," Masefield said.

"No. No proof required. They just get fed up. Followed me on my first trip. Couldn't be arsed on the second, and if they've set someone on to me this time I haven't noticed. Even then, the first time around, some bloke'd be dogging me from breakfast onwards, but by half past three he'd be thoroughly bored and give up. Found I could do what I liked from dusk on. Not that I wouldn't do what I wanted anyway. Not that I'd do anything illegal either. All a bit of farce really. No, there are two things about Moscow you won't find in Baedeker. The KGB give up on you at sunset, and there are no public bogs anywhere, so you'd be well advised to skip that second cup of morning coffee and piss before you leave the hotel. You mark my words, the bloke watching you will vanish before four o'clock. Probably desperate for a piss himself."

Masefield picked up the twist of newspaper holding his pierogi and paid. Potato and cheese, a touch of soured cream—hot, greasy, and filling.

"Sounds like a waste of time to me."

"Oh it is. There's nothing to be gained spying on me. Everything there is to know about English Sewing Cotton is in our brochure."

"But they think you might spy on them, surely?"

"Cloak and dagger nonsense. Load of old bollox. If our people wanted someone to spy in Russia they'd hardly send a cotton rep and a . . . what did you say you did, old man?"

"Metals . . . rare metals."

"I mean, they'd send a proper spy, wouldn't they? Someone trained. You know . . . a Richard Hannay kind of thing."

"Actually Richard Hannay was an amateur."

"Well you know what I mean. It simply wouldn't be blokes like us. But, as I said, they don't give us the benefit of the doubt. I ask you, do I look like a bloody spy?"

Masefield bit into his last pierogi, glanced off to his left. The man in the black mackintosh was still on the other side of the street, fists sunk deep in his pockets. Hiding in plain sight. Cold, and no doubt hungry. He didn't look like a spy either.

It was a quarter past three. Masefield decided he'd lead his tail around for another half hour and put Proffitt's theory to the test.

§28

Perhaps he should be in an art gallery, like the Tretyakov or a literary shrine like Tolstoy's house, or watching the goose-stepping changing of the guard at Lenin's tomb, but he wanted to know the enemy. After all, they were not his enemy, the system was the enemy, not the Russian people—and he wanted to see how they lived, something he knew he'd never be shown, and something most of the men on the trade mission wouldn't care to see. Somewhere there was a "real" Russia not to be found in the hotels occupied by Westerners. He wanted to step past clichés of the USSR . . . adjectives stuck in the rut of "grey" or "colourless" or "identical." If Russia came in colour and 3-D he wanted to see it for himself.

He drifted on, away from the Muromets, out of the city centre past endless, "identical" blocks of flats, past his own knowledge of the map, north and east into he knew not what district, along pavements wet with "grey" slush, into a street of small shops. Every one had a queue, and, as he soon deduced, several queues. He should buy something, anything . . . just for the experience.

His black shadow was hanging back, and Masefield remembered one of Brown's lessons in losing a tail: "Go into a shop. Most unlikely he'll follow. If there's another way out, take it. If there isn't, waste all the time you can and perhaps he'll think you have found another way out."

He decided to buy apples. It could have been almost anything, so long as he joined the queue, conspicuous as the only man, and overheard what one Mrs. Soviet Citizen might be saying to another Mrs. Soviet Citizen, which turned out to be bunions, chilblains, and what a drunken sod her husband was.

The queue moved so slowly it became distinctly possible that his tail had concluded the worst and moved on, and when Masefield reached the counter the apples were unappetizing, almost "colourless," brown-spotted and wrinkly like the back of his mother's hands. He bought two all the same. Then, clutching some sort of invoice, he joined the queue for the pay clerk. It all struck him as archaic, a snail-paced variation on going into a butcher's in England thirty years ago—a process the English speeded up by winging the invoice across to the girl in the wire-mesh booth via a spring-loaded overhead line. The Russian method took twice as long. And when he'd handed over his kopecks, there was yet another queue to collect the apples, with which he was not to be entrusted until paid for. What did this say about the USSR? What meaning could be extruded that might shed light on a nation armed with nuclear missiles that could cross continents faster than the queue for fruit could move five yards? He had last queued like this sometime in 1946 back in Derby, on his demob leave, his mother had told him to hold her place in the queue for potatoes at the local greengrocer's while she nipped into the chemist's. Then it dawned on him—the war had simply never ended for these people. There had been no demob for them. Everything here was either unobtainable, regulated, or slowed down to a grind . . . and the inevitability of that was . . . well, it had to be . . . a black market. "Yes, we have no bananas, we have no bananas today" . . . except on the black market.

The shadow was waiting when he emerged after a good twenty minutes—standing on the next corner, cigarette in hand.

Brown had said, "Look at him as little as possible. You simply don't know he's there."

Masefield turned the opposite way, another two streets on and he found himself at the end of another queue. More women clutching baskets, old men with oilskin bags, all queuing for fruit and veg at one of half a dozen makeshift stalls. Was this the black market—черный рынок?

A uniformed militia man walked by, an exchange of nods with the men behind the stalls and Masefield knew that this really was the black market, out in the open, all kept safe by a backhander, a nod and a wink.

He queued again, and by the time he reached the front, the day had waned, and he found himself looking at an array of apples, carrots, turnips, and potatoes of far higher quality and far higher prices than the shop had asked.

"Ну вы что, черт возьми, будете весь день там стоить?"

Are you going to stand there all fucking day? He bought another apple—just the one—as vividly red and green as a traffic light, paid three times what he had paid in the grocers, and succeeded in annoying the proprietor and most of the others in the queue, one woman heaving him aside with a well-rounded hip and a mutter of

"Дурак!"

Arsehole.

It was an oddly pleasing encounter. Hip to hip. She was dressed in "grey," the only splash of colour being a frayed red headscarf, but he and "real" Russia had finally connected, albeit only via the backside of a monotone fat woman—"dumpy as a sack of spuds"—but she loomed up in 3-D and swore at him in Cyrillic stereo. He was prepared to bet that Arthur Proffitt had never been called а дурак.

And when he emerged from the mob clutching his one red apple, looking like Snow White about to take the poison, his shadow had gone. He walked back to the corner, peered both ways. Gone, just as Proffitt had told him—vanished with the sunset.

§29

Masefield had always been drawn to junk shops. You learnt as much about the culture of a country from its junk shops as its supermarkets. Moscow had no supermarkets. A couple of streets away from the clutter of vegetable stalls he found such a shop. A window full of samovars, a doorway half-blocked with shovels and pickaxes, and a greasy glass counter housing cameras and wristwatches.

The price he paid for listening was greater than the price he paid for the camera.

The man in the junk shop spoke English badly but seemed determined to try, and, it being simply impossible for Masefield to usurp the situation and conduct the transaction in Russian, to pretend and to tolerate English that was compound-fractured rather than broken was the only option. To speak Russian would blow his cover in a single sentence—the second he got past "спасибо" and "до свидания."

Masefield pointed to a Zenit S under the glass counter. A 35mm, single lens reflex camera in a shiny black leather case. It looked brand new, the oddity on a shelf mostly stacked with broken Poljot and Pobeda watches missing hands or lenses. He knew a little about cameras—he had been given a Box Brownie for his twelfth birthday, and throughout his undistinguished war had travelled everywhere with a folding Kodak 620—but he'd never owned a 35mm. Many of his few friends had 35 mils, picked up on foreign jaunts. His boss at New Caledonian had a Leica with which he took colour "slides" rather than "snapshots" and would ruin any meal at his house with a postprandial slideshow of mind-numbing boredom. Skiing in Switzerland, summer breaks in Tenerife . . . snow and sand, sand and snow. For a middle-class Englishman of means it was almost obligatory when taking a foreign holiday to come back with a new camera, a fake Rolex, and a deep curiosity about "when olive oil/aubergines/garlic/anything-else-both-exotic-and-obscure might catch on in this country."

"Is verr good," said the proprietor, handing the camera to Masefield.

Yes. He knew that. It probably was good. It wasn't a Leica, unlike the Zorki it looked nothing like a Leica, but it was OK. And he didn't doubt he knew more than its owner. Focal plane shutter, one thirtieth of a second to one five-hundredth. Sand and snow didn't move much, but with a fast film at one five-hundredth of a second you could catch anything on the hoof.

Masefield did the arithmetic in his head. The man wanted six roubles for the Zenit. At current rates of exchange about £2 10s 6d. Cheap at twice the price, plain, unflashy, the perfect tourist's camera (after all he was a tourist, wasn't he?), the very model anonymous Mr. Brown had suggested to him back in London—but a little further along the counter was a cardboard box full of camera parts . . . lenses, light meters, bodies . . . and sticking edge up was the end of a small, aluminium, rectangular camera, about three inches long—so small it would fit neatly across the palm of his hand.

Masefield pointed at the box.

"May I?" he asked.

The man stared blankly back at him, perhaps the conditional was a confusion.

"Avec votre permission . . . ?"

It worked. The man nodded and gestured an open hand towards the box of parts.

Masefield rummaged, pretended to look at half a dozen bits, and as he did so set the tiny camera on the counter.

It was a Minox Riga, the perfect spy's camera (and he was a spy, wasn't he?), cartridge-loading, and with an attached chain neatly measured off in fractions of a metre so that you had no need to guess at distance. He wondered how the man had come by it. It was Latvian made, World War II, and he supposed many of them had been made, lost, sold . . . but he also supposed that they were impossible to buy in any legitimate shop. What, after all, would any tourist want with a camera uniquely designed to photograph documents?

There was a gamble here. If the chap on the other side of the counter knew as much about the Minox as he did about the Zenit, then his knowledge might extend as far as "verr good" and no further. Doubtless everything in this palace of junk, from the broken car jack he'd almost tripped over to the pile of pre-war Bakelite radios heaped in the corner, was "verr good." In a country that had next to nothing, you threw nothing away. It didn't mean he knew what he had. Even the fact that it was in a box of camera parts told him nothing. The man might just have bought the job lot and not bothered to examine any of them. He might think it an attachment to something larger rather than a camera in itself.

Masefield pushed a lens that might just fit the Zenit, a light meter in a tatty brown leather case and the Minox towards the owner. He glanced down, no more than that, and asked for another six roubles. Done.

He slung the Zenit over his shoulder, looking like a tourist, and with the Minox nestling in his coat pocket, felt like a spy. It was as a potent a symbol as there could be—as powerful as a gun in the unarticulated glossary of his newfound trade. He patted the pocket, smiled, and remembered his enemies fondly.

§30

Up in his room Masefield lay back on his rather lumpy bed. It was as good a room as any hotel he'd ever been in, and he'd been in plenty. It was warmer than most, but that was typical of what he thought of as the "snow" countries. So bloody cold outside they had learnt to heat the inside properly, whereas the English seemed content to shiver and turned off every last vestige of indoor heat between May and October. It was a clean room, smelled faintly of beeswax. He wondered where best to hide the Minox, and wondered more whether he needed to hide the Minox. The hint of beeswax reminded him—daily cleaners, the old babushkas he passed in the corridors. He swung his legs off the bed, knelt down. Put his nose to the parquet, breathed in the scent of fresh wax and looked under the bed. Not a speck of dust. No hiding place free from granny's dusters. He decided the camera was best kept in his pocket along with his spare specs and his fountain pen. If the KGB turned over his room, well . . . it wasn't there . . . and in the unlikely event he was searched, well . . . he was hardly trying to conceal it was he?

He wasn't the only one to buy a camera.

The trade missionaries were all gathered at a table in the Muromets bar. Proffitt was well into fake Russian brandy; mellow and near silent, the French were talking rapidly in low voices to each other and the Dutchman and the Belgian seemed to be Glendinning's captive audience.

On the table between them sat a Zorki, quite possibly the one Masefield had declined to buy earlier in the day.

"Got this in GUM. Absolutely cracking price."

Hellemans, the Belgian, hefted it in his hand, turned it around and looked at the lens and the gadget on the top.

"Looks like a Leica, feels like a Leica," he said. "But what is this?"

"Dunno, o'man. Russki behind the counter couldn't explain it to me in English. So I thought sod it and bought it anyway."

"May I?" Masefield asked.

Hellemans passed the camera to him.

"It's a rangefinder. If you change lenses, you then rotate the range-finder, thus, to match the focal length of lens, that way you're seeing more or less what the camera's seeing."

Glendinning did not roll his eyes up to the ceiling in boredom, but might just as well have done.

"If you say so, o'man. A camera's a camera to me. I'll probably give it to one of my kids and let them figure it out. Did you buy anything? I thought I saw you in GUM. Looking for a bargain too, were you? God, what the buggers will do for hard currency. One Regent Street shop, a Liberty, or a Fenwick for the party apparatchiks and Woolworth's for the rest of 'em. All hypocrisy isn't it. Some animals are more equal than others, eh?"

Masefield reached into his jacket pocket. He'd meant to show them this, was never quite sure when, but the word "hypocrisy" cued him like a drum roll.

He set the shrivelling, brown apple next to the fake Leica.

"That's what I bought," he said.

"Why, for God's sake?"

"I had to buy something, as I'd queued, but really I wanted to be in the queue, to queue for something. Didn't really matter what."

"You need a drink, someone get Masefield a glass."

"Queuing is a fundamental Russian experience. It goes with being cold, wearing leaky shoes, and drinking water that tastes foul. And, however bad you think the food is in a hotel like this . . . this is what a Russian queues up to buy and to eat."

"Have you gone completely bloody loopy? Fundamental bloody Russian experience?"

"Yes. Something like that. I felt it got me closer to understanding Russians."

"You really do need a drink. Listen o'man. There's only one thing to understand about Russians, Russia, the whole bloody Soviet system. Hypocrites. Every last damn one of them. Why you couldn't just hand over a few quid and buy yourself a fake Leica like everyone else I just do not know. They don't want your understanding; all they want is hard cash. They're just like everyone else, it's the ackers that matter . . . they just dress it up in a cloak of principle that doesn't mean shit to a dog. Plonk your average Russki down in a council house in some new town in the home counties . . . I dunno . . . Stevenage or Harlow, some oik hellhole or another . . . and in a couple of years he'll be voting Tory just like the English working bloke does. Because the most fundamental thing on God's earth can be summed up in a single phrase: "they've never had it so good" . . . and my do they know it. Put a few quid in a man's pocket and he'll forget Communism, Socialism, the bloody trades unions . . . all that left-wing claptrap. I say again, hypocrites. Every last damn one of them."

And with that, Glendinning picked up the apple, Masefield's little bit of Russia, and lobbed it neatly into a waste bin on the far side of the room. Masefield had never been very good at cricket, or tennis or any other game involving a small ball, but could admire the skill. He looked around to see if Tanya Dmitrievna had heard Glendinning's rant. But she was nowhere to be seen.

Masefield thought of asking Glendinning if the working bloke in Harlow or Stevenage, be he Russki or English oik, would be permitted to join the golf club, but it seemed like a red rag to an already insufferable bull.

Instead he went up to his room, ate the good red apple and set the last manky brown apple on the dresser between the Zenit and the Minox. Stared at his "souvenirs."

It occurred to him to see if he could strip down the Minox. It came apart easily enough. To his surprise the innards seemed to be brass, which explained its inordinate weight, and to his further surprise, there was an unexposed fifty-shot cartridge inside. That would be . . . no that might be . . . might possibly be . . . handy.

§31

Andrei Semyonovich collected him the next morning in a tatty Mosk-vich, which he drove himself. Of Black Mac there was no sign. Masefield assumed that one at a time was enough and that Andrei Semyonovich now played the same role.

He said very little on the journey. Masefield wondered if he, or any interpreter, had been instructed not to engage in conversation but merely to translate and answer questions. He asked how far they were going, and Andrei Semyonovich replied, "Not far. Not out of Moscow. To Preobrazhenskaya Ploshchad in the northern suburbs."

"And what's there?"

"The refinery you asked to see."

When the car pulled up in a wide suburban thoroughfare, Masefield looked around for anything resembling a refinery. There was none. Row upon row of thirties flats, six and seven storeys high, and in the middle, just as tall, a faded Orthodox church. It might once have been as beautiful as any in the city centre, pointed domes tapering as finely as a Christmas tree ornament, in powdery shades of weathered copper. Walls that might once have been a creamy magnolia could now be best described as dirt-coloured, streaked with black and stained with rust like dragon's tears.

To one side of a doorway, which had been savagely and carelessly widened to take huge steel doors, with no regard for the curve of the arch, was a rotting wooden sign that still bore the inscription

Святая Церковь Преображения.
Holy Church of the Transfiguration.

And on the doors themselves a stencilled line:

МЧМ.

"You're kidding?"
"I don't understand."
"You mean this is it?"
"Yes. МЧМ. Московские Чистые Металлы. Moscow Pure Metals."
Masefield was not at all sure he had heard Andrei Semyonovich right, but the man led off with a terse, "Please, you follow now."

Inside, the church had been stripped of everything. In between walls of fading gilt—scarred and scratched Madonnas in the plasterwork—stood steel-smelting furnaces, and above the furnaces a glowing head of Christ transfigured as though the gigantic sunburst halo was powered by the furnaces themselves. He had stepped into a world where mediaeval onion domes and heavenly spires melded with the earthly remnants of a Stalin-era industrial five-year plan. None of this looked or felt right.

A man bearing a striking resemblance to Peter Sellers playing union leader Fred Kite in the comedy *I'm All Right Jack* greeted him like a long-lost cousin.

"An English visitor. Our first since 1935. We are so proud, so pleased."

Masefield was handed a pair of overalls, whisked around the factory with a commentary from Andrei Semyonovich that was ninety per cent inaudible in the clash of steel and the roar of gas furnaces. It reminded him of open days at the Midland Railway Loco Works in Derby. There was, he thought, beauty in heavy industry—only an idiot would be blind to it—he had thought so the first time he had seen a Jubilee Class locomotive plucked up like a child's toy and hauled over his head. But what did all this heat and noise have to do with indium or any other post-transition metal? Indium melted at scarcely more than the boiling point of water—you could cook it up in a saucepan on the hob like scrambled eggs—in its solid state, at room temperature, you could slice it like a slab of butter.

It occurred to Masefield that in his conversation with Koritsev he had referred to indium as a "poor" metal, a common, and, he had thought, easier term to translate than "post-transition" metal. "Poor" and "pure," phonetically close in English, were perhaps even closer to the Russian ear and Andrei Semyonovich had heard not "poor" but "pure" and hence translated poor not as низший, nizshy, but as чистый, chisty. If the bugger spoke more clearly Masefield would have spotted this the day before. He hadn't. Hence a not uninteresting but otherwise wasted morning observing the smelting of gold and silver—"pure" metals in that they were "precious" metals.

After the obligatory tot of vodka with Fred Kite, the toast to the United Kingdom, and the obligatory second shot of vodka and toast to the USSR, and the obligatory third shot of vodka and toast to nothing in particular, Masefield said, "Andrei Semyonovich, I would like to go back to the ministry."

§32

Tact might be paying off. The look on Andrei Semyonovich's face betrayed no offence taken, and Koritsev still seemed very willing to please. All the same, all explaining the "slight" misunderstanding led to was another, "Leave it with me. Perhaps next time." He'd have to look in the cellar again.

As Masefield left Koritsev's office, the next man waiting to see the minister was waiting by the door.

"I couldn't help but overhear," he said in good English. "The door is open after all, but . . . you're not the Masefield who wrote the paper on post-transition metals for *New World Geology* in '59, are you?"

§33

"Grigory Grigoryevich Matsekpolyev," he said. "Professor of Physics and what have you at the Leningrad Polytechnical Institute."

What have you? A throwaway line or a boastful use of English to show how good he was?

"Come and walk with me a while, Mr. Masefield."

Masefield thought of the line from Lewis Carroll, one his dad had never tired of reciting to him, "O Oysters, come and walk with us" and no sooner had he thought it than his new friend uttered it.

"'O Oysters, come and walk with us!' The Walrus did beseech. 'A pleasant walk, a pleasant talk, along the briny beach.'"

Oh yes, he was definitely showing off. Nothing in Brown's prep and pep talks had prepared him for this. He'd warned him about seemingly random encounters with seemingly harmless individuals, but not this. Not a tall, sophisticated show-off, a man exercising his command of English language and literature—a man who looked less like the shabby apparatchik in the black mac and more like a younger version of Lord Mountbatten, a man dressed far better than he was, far better than Comrade Under-Minister. With a heavy fur collar to his coat, a black sable hat, and pigskin gloves, all he lacked was a furled umbrella. This was one of the party elite. Masefield felt small and tatty beside him—sophistication such as this was beyond his accomplishment, though not beyond his dreams. Come to think of it, he looked a bit like Burne-Jones, and he hadn't even bothered with the moustache.

"Of course I don't have a briny beach, but the Borodinsky Bridge is just over there. We could have all the fun of looking down on a frozen river while we chat."

Chat? What was this man?

"Of course," Masefield replied.

It was not a matter of "what do I have to lose?"—he had everything to lose, but the approach was intriguing, bizarre.

"I thought your paper first rate. Indeed I was a little surprised to find that you were in industry rather than an academic."

In a matter of a couple of minutes they had reached the bridge over the Moskva. A clear, cloudless winter's day with, thankfully, no wind. It was almost tolerable. Masefield wondered if the spot had been chosen for its privacy.

"For my sins, I have to teach the odd class. Recalcitrant bunch of buggers at the best of times. Not the type to win a space race or fill a missile gap. Could I ask you to give a paper? Doesn't have to be the same as the one you published, and you'd be doing me a great favour."

Out of the blue. Unbelievable.

"I've never given a lecture in my life."

"First time for everything and you know more about the subject than I do. I'm heavy metal myself. Transuranics. But I will admit to a fascination with transition and post-transition metals, and, to split a hair, even the d-block elements have a certain charm."

"Yes," said Masefield. "They're beautiful. Almost unreal. I'll never forget playing with mercury as a schoolboy, watching it roll in bright silver bubbles across my desk, knowing all the time that it's a metal."

"Well said. Come and inspire my lackadaisical bunch of students with lines like that."

"You mean in Leningrad? I'm on a trade mission. I can't leave . . . "

"Don't worry about that. The institute will get you all the permits you need. And don't worry about the cost. Koritsev will pay. Absolutely in his own interests. Feather in his cap as you people say, an academic-diplomatic exchange at the industrial level. By the bye, what was the problem with Comrade Koritsev?"

"A little misunderstanding."

"Aren't they all? World War Three will begin with a little misunderstanding."

"I asked to see indium processing. I'm here to buy indium, after all. The UK has none. So I've never seen it processed."

"And?"

"The interpreter mixed up 'pure' and 'poor,' and I got all the crudity of a gold-smelting factory in an abandoned church. Nothing I haven't seen a hundred times before, although never in quite such an odd location."

"I think I can fix that for you. When will you be back?"

"I don't know, but the next trip will surely be set up before I finish this one?"

Matsekpolyev produced a personal card.

"Let me know. Think about a revised paper on the transition metals. Come to Leningrad, give the talk, I'll line up an interpreter for you, and I'll find you a processing plant. It will be a good diplomatic exchange. A Khrushchev-pleaser if ever I heard one. Peaceful coexistence in a nutshell."

"You know," Masefield said. "Peaceful coexistence has to be one of the great myths of our time, only it's Khrushchev saying it not Neville Chamberlain."

This set Matsekpolyev laughing.

"My God, and people think Russians are cynical."

§34

On the Thursday, their last night in Moscow, the seven intrepid industrialists gathered in the bar at the Muromets. Whether out of duty or courtesy, Tanya Dmitrievna joined them.

It was a night to hit the vodka—they were always going to hit the vodka—and it seemed that Glendinning had managed to learn something, perhaps just one something, about Russia . . . that it was bad form ever to put the cork back in a bottle of vodka once opened. He was going to get them all shit-faced and with one exception they did not care.

Masefield reckoned they'd all knocked back the equivalent of three doubles apiece, when Glendinning banged the heavy base of his glass on the bar and got their attention.

"Listen up, you drunken buggers. Drink all you want, drink all you can. No need to worry about the mess bill—old Geoffrey'll be picking that up."

A susurrus of "eh?" "what?"

"Little bet the two of us had, and Geoff lost. So *nostrovya*, comrades!"

And with that he sank a very large vodka in one gulp, slammed his glass down again, yelled, "Set 'em up, Joe!" at the barman and turned around to face the room, both elbows on the bar, a proprietorial grin of measured bonhomie on his face—enough to show he was in charge, not enough for the warmth of fellow feeling.

His gaze fell on Masefield, and the grin became a snigger and the snigger a guffaw, the hearty public school bray that had made Masefield detest evenings in the officers' mess. Then Glendinning turned his back on him to drink again.

"Mess bill" . . . well, that spoke volumes.

Masefield stood clutching his glass, not drinking, not wanting to drink, and looked cautiously to his left. As he had deduced, Tanya Dmitrievna was standing next to him. Perhaps the taunting laughter had been aimed at her too?

She returned his gaze. He could read not a shred of emotion in her eyes, but surely she had worked out the nature of the bet?

"I'm sorry," he said.

"Don't be," she replied.

§35

He had nothing to show MI6 for a week in Moscow, and he knew it. Telling himself that it had cost them nothing, that New Caledonian was picking up the bill didn't help much. Nor did telling himself that their expectation of him must surely be small.

He gave the roll of 35mm film from his Zenit to Tom Radley in Berlin. Radley could have all the delights of the domes of St. Basil's, the goose-stepping guards at Lenin's tomb, and in complete contrast the faded, decrepit old church out in Preobrazhenskaya Ploshchad. All snapped for posterity.

"I'm sorry," he said. "It's all very mundane stuff. Nothing you couldn't find in a back number of *National Geographic* magazine."

"Early days. Geoffrey. Early days. At least you've established your credentials and you've made interesting contacts. This . . . whatsisname?"

"Grigory Grigoryevich Matsekpolyev."

"That's a mouthful and it's also progress . . . progress . . . we're talking to a professor at the Leningrad Poly . . . er . . ."

It surprised Masefield that Radley had no idea what he was referring to.

"The Leningrad Polytechnical Institute. It's the dog's bollocks of Soviet science. He's a professor of physics."

"As I said, Geoffrey, progress. Who knows where this might lead? And you have another meeting set up at the Foreign Ministry?"

"Yes, in January. In principle they'll sell. We still have to agree on a price, and there'll be a lot of argy-bargy about shipping and so forth. I would imagine at least another three trips before we get an ounce of indium. And after that I can think of half a dozen other metals I could be buying."

"Jolly good. The mills of Khrushchev grind as slowly as the mills of God, eh?"

"Something like that," Masefield said.

He had more than an inkling of meetings of infinite boredom and a mountain of triplicated paperwork. And of spelling things out to Radley using only short words.

He decided not to mention the Minox.

He had also decided not to bring it back to Berlin with him. He had tried concealing it wrapped in his flannel at the bottom of his wash kit, but the weight of all those brass components made it a dead giveaway. Any nosy apparatchik who hefted the kit would know at once it wasn't just a shaving brush and a tube of minty Gibbs SR. Instead, and he was proud of this, he had "thought like a spy" and on the assumption he would be at the Muromets for future visits, he had lifted a fire bucket full of sand off its iron hook at the end of the corridor, carefully removed about fifty fag ends, tipped out the sand onto a newspaper, buried the Minox in a stout brown paper bag at the bottom of the bucket, scooped up the sand, carefully replaced about fifty fag ends and hung the bucket back where he found it. It was his one sense of achievement, even if he could tell no one about it. Telling Radley would make him feel foolish, as foolish as he had felt when Radley had jokingly referred to him as "our man in Moscow." Well, it was a joke, surely?

§36

Moscow: January 1961

Masefield had little experience of art galleries. It wasn't as if he knew nothing about art but "knew what he liked"—he'd been dragged to the local gallery in Derby as an adolescent by uninspiring art teachers and come back admiring the way Joseph Wright had with light, and pleased that someone before the invention of photography had chosen to depict scientists at work. Beyond this, he knew nothing or next to nothing. An art gallery was like a pop music chart, you looked for the greatest hits, for Elvis or Johnnie Ray . . . for Van Gogh or Monet. The Tretyakov Gallery seemed to have no greatest hits. No Van Gogh, no Monet, no Joseph Wright.

He'd looked at portrait after portrait of "unknown" Russian nobles and was fighting off the sense of failure that he knew was the end product of boredom as surely as beta decay turned protons into neutrons. He was stuck in front of some bloke in a wig astride a horse, wishing the aspirant culture snob in him would just let go.

"Mr. Masefield?"

It was Tanya Dmitrievna—the "guide" who'd kept a watchful eye on them all during the trade mission last month.

"You are back so soon."

"Oh, it'll take more than one visit to do the deal as it were. And you?"

"A tourist party. Just finished. I work for Intourist, as you know."

Of course he knew. Just as he knew everyone who worked for Intourist also worked for the KGB. Brown had told him so—they might be no more than low-grade observers reporting everything without discrimination, from who got drunk in the bar to who asked about space missions.

"Is Mr. Glendinning with your party too?"

"If he's here I haven't seen him. This trip is a bit different from the last. I'm a party of one, as it were. I have more meetings at the ministry . . . just happens I have nothing on this afternoon."

Suddenly she was transparent. He could read her like a book. Even knowing her trade was deceit, he could read her. She had sagged at the news, a tide of sadness lapping at her eyes. What had that bugger Glendinning told her? What had he done to her? He took out a clean handkerchief and passed it to her. She dabbed at her cheeks.

"Do you know a café where we could have tea?" he asked.

"Yes. Of course. Just not here."

Further down Lavrushinsky Lane she led him into a fogged-up café—puddles all over the floor, a pungent waft of steaming wool, the clank of cast-iron radiators expanding and contracting, the hubbub of forty voices all talking at once.

"We will be OK here," she said.

Did they need to be OK? Didn't they just need tea and time?

She shed two of her outer layers, parked him at an empty table and joined the queue. Masefield looked around, concluded, as no one turned to look at him, that he was of no interest to the proprietors of the ongoing conversations. Perhaps that was the definition of OK.

Tanya Dmitrievna returned with two glasses of black tea, their little silver handles looking to Masefield like tiny remnants of the ancien régime, a touch of curling Russian elegance in the stark new Soviet world of straight lines and plain facades.

"I'm sorry," she said. "I don't know what came over me. I don't know why I have you here."

He did.

"No," he said. "I'm the one who should say sorry. I didn't agree to Glendinning's bet, but I also didn't say no. If I had he might not have boasted as crudely as he did in the bar that night."

"He's not coming back, is he?"

"Probably not. I talked to him at the airport before we boarded in December. He got the deal he wanted. He might be here, I just haven't seen him."

If Glendinning were at the Muromets, Masefield felt certain he would have heard him.

"I see."

"And now you feel used."

"What?"

"Used . . . as in the sense of . . ."

"I know what it means. It just doesn't seem the right word. I gave myself freely. I wasn't looking for a relationship."

"Then I don't understand."

"Glendinning offered to help me."

"Help you with what?"

She lowered her voice as she lowered her eyes, looking at the cracked Formica table, not at him.

"Help me to get out of Russia."

§37

They walked the streets as the daylight faded. Masefield didn't look for a tail and hadn't looked since morning. Either they had given up on him after the predictability of his last visit, or the tail was walking at his side.

After two blocks in silence, she said, "I am not heartbroken, Mr. Masefield. I was not in love with Glendinning, I simply enjoyed him."

"And the offer to help you . . . defect? That is the word isn't it, defect?"

"I would not have taken him at all seriously if it had been his ploy to seduce me. I would have been seduced or not seduced as I chose. But, he said it afterwards, when he had had his way with me, and I with him. He had nothing to gain with an empty promise. And . . . I said 'leave' or 'get out' . . . not 'defect.' Why do you say 'defect'?"

They'd reached a moment he had known they'd reach for at least the last fifteen minutes.

"Because KGB agents don't leave, they defect."

"You think I'm KGB?"

"Of course you're KGB. Everyone who works for Intourist is KGB."

"Is that what they tell you in England?"

"Yes."

"And do they also tell you that the only way to get a job with Intourist is to join the KGB, and that we join the KGB the way schoolteachers joined the Nazi Party in Germany. Simply to have or to keep the job they liked?"

"You make it sound as benign as being a rural postman in Clackmannanshire."

"What is Clockmansheer? I don't understand."

"Forgive me, I was making a joke. You are KGB? Yes or no?'

"Of course I am. But you have to understand what that means. I carry no gun, I have never used invisible ink . . . I cannot kill you with one hand tied behind my back . . . It's just a job . . . do you not have that notion in England . . . it's just a job . . . . I am only doing my job!"

She was tearful again—tears of rage. She pulled out the handkerchief he had given her in the museum and wiped away the tears before they froze to her skin.

"I'm sorry. Of course I understand the idea. I'm not sure I believe it but I understand it."

"Will you ever stop saying you're sorry?"

"You have no gun, no invisible ink . . . so what do you do? Write reports?"

"Yes."

"And what did you report on me?"

"That you were the only one who wasn't a drunken capitalist pig. They like that phrase: 'capitalist' and 'pig' go together. They have little problem with 'drunken' as you may imagine. And . . . I told them you were harmless."

"And Glendinning?"

"I had to lie. I said he was harmless too. I wanted him to get me out. The truth would not have served me so well."

"And the truth is?"

"He is MI6."

§38

Leningrad

A return ticket to Leningrad arrived at the hotel. A travel permit. A covering letter from Koritsev with half a dozen official-looking rubber stamps. And with them a note from Matsekpolyev.

"I trust you are ready. GGM."

He had hoped for a view, for a chance to see something of the country outside Moscow, the lie of the land between the new capital and the old, but for each leg of the journey Koritsev had booked him on the night sleeper. It was already dark when he boarded the train at the Leningradsky Station, but then who could stare out of the window for eight hours? It was a schoolboy fantasy of perpetual trainspotting, but he knew from having tried that at Tamworth junction as a boy that you got bored in less than twenty minutes and looked for something else to do. Perhaps night was best, perhaps sleep was best, perhaps he'd been booked on the night train just to ensure he saw nothing?

The conductor showed him to a compartment, as narrow as an outside privy and containing two bunks. For the first time it occurred to him that he would have to share and when his roommate came in only seconds later he found himself facing a six-foot-two army captain in uniform.

He muttered a greeting that could have been in any language, slung his bag on the lower bunk and so deprived Masefield of any say in the matter.

"Good evening," Masefield said, feeling he should play the polite, innocent foreigner and hoping that this would be the last exchange between them.

It was.

The soldier kicked off his boots, hung up his jacket and was in bed in less than a minute. He seemed to have no interest in Masefield, and Masefield was almost reassured by this. And when the man flicked out the light, leaving Masefield to undress and climb into the top bunk by the firefly glow of a five-watt emergency light, he was wholly reassured. It was just a coincidence. Nothing more. The man had not been sent to watch him.

All the same he could not sleep. Far too many reasons to be apprehensive. Not least that he was about to present a university paper for the first time in his life. Sooner or later the magic of steel wheels on steel rails, the perfect rhythm of clickety-clack at a modest and regular fifty miles per hour, would cast its spell upon him. Meanwhile he might do what he did best. Worry.

§39

The conductor nudged him awake. Horizontal winter sunlight was slicing into the compartment, and Masefield was confused and bleary. The soldier had gone. Not a trace. Masefield wondered if he had imagined him. If he wasn't trapped in an old pre-war Hitchcock film where people simply vanished from trains leaving only a packet of Harriman's tea to tell the tale.

Another nudge, a moustachioed, halitotic face thrust closer to his own.

"Мы приехали в Ленинград, товарищ. Или вы думаете, что вы будете спать весь день?"

We're in Leningrad, comrade. Or did you think you could sleep all day?

§40

"Don't feel you have to keep it simple. They're a dozy bunch, but a bright bunch. Give it them too easy and they can get lazy."

Simplicity bothered him. Matsekpolyev's assumption that he was bright enough to do this at all bothered him. And Matsekpolyev read his mind.

"Don't worry. You'll be fine. Our translator will take her pace from you. When you feel you've said enough . . . perhaps two or three sentences, pause and she'll nip in sharpish."

"Sharpish." Matsekpolyev loved his English affectations. Any second now he's pronounce the entire nerve-racking situation "tickety-boo."

He'd risen, he hoped, to the challenge. Stepped up from the poor metals he knew best to transition metals, and the oddity of combinant inner shell valence electrons and the role of this unique sub-atomic feature in magnetism. Nothing as exotic as indium, all as ordinary, as basic as iron . . . the most common element *in* the planet, pipped at the post for the title of Most Common Metal *on* the Planet only by aluminium . . . but who ever beat a sword or a ploughshare out of aluminium?

Masefield looked out at the serried ranks of students, stacked to the gods, a hundred and fifty or more, and heard himself introduced as "the distinguished English scholar." He wasn't and no amount of flattery would make it so. But he had sought a life of deception, a life in which he was anyone but plain old Geoffrey Masefield from Derby. And he began to warm to the occasion. He would tell no lies, he would bluff no stuff . . . he was the lie, his presence was the bluff, his entire identity but for his name was the lie. He hoped he wasn't smiling too much as the applause died down and Matsekpolyev ushered him to the lectern. He was the lie; the subject was real.

§41

Back in Matsekpolyev's office, the professor was relaxed and expansive.

"Particularly neat account of Coulomb's law, I thought."

"They can look that up in any textbook printed in the last hundred and fifty years."

"Possibly, but your version has the virtue of being succinct."

At this rate the flattery might work. He might even begin to believe in himself.

"And of course, they tend to purity. Theorists all. Won't dirty hands or minds with the commercial value of any of this. You gave them a timely reminder that few of them will stay pure; they'll most of them end up in industry just like you. You drew some interesting illustrations from your work in industry. Impressive. It'll be less of a shock when they're ordered to report to some godforsaken place like Chelyabinsk."

Dare or forfeit?

"I asked Koritsev to let me visit Chelyabinsk."

"Chelyabinsk? Did Koritsev laugh out loud?"

"He didn't say anything."

"I'm surprised they didn't tell you this back in England, but Chelyabinsk is a closed area. Has been for a couple of years. You can't go there, and for that matter neither can I. But I gathered in Moscow that it was a heavy-duty processing plant you were after. I said I could help and I will. Something much nearer home. Sillamäe, in Estonia. A couple of hours from here by car as opposed to the thirty-six hours you'd spend on a train getting to Chelyabinsk if in some moment of folly Koritsev ever gave you permission. Sillamäe's a much better choice. They're just getting started on the refining of transitions and post-transitions in Sillamäe. Niobium, tantalum and, lucky you, indium. We're driving over tomorrow. You'll enjoy it. State-of-the-art equipment. I doubt anything you've seen in the West will compare."

"Not secret, then?"

"Everything in the Soviet Union is a secret, and if it impresses our sense of secrecy upon you its official name is Factory Number 7, Enterprise P.O.B. P-6685, a phrase I would hate to have to utter drunk . . . but there are secrets and secrets. If this were a *secret* secret . . . well, would I be offering if it were?"

Yes, thought Masefield, you bloody well would.

§42

Masefield had read that trains crossing between Finland and the USSR were sealed at the border, so that no nosy parker with his eyes glued to the window could see a damn thing until the train entered Leningrad. Huge metal shutters closed off the windows, and the carriages looked less like public transport than armoured trains left over from the war. It posed a question. What was there to see? And if the answer to that was what Masefield was seeing from the car window as Matsekpolyev drove him at reckless speed across the Pskov Oblast, then it was nothing—trees and frozen lakes and snow and bugger all from Leningrad all the way to the lost frontier with Estonia. But, as his host had told him, everything in Russia was a secret. They didn't even want anyone counting the pine trees.

He could have nodded off. The knowledge that he was a spy and that an important part of a spy's job might be spying would not have kept him awake. He didn't feel much like counting pine trees. What did keep him awake was the seemingly endless, if engaging, prattle of Matsekpolyev.

He learnt more than he needed to about the man's tastes and interests—a fondness for Boccaccio and Chaucer that left him feeling ignorant as he'd read neither, a passion for Shostakovich that he could not share and, far from last, an appreciation of the symphonies of Edward Elgar. At least he'd heard both of those—a couple of nights at the Free Trade Hall in Manchester ten years ago. Sir John Barbirolli and the Hallé.

Yet—it was flattering that Matsekpolyev thought of him, and treated him, as an intellectual equal. Flattering and embarrassing. He wanted to be the man Matsekpolyev took him to be. He wanted the cultural leap from the backstreets of Derby where magazines were called books and books were non-existent, where music was the Billy Cotton Band Show and Sir John Barbirolli, if known at all, was referred to as Rubber Brolly. He knew he'd crawled out of the gutter. He'd scarcely been aware that until now his nose had only just popped up above the kerbstone.

"What do you make of this bloke Kerouac?"

Bloke—he would say bloke, wouldn't he?

Bloke or not, Masefield had never read Kerouac, but that was not the issue.

"Grigory Grigoryevich, how on earth do you get hold of books by Jack Kerouac? Foreign trips? A bit of smuggling?"

"Mostly from visitors like yourself. I don't make foreign trips. I stick within the territory of the Warsaw Pact."

"Why?"

"In case they don't let me back in. Why do you think Pasternak would not collect his Nobel Prize?"

"They wouldn't do that to him?"

"They most certainly would have. He never wanted the damn prize in the first place, told me himself it should have gone to Moravia, but he knew that collecting it in person would be the last straw. A bit like getting excommunicated by the Pope. He'd be stuck in the West for the rest of his life . . . not that he lived much longer anyway, but that's by the by."

"But in the West he would have been . . . fêted."

"I'm sure he would . . . but it's scant reward for losing your country. Don't get me wrong, Mr. Masefield—I may not be an apparatchik, but I am every inch a Russian. And in case you thought otherwise, I am a party member. So . . . I study Western culture, I enjoy Western culture but I've no wish to live it. Could you leave England? Could you lose England?"

He could, but it seemed unwise to say so.

§43

Piotr Ilyich Putkin, technical director of the Sillamäe plant, was nothing like Fred Kite. As different to look at from the manager of Moscow Pure Metals as was possible. Tall and gangly—like Matsekpolyev himself. Well dressed in a three-piece suit—like Matsekpolyev himself. But their managerial practices were identical and Masefield began to think he could go nowhere in the Soviet Union without the top coming off the vodka bottle.

First there was the toast to the distinguished visitor. One shot knocked back. Then there was the toast to Comrade Professor. Second shot. Then Matsekpolyev returned the compliment and they all hoisted a third glass to Comrade Technical Director and only when all three were sufficiently tiddly did they set off on the tour.

Matsekpolyev was right. He had seen nothing like it. One of the advantages, perhaps the only advantage, of being blown to buggery by the Red Army, of being kicked back and forth between the Third Reich and the USSR for five years, was that you had little choice but to rebuild and in so doing modernise. He's never seen so much stainless steel. It was like being inside an Italian espresso machine.

He was about to ask what such-and-such a vast shiny chunk of metal did, when Piotr Ilyich announced that it was time for another toast and he was whisked back to the office to knock back more vodka and drink the health of Her Majesty Queen Elizabeth II, who Piotr Ilyich hoped would visit the Soviet Union very soon.

Back in the factory, Masefield asked if it was all right to take photographs. Piotr Ilyich must have noticed the Zenit hanging from his shoulder in its tatty leather case. All the same he hesitated. Then Matsekpolyev put one arm around his shoulders and said, "What have you got to hide?" and Piotr Ilyich replied, "Everything." Then they both doubled up with laughter and through the laughter Matsekpolyev translated for Masefield—and Masefield, cautious of his cover, refrained from laughing until he'd finished.

Matsekpolyev positioned himself in front of a bank of dials and switches, and beckoned Piotr Ilyich to stand next to him.

"Smile," he said, and they both did.

And it dawned on Masefield that Matsekpolyev had chosen the shot deliberately and the fact that he and Piotr Ilyich were the grinning foreground was as nothing to the technology visible in the background.

Half a dozen more staged shots followed. Piotr Ilyich seemed never to tire of smiling. Nor did he tire of drinking.

Another adjournment to the office and a toast to "our esteemed leader, Comrade Khrushchev." Would sobriety fall upon them only when they ran out of people to toast?

After an hour or more, Masefield had used up an entire roll of film, thirty-six shots entirely staged by Matsekpolyev. He asked if there was a dark or dimly lit place where he might change rolls. Piotr Ilyich showed him to his private lavatory, next to his office, and when Masefield emerged he found it was his turn to propose the toast.

He could think of no one.

Bulganin? Yesterday's man. They'd just laugh.

Macmillan? He'd never voted for him and to drink his health seemed like hypocrisy.

Kennedy? They'd laugh at that too. The man Khrushchev dismissed as a "boy."

"Come on, Geoffrey. Doesn't have to be royalty. We've done the Queen. Give us one of your famous English writers."

"OK. Gentlemen, raise your glasses to . . . Spike Milligan."

And, in Russian, they wished long life upon the creator of Eccles, Bluebottle and Henry Crun.

Halfway through roll two Matsekpolyev called it a day. They shook hands heartily and repeatedly with Piotr Ilyich and made their way back to the car.

"Are you OK to drive?"

"For God's sake, Geoffrey. This is Russia. Everybody is half-cut half the time. If they cremate Khrushchev when he dies, his body will fuel a power station for a week."

On the way back to Leningrad Matsekpolyev played much the same game of cultural chess he had on the way out—more cabbages, more kings. But the ball was squarely in Masefield's court.

Feeling pissed, and pissed almost always making him feel wicked, he asked, "Have you ever read any Kingsley Amis?"

"No."

"Oh you should. Uses humour to create a quintessentially Marxist critique of the English bourgeoisie."

"Sounds a complete bloody bore. Now, name me a writer you *really* like."

"Betjeman," Masefield said, quite seriously. "He's probably my favourite poet . . . 'Come friendly bombs and fall on Slough' . . . If you'd ever been to Slough you'd know exactly . . ."

§44

In his office the next morning, Matsekpolyev threw out a question so casually it might have been possible for a moment to believe that it had not been uppermost in his mind for days.

"Geoffrey, are you a spy?"

He hadn't even glanced up from the pile of papers he was working through.

"No. Of course I'm not. I'm here to buy indium, and I will be buying indium. Why do you ask such a question?"

"Потому что вы понимаете каждое нахуенное слово, которое я говорю."

Because you can understand every fucking word I say.

Masefield wondered what his face betrayed now. Was he card-bluffing blank? Was he transparent as indium itself? At least he wasn't twitching.

"It's all right, you know. I won't be telling anyone."

And Grigory Grigoryevich was smiling as he said it.

Then he looked down at his papers, scribbled his signature on something and said, "OK, have it your own way."

Emboldened, Masefield said, "Grigory Grigoryevich, каким образом вы избежите наказания?"

How do you get away with this?

Grigory Grigoryevich did not hesitate for so much as a moment. Looked up again and launched his answer.

"As I said, I'm a party member. A particularly privileged party member. And, of course, the USSR needs me. I realise that that may sound at odds with my fear of excommunication, but paranoia is a mathematical constant in my country . . . a strand of DNA. You imbibe it with mother's milk.

"They need me. Doesn't mean they won't let me go if they have to. But . . . I know more about transuranic elements than any man in the Soviet Union. I am the king of beta decay, the crown prince of neutron capture. OK, put me up against Robert Oppenheimer or Glenn

Seaborg . . . they'd give me a run for my money . . . but they're not here. They're stuck behind the Iron Curtain, prisoners of the free world."

It was an odd thought. For nearly twenty years now, since Churchill had purloined a phrase originated by Goebbels, Masefield and every other sentient inhabitant of the West had thought of Russia as being "behind" the Iron Curtain. It was odd, a mirror shift, to think that the Iron Curtain had two sides and that to a Russian, America and England were "behind" the Iron Curtain.

Odder still was the man he was dealing with. He began to realise that Grigory Grigoryevich Matsekpolyev might be the most unpredictable person he'd ever met.

"Why did you take me to Sillamäe?"

"You wanted a heavy processing plant. I obliged you."

"In the interests of academic freedom?"

"If you like. There are better reasons."

"Such as?"

"Such as . . . such as . . . the maintenance of the balance of power."

And he emphasised every single word, almost as though he'd spelled them out letter by letter.

Masefield thought hard if quickly about his next question.

"So they are enriching uranium? And I did see a cyclotron?"

"Do you really need me to confirm that? For all Putkin's ducking and diving you surely worked that out for yourself? I'd be shocked if you hadn't. Why else would they need a professor of transuranics on call? To be precise . . . they shipped more than twenty tons last year, and this year'll it'll top twenty-five. Quite enough to build more bombs and power more submarines and who knows, perhaps a bit left over to generate a few volts of electricity for the workers' flats."

"And I thought the English were cynical."

$45

Moscow

The bar at the Muromets was full. Another rowdy group of English-men learning that there was always a vodka bottle that had to emptied.

Tanya Dmitrievna had arrived. He had not seen her for three days. Not since she'd dropped her bombshell on a street corner in Za-moskvorechye. She chatted to the girl in charge of this week's foreign trade mission, waved to the barman, and expressed faux surprise at finding Masefield there.

"I was looking for you. You did not tell me when you were leaving."

Masefield found that, as ever, they could pursue a private conversation in the midst of a din.

"Tomorrow as it happens. Is your friend also KGB?"

"No more than me."

"You should have a standard form printed—English, drunk, harm-less. Might save a lot of typing."

She reached out across the small table, placed her hand on top of his.

"Perhaps. Now it is my turn to say I am sorry."

"For what?"

"I should not have . . . I am searching for the word . . . so many to choose from . . . I should not have burdened you."

The hand squeezed his, and as she drew it back, his squeezed hers and held on to it.

"Will you have dinner with me tonight? Here at the hotel."

She had come looking for him and still the invitation had taken her by surprise. The hand withdrew gently. The lips parted in a gap-toothed smile and unbidden to his brain came Glendinning's "forget the teeth, her tits are pretty damn amazing." And he wished he'd never heard the bastard say it, wished he'd not mentally stripped her. It felt like a betrayal. It was everything he wanted at that moment and still it felt like a betrayal.

"Yes. So kind. Of course," she said.

So kind. He could see himself as less than kind. He could see himself in the dozen or so bladdered Englishmen as clearly as looking into a mirror. "The only one who wasn't a drunken capitalist pig," she had termed him. He'd been all three in his time . . . the strippers, the hookers, the paralytic piss-ups. Every instance a betrayal.

"But," she added, "perhaps I can show you somewhere better. A restaurant."

Restaurants, bars, even cafés were thin on the ground. Closed in the Stalin era. One consequence was open-air boozing, drunks sharing bottles of vodka in doorways, and stairwells that reeked of piss.

"Unless, of course, you like the food here?"

The food at the Muromets never varied—borscht, dumplings, offal . . . tail, hoof and ear . . . cuts of meat the English would feed to a dog . . . and a quivering dish of marrowbone jelly that looked and tasted like the world's worst Turkish delight.

"Well," Masefield replied. "A change would be most welcome. Are we going far?"

"We walk for perhaps twenty minutes. There is a good little restaurant in Malaya Bronnaya. Unless of course you wish to take a taxi."

"No," Masefield said. "Happy to walk if you are."

"It is not so cold . . . sorry that sounds stupid . . . I mean not as cold as I have known it to be."

"And you have lived in Moscow all your life?"

"Yes."

She led him north and west into Tverskaya, out of the Theatre District, across Tverskoy Boulevard and Pushkin Square.

As they walked he told her of his venture into the working-class suburbs on his previous trip.

"Why would you want to see that?"

"Because she was there."

"I do not understand the phrase."

"Sorry . . . I shouldn't be elliptical. Asked why he had climbed Mount Everest Sir Edmund Hillary replied, 'because she was there.' There's even a story that when asked why he had married the Queen of England, Prince Philip also said 'because she was there.'"

"Is a joke, yes?"

"Yes. A joke."

And not one she thought funny.

"Are you sure you weren't followed?"

"Oh, I know I was followed."

"But you did nothing . . ."

There was real apprehension in the blue eyes.

"No. Please don't worry. I'm a guest here. I behaved myself."

She said no more until they reached the restaurant. Nothing announced "restaurant." No painted sign. No menu in the window. You knew it or you didn't.

The proprietor greeted her with glad recognition and a hug of affection. Seated them at a wooden table for two, flung a gingham cloth across it, and rattled off the menu.

Tanya Dmitrievna said yes to everything, and then to Masefield, "They have no written menu. We have whatever he has cooked today."

Masefield knew exactly what he had cooked today and did his best to look blank as she told him of ukha, stroganoff, sweet blinis, kvass, and vodka. Knowing the words was but a fraction of comprehension. He'd never eaten any of the dishes. He'd drunk the vodka—he'd never eaten the food.

Over the first shot of vodka he said, "If it's not impertinent, Tanya Dmitrievna, how old are you?"

"I am twenty-six."

"So you spent the war in Moscow?"

"Yes."

"No . . . evacuation?"

"My mother would not agree. My father was killed in 1942. At Stalingrad. After that nothing would make her leave Moscow."

"Is your mother still living?"

"No, she died in 1957. All I have is my sister. Anfisa."

"Older?"

"No. I am the elder . . . by ten minutes."

"Ah, twins. I am an only child."

"That is sad. I cannot imagine a life without my sister. We did everything together."

And so she told him of a childhood spent as one half of two, in the midst of the bloodiest war in history.

He thought of his own war. Well fed (even though there never seemed to be enough of anything), warm (well, warmish), and never heard a shot fired in anger. A uniform, a ration book and all found. Tanya Dmitrievna had gone cold and hungry and lain awake at night listening to the sound of German artillery as the Wehrmacht came within five miles of Moscow when she was six years old, three weeks before Christmas 1941.

England was an island. He had never felt more insular. And then the bridge appeared. She left nothing. Not a drop of soup, not a sliver of beef, not a crumb of pastry. Nor did he. And he knew that it was second nature to them both. He was ten years older than she was, and still they were children of the same war. To leave a clean plate. The social stigmata of the children of the war.

§46

Out in the street again, he took her hand and risked all.

"Tanya Dmitrievna, would you come back to the hotel with me?"

"No."

"I'm sorry. I shouldn't have—"

"You room is wired . . . microphones in the ceiling. Oh, don't be alarmed. Every room at the Muromets is wired."

She had told him no, but she had not removed her hand from his.

"My apartment is not."

"And where do you live?"

With her free hand she pointed to the upstairs window, two floors above the restaurant.

§47

He was a clumsy lover. Knowing this did not help much. Almost all his experience of sex had been with prostitutes, beginning in the army with the women who hung around the bases, and after a fallow, celibate time in Nottingham ascribed to failure of nerve, the women of the dark alleys and backstreets of Manchester.

He had learnt nothing for the simple reason that a prostitute has nothing to teach a man. She wants nothing from him, other than to be paid for services rendered, and hence has neither the wish nor the means to teach him anything, and the rendition becomes a one-way process. So much so, that Masefield had long ago come to think of sex as a form of dissatisfaction and the male orgasm as a misnomer.

Tanya Dmitrievna lay asleep with her head on his belly.

He thought of the word she had used for sexual intercourse with Glendinning, whilst wishing he could block the idea of Glendinning and sex from his mind permanently . . . She had said she "enjoyed" him. He was not at all sure how this might have started out in her mind before uttered in English . . . наслаждаться, with its suggestion of relishing something sweet, or обладать with an idea of possession, at its crudest "to have him."

But he had enjoyed her, and would dearly love to know that she had enjoyed him. No power on earth would make him ask.

Tanya Dmitrievna stirred.

"How . . . ?"

"About ten minutes," Masefield replied.

She unfurled, wriggled north in the direction of his head. Kissed him.

"Thank you, Mr. Masefield."

Was she smiling? Almost too dark to tell. Was she taking the mickey?

"My first name is Geoffrey."

"You have a second?"

"Stephen, after my father."

"Ah . . . a patronymic . . . how very Russian. Geoffrey Stefanovich. I shall call you that from now on."

No, she wasn't taking the mickey. She was teasing him. Women had never teased Masefield; they'd just hoicked up their knickers and taken his money.

$48

West Berlin

Masefield felt less of an idiot this time. He had next to no idea what, if anything, on the rolls of film he took in Sillamäe would be of use. Would Radley know a cyclotron if he saw one? Should he point them out to him or leave it to the analysts back in London? But to be able to give Radley something that wasn't the tourist take on Moscow, that was out of the city and better still in an industrial complex of the kind Burne-Jones had wanted him to get into . . . that was a step up, and it showed.

"Jolly good show, Geoffrey," Radley was saying as he sifted though the blow-ups. "They'll take a bit of scrutiny, but I can tell you now, we've never got a man into a place like this before. Bound to be something. Has to be."

"It ain't necessarily so," thought Masefield, but he did not deny the possibility or decline what was obviously meant as a compliment.

"Do you think you'll have more contact with your professor pal?"

Masefield could not think of a logical reason why he should but felt sure all the same.

"Oh yes. And, Tom . . . could I ask you a question?"

"Fire away, old man."

"Do we have a lot of men in Moscow?"

"No. We did, but they've been rounded up like sheep. London would dearly love to know who sold them out. There's a leak the size of a sewer somewhere. Fair to say, it's one of the reasons we sent you in. No one knows about you. You have no connection to the embassy there. You're

Burne-Jones's little secret. Not so much 'our man in Moscow' as 'his man in Moscow.'"

"So if there were anyone else doing what I'm doing . . . you know . . . trade mission as cover . . . in and out and so forth . . . "

"Oh, I'd know."

"Terence Glendinning?"

"Never heard of him."

§49

Derby, England: February 1961

Home to Geoffrey Stefanovich Masefield was a Derby suburb—Allestree, on the flat plain where the Derwent spilled out a few miles before it drowned its identity in the Trent. A short trolleybus ride and a far cry from his childhood in back-to-back Normanton. It was where you lived when, in the local parlance, you had "made a bob or two." Masefield hated Allestree. It was managementville—a dreary, interwar development of large characterless houses, housing large characterless men and their large characterless wives—stalwarts all of the Rotary Club and the Townswomen's Guild. It was his own fault. When his career took off, and he proved mortgageable, he suggested to his mother that he buy her a better house. He had thrown the remark away on the rash assumption she would say, "Nay lad, ah've lived in Normanton since ah were a lass an ah'll die here." Instead she had produced the glossy estate agent's brochure of a four-bedroomed house in Ferrer's Way, and once installed had embarked on a spree of hat-buying and a fruitless struggle to locate the letter *h*.

It didn't last. Within a year of assuming airs and graces, the bedrock of drudgery that had been her pre-suburban life caught up with her and she died worn out and bent, leaving Masefield alone in a house that was far too big in a suburb that was far too dull. The job, the travel that went with the job, had saved him. Home was merely camping out, a place to keep a change of clothes and a spare razor.

Home once more, he picked up the spare razor, looked in the bathroom mirror, wiped away the film of moisture and contemplated, as every man must, his moustache. A moustache was not fate. A moustache was choice, and a poor one. A couple of strokes of the blade and it was gone.

The following morning he drove his Austin A40 Somerset (convertible) into Derby, called at an optician's and ordered contact lenses to replace his glasses. He knew no one who wore contact lenses. They were innovative, expensive, and fragile. For the first week they stung and his eyes felt painfully dry. They were worth every penny, every pinch of pain.

If Burne-Jones approved, he would like to move to London. Burne-Jones might not approve; Derby, after all, might be part of his "cover." The job itself was now just part of his cover. He had already used his additional salary from MI6, as he passed through London, to open an account with Foulkes and Fransham (Tailors) Ltd in Savile Row, and on his next visit would have the final fitting for his new suit.

Few things pleased him quite so much as this self-transformation. He was, he mused, sloughing off the chrysalis. Standing in front of one of Foulkes and Fransham's full-length mirrors, hair cut by Teasy-Weasy, moustache no more than a haunting of his top lip, suit in a pleasing dark blue chosen for him by Fransham himself, he looked through his new contact lenses at the man reflected and tried to see himself as Tanya Dmitrievna would. It occurred to him she might have liked the weaselly little man in the cheap suit, but how could she not like the new man? The weaselly man had not been Geoffrey Masefield, he had been the man waiting to become Geoffrey Masefield. He turned sideways. The suit was slimming. He might even be svelte. How could she not like the new man? He turned the other way, ran one hand down his belly, suppressing doubt. But try as he might it did not come naturally to him.

§50

Moscow: March 1961

"Красавец."

He stumbled over the word. Had she called him "beautiful" or "handsome"? Were men ever "beautiful"? To ask what she meant would sustain the pretence, but to what purpose?

Tanya Dmitrievna locked her hands behind his neck and said it again.

"Красавец."

Then her lips moved to the rim of his left ear, her tongue darted into the shell and he didn't care about precision in words any more. The gesture spoke louder.

March nights in Moscow could be bone-chillers. He lay with Tanya wrapped around him squirrel-warm, heard the squeak of wheels or castors in the sitting room and looked at his watch, the luminous hands just visible on the bedside table: 11:30 p.m.

"Anfisa." A whisper in his ear.

"Eh?"

"My sister."

"Your twin sister?"

"I have no other."

"She lives here?"

"Of course."

"What was the noise?"

"A rollout. What you call a truckle bed. She sleeps next to me as a rule. But . . . "

"But what?"

"The knickers on the doorknob. Our sisters' code."

Tanya Dmitrievna buried her head in his side and he realised she was muffling giggles.

She lifted her head.

"Two's company, as you say in English."

He declined to finish the aphorism.

Around seven in the morning he heard the stairs door close, and the soft click of the lock. He was alone. He swung his legs off the bed, felt the bite of cold and wished he had a dressing gown.

Tanya Dmitrievna had one, and stood in the doorway wrapped in it.

"I have made coffee with the packet you have given me. Come. My sister has already left for work. And I shall not have long myself."

He pulled his shirt over his head, socks onto his feet, slithering along the lino to a kitchen no bigger than a closet—sat opposite her at the table, next to a cast-iron radiator slowly creaking into life.

"What is . . . ?" she picked up the packet struggling with the words on the label . . . "Fortnoom and Mazzon?"

"It's London's GUM."

"Ah, a place of privilege. Party members and visitors only?"

"No. And I wouldn't know which party . . . but it's a poor comparison. London has lots of GUMs. Fortnum's, Jacksons, Selfridges, Harrods, what have you."

She sipped at her coffee, grinned her gap-toothed grin at him.

He said, "I haven't got long either. I must get back to the Muromets."

The word seemed to dim her smile.

"Is . . . is Glendinning there this time?"

And the name dimmed his.

"No, and he wasn't last time. He did his deal last December."

He hesitated but knew in his bones he would ask.

"When you came back to the hotel in January . . . the night you brought me here. You said you were looking for me . . . were you looking for Glendinning?"

She said nothing. Put down the cup and stared at him.

"You said, 'I wanted him to get me out.'"

"Yes. I did say that. We want to leave. Me, Anfisa. To go West. He is MI6. He said he could get me out. I don't know how. I assume he has . . . ways. MI6 must have ways."

"Tanya. He's not MI6. He sells ball bearings to tractor factories."

"Why would Glendinning tell me he was MI6, if he wasn't?"

"To get you into bed?"

She glanced down into her cup, momentarily avoiding his gaze.

"No. I told you. He said it . . . after."

"Then, I would imagine . . . I would imagine he was trying to frighten you."

"Why?"

"I don't know. We're all different, aren't we? Maybe scaring you after he'd had sex with you was part of the sex."

"You are certain he was lying?"

"Yes."

"How can you be so sure?"

"Because they wouldn't send two of us on the same mission."

"Oh God, Geoffrey. I wish you hadn't told me that."

§51

A dull day at the ministry. A handshake and a bustle-by from Comrade Koritsev, and entrusted to the care of Third Assistant Deputy Undersecretary Dumsky and the laboured, uninspired interpretation of Andrei Semyonovich. Between them they negotiated the transport of 3.75 tons of indium by rail from half a dozen sites in the Soviet Union to East Berlin, where it would be handed over to representatives of New Caledonian Ores, transferred by road down the Helmstedt autobahn to Hamburg, and thence by ship to Greenock on the Clyde, a few miles from NCO's Scottish headquarters.

The manifest was full and guileless. It pleased him, made him feel vindicated, to note that among the starting points for shipment were both Sillamäe and Chelyabinsk. The loads would be combined in Minsk.

Masefield handed over a banker's draft for a daunting sum of money—the highly sought-after foreign currency—but it was a daunting amount of indium. Over four tons of a metal no one yet knew what to do with, stockpiled against man's powers of invention. It might be his "cover" but it was in its own right a commercial coup that would undoubtedly result in a hefty bonus. Bugger vodka, this called for scotch.

Back at the Muromets he chalked up the ridiculous price of a large single malt on his slate, sniffed, savoured, and gulped. It was a synthetic, almost petroleum taste on the tongue. He asked the bloke behind the bar to show him the label—StrathMcTavish. He'd never heard of it. It looked as fake as it tasted. They might as well have called it Isle of Sporran. No matter, it was the occasion that counted.

He looked around the bar. Another bunch of English, French, German . . . whatever . . . hearties on the usual trade mission, hell-bent on a piss-up and a foreign fuck their wives would never get to hear about. All under the tender care and sloppy surveillance of Intourist. He'd not yet spoken to any of them.

Tanya Dmitrievna was picking her way between the tables, answering questions, scribbling in her notebook, fending off the odd feel-up as though it simply hadn't happened, to end at the bar, next to him. Which of these bastards had bet on her this time?

"Mr. Masefield. Welcome back. Is there anything I can help you with?"

"You seem to have plenty to do as it is, Tanya Dmitrievna."

She glanced around. Smiled a smile as fake as his whisky.

"Ah. Just my little flock."

She dropped her voice.

"There is only me."

"Eh?"

"No one else has been assigned to you. Just me. No one will be watching us. Come to my apartment at seven."

And back to normal.

"Well, if there's anything at all, I shall be here just after breakfast every day. I bid you good night."

Shortly after seven he followed Tanya Dmitrievna up the stairs above the restaurant and into her sitting room.

He'd be able to tell them apart. He was now so familiar with the broken beauty of Tanya Dmitrievna's face that no other would ever fox him, but he had to admit the woman seated at the dining table was pretty much her double.

"Geoffrey Stefanovich, my sister Anfisa Dmitrievna . . . and the person I love most in life."

"Delighted," Masefield said, waiting to see if she remained formal or whether she would bounce up like a Jack Russell with a continental double-cheek kiss. She didn't.

Tanya Dmitrievna drew tea from the small, brass samovar for the three of them and he sat clutching a pleasingly warm glass of tea in its silver cradle.

Ice to break.

"Do you also work for Intourist, Anfisa Dmitrievna?"

"No. I am work at Ministry of Defence."

A stiff silence followed. Masefield wondered whether to continue in Russian or English. Her English was clearly not as good as her sister's and if she really was the "person I love most in life" then she surely knew that he was a spy and that he probably spoke Russian.

"Geoffrey Stefanovich, my sister has an idea she would like to put to you."

"Of course."

Masefield nodded in the direction of Anfisa Dmitrievna.

"To leave. To leave for ever. I . . . we . . . I . . . wish to be deserter."

"Defector," he said. "Перебежчик."

"Ah," she said, as though weighing up the word.

"And you want me to get you to the West?"

Tanya Dmitrievna cut in, "No. That was Glendinning's lie and my fantasy. It was nonsense. We have found a way. A better way."

"A way?"

"A gang. A gang who will get us to Berlin for money. Criminals, but what else would you expect? And in Berlin we walk to the West."

"It would be much easier on your feet to use the S-Bahn."

Masefield grinned, but neither sister shared his levity. It was not a joking matter.

"In which case, how can I help? There must be something I can do or you wouldn't be telling me."

"I work Ministry of Defence. I give you papers. You pay."

"You'll spy for England?'

The sisters looked at each other as though he'd said "fuck" out loud. Then at him, and said simultaneously, "Yes."

Then Anfisa Dmitrievna continued alone, "These men give us fake papers, passports and permits to leave Russia. One thousand British pounds . . . each."

"If," said Tanya Dmitrievna, "we can amass two thousand pounds . . . you and I could meet in Berlin. No more looking over our shoulders. We would be . . . together."

The appeal was direct. The pause was emphatic. "Together" . . . lovers . . . man and wife? It occurred to Masefield to ask if that was what she really wanted, but he didn't. He allowed his head to rule his heart.

"What papers?"

"I am section deputy. Many things pass across my desk. Papers that I must notes make for section chief . . . papers from inside ministry, papers from other ministries . . . from . . ."

Her English dribbled down to zero. She threw half a dozen rapid sentences at her sister so quickly Masefield caught fewer than half the words.

"My sister says," Tanya Dmitrievna said, "that papers arrive from Defence Industry, from Material Resources, from Atomic Energy and sometimes from Trade. All marked 'Secret,' and that there are many times, often towards the end of the day, when she is alone in the office."

"And you would bring me these papers?"

Anfisa Dmitrievna almost dropped her glass in shock.

"No . . . no . . . no . . . I could not . . . we are searched . . . I would . . . be shot!"

Tanya Dmitrievna stood over her sister and hugged her.

"No. Don't say such things."

"But . . . but I cannot take . . . "

"We will find a way."

Now she looked at Masefield across the top of her tearful sister's head.

"Won't we, Geoffrey?"

§52

Tanya Dmitrievna did not speak of it again. They made love in a flurry of sweet nothings in two languages. The hard somethings went unspoken.

They lay in spoons, one hand upon her backside, the other stretched out across the pillow.

The luminous dial of his watch read 2:30. He saw the sitting room light as a sliver under the door. It came on; it went off. A few seconds passed, then the door opened and she slid into the drawer, another spoon curving into the curve he had made with Tanya Dmitrievna.

Anfisa's hand reached for his cock, coaxing the spent vessel back to life. He squirmed, rolled on to his back as Tanya Dmitrievna stirred. And while Anfisa Dmitrievna slowly jerked his cock Tanya Dmitrievna cupped his balls. And when he came, two spunk-wet hands slid across his belly to touch his face—and four Russian lips whispered exotic nothings in his ears.

§53

At breakfast.

"I have it," he said. "A camera. I shall give you a miniature camera. You have only to get it into the ministry once. After that you just hide the camera and bring me the film."

"How big is this camera?"

"It would fit into the palm of your hand."

"And the film?"

"A cartridge. No more than inch or so long. Easily hidden."

Anfisa nodded, sipped at her Fortnum's finest Blue Mountain.

Tanya Dmitrievna said, "And the money?"

"Cash?"

"You think a Russian gangster deals in anything else?"

"I can get cash, of course I can get cash, but I have to ask my people. There's bound to be a going rate for this sort of thing."

"Your people?"

"Back in Berlin."

"Oh . . . of course . . . I see."

He hadn't a clue what Radley would say to this, no idea how much he'd pay, only that he wouldn't turn down the chance.

That afternoon, ahead of the usual drinks o'clock in the Muromets bar, he took the fire bucket into his room, carefully counted out the fag ends and tipped the contents onto a spread newspaper.

The Minox was intact. A little metal mummy in a tomb. He'd picked up a couple of spare cartridges in Berlin. They were surprisingly easy to buy. A bit like walking into Harrods and asking for the spies' supplies department. And just as easy to conceal. He could bring in two or three every trip, and be fairly confident of going undetected.

§54

Paranoia is like a twitch, he concluded. A facial tic that you cannot control. Across Pushkin Square and Gorky Street he found he could not refrain from looking around except by an act of will that was all but vocal, the voice in his head telling him "Stop it." He was, logic chimed, no more at risk that he had been any other day on any other visit. But the camera in his pocket rang as loudly as a passing fire engine. He was surprised that he was the only one who could hear it.

Near the southern end of Malaya Bronnaya, he stood momentarily on a corner and looked back. How does one spot a man tailing? Brown had never bothered to tell him this. And to ask felt like asking how to tell a policeman from a postman—and why broadcast his innocence to a hard man like Brown?

There were people drifting everywhere, most in the typical Moscow posture of head down and eyes averted. All of them and none of them might be following. From what he'd seen on his first trip, the KGB tails were obvious to clumsy.

"Stop it," said the voice in his head, and he did. He walked on in the direction of Patriarch's Ponds and looked straight ahead.

What had Brown said? "Regard every Russian you meet as a spy" . . . "Sex is a quagmire: blackmail is the KGB's strongest weapon and yours is discretion."

Of course Tanya Dmitrievna was a spy. That was a given. They had each lain their cards on the table, as it were. Anfisa Dmitrievna was not a spy—he was about to make her a spy. And sex was not a quagmire . . . it was bliss. He had never felt so loved. He had never felt loved at all until now. And discretion? He would be the epitome of discretion.

§55

"Is like toy."

"I suppose it is rather, but it's really a precise instrument. German invention, Latvian engineering. Watch."

Masefield turned on the table lamp and turned off the room light. Opened a book at random and set it in the half moon of light cast by the lamp.

"That's all you need. I could get a flash attachment, but this is better and easier. You take the cord . . . see . . . and use it to set the distance between the camera and the page."

Anfisa Dmitrievna copied his movements.

"OK. I get it."

"And now press the button between the eyepiece and the lens."

The merest click.

"Is that it?"

"Almost. To move the film on you just close and open the case . . . so."

A louder click.

"You can take thirty-six photographs on a roll, rather quickly I would imagine."

Anfisa Dmitrievna looked at him quizzically.

"Why 'imagine'? Have you not used camera before?"

It was his weakest moment. It felt amateurish to admit it, but he felt he had no choice.

"No . . . no. I haven't."

"So . . . I am . . . what you say . . . guinea pig?"

"Oh, we're all that," he said.

Tanya Dmitrievna came in from the kitchen and set tea in front of them. No quietly stewing samovar—Masefield found he hated Russian tea, and had willingly donated his packet of "travelling tea" to her kitchen cupboard—instead a brown, stripy teapot such as might be found in a million working-class homes in England, and a waft of PG tips as she lifted the lid and stirred.

"Who talks of pigs?"

"No matter," said her sister.

"Monkeys," Masefield said.

"Pigs? Monkeys? Do we run a zoo here?"

"I was about to say . . . at home they advertise this tea with a troupe of performing monkeys."

"Amazing," Tanya Dmitrievna replied. "And they say capitalism is decadent."

§56

No more creeping to the bed. He rolled between them and lay like the Constant Tin Soldier in Hans Christian Andersen's cutlery drawer. He had never felt so loved nor so twice-loved.

§57

London: April 28

In the years he had worked for Burne-Jones, Wilderness had bumped into Jack Dashoffy dozens of times. They'd first met in Berlin in 1947. Jack Dash, as he was known, was a breed of American that Wilderness thought quite common, the dyed-in-the-wool Anglophile. Odd in a man of largely German and Hungarian descent, odder still in a CIA agent. Nonetheless, Jack loved all things English from royalty to rose-pattern, ornamental tea caddies. Wilderness was not Jack's kind of Englishman—that was Burne-Jones—but they got along well enough in that they each recognised the limited value of secrecy and were prepared to swap notes from time to time.

One sunny afternoon in April Jack sought him out in London. Wilderness did what was expected of him and offered tea at Fortnum and Mason's in Piccadilly. Jack could bask in an Englishness that Wilderness found utterly alien. Wilderness would simply listen in the hope that Jack's natural indiscretion would lead somewhere. The speed with which Jack got to the point surprised him all the same.

"The summit's on."

"What summit?"

"The one Khrushchev wouldn't have with Ike after the U-2 thing."

"He'll have it with Kennedy after the cock-up at the Bay of Pigs?"

"He'll have it with Kennedy *because* of the Bay of Pigs. It's being set up for June, in Vienna."

"And you're on the team?"

"Yep. And so could you be. I can get you clearance . . . of sorts."

"Of sorts?"

"You won't be in the room with JFK and Khrushchev. But I can get you an embassy pass on the Company, you'd be in on briefings and anything I can tell you short of treason. Day one, Mr. K meets Mr. K at the residence."

"Residence?"

"Our ambassador's official home in Vienna. Still US territory, but not the embassy if you see what I mean. Lends a little informality to something that couldn't be informal if it sat on the can and strained to gut busting. Day one is OK, you'll be with me. Day two is their call. Most likely they'll shift the whole three-ring circus to their own embassy. Nothing I can do for you there, but stick with it. We'll see how it all rolls out."

How it all rolls out? Burne-Jones would kill for this. To be second fiddle at a summit conference when the most they could ordinarily expect was the back row of the choir.

"And you might find it handy to be genned up. JFK'll be in London for talks with Prime Minister Macmillan as soon as it's over. You'll be ahead of the press releases. That's all I can guarantee you. You'll know what's going on ahead of the *New York Times* and whatever lies the Commies decide to print in *Pravda*."

"All the truth that fits."

"You said it, kid."

"Any expectations, Jack?"

"Expectations? Nah. Wishes? Sure. I wish that we could come out this year of unstoppable crap storms into a world that isn't about to boil over like Mother Murphy's chowder."

Wilderness wondered what most might. How would President Kennedy get on with First Secretary Khrushchev? He'd followed Khrushchev's career since the late forties, when he ruled the Ukraine, and he'd watched him oust every other rival to succeed Stalin. John F. Kennedy? Kennedy appeared to have come out of nowhere. A brief spurt of national attention as he lost out in the 1956 nominations for vice president, and then the merest pause before a roller-coaster campaign for the presidency itself, seeing off Hubert Humphrey, Lyndon Johnson, and finally Richard Nixon.

It could hardly be a meeting of minds or character . . . the sophisticated Boston millionaire, brought up to unimaginable privilege, versus the Russian peasant. Even age and height were against them. Khrushchev was sixty-seven and clocked in at just over five foot, Kennedy forty-three and six foot tall. Experience mattered more than either statistic. Two years ago Khrushchev had run circles around Nixon, in public and on camera. If the little man decided to get rude or funny or just vulgar no one could keep up. He'd dismissed Nixon as little better than an idiot with, "He shows the Russian people a dream kitchen from some impossible future and expects them all to convert to capitalism. Only Nixon could come up with nonsense like that."

"Snap out of it, Joe, you're daydreaming!"

Indeed he was.

"Now . . . the quid pro quo. What's the dope on George Blake?"

"The dope, Jack?"

"The damage. You guys must have been doing damage assessment at the speed of light."

"It may be that Blake has cost us everything. We are getting sod all out of Russia. We are Russia-blind, to coin a phrase."

"Because you no longer have any agents that Blake hasn't blown to the Russians?"

"Well . . . Blake didn't know everything. We still have the odd one."

Wilderness wasn't about to qualify "odd" and was pleased Dashoffy didn't ask.

Instead he said, "That's fuck all quid pro my quo. You owe me Joe, you owe me."

§58

London: May 17

"Joe? Would you mind popping down to the tech room?"

"Pop"—such a toff word. The concealment of whatever inconvenience might be caused in a nonsense syllable implying that it was all low key, harmless even, when the opposite might well be the case.

"Tom Radley's in town. Bit of film I'd like you to see."

Yes, it would be a "bit," wouldn't it? A word in the Burne-Jones vocabulary that might span an ocean.

Ten minutes later Wilderness went down to the basement, to the room with no windows, where stills and moving footage could be projected.

He'd met Tom Radley, Berlin station, half a dozen times—but Berlin was not his "beat" any more. This would not be a German matter. Burne-Jones would not have sent for him about anything German. He was on his own turf with Germany, but affected a form of bafflement when it came to Russia and regarded Wilderness as his repository of knowledge.

Burne-Jones said, "We've been looking at photographs Tom's brought in. Not the best either of us has ever seen, bit blurry to say the least, and neither of us is quite as good at Russian as you."

Wilderness shook hands with Radley and took his seat. If Radley's Russian was less than good, what was he doing running the Berlin station?

They watched the thirty slides through once, and then again, slowly, one by one.

"We know what they are, just a few gaps here and there . . . and I wondered if you concurred."

"Concurred with what?"

"They're Soviet Ministry of Defence documents dealing with spy-plane flights over the last five years."

"Yep. Reports from pilots, ground control, radar operators. Sightings, trajectories . . . cock-ups."

"Cock-ups?"

"I meant . . . these are the flights that they didn't manage to shoot down. The flights Eisenhower wasn't boasting about and Khrushchev wasn't mentioning until he actually had shot one down."

"Ah . . . then we do agree."

"Useful all the same."

"In what way?"

"Well, they tell us nothing about Russia per se, but did we know the Americans had flown quite so any missions? These papers seem to be recording at least twenty."

"Ah," Burne-Jones hesitated. "We did know. In fact the missions between 1959 and early 1960 were flown by us."

"What?" Radley spoke for the first time since greeting.

Burne-Jones flicked the lights back on.

"I'm sorry, Tom, but I think there's nothing here of any use. We know all this . . . because it was us."

Radley looked deeply unhappy, and all he said was "bugger."

"Ike didn't want to risk U-2 flights over Russia while Nixon was visiting. All the same he didn't want them suspended, so the PM agreed to RAF pilots flying them out of one of our bases in Turkey. Gave Ike the deniability he needed. The minute we knew Powers had been shot down we pulled our chaps out of Turkey and sent them off on extended leave. Free holiday on the Costa del wotsit for some of them, and there were a couple of gongs handed out in New Year Honours, with the vaguest citations. It was all on a need-to-know basis . . . and you didn't need to know."

"So our man has wasted his time?"

"'Fraid so."

"I may be a bit in the dark here," Wilderness said. "But who exactly is our man?"

"Geoffrey Masefield," Burne-Jones replied.

Wilderness said nothing to this, kept his thoughts to himself, just nodded and asked for the lights to be turned off and slides 28 and 29 to go up again.

"They're the blurriest of them all," Burne-Jones said.

Slide 30 had been nothing more than a black smudge.

Wilderness stood up, walked to the screen and tried to make sense of the Russian typeface, odd at the best of times to Western eyes, odder seen madly out of focus.

He had been wondering what part tact might play in what he had to say. It would be a typical Burne-Jones ploy to have got him in just to avoid having to say something himself. A way of sweetening whatever dose he might hand out to Radley.

"I could be wrong, but these two appear to deal with the flight of April ninth last year."

He looked at Burne-Jones and Radley, waiting, knowing he most certainly could not be wrong and that saying he might be was all the tact he was prepared to display.

"Quite possibly," said Burne-Jones.

"The flight Khrushchev has mentioned precisely once and the Americans not at all. In all the rounds of recriminations and fudges amounting to somewhat less than an apology . . . this has been utterly eclipsed by the U-2 that was shot down on May Day last year just north of Chelyabinsk."

"Your point, Joe?"

"In a moment. The RAF flew flights into early 1960 you said. The Americans climbed back into the cockpit when exactly?"

"End of January."

"So, an American flew the April mission. The last one that succeeded. That's why neither side will talk about it. Khrushchev does not want to admit his people failed to shoot it down; Ike didn't want the Russians to know what he'd got. Now, let me ask this: as we flew missions for the Americans was the data gleaned shared with us?"

"I can't answer that, you know damn well I can't."

"I'll take that as a maybe. And let me further ask . . . have the results of the April ninth mission been shared with us?"

Burne-Jones hesitated a fraction too long before saying, "Can't answer that either."

"I'll take that as a no."

Radley said, "Joe, I'm beginning to feel like the outsider here. I brought my own bat and ball to the game and I don't get to play. What are you saying?"

Wilderness pointed to slide 28.

"If this were a clear shot I'd be certain, but as it is . . . call it an educated guess . . . the Russians have recorded the flight path . . . and the flight path would tell us what the Americans aren't . . . that is where they think the Russian missile sites are, and the fact that the Russians have not raised all hell about this, the way they have about May Day and Chelyabinsk, tells me the Americans found them. Shooting down Gary Powers let Khrushchev go on the attack knowing full well the USA would not be boasting about the flight that took place three weeks before. It suits everybody. America keeps its film secret and Khrushchev avoids looking like an idiot in the eyes of his own politburo. The USA now knows where the Soviet ICBM launch sites are, Khrushchev knows they know but is able to trumpet shooting down a U-2 as his success and their failure."

"I'm sorry to appear dense, Joe," Radley said, "but where are their ICBM sites?"

"I don't know, Tom. Our allies aren't telling us and I can't read any of the words after 'Пермь', Perm. You're going to have to ask our Geoffrey to photograph the pages again. Think of it as spying on a friend."

"Bugger," said Radley, as he was wont.

§59

Wilderness contrived to be in the lobby as Radley was leaving.

"Are you in London for long, Tom?"

"Just overnight, staying with my mother in Highgate."

"Oh," said Wilderness. "I'm going your way. Can I give you a lift?"

If Radley had said Croydon or Ealing, Wilderness would still have offered the lift.

As they rounded Russell Square he cut through the small talk and said, "When did you decide to switch Masefield from observing to being a courier?"

"I didn't. In fact he quite surprised me. He suddenly turned up in Berlin with a roll of microfilm in March, after his third visit. Said he'd had to pay for it, asked for money."

"You paid him?"

"Burne-Jones approved two hundred. Bit of a cock-up. He clearly didn't know how to use a Minox and every single frame was practically black. But he seems to have got the hang of it now."

"You gave him a Minox?" Wilderness hoped he had kept any note of incredulity out of his voice.

"No, no. I didn't. That was another surprise. He seems to have gone out and bought his own. Useful. Initiative even—after all, he nips in and out of Moscow a couple of times a month now."

"How much bloody indium does Russia have? Has he bought the lot?"

"Oh, he's onto unobtainium now . . . he reckons Russia is sitting on tons of the stuff . . . an almost infinite supply."

Radley, clearly, had no idea when his leg was being pulled—but Wilderness admired Masefield's cheek all the same in perpetrating such a schoolboy spoof.

"And you've gone on paying him?"

"Well . . . I'll go on paying him . . . Burne-Jones has approved that . . . I'll go on paying him . . . and he'll go on paying his source as long as he delivers. Two hundred a pop. Hardly a fortune."

$60

In the morning, Wilderness was waiting for Burne-Jones, sitting in his office nursing a cup of strong black coffee.

"I'd've called you at home, but . . ."

"I know. Wives. I appreciate you not calling. There are times we must appear like a conspiracy to the two of them."

Wilderness was damn sure they did.

"This is about Masefield, I take it?"

"It's as much about Radley as him. Why did you let Tom turn Masefield from passive to active? You wanted someone just looking around, you said."

"All looking around got us was pretty photographs of the onion domes of St. Basil's, the changing of the guard at Lenin's tomb and so forth."

"Well. We both knew he wouldn't get within a hundred miles of Chelyabinsk."

"Can't deny that. All the same I felt I had to let him try . . . and then he turns up with this."

"He was approached?"

"Apparently."

"Radley mentioned a source, and his source is?"

"Hang on, these long names always tire me out . . . Grigory Grigoryevich Matsekpolyev. Professor of physics at the Leningrad thingumajig. Their top man, or so he says, in . . . trans . . . trans . . . "

"Transuranics. It means all the radioactive elements heavier than uranium . . . neptunium, plutonium, americium and so on. What's odd is that I've never heard the name before. Doesn't ring any bells. That big a fish and he's new to me? Seems odd. What do the files say about him?"

"Nothing. We have no file on him. There are articles by him in half a dozen languages in the science journals but beyond that we know nothing about him. If he'd been to the odd boffin conference anywhere beyond the Warsaw Pact we'd have a file. But he hasn't. I rang a pal at the Cavendish and, needless to say, he knew him. Met him in Leningrad a couple of times . . . but asking boffins to report on anyone is pissing into the wind . . . violates their scientific integrity. Or something."

"Or something? And so we have . . . nothing? And yet this bloke told our Geoffrey he's their top man. Is he just boasting?"

"Joe, George Blake cost us pretty well our whole operation east of Berlin. It's hardly surprising we have nothing on this bloke. It now appears we've been getting nothing but rubbish from Russia for years. Our people have been rounded up or turned and we've been fed porridge."

"Then it's possible Masefield is being set up right now. They're giving us stuff we already know. It looks like porridge to me."

"To be precise, Joe, in fact to be precise in your own words, it's not that we know—as you have pointed out there are things on those pages we don't know, but as the Russians think we surely do it's information they have nothing to lose by imparting—it's only that they think we know."

"You just lost me."

"I don't think Masefield is being set up and nor does Tom. I think it more likely to be a matter of his source not knowing what to give him, and Masefield not knowing what to ask for. That can be fixed. For now, I prefer your first idea, that there is gold dust on those two muddy frames you suggested he re-took."

"I suggest. You order."

"Meaning?"

"It's putting our man at risk."

"No risk no gain."

"And what do we have to gain?"

"As you said, if we can read the flight path of the April ninth U-2, we know what the Americans were looking for."

"It would be easier to ask them."

"No . . . can't do that. Special relationship isn't that special."

It crossed Wilderness's mind to ask what the special relationship amounted to if they could no longer exchange information, but he said nothing.

"Let me," Burne-Jones went on, "ask you. Where do you think that plane went after Perm?"

"Plesetsk, up on the Arctic Circle near Archangel."

"And if I ask you 'Why Plesetsk?' you may answer without teaching your father-in-law to suck eggs."

"Whatever ICBMs the Russians have will be of limited range—a disadvantage they will surely overcome with improvements in rocketry— but in the meantime their only option is to move the missile closer to its target and, short of opening a base in Toronto, their best bet is to get into the Arctic Circle and send missiles over the pole. In that respect Plesetsk is well placed. Only six hundred odd miles from Moscow, not too close to the Finnish border. Further east and their communications would be stretched . . . and we know they've been laying rail track in that direction. I may be wrong, but it will be somewhere like Plesetsk and on pretty much the same latitude."

"Suddenly I can taste raw egg. But . . . no matter."

"Then you might as well accept my guess and let Masefield off the hook."

"We must let him try again. We really must."

"Blake?"

"Blake?"

"Is this about national pride, perhaps only Service pride? You said it. George Blake has rolled up our Russian operation like an old rug in some Turkish market. You, that is we, want sources inside Russia, we want 'our man in Moscow' . . . we want to be able to tell ourselves, as we are made to look like a bunch of twats at Blake's trial, that we still have something . . . anything. So we put in place the first man we can, who has fuck all going for him."

"A harsh appraisal, Joe. Harsh. Masefield has one rare quality going for him . . . innocence. Not a career agent. Below the radar."

"You mean no track record, no experience."

"Joe, all caveats duly noted. But I say again, we must let him try. We really must.

"The U-2 photographs are not the only thing he's brought us. Matsekpolyev took him round a metals refinery in Estonia, he got a look at their indium processing, for what it's worth—only a cover story after all—but he's confirmed that they're enriching uranium. And that's a gem. That's close to priceless. OK, it wasn't Chelyabinsk, but we also have the photographs he took. Managed to shoot two rolls inside Sillamäe. They're both confusing and inventive. Some very interesting shots, we're still analysing.

"Ostensibly the Russians are refining indium and a few other metals. But now we know what they're really up to. More than enough enriched uranium every year to keep their weapons programme going. We'd never have got anyone else in there. His innocence worked for him. And if we'd sent a career agent, a man like you—or worse, a man like me—well . . . would either of us have been able to tell a uranium enrichment plant from a Tizer bottling plant?"

"That's the part that makes sense. This doesn't—where did Grigory Grigoryevich Matsekpolyev, professor of physics in Leningrad, get hold of papers on the U-2 flights, presumably housed at the Ministry of Defence in Moscow?"

"I've no idea."

"Alec, it's a trap."

"I cannot agree."

"Tom's story doesn't ring true. Wouldn't you expect a professor of physics to be an idealist? Yet I gather we are paying for these photographs. It's a trap."

"I say again, I can't agree with you on that."

"Suit yourself. If they catch him what's another dull, little Englishman more or less?"

"You don't like Masefield much, do you?"

"I have no feelings about our Geoffrey. It's Radley I don't like."

"And why's that?"

"He's a chancer."

"And how many times do think I've heard the same word used to describe you?"

§61

Vienna: June 3

On the Saturday of the summit, Wilderness stood with the US Secret Service, the CIA, and half a dozen blokes in uniform and medals he hadn't been introduced to and about whom he had no curiosity.

The Ks had arrived by very differing means of their own choosing. Kennedy had flown in from Paris after a meeting with de Gaulle and was accompanied by his wife and mother. Jackie Kennedy had wowed Paris. Khrushchev had taken the slow train from Moscow via his satellite capitals, accompanied by his wife, Nina, and by Minister for Foreign Affairs Gromyko. Nina Khrushchev had wowed nowhere and no one.

As they waited, only feet from the red carpet that had been rolled out down the steps of the US ambassador's residence, Dashoffy tapped him on the shoulder and pointed up at the sky.

Soviet MiGs and helicopters were orbiting Vienna. A sky-high riposte to the overblown motorcade that had been Kennedy's journey from the airport. More stars and more stripes than anyone could ever be bothered to count.

"Lest there be any doubt," Jack said softly.

Before Wilderness could say anything the Russian limousines swung into the drive, and the Secret Service parted like waves to let John Fitzgerald Kennedy trip lightly down the steps to greet Nikita Sergeyevich Khrushchev, who was far from lightly swinging fat little legs from the car. Fred Astaire meets Oliver Hardy.

"The drugs must be working today," Wilderness heard Dashoffy whisper.

Khrushchev seemed to Wilderness to take in everything in a slow, sweeping turn of his very round, very bald head. For a moment he could even kid himself that their eyes had met, but then the Russian leader was glad-handed by the president of the USA with a hearty "How are you?"—a phrase that needed no translation, but got one anyway, and no answer.

They posed for the press. For some reason Khrushchev had chosen to wear his wartime medals on his civilian suit. Wilderness did not doubt that Kennedy had won some medal or other in the same war—he had vague recollection of something about rescuing his crew after the sinking of a boat he had commanded in the Pacific—and he doubted it had occurred to JFK to wear it. It was move two in gamesmanship . . . first the MiGs, now the medals. First the might and the metal; now the superiority of age over youth, of suffering over privilege.

If Khrushchev had taken them all in with a curiosity amounting to suspicion, JFK only had eyes for Khrushchev and regarded him with an intense gaze amounting to scrutiny. Wilderness wondered about the lives they had led. Had Kennedy ever met a man like Khrushchev before? A Ukrainian peasant, illiterate until well into his twenties, who had survived in a political pit that had seen many of his contemporaries eaten by the bear. He was certain Khrushchev had met rich aristocrats before—but only to shoot them.

And they were both of them bound by good manners, smiling for the cameras, smiling for the watching world. It meant nothing and would count for nothing.

§62

They agreed to meet after the "show," in the bar of the Hotel Sacher on Philharmonikerstraße. The British hotel . . . British in that they had billeted themselves there for ten years after the war and only left in 1955.

Dashoffy was late, and the bar at the Sacher was clearly not the only one he had visited en route. Wilderness had nursed one glass of claret for over an hour waiting for him. Jack ordered double scotches for both of them, downed his in a single gulp and eyed Wilderness's so covetously that Wilderness pushed it across the table to him and watched it vanish in an instant. Jack's hand went up to summon refills. Wilderness smiled at the waiter trying to convey silently that his friend would not be a problem and waited until they were alone. Jack had always liked a drink. Wilderness had never thought of him as having a problem with drink. The problem lay elsewhere.

"What's the problem? I'll tell you what's the problem. You remember the old Charles Atlas ad from the magazines a few years back. Some scrawny kid gets sand kicked in his face by the beach bully? That's what's happening. Our scrawny kid is getting sand kicked in his face by their five-foot lard butt of a beach bully. And you know what? It's humiliating. It is so fucking humiliating. We have a Khrushchev-monitoring team back in Langley. Physicians, psychiatrists, you name it. We know his hat size, his favourite food, his favourite colour. Whether he's manic-depressive or depressive-manic or just plain nuts. Hell, we even have the results of his blood-pressure tests. We've seen the inside of the man's arteries. We know what Khrushchev is like, what he's capable of. And if we know, the president knows . . . so why in God's name is he underestimating the little guy at every turn?"

"Well, he's never met him before."

"You're forgetting the comrade's US tour. Y'know. Sinatra, Shirley MacLaine, *Can-Can*? They met then."

"OK. Then it's his first summit."

Wilderness felt odd. It was odd, to be justifying an American president to an American. To be showing sympathy where the man had none.

"Then I hope to God it's his last. Joe, he knows nothing. Choate, Harvard . . . Congress . . . the Senate . . . but he knows nothing. He mangles ideas the way he mangles foreign languages. He hasn't an original thought in his head. Khrushchev tackles him on Marxism and history . . . the inevitability of this and the inevitability of that. Kennedy looks at him as though this is the first fuckin' time he's heard any of it. And instead of waving it aside and saying 'Let's talk peace, let's talk nukes or let's talk war,' he lets Khrushchev bang on, lets him set the agenda. And you know what? It's as plain as the nose on your face that Kennedy has never heard all this crap before, that he's never read a word of Marx and thinks a dialectic is the funny accent a guy from Arkansas has. That fuckin' Russian peasant in there is wiping the floor with him like he was Rocky Marciano and Popeye rolled into one and the president, my fuckin' president, is . . . is . . . Huntz fuckin' Hall . . . the dopey one from the Bowery Boys, the one with his brains in his fuckin' shoes."

"Keep your voice down, Jack."

Dashoffy looked around, satisfied himself that he hadn't turned any heads with his outburst.

"Yeah. Right. I shouldn't be another diplomatic incident. I don't think the fans in this city could handle that much shit right now."

"I read his book, you know."

"What?"

"*Why England Slept*. It was in what passed for a library while I was attempting basic training just after the war. It's more than generous to us. Took some brains to write that."

"Yeah, well . . . maybe, just maybe I'll make it my life's work to find out who wrote it for him, because he sure as fuck didn't. One of Joe Kennedy's tame eggheads probably did. Because I tell you now . . . I was at Harvard the year behind Jack Kennedy and all he did was chase tail."

"Jack, you sound sorry you voted for him."

"Hell, kid. I voted for Nixon. I had my doubts at the time, the man can be a prize prick when he chooses, but right now I have no regrets. None at all, and if he runs again in '64 I'll vote for him again. I'll even buy that used car he has for sale."

Now Wilderness looked around. Every other person in this bar had to be attached to one foreign delegation or another. They still weren't turning heads, but if he didn't get Jack into the street and into the noise of traffic they soon would. If he didn't get Jack away from the scotch bottle they most certainly would.

He steered him out of the hotel and down Kärntner Straße towards the Ring. A warm, midsummer night, full streets, a city buzzing with activity—enough to drown out Jack, but Jack seemed to have shot his bolt.

He looked across the Ring towards the Naschmarkt and the golden oddity that was the Secession Building. He seemed to be breathing in petrol fumes like they were fresh air. Then he leaned against one of the iron columns that carried the tram wires, stretched out his neck and for a moment Wilderness thought he was going to puke, but he drew back, wiped a strand of phlegm from his lips.

"Hell, kid. You remember the first time we ever saw this place?"

It had been 1951. The three of them together. Jack, Wilderness, and Frank Spoleto. A city of shadows. Spook paradise.

"A mess of a city. A train wreck of a city. But it was fun, right? Tell me it was fun?"

Some of it had been. There was no lie in agreeing to that.

"Where's this heading, Jack?"

"I dunno where it is heading, but I'm heading home."

"Aren't you supposed to be out at Schönbrunn in your tuxedo?"

"Fuck the tux. Kid, just flag me a cab, stick me in it, and tell me to keep my big mouth shut. I have drowned my sorrows and needs must I am sober in the morning. And thanks. I really didn't mean to bend your ear quite so damn much."

"That's OK, Jack. My ear came to be bent."

Dashoffy was still laughing at that as Wilderness closed the cab door on him.

He rolled down the window for one last word.

"Tomorrow it's at their place. Can't get you past the door, but it'll be all over by lunchtime. Let's meet for lunch. Not the hotel. Somewhere where I don't feel I'm looking over my shoulder the whole time. You pick."

"Frauenhuber in Himmelpfortgasse."

"OK. I know where you mean. Passed it. Never been in. At one. OK?"

"OK."

§63

Jack turned up sober, if grim.

Looked around.

"Kinda corny."

Looked at the menu.

"Kinda limited."

"Possibly, but in both cases very Viennese."

"Hmm. Why d'you pick this place?"

"The romantic in me. Mozart played here. So did Beethoven. In fact for a while he was the resident pianist. Sat over there and improvised."

"What? Like in a New York jazz club? Like he was Monk or Mingus?"

"Pretty much. I'd even be prepared to argue the case for Schubert being the first jazz musician. You look at his life it wasn't a lot different from the one Charlie Parker led."

"Booze, drugs, and dames, eh?"

"And not necessarily in that order."

"Well . . . other guys used to put Beethoven on the turntable when I was in college. In one ear and out the other. Did he write a fifth something or other?"

"Everybody wrote a fifth something or other."

"Whatever."

Jack pointed to the menu. Subject abruptly changed.

"Boiled beef and carrots? Did Vienna learn to cook in an English NAAFI?"

He ordered it just the same, ate it just the same, and only over coffee—coffee and two large brandies—did he unwind enough to want to talk shop.

"I may be around a little longer. There was no scheduled afternoon session, but JFK has asked to see Khrushchev alone."

He glanced at his watch, a dual-face giving the Continental and US Eastern time.

"They're probably closeted together right now. Jaw jaw, war war."

"On what topic, I wonder?"

Jack looked around, much as he had done at the Sacher, sighed, shrugged, and muttered, "What the heck."

"You're rushing back to London, right, kid?"

"Of course."

"OK, when this farcical parade is over, when Macmillan is wondering 'What the fuck was that about?' and when Burne-Jones finally asks what difference any of this has made . . . you have one thing to tell him. There is only one topic . . . Berlin. And if being a desk jockey doesn't suit you, Joe—and I figure it sticks in your craw like fishbone—tell old Alec you want to go back to Berlin. Because right now, and maybe till the end of fuckin' time, Berlin is it. The bellybutton of the world—*l'ombelico del mondo*. You want to be where the action is you go to Berlin; you want to be there when the world ends you get to Berlin. Forget postings to Paris or Beirut . . . Berlin."

"You think they'll really go to war over Berlin?"

"I cannot speak for the Commie lard-ass, I will speak only for the ignorant streak of piss that is my elected president. No, we will never start a war over Berlin. Khrushchev can roll his tanks all over West Berlin, he can surround it with a solid ring of ICBMs . . . there is no way the US of A is going to start a thermonuclear war over Berlin. There is no way the US of A is going to start even an old-fashioned boots 'n' bayonets war over Berlin. We'd need half a million troops to hold Berlin. We couldn't supply them, feed them, or even billet them."

The prospect was interesting. Did Wilderness want to go back to Berlin? He had been in and out many times since he left there in 1948.

"Did we go to war for Berlin in '48? Did we go to war for Berlin in '53?"

He'd been in and out many times—with eyes closed and his head down. He'd avoided almost anything that reminded him of his years there after the war, but, of course, everything did. Every time, he would call Erno Schreiber, and Erno would say, "I'm always home," and every time Wilderness would talk him into meeting in a restaurant rather than climb the staircase at Grünetümmlerstraße, and watch the old man torn between pleasures of a menu and the taboo he would not break. He wouldn't mention Nell Burkhardt and Wilderness wouldn't ask.

"Of course we fuckin' didn't. And we're not going to do it now. Khrushchev has Berlin by the pips. All the bastard has to do is squeeze."

Berlin had its "man"—Tom Radley still ran the Berlin station. Had done for four years now. Perhaps Tom would like to move on? Perhaps Burne-Jones would move him on. He was hardly the brightest bear in the woods and certainly not the man to have in charge if all Jack's gloomy predictions came true. Wilderness's last meeting with Radley had left him thinking the man was a fool. Pleasant enough, a man you might enjoy propping up a bar with . . . but running a station a hundred and fifty miles behind the Iron Curtain was a different matter.

"Are you sober enough to talk sense?"

"I thought I was talking sense."

"Tell me what you think Khrushchev will do, and try to avoid the genital metaphors."

"It's not a whit different from that tirade of his at the UN a while back. Was it last year or the year before? And that was not a whit different from the ultimatum he handed out in '58. He seems to sound off all the goddamn time. Anyone can get frustrated. Some guys beat their wives, some guys get shit-faced, Khrushchev delivers ultimatums on Berlin. Basically it's this . . . he fears a united Germany that might be just a tool of the West and on a lesser level he fears a Germany that will do what Germany did best all over again. On that score, you can hardly blame him. So . . . he wants a Germany free of the guys who won the war; he wants us all to withdraw. If we don't . . . he's threatening a separate peace treaty with the DDR . . . effectively ending the Second World War and Allied Occupation, and to turn Berlin over to them. Basically he'd nullify all the claptrap that came out of Yalta and Potsdam by pushing it all to the next stage. It has its logic. What I think it conceals is an intention to set the tanks rolling for the Rhine."

"You know how many men the USSR demobilised after the war?"

"No, do you?"

"More or less."

"Well, I don't buy it. So they got rid of a few thousand guys fifteen years ago? They still have the draft and there's no shortage of comrades in uniform."

"Actually Jack, it was eight million. And another three and a half million in the last five years."

"Sheeeit!"

"Quite," said Wilderness, much as Burne-Jones might have done.

"But . . . it makes no never mind. You know what I think? I think he'll give us 1948 all over again."

"Jack, that's not possible. That stunt could not be repeated. The world has moved on since then. We're not about barbed wire and armoured cars any more . . ."

"Yeah, yeah, yeah . . . I know rockets, sputniks, and dogs in space. I heard it all."

"Besides. It didn't work the first time. Why would blockading Berlin work a second?"

"Did I use the word 'blockade'? Did I? I'm not saying blockade . . . but . . . but . . . Khrushchev will cut us off somehow."

"Somehow? What assurances has Kennedy given to Brandt?"

"Nothing that could possibly mean anything. He may swear with his hand on his heart that we will stand by Berlin. But we won't, we can't. If Berlin comes up in the next few weeks you're just going to hear sabres rattled . . . that's all it will amount to."

"Depressing. You ask me if Vienna was fun. Of course it was. But nowhere near as much fun as Berlin."

"Even though you got busted and ended up with a Russian bullet in your gut."

"I was young enough to ride out all that and more. Berlin was fun. Berlin might just have been the time of my life."

"How old were you when we met in Berlin, kid?"

The 'kid' all but begged the answer.

"I was nineteen."

"I was twenty-nine. I'd been in the army since 1942. I'd seen Europe all the way from Omaha Beach to Berlin. I felt old then. I'm forty-three now. I feel even older. Young enough for some grey-beard of a guy to tell me I have my whole life ahead of me, old enough to tell him to go fuck himself. Joe, I am tired. I've had this way of life up to here. After London I'm going to quit. My old man is nearly eighty. He can't run the farm on his own any more. I had two brothers. Rick died in the Battle of the Bulge. Tony is some hotshot lawyer in LA. I'm all he has. I'm going to go home and run a farm. To hell with the spying game. To hell with the Cold War. It stinks. I'll be happier with the smell of new-mown grass and fresh horseshit."

"You're a country boy? I would never have guessed."

"Four hundred acres in south Pennsylvania. You can all but spit into West Virginia from the kitchen window. It's not a lot, but enough to do what I want to do."

"And what's that?"

"Dig a fallout shelter. What else? It isn't going to be Berlin . . . but it'll be something else, someplace else. I'll dig me a shelter with the old man's steam shovel. I'll line it in concrete three feet thick, put in a water purifier, bunk beds, a ton of canned food . . . and maybe a hi-fi . . . while away Armageddon listening to that Beethoven guy. Turn him up loud enough maybe I won't hear the bang when the bomb drops."

"Ah," said Wilderness. "For that you'll need Tchaikovsky."

Dashoffy laughed. Wilderness had always been able to make Jack laugh, and now he wanted above all to take advantage of the upward surge in his spirits.

"Jack, before you call it quits and dig your hole in the ground . . . one last professional question."

"Fire away, kid. Anything. My big mouth will open one last time for your one last question. Name it. Jackie's dress size, name of McNamara's dentist . . . my parting gift to you."

"Is there an ICBM launch site at Chelyabinsk?"

"Dunno. We never got the shot."

Nothing in Dashoffy's demeanour led Wilderness to think he was being anything but honest—and that they never got the shot was undeniable.

"Is there one at Plesetsk?"

"No."

"Ah."

"There are three."

At last. Always a frisson in being proved right. Try not to be smug. In a fair world he could tell Tom Radley to stand Masefield down now, let him go back to snapping tourist photos and looking for transition metals. But it wasn't a fair world, and Geoffrey Masefield wasn't his problem, he was Berlin's.

§64

London

Wilderness pondered Berlin.

All the way back to London.

Wilderness pondered Jack Dashoffy.

He did not ponder Geoffrey Masefield.

It was late evening before he got back to his house in Hampstead. His wife had left a note, scrawled, with her customary sense of melodrama, across the sitting room mirror in red lipstick.

"Stuck in all-night edit. Jxxx." This happened a lot. The hours of a BBC producer were hardly any more predictable than those of a spy.

He phoned Burne-Jones.

"I do hope you had a productive weekend, Joe?"

"Perhaps."

"So non-committal. Tell you what. Let's make an early start tomorrow. Come over for breakfast. Tell all and we'll make our minds up whether any of it matters over scrambled eggs and bacon."

Burne-Jones was an old-fashioned man. About as domestic as a rhinoceros. Years in the army had taught him how to darn socks, and somewhere along the line he had learnt to cook just one meal. Breakfast was the one meal Burne-Jones would cook. It would never vary, as though he was stripping down a Bren gun in darkness . . . every component to hand and in its rightful place. Breakfast at Campden Hill Square would begin with tea and porridge by the fireplace. Wilderness would let his tea go cold on the mantelpiece and wait for coffee. Burne-Jones never seemed to notice. What mattered, he had learnt early on, was that one should be standing up for porridge.

"Only a complete cad eats his porridge sitting down," Burne-Jones had told him. And Wilderness had silently despaired of his father-in-law ever making it into the twentieth century.

Porridge would be followed by scrambled eggs, whipped up over a flame at the table, with streaky bacon (kept warmish under silver) and wholemeal toast (allowed to go cold in its rattan rack). At the toast and marmalade stage if it was shop talk, Madge Burne-Jones might appear in topcoat and headscarf, clutching a shopping basket, peck Wilderness on the cheek and tell her husband that she was "orf now."

And then they'd talk.

Wilderness unwound the skein of Dashoffy's argument.

Burne-Jones listened without interruption, occasionally sipping coffee or crunching toast. At last he said, "Poor Jack. So young and yet so jaundiced."

"He's ten years older than me," Wilderness replied to no reaction.

"And there's nothing new in what he said, is there?"

"Perhaps."

"Ah, that word again."

"Perhaps telling us that Berlin is the bellybutton of the Cold War is nothing new. We've known that all along. I doubt Khrushchev said a word to Kennedy on the matter that couldn't be gleaned from last year's newspapers. Even his idea of Berlin as a free city isn't new . . . "

"Quite. It does rather make one query Khrushchev's use of the word 'free'—if he only 'frees' West Berlin and hangs on to his bit then it's only half a city and only questionably free."

"Perhaps what is new is Jack's conviction that the new component, that is a newly elected US president, a man in office less than six months, has changed nothing, that he means to do nothing about Berlin. Quite possibly less than Ike might have done."

Burne-Jones and Wilderness had long agreed on Ike—that having run the Second World War, been an enforced bystander to the Korean War, he would never allow the USA to commit itself to a conventional war again. He'd build up the nuclear arsenal instead and risk all.

"What was it again? Pay any price, meet any foe?"

"Pay any price, bear any burden, meet any hardship, support any friend, oppose any foe."

"Hmm . . . almost poetry."

"Almost but not quite."

"Imagine Baldwin or Eden saying anything quite so lyrical. However . . . you and Jack Dash would appear to have concluded it's what? Bluster?"

"More or less. Although the temptation Jack has succumbed to is not one I feel . . . he's not my president; I feel no need to rush to underestimate him."

Burne-Jones smiled at this.

"How precisely you put it, Joe."

"And of course Jack may not be the only man in a hurry."

An eyebrow raised at this.

"Khrushchev may be as rash as Jack. Jack beats a path back to the family farm in Pennsylvania to await Armageddon. Khrushchev returns to the Kremlin basking in glory thinking he's kicked JFK's arse for him . . . and they might both be wrong."

Burne-Jones glanced at his watch.

"Macmillan and Kennedy should be meeting just about now. Single topic, I suppose?"

Burne-Jones paused for a bit of marmalade munch. Then added one word: "Berlin."

Wilderness waited, wondering where the one word might lead.

"What Vienna has confirmed . . . is that Mr. K will do something. The status quo that has held since the end of the blockade in '49 is probably over . . . it was probably over the day we let West Germany into NATO in 1955 . . . bloody stupid move, but there you are. If Khrushchev had been in a stronger position then, all this might have happened much sooner. Right now he's not getting what he wants . . . ergo he has to do something . . . and now he thinks he has wrong-footed the American president, and in so doing has wrong-footed us all. So he'll do something simply because he can do something. The little fat bloke's moment has come. The man, the moment, the place . . . Berlin."

Wilderness said nothing. His boss was meandering. Let him.

"So . . . how would you feel about going back?"

How much does a man whose job is to know everything actually know? Wilderness had never mentioned Nell Burkhardt to Burne-Jones. This did not mean that Burne-Jones didn't know. Burne-Jones had mentioned Nell to him. Once or twice. Good mannered enough never to have used the word *Schatzi*. He might even know that Wilderness had found trips to Berlin a tad disturbing over the last ten years. And he would readily conclude that Wilderness should and could separate his private and professional lives. After all he'd married Burne-Jones's daughter, and the compartmentalisation of mind that required was monumental.

Her timing was immaculate. He had not mentioned Judy's name, simply thought of her . . . and there she was, kicking the door shut behind her, dropping a satchel full of papers and tearing off a tatty red beret that told Wilderness she had driven from Lime Grove with the top down on her MG.

"I am nicknackpaddywhacked . . . any coffee, Pa?"

Burne-Jones lifted the top on the coffee pot and shook his head.

Judy sloughed off her shoes and headed for the kitchen.

"Fuckfuckfuckfuckfuckfuckettyfuck."

"I did not pawn the family silver, mortgage the stately home and sell your grandmother into white slavery in order to pay your school fees to have the net result be a string of obscenities!"

Judy yelled back, "Don't mind me. I just pulled an all-nighter. Always makes me grumpy. You two go on talking state secrets."

Wilderness had not spoken to her, nor she to him. All the same he was grateful for the interruption. Without doubt Burne-Jones would repeat his last question some other time, but right now he'd not expect an answer.

§65

Judy told Wilderness to drive. It would be a pleasure to be at the wheel of her father's old pre-war MG on a bright June day . . . top down, blonde in the bucket seat.

"I won't nod off with the top down," said the blonde. "But I might just relax."

"What was it kept you in the edit suite all night?"

"The Baschet Brothers."

"A couple of French dogs?"

"Baschet not basset!"

Wilderness was sure she'd told him this before and he remembered next to nothing, but when talking to Judy bluffing never paid—she could be as resilient as her father. Better to come clean at once.

"Remind me."

"Bernard and François Baschet. Inventors of *Les Structures Sonores*. Been around about ten years now. Scored Cocteau's last film. Time for a bit of a retrospective. They invent instruments. I played you some of their music. You called it 'wibbly-wobbly.'"

Indeed he had. It was not unpleasant, just unfamiliar.

"And you?" she said.

"Eh?"

"I clearly interrupted something."

"Yes. A timely appearance. Your father had just asked me if I would like to go back to Berlin."

"Hmm . . . not as if you haven't been back."

"This is different. He wants me to run the Berlin station."

"Good Lord! He asked you that?"

"No . . . but he was about to. Not a lot of confidence in our man in Berlin."

"Fuckywuckywoo. Good job I showed up when I did. Do you think he's trying to drive a wedge between us or is it just carelessness?"

Wilderness said nothing.

"I wonder sometimes if he and Ma ever talk to one another."

"Meaning?"

Judy hesitated. Long enough for Wilderness to know exactly what she was going to say.

"We've been married for six years. She wants grandchildren."

"You have three sisters."

"None of whom are married. Imagine the scandal of a Burne-Jones bastard. The sky would fall. No, Wilderness. We are the chosen vessel for the propagation of her line. It's just . . ."

Judy trailed off, waiting for Wilderness to pick up.

"It's just that she thinks it's me and my frequent, nay, prolonged absences. She hasn't worked out that it's you."

"Thank you. Almost on the button. She hasn't worked out that it's me, my choice, my decision."

§66

Stuff, things, documents, passed across Wilderness's desk, more often than not with a scribbled note from Burne-Jones and sometimes, only sometimes, with just a question mark in the margin. Most were marked "FYI" or "FYEO" and required no response from him.

Not long after his return from Vienna a manila folder with half a dozen enlarged photographs appeared in his in-tray—Masefield's latest attempt to clarify the smudgy roll from his Minox.

Burne-Jones's note read, "Looks as though you and Jack Dash are right. The U-2 passed right over Plesetsk."

But it was of no importance.

The last two photographs were not from the same sequence. They were not photographs of documents but photographs of photographs. Two blurred aerial shots. In the bottom right hand corner the date had been written in a white crayon, and was the clearest thing in either shot. Burne-Jones, in turn, had ringed the dates in red pencil.

Wilderness took a magnifying glass to them just to be sure: 1.5.60—in each case.

He stuffed the photographs back in the folder and walked down the corridor to Burne-Jones's office.

Burne-Jones was in his customary, laconic pose, feet up, a chewed pencil twirling in one hand—thinking.

Wilderness spread the photographs out on the desk.

"No comment?" he said. "Not even one of your infuriating question marks?"

Burne-Jones swung his feet to the floor and stood up.

"I was rather hoping to let you have the first shot."

"It's obvious isn't it?"

"Quite. Do we agree it's Chelyabinsk?"

"Alec, it could be anywhere, any large industrial complex snatched through a haze of cloud and pollution."

"But we know it isn't, don't we?"

"We know. Does Tom Radley?"

"Passed it to me as I did to you, without a word."

"So he hasn't figured it out?"

"Apparently not."

"The Russians retrieve Gary Powers's camera intact from the U-2 they downed on May first last year and Tom doesn't spot it?"

"Well, either that or he didn't think it important enough to mention."

Wilderness realised he had to change tack, had to risk upsetting Burne-Jones.

"In that respect he'd be right."

"What?"

"Of course it's Chelyabinsk, but it tells us nothing. There's nothing in either shot that would enable us to tell a missile silo from a grain silo."

"I agree. Tom is missing the point, but so I fear are you."

"You just lost me. The photos are next to useless. What is there to miss?"

"This—we have them; the Americans don't. We got them out of Russia when the Americans hadn't a clue the film had even survived. It means we're back in the game."

Wilderness's heart sank. They were going to have the same conversation they seemed to be having every six or seven weeks. Uncle Sam . . . the elephant in the room . . . *The Man Who Came to Dinner.*

"Alec, they're just blurs."

"I can see that, Joe."

"The Americans won't thank us for sharing them. Half of nothing is still nothing."

"No. Perhaps not. But they won't begrudge us a bit of respect."

Wilderness hated this. The special relationship that was about as special as fish and chips on Fridays. One-upping the Americans was pointless.

"A game, you said."

"No, Joe. The game."

And Wilderness wondered if it was a game he wanted to go on playing. It was tempting to ask where Masefield's source, the elusive Professor Matsekpolyev, had obtained film from the destroyed U-2. It made sense that the camera had survived—the Russians had, after all, gleefully displayed the pieces of the plane in Gorky Park for all to see—but how the film got from Matsekpolyev to Masefield mattered more. He did not ask. It was—so clearly—not part of the game.

He let it pass. He would not be the one to utter what no one wished to hear.

Towards the middle of July an oddity appeared among the morning pile sent in by Burne-Jones.

Wilderness looked blankly at a copy of an order placed with a firm of wiremakers in Ambergate, Derbyshire, for what amounted to over a hundred miles of barbed wire to be shipped to Poland. The kind of overseas order to delight the politicians who exhorted "export or die."

Burne-Jones had jotted in the margin . . . "How long is the green line between us and them?"

Wilderness sent a note back saying, "If you mean Berlin, less than thirty miles down the middle, more like a hundred if you take in the entire perimeter with the DDR."

Burne-Jones replied, "I wonder what else we could sell them? I've an old Nissen hut in the back garden that's going begging. To say nothing of my old man's ARP tin hat."

And Wilderness in turn replied, "Now you mention it, I feel I'm living in a nation of wartime spivs . . . stolen nylons . . . frilly knickers . . . dodgy coffee . . . and enough barbed wire to carve up a continent. Hang on to your tin hat."

But neither of them raised the matter of whether the order should be prohibited or even investigated further.

§67

West Berlin: August 12

Nell had worked at the Marienfelde Refugee Centre since 1956. It was the hub of the universe. The bellybutton of the world. It said "Germany" as clearly as the Statue of Liberty said "America." That is, if symbols were to be readily appreciated, and they weren't.

The more appreciable interpretation was that Marienfelde was Ellis Island. You glimpsed the great green woman as you sailed through the Narrows into New York Harbor—but you landed at Ellis. Marienfelde was where the fluctuating tide of refugees landed in Berlin.

To be the refugee, the *Flüchtling*, was to Nell the European condition. She'd been one herself. Leaving Berlin by train in 1945, a step ahead of the Red Army—returning on foot eight months later to find her hometown occupied by the French, the Americans, the British, and the Russians. All of whom were still there in 1961. She'd watched the dribble of returning prisoners after the war, among them her own father, and with every Soviet-induced crisis . . . 1948, 1953, 1956 . . . she'd seen the dribble become a tidal wave. It was the Hungarian uprising, or to be precise its defeat, that first drew her to work at Marienfelde in 1956. Since then the tide had ebbed and flowed with every passing week, but almost always in the thousands.

There were endless individual types of refugee, but only two generical species, she concluded. Those who came from the east of the country, from the DDR, were pasty, lacking vitamins, lacking joie de vivre, as though hidden too long from the light of the sun. Those from East Berlin looked better fed. You couldn't tell a Berlin Oster from a Berlin Wester just by looking. It was the easiest thing to live on one side of a scarcely guarded line and work, eat, and shop on the other. Indeed, the cheap deal for years now had been to work in the West, to be paid in Western Marks, and to live in the East and pay rent in Eastern Marks at a very favourable rate of exchange. To be a *Grenzgänger*. Nell had never been tempted to do this. She was happy, although she would never have used the word, in Wilmersdorf in the American Sector. Her old school friend Eva Moll mocked her for her lack of pragmatism. Eva lived on Bernauer Straße in Mitte in the Soviet Sector. Her front door opened into Wedding, in the French Sector. One small step and she was in the West, with its shops and its better-paying jobs, one step back and she was in the East with its subsidised rent. It was, she said, "Sweet."

None of the East Berliners pouring into Marienfelde on the second Saturday of August was starving—but they were hungry. While they were in line to be "processed," a word whose use Nell had tried to discourage, they could not be fed and got hungrier. And when a line became a queue, and a queue became a crowd, the refectory retreated to infinity. By lunchtime, not that lunch was on offer, an additional two thousand had crossed from the East and sought refuge. The centre ran out of food.

Nell sat at her desk and thumbed her tatty black book of telephone numbers. What were the chances of anyone on the mayor's staff being in the office on a Saturday afternoon? What were the chances of anyone on the mayor's staff being in the office on a Saturday afternoon in the middle of Willy Brandt's election campaign for the chancellorship in West Germany? They'd be in Nuremberg. Or was it Hanover? Or Timbuktu?

Her eyes fell on "Marcus Dürer," whose title was something like deputy assistant chief of staff. She had his home number. She could not remember why. She could not remember that they'd ever met.

A grumpy Frau Dürer answered.

"We are in the middle of lunch!"

"Some people won't be getting any lunch, Frau Dürer."

Dürer came on the line.

"How can I help you, Fräulein Burkhardt?"

"I'm the assistant administrator at Marienfelde."

"I know."

"We're running out of food."

"Why are you running out of food?"

"They're coming over in their thousands. We're out of everything, coffee, tea, bread . . . you name it. We feed all we can and still they keep coming."

"Thousands?"

"Something's happening, something's about to happen . . . they all know it. The numbers won't drop. There'll be a few thousand more overnight."

"Oh God. Give me a quarter of an hour. Stay by the phone."

It was three quarters of an hour before Dürer called her back.

"I've found none of the people I need right now. I've left messages for the mayor in Nuremberg and Kiel, and for Harry Kempson."

"Kempson?"

"He's with the American mission. Something on the political staff. His people tell me he's having lunch somewhere in Charlottenburg. Didn't seem to know where. You might try ringing around yourself."

Nell tracked Kempson down at Café Kranzler.

He was as grumpy as Frau Dürer, but heard her out.

"And what do you expect me to do?"

"Do, Mr. Kempson? I expect you to open up some of those vast warehouses you have to keep the PX and every smuggler in Berlin happily supplied with the fruits of the Western World."

"Lady, you got some nerve."

"And I also have two thousand hungry and homeless."

"Is two thousand a lot?"

"Not as such, but we have been running at a thousand a day for weeks now. Last month more than thirty thousand crossed over. Last week alone, eleven thousand."

"Jesus H. Christ."

One of the things Nell liked about Americans was the combination of bluntness, reasonableness, and flexibility. A German in Kempson's position would be readjusting his dignity the better to stand upon it right now. Kempson, adjusted his view, his tone, and his mind.

"The PX, I can't raid on your behalf, but I've got C-rations by the ton. The stuff we gave out to combat troops. Not the most appetising chow in the world, but it got us from Normandy to the Elbe. I reckon it's about three years old, dates from '57 or '58 but it should still be good."

C-rations might be perfect. Pre-packed. Pre-cooked. Cereal bars, fruit cake, processed cheese, chocolate . . . all-American chewing gum. It could all be handed out in the queues. No pans no, plates.

"That would . . . suffice."

She knew it was the wrong word, perhaps even rude, smacking of ingratitude in its precision, but it bounced off Kempson.

"How much do you need?"

"I have over two thousand refugees already, I anticipate more than four thousand by this time tomorrow. Some move on quickly, some do not. So let's say . . . enough to feed . . . to feed . . . five thousand for a week."

"Sure. I'll throw in some loaves and fishes too. And after tomorrow?"

"I'm sorry?"

"Are you saying you're not expecting more refugees in the next few days? Another what? Another five thousand? Another ten thousand?"

"No, I'm not saying that. But I'm expecting something else."

"Such as?"

"Such as . . . something."

"Something like the shutters coming down on the East?"

"Aren't we all expecting that, Mr. Kempson? I can read it in the faces of my *Flüchtlings*."

"Miss Burkhardt, I don't know what to expect. Nobody tells me a damn thing. And your something could be a wooden No Go placard stuck up at the Brandenburg Gate or a nuke on Washington. We're dealing with Nikita Khrushchev, here. A wagonload of monkeys does not begin to describe the man."

By 6:00 p.m., lorry after lorry, each with its US Army white star on the cab door, pulled into Marienfelde. Kempson had been as good as his word.

Around 10:00 p.m., a warm August night, after one of those blistering Berlin summer days that rendered its winters such an unwelcome surprise, Nell packed up, locked her office, wheeled her bicycle past the long lines of *Flüchtling*s and went in search of her something. Rode her bike out to Bernauer Straße, up to Eva's apartment, up to the line.

Eva was in her room on the second floor front, the sash window propped up with a broken piece of broom handle in the vain hope that a breeze might stir the evening stillness. She was hunched over her treadle-operated Singer sewing machine. Joe Wilderness had bartered for it just before the airlift in '48. A small mountain of coffee handed over to a USAF sergeant out at Tempelhof. Wilderness had not asked Eva for anything. In return Eva had stopped referring to him as 'Nell's *Schieber*'— her smuggler, her black-marketeer—words from which Wilderness had never shrunk but Nell would. Eva had welcomed the gift as a symbol of freedom—not just the freedom from post-war Berlin shop prices and shop shortages, but the freedom to supplement her income by making clothes for others. Her eye and her sense of what might look good, whether following or defying fashion, were flawless. Eva was always better dressed than Nell, always better courted. Not that Nell gave a damn.

It was another summer frock. No doubt Eva's own copy of something seen in an expensive store on the Ku'damm. Yellow pansies on a translucent, sage green. Flimsy and seductive. A man-catcher. Eva was younger than Nell, but not by much. At twenty-nine, men were still abundant. She felt no need of marrying. At thirty-two, Nell was still seared by her time with Wilderness. If the men since did not remind her of Joe Wilderness, what use were they? And if they did, what use were they?

"I'm surprised to find you out on a Saturday night," said Eva.

"And I'm surprised to find you at home."

"No, you're not or you wouldn't have biked all the way out here."

"There is . . . there is . . ."

"Nell, for Christ's sake spit it out."

"It's going to happen."

"Oh bugger, if you're going to talk in riddles I'll get the gin."

Listening to Eva rummaging around in the kitchen, Nell paused to wonder. Was the "riddle" any more than a hunch? What was it Kempson had said . . . no one had told him anything? And surely the Americans would be the first to know?

"The Russians are getting ready to cut Berlin in two."

Eva stuck a warm gin and tonic in her hand. No ice, no lemon.

"Nicely spat. When did you have in mind? Tonight? Tomorrow?"

"Oh no . . . not that . . . I mean I don't know. I just know they're panicking in the East. Marienfelde is full to bursting."

"Well . . . we are in the East and I'm not panicking. Don't you think I might have seen something . . . more soldiers, more . . . more stuff?"

"Stuff?"

"I don't know. Wood, concrete, barbed wire . . . stuff the silly bastards might build a fence with. And if Marienfelde is overflowing . . . well hasn't it always? Haven't you come here twice a week for five years to tell me your job is impossible?"

Had she? Was that how it looked?

"And if they build a fence . . . well the Flüchtlings will jump over it or crawl under it, won't they? And if they mean to build a fence . . . why are they getting snotty about me paying my rent in ostmarks?"

"Are they?"

"Last week. Another silly edict from City Hall . . . those of us working in the West must pay our rent in deutschmarks not ostmarks."

"Of course, they want Western currency . . ."

"Exactly. And if they do, why would they cut us off? No more Grenzgänger, no more deutschmarks. It's all just too emotional. It's Torschlußpanik. Last-minute panic. Ulbricht needs us. Ulbricht needs our currency. So, a bit more rent to pay. I can live with that."

It was a convincing argument, presented with Eva's customary rattiness—the occasional skyward roll of the eyes as though she felt she was suffering a fool ungladly.

It did not deter Nell. Few things, few people, could.

"Eva, leave with me now. Pack a bag and come home with me. I have a bad feeling."

"Not tonight. I have a date, and before I have a date, I have a dress to finish."

"Where?"

"Don't you mean who? Since you don't ask I shall tell you. Ulrich—likes to call himself Rick because it sounds American. A meal out, and then back to his place."

"Where?"

"Is there an echo in here? Where? Friedrichsfelde."

Further east, about twelve kilometres from where they sat now.

"You'll spend the night?"

Another skyward roll of the eyes.

"Y'know Nell, for a thirty-two-year-old woman you sometimes have a way of sounding like a born-again virgin. If you could give that to the Catholic Church they'd bottle it and sell at Lourdes."

§68

West Berlin: August 13

Around two in the morning Nell was woken by the telephone. She ignored it, but whoever was calling did not ring off. She wrapped her dressing gown around her and barefooted into the sitting room.

"It happens."

"I'm sorry, who is this?"

"It's happening, right now. Pick a spot. Anywhere from Blankenfelde to Schönefeld. It's happening."

Then the line went dead.

She dressed quickly, lugged her bicycle down the stairs, and set off. She had chosen her spot. It required no thought—the Brandenburg Gate, where the British and Soviet sectors met.

$69

Nell was not a night person. The hours at Marienfelde could be so long that more often than not she would go home after work, cook, eat, listen to the radio, and sleep.

Eva Moll thought differently.

"It's nothing to do with the job. It's you. You're hiding."

"From what?"

"From yourself, and for that matter from Berlin. When did you last go to a nightclub, the theatre or even just sit in a bar after dark?"

All the same there was an unexpected pleasure in cycling across the Tiergarten in the dead of night—perhaps because night was never dead. For one thing she could hear it breathing.

Usually the Brandenburg Gate was visible for almost the length of the East–West avenue, floodlit by the Russians. Tonight it was dark, only moonlight to see by. She dismounted by the sign, the commonplace white board erected at every point where sectors met advising "You are leaving Such-and-Such Sector" in four languages. She had always seen it as advice—and superfluous advice at that—but perhaps it was now taking on the nature of a warning.

By the sign two British Tommies leaned on a jeep, utterly indifferent to her arrival. Half a dozen West Berlin policemen stood closer to the Gate. One turned to look and perceived no threat in a girl on a bike. And a dozen or more curious Berliners stood and stared as grey-uniformed East Berlin Factory Fighters rolled out barbed wire and hacked at the cobblestones with crowbars and pickaxes.

The Kampfgruppen der Arbeiterklasse, almost literally the Workers' Struggle Group, were factory-based. Somewhat like joining a trades union, and somewhat not. Formed in the wake of the 1953 protests it had probably done very little since, except dress up at weekends and drill after the fashion of the Third Reich Home Guard her father had been in during the war. It was voluntary. Nell could not understand why anyone would volunteer, but she knew people who had. One of them was facing her right now—Jürgen Fleck. They'd known each other since the thirties. They had survived the war apart, and got to know each other all over again in the deprivations of the peace. He fancied her. She knew that, but the boy had good manners and could take no for an answer. They had salvaged a good friendship over the years.

The boy was now a man. Thirty-one or thirty-two years of age. Standing with three other Factory Fighters, all in their baggy uniforms and soft forage caps—and all clutching tommy guns.

"Hello, Nell."

Smiling as he greeted her.

"Have you come for the show?"

"Jürgen . . . I've never seen you with a gun before."

"Oh, this . . ."

He shifted the angle of the barrel, and looked at it as though she'd mentioned a particularly tasteless tie he might be wearing. Spoke of it in the same "this old thing" tone of voice Eva used if you tried to pay her a compliment.

"It's not loaded. None of us have loaded guns. There's nothing to be scared of. Except them."

He nodded in the direction of the West German policemen.

"They won't be shy of wielding their truncheons or bringing in the water cannon if things get a bit rough."

"Is this happening everywhere?"

"Probably. My entire hundred was mobilised last night, and dozens more from other factories."

She looked around at the snagging rolls of barbed wire, uncurling, twisting and turning on their own stored kinetic energy as though alive—gigantic metal worms.

"And this is it? Barbed wire and empty guns. Do you expect to cut off a city with barbed wire and empty guns?"

The man standing next to Jürgen nudged him. A West Berlin cop had come up behind Nell.

"You shouldn't be here. Move along."

"No."

She pointed east.

"That's the police state. This is free Berlin."

Jürgen and his comrades laughed out loud at this, enough to embarrass the cop into moving on rather than pestering Nell, and as soon as he'd gone two Factory Fighters with a roll of wire on a steel spindle cut right between Nell and Jürgen with a cry of "Mind yer arses" . . . and it was done.

She almost wept. The simplest and crudest of symbols. A fence across her childhood.

"Jürgen. Jump. There's still time. Jump."

§70

She cycled north, past the ruined Reichstag, and, thinking it unwise to leave the West, cut a dogleg to approach Bernauer Straße from the northern, French side, down Ackerstraße.

The south side of Ackerstraße was already closed, and so was every other side street that crossed Bernauer Straße. At Brunnenstraße where the steps led down to the U-Bahn, the station had been shut off.

It was a difficult border to close. The line being the front wall of the apartment blocks in the Russian Sector, the Factory Fighters had no mandate to patrol the street itself. Closing the U-Bahn and the side streets seemed to be about the most they could do. She stood half an hour and her point was proved. No one took on the troops in the side streets, but as news of what was happening spread, half the doors on Bernauer Straße opened, and in twos and threes and fours, entire families slipped out, clutching suitcases and parcels. From an upstairs window she watched a man throw down a sheet, knotted around whatever possessions he had wrapped, for his wife to catch and drop . . . the sound of rattling cutlery and breaking china.

Where was Eva?

Where was Eva?

Why wasn't she . . . ?

And then Nell remembered. A night with "Rick" in Friedrichsfelde. Wrapped up in yet another man. Oblivious to what was happening on her own doorstep.

How long could it be before the doors were nailed shut and the windows bricked up? She did not doubt that Jürgen had told her the truth when he said his gun was empty . . . but how far off were the tanks and the armoured cars? Tucked away? Around every corner? Merely out of sight?

The couple with the bedsheet gathered up their belongings. The man slung the bundle over his shoulder like a tramp with an outsize spotted handkerchief and walked off into the night.

Nell knew exactly where they'd end up, and where she should be.

She rode home, locked up her bike and rang for a cab to take her to Marienfelde.

Khrushchev had murdered sleep.

§71

On the fourteenth Harry Kempson of the US Mission, Berlin, sent a note to Marcus Dürer:

> That young woman you set onto me is good. Won't take no for an answer. I went down to Marienfelde to see for myself. I think she averted a crisis.

Dürer passed this on to Mayor Willy Brandt, adding a note of his own.

> Soon, if not today, the westward flood of Flüchtlings will become a trickle. It may even stop altogether. At that point there'll be no need of Marienfelde. If you haven't yet found a replacement for me when I move to Bonn next month, you might consider Nell Burkhardt. Knows how to deal with the Amis. So few of us do, after all.

The last line stung. Too true for comfort. All the same Brandt made a mental note of this, left the paper version sitting on his desk for a week. He had to deal with the Amis. And that meant sitting on his hands and biting his tongue as the United States said and did nothing.

§72

London: August 18

Less than a week had passed. Wilderness had been shown none of the official reports from Berlin, nor had he asked to see them. He had relished being a spectator, standing at the touchline, and gathering all he needed to know from the newspapers and the BBC Home Service.

It was past five on the Friday evening. He had today's *Times* open on his desk. He liked *The Times*, simply because it ignored any sense of priority and gave over its front page to small advertisements tailored to the upper classes . . . Thomas Cook travel, Boon and Port Jaguars, Jack Barclay Bentleys and numberless ads for Rolls-Royces. Those in need of a news fix had to turn to the inner pages. It couldn't last. The next prominent death . . . Churchill, Mountbatten . . . and *The Times* would discover headlines and Burne-Jones would read into this the end of an era, not in the passing of statesmen but in *The Times* dropping its small ads . . . all those Bentleys and Jags. Debutantes were no longer presented at court, Prince Charles was not at Eton, the Queen probably listened to Jimmy Clitheroe over fish fingers and tinned rice pudding at Sunday lunch . . . but *The Times* hung on grimly. What was a charming anachronism to Wilderness was little short of sacred to Burne-Jones.

"It's a pickle."

Burne-Jones had appeared almost silently, a finger poking at the page-three news Wilderness had been skimming.

**US 18th Infantry at East German Border—
Autobahn to Berlin.**

Wilderness folded the paper hoping to kill the subject, but Burne-Jones sat down opposite him and the game was so very clearly afoot.

He tried again to be dismissive.

"A predictable pickle. Every political hack in Fleet Street, every Washington pundit, saw this coming."

"And now they're all saying things like 'a lamentable failure of Intelligence' . . ."

"Hold on . . . whose Intelligence?"

"Ours, theirs, everybody's I suppose. Next thing Gaitskell will be on his feet in the Commons asking for explanations. 'Why did no one know?' and so forth."

"But we did know. I just bloody said that. Not the precise what or when, but we most certainly knew the where."

"Of course. But we're not going to admit anything, are we?"

"And why not?"

"Because, o son-in-law mine . . . it is far better to say nothing and appear ignorant than to admit we knew and appear futile. We knew what we knew and discretion was the better part of thingy . . . and in the meantime a hundred miles of best British barbed wire has by now surely found its way from darkest Derbyshire to Warsaw and thence to Berlin."

Burne-Jones waved a hand in the air. Now he was the one aiming at the dismissive. Wilderness didn't know how to read it. We should have stopped that shipment or we shouldn't have? So he tacked away instead. Impossible to change the subject, perhaps possible to move it along.

"I can hazard a guess at what comes next."

"I'm all ears."

"Kennedy jetting in."

"Hmm. Not exactly."

"What do you mean 'not exactly'? He is or he isn't."

"He isn't. He's sending LBJ to Berlin."

"When?"

"ASAP."

"Any point to it? What can he do? Wave to the troops? Look at our rolls of barbed wire and tell them all 'something will be done!'?"

"Edward VIII? Right?"

"Yep. And we both know the hill of beans that amounted to. I just hope the Russians took the labels off the wire before they strung it out in the streets. I doubt we'd survive the diplomatic fallout if LBJ sees the city divided and the barriers labelled 'Made in Great Britain.'"

"Ah, Joe. So cynical. Perhaps, the main point might be to get LBJ out of Washington. They have to be the oddest of bedfellows. Odder even than

Nixon and Ike, although it might be fair to say that Kennedy fears rather than despises Johnson. To have him fly the Stars and Stripes, hand out a couple of hundred monogrammed biros, glad-hand a few Allied leaders and make speeches that amount to bugger all may well suit both of them. What else does a vice president have to do with his time?"

"Well . . . technically he's in charge of the American space programme. NASA answers to him."

"Which says very little about either. Vice president of Dogs in Space. Up there with the King of Cornflakes and the Duke of Doughnut, I should imagine."

"Actually, the Americans favoured monkeys not dogs for their space missions."

"Well . . . this monkey's going to Berlin. And so are you. LBJ is flying in overnight. Your flight gets in a less than an hour ahead of him."

Wilderness said nothing to this. There was no argument he could make that he had not already made. Following the vice president around had to be less interesting, less informative than following the president. And there was no mention of accreditation this time. The most he'd get out of this might be one of the monogrammed pens—an LBJ souvenir, like an Isle of Wight ashtray or a stick of Blackpool rock. The least would be that he was bound for Berlin again, wearing the old ball and chain.

"It may well be that Berlin is the place to be," Burne-Jones went on. "There's even been talk of moving the UN, or part of the UN, to West Berlin."

"What's that supposed to do? Scare Khrushchev? Invoke a visible if silent 'you wouldn't dare' to a man who dares almost anything? A man whose mind is like a dozen weasels in a potato sack. I think prefer the opposite idea."

"And that is?"

"It was a *Guardian* leader a while back . . ."

Burne-Jones was not a *Guardian* reader and still referred to it somewhat scornfully as the *Manchester Guardian*, implying it was "provincial."

"Abandon West Berlin, blow up anything the Russians might value . . . leave them scorched earth . . . and move the entire population to a new site somewhere in West Germany."

"And you wonder why I stick with the *Telegraph*? You're on the morning flight," said Burne-Jones with calm finality.

§73

He went home to pack for Berlin. He packed and repacked, wondering how short he could make this trip and hence how little he could get away with taking, while Judy fussed around him, saying, "But Pa hasn't actually asked you to run the Berlin station, has he?" and "You will say no, won't you?"

It was her constant refrain throughout the night and cost Wilderness badly needed sleep.

As Wilderness was knocking back a last cup of coffee at seven the next morning—a car waiting in the lane—Judy picked up the pile that was yesterday's unopened and ignored second post. She clutched half a dozen envelopes to her chest and tossed a lone postcard down on the breakfast table for Wilderness.

A view of nothing much in shades of green, a landscape somewhere unmemorably nondescript. An American eagle stamp, and a scrawling hand he did not recognise.

Broke turf on the shelter yesterday. When they drop the big one, I'll be ready. Saving a place for you.

Jack

PS Hold 'em off as long as you can, I can't get a plumber till September and I figure the survival of civilization rests on me getting the john plumbed in.

Wilderness thought this might be his mission. So much more specific than anything Burne-Jones had said. No longer the passive observer of Berlin unravelling, of LBJ touring, he was there to fend off World War III till Jack Dashoffy had a working lavatory. And all on Her Majesty's Secret Service.

Beneath his postscript Dashoffy had drawn a crude Looney Tunes character . . . crude but recognisable, and a dustbin lid, creating the equation: "Daffy + a garbage can lid = ?"

Wilderness knew the answer. "Duck and cover."

§74

West Berlin

Wilderness had been in Potsdamer Platz the last time they'd rolled out the wire in 1948. It hadn't lasted long. All the same he'd not been there to see it rolled up again in 1949. Shot by Yuri Myshkin, thrown a few thousand dollars in consolation by Frank Spoleto and dragged home in disgrace by Burne-Jones—except that the disgrace had been in Burne-Jones's eyes only. He'd kept it off the record rather than admit to anyone that Berlin's biggest racket—the smuggling of coffee, sugar, penicillin, morphine, and anything else that could be nicked—was down to one of his own men. He'd made Wilderness a sergeant. He still was a sergeant. He'd never get promoted again.

At Tempelhof, Radley had met him with, as he had requested, a second car and driver. Radley had a copy of LBJ's itinerary, from the press office of the US Mission, Berlin. His arrival would be met with a row of tanks and a seven-gun salute—who, Wilderness wondered, decided how many tanks and guns a man was worth? 'Sorry, Senator Frisbee, you're only a two-tank man'?—and then go through all the tedious motions of being a semi-head of state on a semi-state visit. The inspection of a guard of honour, which must be close to meaningless to a man who'd spent World War II as an observer in the Reserve. Then, a motorcade to Potsdamer Platz, followed by a public address to anyone who cared to turn up, outside the *Rathaus* in Schöneberg.

Any hope that Adenauer might fly in with him from Bonn was dashed by the old man himself, who'd made it perfectly clear that Berlin was not a mess of his making and he'd no intention of helping Brandt out by showing up.

Wilderness looked at the press release and was succinct.

"I don't think the old bastard would so much as piss on the flames if Brandt were on fire. There's nothing for me here. I'll get out to Potsdamer Platz."

"I thought we were supposed to observe the vice president?" Radley said.

"You observe him, Tom. I'm nipping out for coffee."

What he was reluctant to spell out to Radley was that they were not observing LBJ, but the Berlin reaction to LBJ . . . and if he didn't get it he didn't get it. LBJ would say nothing that meant anything. If Wilderness felt wicked he might just jot down his version of Johnson's speech on the back of a menu while he had coffee and bet anyone a fiver that he'd be proved mostly right.

"Honour"—LBJ was bound to work in that word somewhere. A touch cynically, Wilderness had always agreed with Joseph Conrad about honour . . . "he made so much of his disgrace, while it is the guilt alone that matters."

No one was ever guilty. They were all honourable men or they were not, and when the promises LBJ was about to give Berlin were broken—in a week, a month, however long—it would not be a matter of guilt but only of dishonour.

He was feeling wicked.

He sat in the Hotel Esplanade in Bellevuestraße. Sipped coffee and looked out at the square. The Esplanade had been central. A Berlin landmark. A survivor. The RAF had destroyed most of it in '44. When he first saw it in '47 only a couple of the public rooms were useable. But Berlin had not wanted to see the Esplanade die, and over the years, while bits of Berlin lay as rot and rubble, something magical arose out the old hotel. More than a hint of its pre-war Weimar glamour. It was central once more. Where the sectors met, where Russians rubbed shoulders with Americans who rubbed shoulders with British. Most of the shady deals he and Yuri had done were set up in bars and clubs not a hundred yards from this spot, and one or two of them in this very room. It was the heart of the party. At the edge. And now, the wire was back, and as the wire became a wall, as it surely would, it looked as though the Esplanade would become peripheral again. It was too close to the new edge. And the new edge was going to be a cul-de-sac, because West Berlin was going to be a cul-de-sac.

He gave it an hour—skimmed the *Telegraph*, the *Guardian* and the *Frankfurter Allgemeine Zeitung*, and watched the crowd gather. He stepped out among them—a sea of Stars and Stripes, many of them homemade, kids' wax crayons on lined schoolbook paper.

There were more than he could ever count and more arriving all the time. As his driver had struggled to find a clear route from Tempelhof to Potsdamer Platz against the tide of people heading the opposite way, he'd taken a guess at the size the reception awaiting LBJ, tanks and all—ten thousand, fifty thousand? Pointless, and just as pointless here. It didn't matter what LBJ might say, and Wilderness was resolute in his cynicism, it was simply that he said it at all. He could stand up and say "Donald Duck for President," and they'd probably cheer.

Another half hour passed. The veep was running late. He looked at his watch. And another half hour. The veep was running later. Berliners were starting to drop their paper flags and drift away. Then he realised.

The bugger wasn't coming.

§75

East Berlin: August 13

Eva and Rick had fucked themselves into a stupor on the night of the twelfth. She slept soundly; he slept with one arm around her, one foot dangling off the bed not quite as deeply in oblivion as she. Her gentle snoring penetrated his dreams, and every so often brought him to the surface.

That wasn't anyone's snore; that wasn't human. It was a sound that pushed every button, jerked every string and dragged him back sixteen years to April 1945—he was fourteen—hiding in a cellar—it was the steel rattle of Russian tank tracks on Berlin cobbles.

He pulled back the curtain. Nothing. Had he dreamt it? He flicked on the light, looked at his watch: 6 a.m. It had been light for half an hour.

"What's wrong? Put the light out."

Eva pulled a pillow over her face.

"Nothing. Just my imagination. Go back to sleep."

There it was again, and this time she'd heard it too.

He went to the other window, the one that looked out in the alley. A T-55 had backed in with inches to spare on either side, killed its engine and sat like a brooding monster.

"Eva, there's a Russian tank out there. Put the radio on."

"What?"

"A tank. A Russian tank."

"What? Have they invaded?"

"How should I know? Put the radio on."

She fiddled with the dial, coursing through the static.

"No, forget anything local. Tune to the BBC World Service."

And then they knew.

§76

Rick would not let her leave.

They had breakfast and went back to bed.

Eva was surprised to find that she had slept at all, but Rick woke her in the early afternoon.

"Tell me it's a dream."

"It isn't."

He improvised lunch around two, listened to the BBC once more, and said, "What's the point in you even trying to get home? The streets are full of those Factory-Fuckers and VoPos . . . the tank in the alley is on standby in case things get worse, and your apartment is the front line. If they've closed off the Brandenburg Gate, think what's going on at Bernauer Straße. Besides it's Sunday. You don't work on Sundays."

"Why, do you think it'll be different on Monday?"

It wasn't.

On Monday morning more than fifty thousand *Grenzgänger* did not and could not report for work in the West.

On Tuesday Rick finally agreed to let her walk around. Manliness and authority were all very well. She would not deny a certain pleasure in being so protected, but it took no account of the need for clean knickers and when he said "I'll lend you a pair of my underpants," the silent stare she gave him would have frozen nitrogen.

It was Wednesday before she got back to Bernauer Straße.

At the back of the block of flats, there were VoPos and border guards milling around. She got as far as the southern side of the Ackerstraße barrier before one of them shooed her back. She'd had a glimpse of a sizeable crowd in Bernauer Straße. At least they weren't giving up just yet. But when she tried to enter the building she was refused.

"You have keys?"

"Of course I have keys. I live here."

"You must hand them over, that is now the law."

"Why?"

"All keys to Bernauer Straße must be handed over."

And taking him at his word, she'd given him her front door key, and held on to the back.

She went back each day. Each day it was worse. On Thursday trucks of sand and cement blocked her way. On Friday a crisis at the front, which she could hear but not see, had thrust the VoPos into panic mode and they'd cleared the southern side with drawn guns.

"You could stay," Rick said.

She hated male sentimentality. The idea that they could nest together like small, furry animals and let the world pass them by.

"Don't be ridiculous. You have no idea what life is going to be like in the East from now on. This isn't just a change that affects them, it affects us as well."

"We've got each other."

That was the last straw. On Sunday afternoon, August 20, as Vice President Johnson whistled his way around West Berlin, out in East Berlin, Eva Moll stole Rick's bicycle.

§77

Perhaps it was something to do with it being Sunday. Perhaps more to do with the American ballyhoo taking place in the West, but it was quieter at Bernauer Straße.

As she arrived, workmen emerged from the back door, slapping the dust from their clothes with the flats of their hands. They upturned half a dozen wooden crates, set out their bread and sausages, flipped the caps on their bottles of beer. Quite by chance she had arrived at their lunch break.

She'd heard the lock click as they came out. Her key was clutched in her hand, but she waited until the first dirty joke of lunchtime had set them all laughing before approaching. No one looked around as she turned the key.

Up on the second floor she found they had been working in her apartment. They'd respected her property, moved her possessions away for the windows and put down dust sheets. Ironic, the persistence of good manners—after all she was quite certain no one would ever be allowed to live in this building again, and the evictions would lack all semblance of manners.

In her bedroom, the workmen had laid a dozen rows of bricks inside the window frame, the cement still wet. It would be the work of seconds to demolish the barrier.

First she needed to find everything she meant to take with her. No souvenirs, no treasured childhood toy, no favourite book. She'd be practical—clothes and shoes. Nothing that would not fit in her smallest suitcase. And when the suitcase was full, she dragged the dust sheets off her bed, and upended the mattress against the wall. Two storeys was what? Twenty feet? More? The mattress looked too insubstantial to break her fall.

She went out into the corridor. Every door was unlocked. In Frau Schocken-Hauser's apartment she found a solid, goose-down mattress, so overstuffed it took all her strength to drag it back to her own bedroom.

What happened next needed to happen quickly.

One kick and the rows of wet bricks tumbled into the street below. She looked out. Some hoo-ha, some other jumper, was preoccupying people fifty yards up. No one had paid any attention.

Then her mattress, shoved through the window to flop down lightly. Then Frau Schocken-Hauser's mattress, hoisted, dragged, and shoved to crash down with a bass thud and a hiss of air as though some fairy-tale giant had breathed his last.

That did not go unnoticed.

And all she had to do was jump.

Standing on the windowsill.

All she had to do was jump.

Now men were running down the street and yelling up at her.

Jump—before the buggers at the back heard the commotion.

With her suitcase in her hand, Eva jumped.

Bumped down, arse first on the spot she had aimed for.

She had closed her eyes. When she opened them, two young men were standing over her with a blanket, held out like some sort of safety net.

"What kept you?" she said.

§78

West Berlin: August 20

Berlin had built the Marienfelde Centre to be redundant, or, rather, in the optimistic expectation of redundancy. It was designed to be easily reconfigured as apartments once its primary purpose had lapsed. It was said that it looked like a post-war housing project for the proletariat. More fancifully, a backlot set for a dystopian film in a totalitarian state directed by someone like Fritz Lang—a grid of clean lines, symmetry and regularity. The boxy shape of things to come. To Nell it had always looked like a prison, even its name Notaufnahmelager sounded like a prison, and she had made it her mission to ensure that it never felt like one.

The flood of refugees had slowed in the last week, but it was hardly a trickle even now. Somehow they were getting through, and a camp designed to house 1,200 was still overcrowded. They sat in corridors and in the yards, perched on their suitcases and bundles—Nell always wanted to ask "What did you bring?" wondering what she might take if she ever had to abandon almost everything. In a sense she had. Twice. Leaving Berlin a few months before the Russians arrived, her mother's last warning "Don't look back," and leaving Celle to walk back to Berlin in summer the same year with only a knapsack, two days' food and a copy of *Andersen's Fairy Tales*. She had not starved . . . the kindness of strangers . . . nor would these, the stragglers . . . those who had waited almost too long.

Her secretary, Cosima, appeared in the doorway, breathless and flustered.

"They're coming here!"

"Who's coming here."

"The mayor . . . Brandt and whatsisname . . . you know, the American vice president. The motorcade's on its way, they'll be here in fifteen minutes! What do we do?"

"Do?" said Nell. "We do nothing. What did you have in mind, a quick whip round with a mop and a duster? We run a refugee camp, so that's what we'll do. Run it."

"Oh God, Nell. You're impossible."

A quarter of an hour later, she heard a tap on the open door. A man in his early thirties, the two-piece suit and rimless glasses that seemed to be the uniform of the professional men of her generation. And, yes, she knew him now. Marcus Dürer, the mayor's dogsbody.

"Fräulein Burkhardt. How pleasant to see you again. I'm afraid we are pressed for time, so if you would be so kind as to line up your staff for the vice pres— "

"Which way did you come in Herr Dürer? The main gate?"

Nell returned to her papers, scribbled a note in the margin, not looking at Dürer.

"Why? Yes."

"Then you may have noticed a hundred or so people in the courtyard, and perhaps as you came down the corridor to my office a hundred more to trip you up? And as you look out across the lawns the row upon row of tents housing all the *Flüchtling*s who came through in the last days before the present crisis and for whom we have no beds? So where do you think my priority lies. In lining up on parade for the Amis or getting on with the job?"

She looked at him now.

"Fräulein Burkhardt, I would appreciate your cooperation as I'm sure you appreciated mine last week. And I take your point. The job must come first. Perhaps if you, and only you, gave us ten minutes of your time, we might be able to accommodate a vice presidential whim without making it seem that we lack respect?"

"Does he have many whims?"

"Rather too many. We run around like scalded cats. We have two men assigned just to go shopping for him."

"All right, let's take a walk through the canteen. Mr. Johnson can press the flesh and kiss what few babies there are while our *Flüchtling*s eat. He might find it an education."

"Your sarcasm notwithstanding, thank you. Please lead the way."

The motorcade had stopped just inside the main gate. Johnson had stepped out of the open-topped car and was holding a girl of seven or eight in his arms—every inch the politician on the campaign trail. The girl frowned, unhappy at being singled out. Brandt stood just behind him, and big men with crew cuts and bulging jackets seemed to be dotted about everywhere like pieces on a chessboard.

Johnson set the girl down, one of his huge hands ruffling her hair, acknowledging Nell's approach with a stare of curiosity. He was, she thought, unprepossessing—big nose, donkey ears and a chin that rippled in contours of flesh to bury itself in his neck. The child was still not smiling. Johnson almost was—as much as letterbox lips would allow.

"And you must be the Miss Burkhardt these gen'lemen have been tellin' me about?"

Johnson spoke no German, and his interpreter moved closer, poised to speak. Nell did the merest double take at these words, glanced at Dürer and got in first—in English.

"Welcome to Marienfelde, Mr. Vice President. Have you had lunch?"

§79

Cosima passed her in the main courtyard.

"I can't believe you did that. Feeding the vice president of the United States C-rations!"

"Really? He seemed quite partial to the processed cheese. And he pocketed the chewing gum and took it with him."

"One day, Nell, you'll get us both shot."

Dürer had vanished without her noticing. No doubt speeding ahead to prep the way for the next pointless display of concern and futility. She had meant to thank him for the food and to apologise for her rudeness. He hadn't asked for that. He was only doing his job and had let her get on with hers. As she crossed the footpath a tall man in a pale, stylish suit detached himself from the gaggle of prominenti and walked quickly towards her. It was Brandt, alone—no guards, no flunkies.

"I'm sorry we didn't get a chance to talk, Fräulein Burkhardt."

"The show must go on, Mr. Mayor."

Did Brandt frown at this? Did she bite her tongue?

"I might agree with you that politics and show business often look alike, but I know we can achieve more than the clowns and lion tamers. Marcus thinks your work here will soon be over. Do you?"

"Yes. The Russians will tighten and tighten their grip and perhaps in a month or two the Flüchtlings will run at one or two a week. The centre will be an expensive indulgence and one you will doubtless wish to spare the city."

"I agree. The Russian grip will become total, and we shall learn to live with it. Defiance will give way to pragmatism—to a new politic. One the Americans may not understand. One I feel you could help us create. When you want to move on, phone my office, give your name, and ask to be put through to me. They'll be expecting your call. I can hold the post until Christmas, no longer. The choice is yours."

He didn't say goodbye, simply turned on his heel and walked away. Had he just offered her a job?

Nell called after him. "You mean a job?'

He turned for a moment.

"Yes. A job. Don't wait forever."

§80

It was close to six in the evening. Nell was tired, self-recriminating, and felt like calling it a day. She couldn't. For a week, each day had seemed like no other; the unpredictable was to be expected. Instead she would play the deputy headmistress, get up from her desk and inspect—inspect everything and everyone, down the corridors out onto the courtyard where the fresh *Flüchtling*s of the afternoon sat with bags and bundles, relieved and scared, free and homeless.

A dozen or so from the end of the line was Eva Moll. Her left leg was propped up on a suitcase. She winced with pain as Nell approached. Rubbed at her ankle.

"Eva?"

"It'll pass. I twisted my ankle when I jumped. Nothing's broken."

"You jumped?"

"Well . . . the buggers nailed up the doors and bricked up the windows, didn't they?"

"Why didn't you come to me?"

"I have come to you."

"I mean . . . to me . . . at home."

"What? And have you tell me 'I told you so'? Remind me that I didn't listen when you warned me? No, I prefer to meet you in your professional mode. If you are going to be schoolmarm-strict and po-faced then at least you're only doing your job. In your apartment I'd find you insufferable and I'd take it personally. This is better by far. I fucked up, I am homeless, a refugee, I go where the hopeless fuckers go, to Marienfelde, to Fräulein Burkhardt."

"You don't have to . . ."

"Nell, please . . . I expect no favours. I don't want to jump any queue. I've jumped far enough for one day. So stamp your foot, put on your cast-iron face and oblige me by asking if there's any ice for my ankle."

"I am not po-faced!"

"Really?"

"No."

"Oh God, Nell. You're impossible."

§81

Nell found ice. And then she found a wheelchair. Stuck Eva in it and pushed her to the S-Bahn station.

"What are you doing?"

"You're coming home with me. To Wilmersdorf. You will have to learn to live with my 'po-face.'"

§82

Tom Radley lived down to Wilderness's expectations. The news that LBJ had left Berlin, scooting through the cloud of dust that had not yet settled from his arrival, brought forth only scorn, when Wilderness wanted insight and interpretation.

"Heard the one about the Yank at the Louvre? Quick, quick, where's the *Mona Lisa*, I'm double-parked! He even skipped out on his own troops arriving to fit in a bit more shopping."

"Where do the mayor's apparatchiks hang out?"

"I'm sorry?"

"The mayor's staff. Surely there's a bar in Schöneberg where they gather to grouch and grumble after work."

"Of course there is. But why would you want to go there?"

Wilderness ignored this and said simply, "You drive, Tom. Make yourself useful." And he knew from Radley's cheery "okey dokey" that he had not heard the insult.

In the Jägerkeller, a bar Wilderness did not think he'd ever been in before, they were surrounded by men the best part of ten years younger, men in stylish Italian suits, men with close-cropped hair, men striving to look like their bosses—the bright young things of the Brandt administration. The complaining bright, young things . . . forced to work a weekend just to accommodate the vice president of the United States.

"*Das Einzige, das er getan hat, war das Schuhekaufen. Es hätte auch eine Visit von Jackie sein können.*"

All he did was shop for shoes. We might as well have had a visit from Jackie.

"*Hätten sie Jackie geschickt, würden wir wenigstens auch Jack bekommen haben.*"

If they'd sent Jackie at least we would have got Jack. "*Glauben Sie, dass Kennedy jemals kommen wird?*"

Do you think Kennedy will ever come?

Who cares? It's all over. The wire is up. The slabs are down. Soon the slabs will be a permanent wall and anyone stuck on the other side is fucked. What can the Amis do about that? Buy more fucking ashtrays? Hand out more fucking pens?

So saying, the man took a handful of vice presidential LBJ monogrammed biros out of his pocket and tossed them up in the air like rice at a wedding, to clatter down on the table and the floor.

I'm the Texas cowboy. I'm the vice president. Have a pen. Oh fuck me, I forgot the fucking paper hats and the fucking campaign buttons. Rah fucking rah.

While they laughed, Wilderness bent down and picked up a pen. It might just prove a point to Burne-Jones when it came to convincing him of the truth of what he'd just overheard. LBJ's rapturous reception by the Berlin crowds was no reflection of his reception at City Hall. What these arrogant young brats were saying was not diminished by their youth or their arrogance. They were Brandt's Camelot. This was what Brandt was saying, and if not saying thinking so clearly they had read it in his face.

When the laughter finally died, another of the young suits said to the one who'd been making all the jokes, "*Haben Sie gehört, was Brandt sagte zu Kleist?*"

Did you hear what Brandt said to Kleist? "*Zu Kleist? Wann?*" To Kleist? When?

"*Vor etwa einer Stunde.*"

About an hour ago. "*Ich hörte ihn. Er sprach sehr leise, aber ich schwöre, dass er sagte: 'Kennedy macht Hackfleisch aus uns.'*"

I heard him. He was very quiet but I'd swear he said, "Kennedy is making mincemeat out of us."

"*Scheisse!*"

It seemed to Wilderness that every young man in Brandt's entourage had uttered the same crude German syllables and with them all doubt as to what Brandt was thinking vanished.

He had no difficulty persuading Radley to go home, that there was nothing else to be done. If they had office jobs, Radley would be the kind of bloke who always managed to sneak off after lunch on a Friday.

Such as it was, Wilderness went back to their "office" and phoned Burne-Jones on the scrambler.

"It's a fiasco."

"Not according to the BBC news. Johnson seems to have gone down rather well."

"Mickey, Goofy, and Pluto would have gone down rather well."

"Meaning?"

"It is close to irrelevant who the Americans sent. The crowd was always going to rip up its bed linen for flags, throw flowers, and cheer. I'm not sure LBJ even saw the bloody wall, he was so busy glad-handing. Berliners wanted a gesture, and they got it. Brandt wanted action. He got nothing. The closure of the East is a fait accompli. There's nothing he can do about it and he knows it. There's nothing the Americans will do about it. And he knows that too."

"What next?"

"Next?"

"I suppose I'm asking what you think Brandt will do."

"I think he'll accept a new status quo. He'll find a way to live with the wall and work with the Russians. I think he'll probably never trust an American again."

"Bad as that, eh?"

"Closing the East suits almost everyone. The human drain stops, so Khrushchev is happy. The barriers going up suits Kennedy. It's as clear a statement as could be that Khrushchev has no designs on the West. We win, they win. The losers are Berlin and Brandt."

"How succinctly you put it, Joe."

"There's more."

"I'm sure there is."

"Tom Radley is a twat."

"Now, Joe . . ."

"A complete and utter twat."

There was a silence Wilderness would not be the one to break.

"I can't just relieve him of his post."

"Yes, you can."

"For one thing . . . there's Masefield. He has . . . built up a relationship with Masefield."

"Has he now?"

"For Christ's sake, Joe. You're making this personal."

"Alec. He's an idiot. He has no handle on what just took place in front of his eyes . . . he sees nothing . . . I asked him what he had to report . . . and he recited chunks of LBJ's speech . . . I could have got that from any newspaper . . . it was Brandt's reaction that mattered . . . he can't see Brandt . . . he can't see Berlin, he can't see Berliners . . . and I'd be amazed if he has a handle on our Geoffrey. Bring Radley back to London. If you think his relationship with Masefield matters, he can run him from there. In Berlin the man is a liability."

More silence.

"Stay there."

"What?"

"Just stay there. Work with Tom for a while."

"Alec—"

"Joe. You cooked your own goose with your opinions just now. If you really think Tom is that bad, then you must stay there until I can resolve the matter."

"I'm not taking over the Berlin station."

"And I'm not asking you to."

More silence. Wilderness's silence. A silence Burne-Jones would not be the one to break.

§83

On the Tuesday morning following, Ida Siekmann, a fifty-eight-year-old nurse, long-widowed and a resident at 48 Bernauer Straße, just a few doors away from the former home of Eva Moll, jumped from the fourth floor window of her apartment. Jumping now being a regular occurrence, if not yet an actual tourist attraction, the West Berlin Fire Brigade had become an almost permanent presence somewhere along the East–West axis that Bernauer Straße sliced through the post-war division of the city. Politically, jumpers leapt East to West, geographically, South to North, from the Soviet Sector to the French. Alas, Ida allowed too little time for the fire crew to scuttle house to house and open the catching-blanket—she threw down her bedding, blankets, and an eiderdown, and jumped. Her old bones shattered on the stone pavement and she died on the way to hospital.

The first death of the new crisis.

Eva Moll received the news with little less than rage.

"What future do you think you have here? What future can anyone have here?"

And Nell replied, as she always would, "It's where I belong."

"I know. You keep telling me. You're a Berliner, if not *the* fucking Berliner! Nell, Berlin is an island. An island you haven't left since . . . since God knows when."

"It was 1945."

"Almost twenty years . . . you make my point for me. You may think you know Berlin, but you don't know Germany. You haven't been to Germany for twenty years. This isn't Germany . . . this is the artificial island, a great pontoon floating on the almighty dollar . . . but the dollar's not as mighty as the Red Army. The Russians can take Berlin whenever they want."

Nell was keeping calm by an effort of will. Sipping at her cup of herbal tea in the pretence that they were still girlfriends chatting. A pretence she could not sustain.

"I know they can. But . . . they won't."

"A hunch?"

"An opinion."

"Same thing. You're going to gamble your life on a hunch?"

"Yes."

"Then I won't be around to watch you do it. I'm going West. I'm a trained legal secretary. If I can't find work in Bonn or Frankfurt . . . well what is the world coming to?"

The last throwaway piece of rhetoric was a question Nell would dearly have loved to be able to answer, but she had no answers, just more opinions to be dismissed as hunches, so she said nothing.

Eva's ankle was normal by Thursday morning, the twenty-fourth. She took her bag to the Charlottenburg Bahnhof and boarded a train for the West.

Later the same day the DDR policy of shoot to kill claimed its first victim. Günter Litfin, aged twenty-four, a tailor, who, like Eva Moll, lived East and worked West, was shot by a sergeant of the transport police as he tried to swim the Humboldt canal.

§84

Moscow: August 24

Masefield had another audience with Koritsev. Such a good customer after the indium deals that he merited a full-blown undersecretary once more—no more deputies, assistants, deputy assistants or assistant deputies—and the relayed good wishes of Comrade Minister Patolichev himself, as they discussed the possibilities of a deal for zinc.

Zinc bored Masefield. He could not think of another metal quite so boring as zinc. Even lead was more interesting than zinc, and neither of them could hold a candle to bismuth, pretty in pink with a hint of ruby red and verdigris. But . . . the Soviet Union had zinc galore. Close to a million tons produced every year. The UK? Bugger all.

As he was leaving a less than memorable encounter with Yevgeny Vasilievich and the excruciatingly mangled translations of Andrei Semyonovich, Masefield met Matsekpolyev, almost exactly where he had first encountered him.

Matsekpolyev waved Andrei Semyonovich away before he could attempt a fatuous reintroduction, and shook Masefield's right hand with both of his, vigorously.

"Comrade Masefield. A delight to see you again."

And Masefield felt something small, flat, and square pressed into the palm of his hand.

"I cannot stop to chat, comrade. Duty calls. But who knows, perhaps there will be other occasions while you're in Moscow?"

He followed Andrei Semyonovich into Koritsev's office. Masefield had not spoken. Matsekpolyev's manner had been one of hearty bonhomie so unlike his usual dry, near-scathing wit. Masefield had no idea why, but he felt sure that all he had to do was unfold the note.

He waited until he was out on the bridge, the summer sunlight dancing like crystal upon the water.

Meet me in front of Moscow University, Lenin Hills. Today at 4 p.m. The large terrace, facing the city. Bring yr briefcase—empty. Now, burn this.

Masefield strolled to the far end of the bridge, chewing on the note until it was soft enough to swallow. Spies didn't burn notes; they ate them. Everyone knew that.

§85

The Lenin Hills turned out to be less hills than bumps. Masefield found he could get there easily by public transport, and he had long felt that one learnt far more about a city from using its trams and buses than its cabs. Less than a mile from Moscow State University was the Universitet Metro station on the Sokol'nicheskaya Line. It was spanking new, only a couple of years old, shining white in its marble walls and a sharp contrast to the miles of dirty, yellowing proletarian flats that lined the track as it ran southwest from the city.

He tagged along behind a gaggle of students. Students were not what they were in his day. In his day students had been simply younger adults. You could not tell them from the grown-ups by their clothes, by their fashion sense, since there was no such thing as fashion sense. At best an affectation might single out a student as being a student—a pipe clamped between lips too young for a pipe, or an outrageous choice of tie. Or, worse, a faceful of fluff struggling to be a beard.

These young Russians might be poorly dressed by Western standards and the ubiquitous blue denim had not yet rinsed the red Soviet Union purple, but did they really look any different? He might be following a bunch of students in London, or Paris or New York.

The university looked like the Foreign Ministry, but then so many buildings did. The giant, lurid, demonstrative, showy braggadocio of the great Moscow wedding cake.

Matsekpolyev was waiting on the terrace, standing in the shadow of a huge statue of a huge woman in full skirts not reading a huge book but gazing off as though daydreaming. Matsekpolyev wasn't daydreaming. He was looking at his pocket watch with some impatience, but when he saw Masefield approaching he twirled it, with all the panache of Will Hay playing a stationmaster, and landed it neatly in the fob pocket of his waistcoat.

"Comrade Masefield," he said still using his fake, hearty voice.

And as they shook hands he whispered.

"You're here as my guest. The famous English scholar. I'm showing you this architectural obscenity as an act of East–West goodwill or some such guff. Just follow me, smile a lot, look as though you're enjoying it and say nothing of any consequence."

"Of course, Grigory Grigoryevich. Follow you where?"

Matsekpolyev pointed up, and up and up . . . past Lomonosov's statue, past the clocks and the barometers, past the stone women representing industry and agriculture and whatever, to the laurel-wreathed Soviet star perched eight hundred feet above.

"Believe it or not, there's a viewing room in the star. Only holds two or three people, and you have to book it, so I did. Guarantees we won't be disturbed."

"Supposing it's bugged? My hotel room is bugged."

"It isn't. Now, shut up, smile, and follow me. Look as though you're enjoying Russia."

Well, at least that was one thing he wouldn't have to fake.

§86

The view was amazing. He knew from guidebooks that this was the tallest building in Europe. Moscow sprawled before it. Unfortunately he didn't get much chance to look at the building. The urgency in Matsekpolyev's voice was inescapable.

"Swap briefcases."

"Eh?"

For the first time he noticed that Matsekpolyev had acquired a briefcase identical to his own.

"OK. Mine's empty, as you asked. What's in yours?"

"Everything you ever wanted to know about Chelyabinsk. Production figures, ground plan, staff lists . . . the lot."

"Good Lord. However did you—?"

"No. No questions. We just walk out of here. Two professors with matching briefcases. Nothing has happened, nothing has changed."

"Grigory Grigoryevich, you can't just—"

"Yes I can and we just did. Stop asking damn fool questions, Geoffrey. You have twenty-four hours. This time tomorrow, we meet, chatter inanely and walk off with the right briefcases. You have . . ."

Will Hay's pocket watch came out again, the silver cover flipped with the merest of clicks and the whole faintly ludicrous apparatus swung back into his pocket in an effortless motion.

". . . Twenty-three hours and forty-one minutes to copy them. I must have them back by then. I'm on the night train to Leningrad."

Was this panic he felt? A bit of a twitch, the sensation that he could not get enough air, a grumble deep in his bowel that he hoped wasn't an imminent fart?

"I don't know how to. I mean . . . I . . ."

"Geoffrey. Think!"

There was only one way, he thought. Somehow, he had to get the Minox back from Anfisa Dmitrievna tonight.

§87

No one was home at the apartment on Malaya Bronnaya. Tanya kept unsocial hours; it was part of the job. Anfisa kept office hours. He had thought her likely to be home at 6:30.

Then it occurred to him: 6:30 p.m., a warm August evening . . . an apartment that overheated from May onwards, where by July you threw even the sheet off and slept naked, sweated naked . . . and, if lucky, fucked naked. Of course she wouldn't be at home. She'd get in from work, grab a book and be sitting out in the nearest bit of green space—Patriarch's Ponds.

Comparisons might be meaningless—it is what it is what it was. But the Patriki, Patriarch's Ponds, always reminded Masefield of St. James's Park in London. It was a beautiful spot . . . walkways lined with cast-iron railings and mature trees that had withstood revolution, war, and countless five-year plans . . . a neat wooden boathouse that would grace any London park, and a neater café-kiosk. Anfisa Dmitrievna was sitting a couple of benches past the kiosk, her nose, predictably, in a book, facing the still, metallic-green pond but not looking at it. Seeing her in her summer dress, a creamy yellow with some sort of cornflower blue worked into the pattern, he noticed for the first time how thin her arms were. He'd seen her naked countless times, but by the light of a single candle, by the shaft of a moonbeam between half-drawn curtains. She looked undernourished; something he'd never think of her sister.

She looked up only at the last minute, and more from the shadow he cast than the sound of his feet.

She closed the book, using both thumbs to keep her place, a look of mild surprise on her face, and peered around him at the path he had taken.

"Oh," he said as he sat down. "Nothing to worry about. They don't follow me any more. Haven't done in ages."

"Don't get *cocky*." A word he had taught her. "Tanya tells me there is always a man outside your hotel."

"Of course there is. Usually two or three. And if I bought a ticket to Kazakhstan they might perk up. But I had an appointment at the ministry today. Routine stuff. Visits I've made half a dozen times. They're too preoccupied or too lazy to bother with what has become familiar to them. What are you reading?"

Habit had its forces.

She showed him the cover, splayed it with her thumbs.

L'Âge de raison, by Sartre. He'd bought it for her at Hachette's in London. He'd read it himself just after the war and not cared for it.

"Hard," she said. "Grim and grey. So refreshing after years of Soviet optimism."

To be a шестидесятник (shestidesiatnik)—a child of the sixties—was to understand irony in a rather English way. Not least among the ironies was that the term had been thought up not to describe the "liberals" of the Khrushchev era, but of the 1860s—the reign of Alexander II that had seen the "flowering" of talents such as Tolstoy and Rimsky-Korsakov.

She was smiling still. Pleased at her own wit. It was a shame to wipe the smile away.

"Anfisa Dmitrievna, I need the camera back."

The book slammed shut.

"Oh God, Geoffrey Stefanovich. Do you know what I had to do to get it into my office? Do you?"

"Well," he fluffed. "I just assumed you'd found a way . . ."

"Geoffrey Stefanovich. They search me. Going in and coming out. The camera is three inches by one. How do you think I got it past the guards?"

"Oh."

"Oh, indeed."

She stared ahead, across the pond, at nothing. Her face reddening as she held anger below the surface.

"I wouldn't ask, but . . ."

"But you have."

"Because it's important."

"How important?"

"I'm sorry?"

"So far, you have given to me and my sister twelve hundred pounds sterling. You know what we need. Two thousand pounds. Make up the difference and I will bring the camera out."

"Eight hundred pounds? I don't have that much with me. I have about half that to cover the next two rolls of film. I can't get more until I go back to Berlin."

"I trust you. We trust you. You have always been as good as your word. Four now, four . . . later. And I bring you the camera. And it will be the last time."

"Will it?"

She looked at him as looking at a particularly stupid child.

"Of course. When we have the two thousand we leave Russia."

So, that was it. His source would cease. It was endgame, but endgame with a royal flush . . . if Matsekpolyev really had given him the "goods."

"And then, we meet in Berlin."

She was smiling again.

He was not sure he believed her. He had made fantasies of life after Moscow; he had not made plans. He had dreamt of life with Tanya—much as he had enjoyed her, he had not dreamt of life with Anfisa. Yet, the two were inseparable. In his heart he wanted a life with Tanya. In his gut he knew he'd never see either of them again once they got to Berlin.

"Berlin," she repeated.

And she was smiling far too much.

"I need it tonight."

Anfisa stood, all but stamping her feet.

"You want the fucking world, don't you?"

"I have less than twenty-four hours."

Still with her back to him, still staring out across the water.

"Twenty-four hours for what?"

"To do what I have to do."

She turned now.

"Not going to tell me, eh?"

"Knowledge isn't power, Anfisa Dmitrievna, it's danger."

§88

Back at the apartment on Malaya Bronnaya, Tanya had returned home and took Masefield's news more calmly than her sister had, but then none of the responsibility rested upon her, yet.

"I can't do this tonight. It is nearly eight o'clock. Asking to go back in would arouse nothing but suspicion. I can't even think of a phony reason why I should want to be in my office after six let alone a real one."

"I could meet you," Tanya cut in.

"Meet me? Where? When?"

"At lunch tomorrow. I can get away by twelve. We find a café. I pick up the camera from you. And as no one will look twice at me in the Muromets, I give the camera to Geoffrey."

Anfisa stared back at her.

"What are you suggesting. A trip to the ladies' lavatory while I remove my brass tampon?"

Tanya looked from her sister to Masefield and back again, not quite believing the rage to which this had roused her twin.

"Pretty much."

Anfisa was hugging herself, entwined in her own arms, so self-wrapped her fingers almost seemed to meet across the back of her ribcage. As though she hugged herself because no one else would.

Tanya Dmitrievna did.

Masefield heard sibling whispers. Darkly incomprehensible.

Then he thought he heard, "Это не ваша пизда."

It's not your cunt. And . . .

"Do this and we are free."

Silence, then the sound of the two of them breathing in sync.

"Сделаем это и мы будем свободны." Do this and we are free.

And more silence.

Tanya's right arm unwound from her sister and the hand reached out blindly to Masefield, her head buried in Anfisa's neck. He took the hand and let himself be drawn to them, his left arm embracing both of them. He squeezed once and felt both bodies respond, a contraction, a spinal shiver.

"We are free. We are free. All of us. We are free."

§89

It was a dilemma. Leave the briefcase in his room or take it down to breakfast and look like a swot. He'd given the plans a once-over. It was Chelyabinsk, he'd no doubt about that, but he'd neither the skill nor knowledge to interpret the seventy-seven pages Matsekpolyev had given him. He opted for looking like a swot, stuffed in a couple of American science journals, which he could read, or pretend to read, over breakfast—the case itself perched on the spare chair—and both might deter any other Englishman from joining him.

They didn't.

He was halfway through an article on the geology of Arizona, rhyolite columns and such, when a figure loomed over him.

Glendinning.

"Mugging up over breakfast. Bit bloody much, old man."

He picked up the briefcase and dropped it casually to the floor. Sat uninvited in the chair. A page of Matsekpolyev's file slipped halfway out. Glendinning did not notice. He was looking around for a waiter and muttering about another pot of their awful bloody coffee.Masefield bent down, slipped the page back in and clicked the catch.

"I wasn't expecting to see you again," he said.

"Well. Here I am. Can't be helped. Last place I wanted to be. On a par with Scunthorpe or New Brighton. Absolutely no need to visit any of them twice. But . . . I take orders. We all do, or the bloody world would fall apart. Your first time back too?"

Masefield put one foot on the briefcase, drew it slowly under the table and hoped Glendinning might die of a stroke in the next ten minutes.

"No, no. It's become a monthly sort of thing. In fact I've been back several times since we last met."

"Oh. Tough titty. Things going well in the world of cotton, are they?"

"Er. That wasn't me. That was Proffitt."

"Eh? Oh. So it was."

Both elbows came on the table—something his mum had told him never to do—and Glendinning's face was in his, the voice an unsubtle, gravelly *sotto voce*.

"I don't suppose you've seen anything of the totty with the wonky teeth and the big tits, have you?"

§90

Glendinning was tenacious as a limpet.

A simple, "Oh, I've seen her around" had not sufficed, and Masefield had retreated to his room. He gave Matsekpolyev's seventy-seven pages the twice-over, checked that he had enough film. He hadn't. He'd two cartridges. He was short by five frames. And then he remembered that there would be an unused cartridge in the camera.

It was the longest three hours of his life. He knew they required restraint. It would be half past one before Tanya would arrive at the hotel. But at half past twelve found he could sit still, lie still, stare at the ceiling no longer.

He went down to the bar. Ordered a glass of tea and sat staring at it until it went cold.

Just after one he heard the toff bray of Glendinning in the lobby, talking, as ever, as though he meant to be heard over the sound of a passing steam train.

"Keyski, chappie, keyski. *Ponimayesh?* Understand? Room 405."

He was going up to his room. A small mercy.

As his second glass of tea was cooling, Tanya Dmitrievna finally appeared. She went up to the bar, asked a question, turned, and faked surprise at seeing him sitting there.

"Mr. Masefield. So glad to see you again."

Masefield rose for a formal handshake.

"You asked me about the autumn season at the Bolshoi. I have their programme for you. I believe they will be performing *Yevgeny Onegin* in September."

She set down her bag and pulled out an A4 brown envelope stencilled with a conspicuous image of the Bolshoi theatre and the word "Большой."

As she handed it to him, she gripped a bulge in the bottom right hand corner, where the camera lay, and as she let go it slid down the envelope to be trapped between his thumb and fingers.

"Enjoy, Mr. Masefield. Enjoy."

She bent down to close up her bag, and behind her Glendinning was approaching, one hand raised in greeting, a stupid grin on his face. He was waving at Masefield and clearly had no idea who the crouching woman was.

"Ye gods, Masefield. The way these buggers can drink at lunchtime."

He belched into his fist. Tanya rose, her back to Glendinning, a look of desperation on her face.

Their eyes met.

She turned, tried to smile at Glendinning.

"Sorry, old man," Masefield said. "We have to be going."

"Well, well, well. Heeeelllooooo."

Masefield took a risk, took Tanya by one arm and tried to lead her past Glendinning. But Glendinning had her by the other arm, saying, "Half a mo'. Been an age since we three got together. Let's have one more for the road, eh?"

He attempted to steer Tanya back to the bar.

Masefield held on. She was momentarily the baby at the judgement of Solomon. But Tanya detached herself.

Softly, "I can handle him. Let go."

Loudly, "Of course. Mr. Glendinning. All part of the service."

"Jolly good, old girl. And what can I get you, Masefield? Something to wipe that miserable expression off yer northern fizzog?"

Masefield looked at his watch. It was almost two. He had next to no time to take the photographs and get out to the university.

"Not for me, old man. Business before pleasure."

Glendinning let go of Tanya and lurched for the bar. Masefield heard him mutter about a fucking killjoy and order a bottle of vodka and two glasses, "Chopsky chopsky, Ivan!"

"Please, Geoffrey. Go. I can handle this. If you stay, there will be the scene neither of us wants. I will be home by seven. Now go."

§91

It took a matter of minutes to photograph the file. Far less than he had thought. Far longer to work out what he did next.

He could not, dare not, take both camera and file out with him. He wrapped the Minox in brown paper and stepped out into the corridor. The fire bucket was not there.

He walked down to the next turn in the corridor, to find another vacant hook sticking out of the wall. He nipped up to the next floor. They'd all gone. Every single fire bucket taken away for a new coat of paint or fresh sand or something.

He did what he swore he'd never do. Stuffed camera and exposed cartridges under the mattress. It was a risk, hardly much of one. He'd be back by 5:30. Six at the latest. If the bucket was back on its hook, all well and good. If not he'd find a better hiding place.

§92

Matsekpolyev was on the terrace, a few feet from the statue of Woman-Not-Reading. He had his backside resting on the stone balustrade and was looking up at the university tower.

Masefield's briefcase was resting on the balustrade.

He put the other case down next to it.

"Shall we walk a while?" Matsekpolyev said.

Pretty much what he'd said the first time they'd met. He led off and they walked thirty or forty feet, Matsekpolyev still staring up at the building.

"Geoffrey. What do you think architecture says about a country?"

"Dunno. I never thought much about architecture."

"Do you think it says as much as a book? Can you read Russia in this monstrosity as clearly as in a page of Dostoevsky or a Pushkin poem? Can you tell anything about the British from Big Ben or the Tower of London? One can read Imperial Germany in the Brandenburg Gate . . . but monuments are plain statements. Not every building is an obvious monument."

They were back with cabbages and kings, conundrums for which Masefield had neither opinion nor answer.

"I've tried counting the windows, but I've given up. I get about as far as my cat would . . . one, two, three, many."

He turned on his heel and set off back towards the statue.

"When I was a boy this place was known as Sparrow Hills. It was Stalin who changed the name to honour a man he despised. And there is poetry in neither title. Whatever meaning there is, it's all in the building."

They stopped where they had begun.

Masefield still had no idea what Matsekpolyev was on about. Another of his non-sequential tangents.

"A present for you, Geoffrey."

Matsekpolyev handed him the small package he'd had tucked under his arm since they met.

"I don't know what to say, Grigory Grigoryevich."

"Say nothing. Just open it now and let anyone with eyes see that it's just a book."

It wasn't just a book, it was *the* book.

История Московских Улиц

A History of the Moscow Streets, by P. V. Sytin, first published in 1948. He'd been looking for a copy for ages, had looked, he thought, in just about every second-hand bookshop in the city.

Inside Matsekpolyev had written

"Моему близкому другу, уважаемому английскому ученому, Geoffrey Masefield. Наука не знает границ."

To my good friend, the distinguished English scholar, Geoffrey Mase-field. Science knows no frontier. And under that a florid signature in letters two inches high: "Grigory Grigoryevich Matsekpolyev August 25th, 1961."

"I don't know what to say."

"I know. You told me. It's just our cover. We met so I could give you a parting gift. Now, shake hands, pick up the other briefcase and . . . and . . ."

"Nunc dimittis?"

"Indeed I do."

Matsekpolyev looked up at the tower once more, tilted his head back to see the star.

"I'll guess. Unscientific, but I'll guess. Ten thousand windows, ten thousand watching eyes. The perfect symbol for Russia. Ten thousand watching eyes. And fukkemall, Geoffrey. Fukkemall."

"Grigory Grigoryevich, I have to ask—"

"No you don't. I already told you why."

"Yes . . . but why now?"

"Because the balance of power has shifted yet again."

"It's always shifting . . . the U-2 thing—"

"That was nothing, Geoffrey. A damp squib. Not even a sparkler. Nothing you could measure on the Richter scale."

"The Bay of Pigs."

"One step forward, two steps back. No, it's one step and one word, Geoffrey—and the word is 'Berlin.' What's happened in the last ten days has been seismic. It has set the shape of things to come. Now, do your best with what I have given you."

§93

Riding the Metro back into the city centre Masefield opened the book a dozen times just to read the inscription.

"Just our cover," Matsekpolyev had said, but the inscription belied that. "The distinguished English scholar."

He'd have loved it to be true. He wanted to believe it. He was fairly certain Matsekpolyev believed it. But that didn't make it true.

He made good time, and was back at the Muromets by half past five. A quick glance around the lobby and the bar, on the off chance that Tanya might be there, and then up to his room.

The first thing that hit him was the smell. Fresh beeswax. A new gleam on the parquet. The cleaner had been in.

The second thing that hit him was the flat of someone's hand. Squarely between the shoulder blades with enough force to put him facedown on the mattress.

§94

West Berlin: Late August—the 25th or perhaps the 26th

Every couple of days there was news of someone managing to escape to the West and every couple of days, or so it seemed, news of someone who'd tried and failed and got shot in no-man's-land or had broken every bone in their body leaping from one window or another. Wilderness did not even bother to report such incidents to Burne-Jones. They'd be on the radio and the television back in London as surely as they were in Berlin. Nor did he mention the panic buying . . . the brushfire rumours that told Berliners they would soon run out of sugar, flour, butter, and sent them hurrying to the shops.

He walked the course of the rising wall. Watched it change and grow from day to day, the slow accretion of solidity. Not that he knew it, but Nell Burkhardt walked the wall most days, and on several occasions they passed, unseeing and unseen, within fifty feet of each other.

Nell had walked down from the direction of the Reichstag. Had stood in front of the Brandenburg Gate. She remembered when the Russians had taken Viktoria, her chariot and her horses down, saying they had to be restored. Years passed with no sign they would ever be back and the plinth stood bare. She had come to think of it as the Russians' final act of looting. Then . . . when was it? Two years ago? three? . . . in '57 or '58 cranes appeared and the Quadriga was hoisted back into place—eyes east—to stare down Unter den Linden, a street of broken walls and rubble that somehow did not need to be "restored."

Wilderness had walked up from Potsdamer Platz only minutes later. Looked up at the Gate and noticed for the first time that the statue was back in place. He had the vaguest memory of it when he had first arrived in Berlin in 1947—then it was gone. Sold for scrap, Eddie Clark had said. Yet, here it was, back again. A gigantic symbol of victory in a city where there was nothing but defeat. Odd. He could have sworn it faced the other way, looking out into the Tiergarten—eyes west. No matter. It was theirs. The Russians. They could do what the hell they liked with it.

One afternoon, one bright summery August afternoon, he walked over to the junction of Zimmerstraße and Friedrichstraße along the line that divided the Soviet Sector from the American, where the Russians were establishing a checkpoint, a crossing for foreigners and representatives of the Allied Forces and Governments—no Germans, no Berliners. It was run-down still. Very little seemed to get renewed where sectors met, as though neither side would quite take responsibility for the frayed edges, and consequently it was possible to timewalk from 1961 to 1945 in the length of a block or two. Wilderness stood outside the old Café Köln and stared at the gap-toothed ruins on the other side of Friedrichstraße. The same ruins he'd stared at in 1947 over his cup of black-market coffee. Up ahead the checkpoint was barely taking shape. The "wall" was mostly barbed wire, but the Russians had sunk concrete posts into the ground ready for something more substantial. In the middle of the street the Americans were engaged in erecting a wooden hut, which looked about as substantial as his grandfather's bike shed, and at ground level an East Berlin border guard was on his knees with a large can of paint, defining the border in a single white stripe, and looking about as happy as if he'd drawn spud-peeling duty for the third day in a row.

Wilderness approached the wire. The Americans ignored him; the guard glanced up but carried on painting. A greying cardboard label dangled from the wire about ten feet from the guard's hunched backside. Wilderness tilted the label to read what it said.

J[as.] Wilde & Sons
Wiremakers,
Ambergate,
Derby[s.]
Made in England

And as if that were not enough, they'd added a tiny Union Jack . . .

. . . just to complete the embarrassment. Burne-Jones was going to love this.

Wilderness gave the label a quick tug and with a snap it came away in his hand. The guard turned.

"Was machen Sie?" What are you up to?

"Zum Andenken." Souvenir, Wilderness said, smiling.

"Fotze." Twat, the guard replied, not smiling.

Most days he'd find his way to Bernauer Straße—something always seemed to be happening at Bernauer Straße. The enterprising Germans even ran tourist buses out there.

§95

West Berlin: September 25

There were people and cars and cops everywhere. It struck Wilderness as being like the circuses he had been taken to once or twice in child-hood, on the eve of the last war. Between the elephants and the liberty horses the Italian clowns would appear, baggy pants and bowler hats, big shoes and boozer's noses, and the white-faced clown who seemed tearful, serious, and disapproving of all the manic speed, comic violence, and utter incompetence. There'd been a skit he'd seen in 1939. A woman, a caricature woman with balloon breasts and frilly knickers scarcely smaller than the marquee they were in, stood atop a burning tower while clowns below rushed around with the safety net. Whenever they got it in place the tower would sway and they'd dash to the other side of the ring, only to dash back again thirty seconds later. At last, when "she" jumped, the safety net turned out to be a trampoline and the damsel in such distress found herself more bounced than rescued.

He saw himself as the white-faced clown, the *pagliaccio*, in this scenario. The too sad, too serious bystander. He glanced over his shoulder, distracted by some noise or other and saw another clown, a baggy-pants *auguste* dressing for an entrance. The rear door of a dusty Merc 220 had opened and a warty, little fat bloke in a brown mac—overdressed for late September—had stepped out of the car. Wilderness saw disembodied hands pass out a cloth cap, a muffler, and wire-rimmed spectacles. The illusion thus effected, the little fat bloke ambled towards the back of the crowd, just a few feet from Wilderness, looking for all the world as though he was on his way to support one of the lesser northern soccer teams . . . Tranmere Rovers . . . Accrington Stanley.

Wilderness stood at the back of a crowd gathered in front of an apartment block—one that had not yet been bricked in, although without a doubt the ground- and lower-ground-floor doors and windows were boarded up and nailed shut. A rope was dangling from a first-floor window. An old lady, white-haired and black-clad, climbed out onto the window ledge some fifteen or twenty feet above the ground and clutched not the rope but a cat.

The West Berlin Police scurried to the spot below the window . . . Over the heads in front of him Wilderness could see the archaic, opéra-bouffe hats of the police and the tin helmets of the fire brigade.

"*Springen Sie, Oma, springen!*" went up from the crowd.

Jump, Granny, jump!

Wilderness couldn't see it, but it was obvious that a net or blanket was being held out for her.

She didn't jump. She threw the cat into the blanket and froze. In the precious seconds wasted the VoPos came up behind her. Wilderness would have bet a fiver they hadn't known what was happening until the chant of "Jump!" had begun.

A VoPo grabbed her by one arm, a cloth-capped workman off the building site by the other. She slipped off the ledge, her own weight jerking her free of the VoPo, and dangled by her left arm fit to tear it from its socket.

"*Springen Sie, Oma!*"

Both men tried to pull her back inside.

"*Springen Sie, Oma!*"

Out of nowhere a young man in a singlet leapt at her as though in a rugby tackle and missed. A brief tug-of-war followed. Two men above, two below, arms versus legs. The German version of the judgement of Solomon. Pull grandma in two.

Gravity won and the old lady toppled into the hands of her rescuers. A cheer, followed by blown raspberries, and a host of two-fingered "fuck you"s held up to the defeated representatives of the East.

He'd seen enough. He'd had enough. There'd been no death or injury, not so much as a bruise, but if not fatality then there seemed to be finality in the leap of an old woman. This . . . whatever it was . . . seemed to have hit rock bottom. Here he was, a British Intelligence officer, at the geopolitical crossroads of the world in the twentieth century looking up an old woman's skirt on behalf of Her Britannic Majesty's Government. It was a circus, the Cold War Circus . . . roll up roll up.

He turned to leave. The West Berlin cops were pushing the crowd back. Everyone between him and the little fat bloke had left.

The little fat bloke stared at him and said,

"Вена, не так ли?"

Vienna, am I right? Bugger. Who would have thought the little man took in quite so much? To remember his face out of dozens, perhaps hundreds.

"Да."

"Если бы я был нервным характером, я мог бы думал, что ЦРС следит за мной по всей Европе."

If I were a nervous man I might think the CIA were following me around Europe.

"А я MI6, товарищ Хрущев."

I'm MI6, Comrade Khrushchev.

"Ага. Что привело вас сюда, это не ради меня, что ли?"

Ah. What brings you here, surely not me?

"Did anyone know you were coming?"

"Of course not, and unless you tell him Ulbricht will never know."

"You just had to see?"

"Yes. I had to see for myself."

"From this side?"

"Yes. To see what you see."

It was irresistible. The only man Wilderness could think of who would resist this temptation was Burne-Jones, and Burne-Jones was a thousand miles away.

"Comrade Khrushchev, if the British or the Americans were to just come over here and rip up the barbed wire and concrete blocks, what would you do?"

"I have thirty-four divisions surrounding Berlin."

"Doesn't answer my question."

"Your question is hypothetical. A month ago it probably wasn't, but you did nothing and your moment passed. It's here to stay."

"If you're unlucky, comrade . . ."

He cocked his head momentarily back towards the nailed-up Bernauer Straße apartment block.

". . . This will be your monument."

"How so?"

"You want to bring peace, you talk about a united, free Germany. If this . . . barbed wire and concrete . . . this . . . I almost said 'wall' but it's hardly a wall yet . . . if this stays, it will be what the world remembers Nikita Sergeyevich Khrushchev for . . . and I'll remember the day I stood with the leader of half the world just to look at an old woman's knickers."

"You English can be so damned cheeky. Хуй тебе! Fuck you!"

Hackles raised, Khrushchev returned to his car. Wilderness was about to walk off himself, slightly disappointed not to have kick-started World War III, when the window wound down and a finger beckoned.

"What's your name, English?"

"John Holderness."

"Before you make this my monument you should come and see the Soviet Union. Come whenever you like. My people will have your name. There is so much more that the world will remember me by far better than Berlin, barbed wire, concrete blocks and an old lady's knickers. You'll see. You are wrong, comrade, but вы увидите . . . you'll see."

Later, on the nightly news, Wilderness finally learnt the name of the old woman he had watched leap to freedom—Frieda Schulze.

§96

Wilderness called on Radley after breakfast the following day. He had no intention of mentioning his brief encounter with Khrushchev. He had no intention of ever telling anyone.

And if he had, Radley would not have heard him.

Radley looked awful. He hadn't shaved and had the raggy look of a man who'd been up all night. The blinds were still drawn. The ashtray was full, and a bottle of Bell's stood, cap off, on his desk with less than an inch in the bottom.

"Tom?"

Radley stood up, ran his fingers through his hair, dusted the fag ash off his lap.

"Sorry, Joe. Wasn't expecting you today. Well, not this early at any rate."

"It's after nine, Tom."

"Fuck me. Is it?"

"Tom. Just tell me."

Wilderness swept a pile of documents off the chair, sat down and waited for Radley to do the same.

Instead he scrabbled around among the mess of papers on his desk to retrieve just one teleprinter page.

"TASS release. Midnight Moscow time."

He handed it to Wilderness, sat down and helped himself to the last of the scotch.

On August 25th, officers of the USSR arrested the British secret agent known as Geoffrey Stephen Masefield. Masefield has made a full confession of his crimes against the USSR and will be tried accordingly. Trial commences Thursday September 28th.

"August twenty-fifth? They've had him for a month and you didn't know?"

"It was due to be a longish trip this time. He was supposed to tour half a dozen zinc or iron smelters or something. I didn't expect to hear from him at all while he was there. Off radar. Par for the course after all. Truth is he's only a week overdue. They busted him the third day he was there."

"A week overdue. Tom. For fuck's sake. Why didn't you tell me?"

Radley was weeping now. Salt tears and scotch.

"Did you tell Burne-Jones?"

Radley just shook his head.

"Why not?"

"It's . . . it's messy."

"How messy?"

"His sources . . . I wasn't wholly straight with BJ about Masefield's sources."

Wilderness stood up, kicked the chair backwards and hauled Radley to his feet by the front of his shirt.

"You stupid sod. Are you saying this professor of his set him up?"

"Joe . . . Joe . . . please put me down. I might puke any second."

Wilderness threw him back in his chair.

"You fucking idiot."

Radley was rummaging around in a desk drawer only to surface with another bottle of scotch.

Wilderness threw it against the wall, only to hear it bounce off without breaking.

"Tom. Tell me everything."

He picked up the scotch bottle, righted his chair and stared back at the weeping Radley.

"No. It's not that. Matsekpolyev was . . . is real . . . completely kosher I would imagine . . . but he wasn't the source for the rolls of film Masefield was giving us . . . you said yourself that it seemed odd a professor of physics in Leningrad would have that kind of access . . . truth is Masefield had . . . had got off with his Intourist guide . . ."

"Got off?"

"A relationship . . . developed."

"Jesus Christ, Tom, did you not tell him they're all KGB?"

"Of course I did, but . . ."

"You mean they were lovers? He's been fucking her?"

"Yes. But there's more than that."

Wilderness waited. Radley was sucking in air like a man surfacing from near drowning—head back, eyes up, tears coursing down his face.

"There's more. He was fucking this woman. He was. But . . . but . . . he was fucking her sister too."

More desperation-breathing. Head down now. Trying to look anywhere but at Wilderness.

"The sister . . . she works at the Ministry of Defence. It was her. She gave him everything we've seen. The U-2 photos. The lot. Matsekpolyev was a useful bit of cover. The truth is he gave us nothing. It was . . . what? A purely academic relationship. They swapped ideas about physics and metals and what have you. He got our man into that plant in Estonia, but that was all. But if I'd told you the real source of the photographs you'd have thrown them back at me."

"*Provokatsiya.*"

"Eh?"

"It's the nearest I can get to 'honeytrap' in Russian. Our Geoffrey walked into a honeytrap and you, you stupid bastard, let him. One woman I might just have found credible. He's an unprepossessing creature, but God knows, some woman might want to fuck him. But two? Two sisters? For Christ's sake! Tom, where's your brain been holidaying the last six months?"

Wilderness unscrewed the cap on the bottle of scotch, took a swig and offered none to Radley.

"Joe . . . I'm so . . . so sorry."

"Tom, bugger off home and sober up."

Wilderness opened the blinds on a bright, Berlin morning. Waited twenty minutes or more until Radley's assistant got in at ten.

"Gretchen?"

She stuck her head around the door, blinked a little at the mess but showed no surprise at seeing him instead of Radley.

"It's nine o'clock in London. In an hour I'll need a secure line to Burne-Jones. Make that an hour and a half. He likes a lazy breakfast. I'll be here all day. And I want to see anything TASS has to say as soon as you get it. OK?"

§97

"I heard," Burne-Jones said. "Of course I bloody heard. Why in God's name did I not hear it from Radley? Why didn't the bugger get me out of bed for this one? He's never held back from doing that in the past."

Wilderness said nothing.

"The BBC won't be reporting it until the evening news. Gives us a few hours. We deny it all, of course. Innocent British businessman. Do you have the exact wording in front of you?"

Wilderness did not embellish. Burne-Jones heard him out in silence as he read TASS's midnight release to him.

A long silence, then he said, "I do feel I have fucked up."

"Alec, we both fucked up. You overestimated Masefield and I for my part underestimated him. But that's not the point. The point is Radley. Not telling you in person is just the tip of the iceberg."

"I'm not following you here, Joe."

"Radley told us that Masefield had a tame professor in Leningrad, of whom neither you nor I had heard."

"No names over the phone, but the feller checked out. He's real."

"I know. A published scholar. A distinguished scholar. That's as may be, but he was not the source of the documents Masefield gave us."

"What?"

"Masefield had a Russian lover."

"Oh Christ, I can hear this one coming."

"More than that, he had two Russian lovers."

"Oh shit."

"They were feeding him the documents."

The line went quiet for a while. All Wilderness could hear were the sighs of a deeply unhappy man.

"A honeytrap?"

"What other conclusion could we draw?"

"And Radley knew?"

"Yes."

"Jesus Christ. The fucking idiot."

"Masefield was set up from the start. The Russians have fed us stuff just one degree above useless to keep us interested. They must have got bored with the game and decided there was more international fun to be had with a show trial. There's been a second TASS release, less than half an hour ago. They'll be making a statement this evening—television and radio. At 6:00 p.m. their time. That's a couple of hours ahead of the BBC news, so short of a D-Notice you can be pretty certain both that and last night's statement will be on the news in London tonight, closely followed by the usual diplomatic protests."

"Jesus Christ."

"Alec, if you have any thoughts of tempering your explanation of this cock-up with your resignation, don't. Radley knew what the source was, he could see the implications as clearly as you or I would have done, yet he let Masefield go back to Moscow when the only sensible course was to pull him out for good. He lied to you . . . reel him in. Get someone else out here as soon as possible. Assign Radley to guarding Princess Anne or the royal corgis. Somewhere, anywhere, just bury him for a while. And when the shit hits the fan, let them have him."

Another long silence.

"Would you consider staying on?"

Again, the same old question.

"Only till you can get a replacement."

"I could do with you there. I need someone I can rely on."

Wilderness wished this could have waited until he got home, till scrambled eggs and toast and Twinings Blue Mountain, but Burne-Jones would ask now, and if Wilderness failed to speak his mind he would go on asking.

"Alec, I'm through. I'll be putting my papers in as soon as I get back."

The silence didn't last long. Wilderness had barely counted to twenty.

"Ah . . . I see. Masefield?"

"Partly. As I said. We both fucked up. They won't shoot him, but we just bought a tubby little Englishman a lifetime stay in the Lubyanka."

"That's not your fault."

"Alec, one of the things you pay me for is to say no."

"You offered plenty of warnings. I just —"

"But I didn't say no. As we used to say in Stepney when I was a kid, I just farted into a colander. I should have put a gun to your head."

Another silence. A world spinning.

"Joe, you say 'partly.' Why 'partly'?"

"Frieda Schulze."

"Who the hell is Frieda Schulze?"

§98

Wilderness had had moments of feeling lower, but at this low moment he could not quite bring any of them to mind. Try as he might he could not dismiss the idea that he was letting Burne-Jones down. Burne-Jones was one of those people in his life "but for whom . . . ," and it was possible he was the person "but for whom . . ." He waited three days, between Radley's recall and the arrival of the new bloke, Elsworth "call me Dickie" Delves, a man he had met but scarcely knew, a man whom there was no necessity to know more than scarcely.

The three days were a waste of time, racked up only because Delves had chosen to use two of them driving from London. He pulled up at the "office" in a two-seater 1954 Austin-Healey 100M roadster in British racing green. Bonnet down, windscreen folded, open to the elements. The sort of car that was incomplete without a leather strap across the bonnet. The sort of driver that was incomplete without corduroy trousers and a cravat.

"Couldn't leave the old bus behind, could I?"

This man looked likely to be as big an arse as Radley. If this was the kind of man to run the Cold War, the same "breed" that had only lately run the Empire, a bunch of rugby-playing, yard-of-ale swilling Hooray Henries and Bullingdon Billies, then Burne-Jones was welcome to them.

A line had been drawn.

Wilderness wished him good luck, offered not a word of advice, left him standing on the pavement and caught a cab out to Tempelhof before Delves had even hefted his suitcase from the car.

A line had been drawn. Drawn at the sight of Frieda Schulze's knickers. He had been the one to draw it. He was through with Berlin. How many times in the last fifteen or so years had he been through with Berlin? He was through with Berlin.

§99

London

"You heard?"

"Do I work for BBC or behind the biscuit counter in Woolies? Heard? We hoicked buggers out of bed to deal with this one. Hardly enough pundits to go round. Muggeridge, Huggeridge, and Buggeridge. Can I take it Mr. Masefield is one of yours?"

"Not really. I knew him, I met him a couple of times. He was your dad's man not mine. But . . ."

"But?"

"But I meant . . . you've heard about me. I put my papers in."

"Oh sweetie pie, of course I heard. Do you think you get sirloin, Brunello, candles, the red dress, and matching knickers just because you've lost a spy and created the biggest international punch-up since the Bay of Pigs? Noooooo . . . you only get this when you quit. Think of it as a version of the Last Supper, only with sex."

"Have you seen your father?"

"Just the once. I dropped in on the way home. Didn't say much. In fact didn't say anything."

"I think that's his version of being furious."

"Yep."

"And . . ."

"And he'll get over it. You've given my old man fifteen years of your life. More than you've given me. He may not think you've done the right thing for Queen and Country, the right thing for him, or the right thing for you, but you've done the right thing for us."

"Us. Such an odd word."

"Us. Such a nice word."

$100

Judy, product of a girls' boarding school that prided itself on lacrosse, tennis, and cricket, had excellent hand-eye coordination and took a childish delight in being able to lob her knickers onto the lampshade, backhanded, looking over her shoulder.

An hour later, Wilderness found himself staring up at today's red skimpies, in a gentle, but wakeful post-coital sloth. Hands locked behind his head. His wife curled into a ball next to him.

Her head popped up from beneath the sheets.

"Good shot, eh?"

"The things you learnt at that school."

"I never told you about the farting contests, did I?"

"No. And don't tell me now."

"Or the things Sarah Hammond-Smith could do with ping-pong balls?"

"I have better, more interesting things to think about than your wasted adolescence."

"Such as?"

"Are we serious now?"

"Yes. We have entered serious mode. I heard the click."

"I've been asking myself . . . for ages now . . . what am I to Alec? What have I become?"

"Well . . . you were hired for your natural criminal tendencies, sweetie."

"That's a bit bloody harsh."

"OK, in the interests of marital harmony and the defence of truth, remark withdrawn and I leave it to you to find a definition."

"Could you try to be less BBC?"

"Only kidding."

"I'd've said I used to be his hands, feet, and eyes . . . and yes, I did shin up drainpipes, crack safes, and nick stuff on his behalf."

"Told you."

"It was the 'natural' I was contesting, not the 'criminal.' Anyway. What have I been the last couple of years, what have I become? I've become his memory . . . I'm his walking filing cabinet, his *Encyclopædia Cocknicca*, his expert on things Russian."

"And you don't like that?"

"Judy . . . it's a desk job."

"So you like being out and about . . . toting a gun . . . spying on people . . . nicking things?"

"I suppose I do."

She snuggled up, made him unlock his hands and lie on his side, embraced his back and arse, spoons in the cutlery drawer, her head pressed between his shoulder blades.

"Then I suppose we have to find some other occupation in which your talents, natural or not, will be appreciated and paid for."

"Y'know. There are times I hate you."

"Fibber."

"Go to sleep."

§101

West Berlin: June 1963
Reprise

"Sign on the dotted, Joe, and all this will just go away."
Wilderness read the page in front of him.
"So . . . I'm re-enlisting?"

Burne-Jones said nothing. Just stared back at him, accepting no contradiction.

He'd drawn a line that day out on Bernauer Straße . . . and now it was being handed back to him with dots . . . lots of dots . . .

"Sign on the dotted, Joe, and all this will just go away."

And it did.

IV

Bogusnik

Old age is the most unexpected of all things
that can happen to a man.

—Leon Trotsky

§102

London: June 1965
It doesn't matter what day

Wilderness had few memories of his mother. None of them fond. He had more of his father, all of them lethal. His mother had died in the Blitz when he was thirteen, and if the ideal condition in which to meet one's maker is, as cliché has it, to die "on the job," then Lily Holderness had died happy, "on the job" . . . alas the job was propping up a bar and knocking back gin. The absence of fresh lime in wartime had caused her no end of annoyance.

His father, Herbert Henry Asquith Holderness, known as Harry, or, if he was out of earshot, as "that big bastard," had been a maniac capable of psychopathic violence, and hence had served His Majesty well throughout the Second World War.

About a year after the war ended Wilderness had watched his father walk bollock-naked into the North Sea, never to be seen again. His last words echoed in Wilderness's mind as vividly as all the beatings—"hope you make a better job of this life thing than I could"—and that was the only positive thing he had salvaged from the brief encounter with Harry Holderness that had passed for childhood.

The relationships that had mattered to the young Wilderness had been with his maternal grandfather—a small-time crook who had taught Wilderness all he knew about burglary and safe-cracking before meeting a timely end falling from a Hampstead rooftop less than a mile from where Joe and Judy now lived—and with the old man's . . . what to call her? Abner and Merle had never married, she was half his age . . . mistress seemed wide of the mark, floozy too rude . . . with the old man's "concubine," Merle, a good-looking London prozzie who had seen fit to deflower Wilderness for free on VE night.

All in all, there were no fitting paradigms in his personal history to prepare him for parenthood. All the same, parenthood fell upon him on April 1, 1964, in the shape of twin girls. Wilderness and Judy readily agreed on names, neither having the desire to perpetuate any family forenames—so Joan (the elder by seven minutes) and Molly Holderness, known, in utter secrecy, to their parents as "our foolish girls."

Lady Margaret Burne-Jones, known to her husband as Madge, except when he was cross with her—a rare occurrence, most of what little anger he had being reserved for his daughters—when he would adopt a formal and rather arch "Margaret," was the better example. Madge had brought up four daughters and Judy, being the eldest, was the first to make her a grandmother.

"I was born to play this part, Joe," Madge said far too often.

And he would think that perhaps he wasn't, and that all he could do, the best he could do, was live up to the last wish of a dying bastard and make a better job of the life thing.

They sat in the kitchen one warm summer's afternoon, at Campden Hill Square.

The life thing in full swing.

He had set the new lives in their high chairs. Madge had set Beatrix Potter bunny bowls in front of them with an assortment of sliced and chopped fruit. Joan had woofed hers down as though she hadn't eaten in a week. Molly was dissecting the banana in search of a backbone, and looked up disappointed when she found none.

"Fish," she said.

"No," Wilderness replied. "Banana."

"Banananananan."

"Close enough. Now eat what you just killed. Rule of the game, Molly. Don't kill what you can't eat."

"You know, Joe," Madge said, leaning back to indulge one of her many vices, the filter-tipped king-size cigarette. "You're a damn sight better at this than I had thought you'd be."

"Better than Alec?"

"Not sure comparisons help. He had amazing patience with our girls. Just as he has with yours, but he's a great tendency to be off in the clouds. That he's in 'the game' as you call it . . ."

"No. I take no credit for that. I pinched it. Kipling, I think."

"That he's in it at all never ceases to baffle me. I mean just look at him, just listen to him. Wouldn't you take him for a professor of classics rather than a spook?"

"Perhaps Her Majesty needs the odd professor behind that particular desk. Can't all be in the field."

"No, I suppose not. I could never see Alec playing baccarat, wondering about the mix of his martini or holding a gun. But you were in the field weren't you, Joe?"

"Yes, and inasmuch as I like martinis at all I prefer them stirred not shaken."

"Do you miss it, Joe? Do you miss 'the game'?"

"No," he lied. "I don't."

Molly burped. Burping gave way to giggling, readily amused at the noises she could make, and when one of the girls giggled the other always joined in. Laughter was addictive—every joke a shared joke. Something Wilderness had never known as a kid.

"It's been a good year," he added. "One the best."

And that was no lie.

§103

London: November 1965
Queen Anne's Gate

Suddenly the ghost of Nell was in the room—looking over his shoulder. Hands moving swiftly, invisibly above his head. Do the living have ghosts? Wilderness thought there must surely be a word for it. He had a vague recollection of something like "avatar." Any minute now he'd get up, cross the room and heft a dictionary off the shelf and look— but for the moment he was transfixed by the work of his own hands, not ghost hands. He had rearranged all his pens and pencils in order of length. It had to be him. Or it had to be Nell. He had stacked all his files according to colour coding—from Who Gives a Fuck to Top Secret. And the contents of his rotary paperclip holder were arranged clockwise 1–12, small to large. Yes—Nell Breakheart was in the room with him. The hands were his, the strings were hers, pulling him this way and that like some loose, shambling Pinocchio.

The temptation was to treat the pile of folders like a house of cards, behave like a spoilt child and send the lot flying—the floor strewn with secrets from the price of tea in the NAAFI canteen in Bielefeld to the "your guess is as good as mine" location of Russian nuclear submarines in the Denmark Strait.

The Cold War had become a bore. Wilderness a puppet. The puppetmaster not so much his long-lost lover Nell as his employer and father-in-law Lt Col Alec Burne-Jones, nominally of the Coldstream Guards much as Wilderness himself was still nominally an RAF sergeant. None of it meant a thing and he was baffled that SIS held on to any notion of rank among those recruited from the armed forces, when no such thing would matter with the legions of toffs recruited straight from the universities, the BBC, or the Foreign Office. It was not a world of pips and stripes, but smoke and mirrors. What he wouldn't give for a whiff of smoke or a reflection glimpsed in the mirror. Anything not to be stuck behind a desk doing paper penance for past sins.

Fukkit. Fukkit. Fukkit. He knocked the folders to the floor, just as Alice Pettifer, his secretary, opened the door.

"Oh God. Are you in one of those moods again?"

"Yes."

"Well you can bloody well pick them up yourself this time. I'm not ruining another pair of tights scrabbling around on the parquet just 'cos you've thrown your rattle out of the pram."

Tights. Ye gods, whatever happened to stockings and the irresistible allure of seams that seemed to lead somewhere?

"He wants you."

"Lost the use of his legs has he?"

"For God's sake, Joe. Try not to rubbish everything. He's the boss; he wants you. That's all there is to it. Now, go on, bugger off and I might just clean up your tantrum."

Burne-Jones was two doors down the corridor.

He didn't look up as Wilderness came in. Long legs up on one corner of the desk, busily annotating something or other in the verdigris shade of ink he favoured—his notes in green, his superior's in red and Wilderness's, when on rare occasion required, in blue pencil, creating a rainbow of confusion and hesitation. Wilderness had known documents circulate at several levels only to come back to him with "What's the chap with the blue pencil on about?" or "Blue cannot be serious" and "Has Blue actually read FO472/1?"

Wilderness pulled out a chair and waited.

Every meeting with Burne-Jones reminded him of the first. The day, long ago and yesterday, when he had pulled Wilderness from the RAF glasshouse and offered him a choice between military prison—and its endless square-bashing—and learning Russian and German at Cambridge. Such a choice. Wilderness had hesitated, on the grounds that eagerness was not next to godliness and gratitude a vice, just long enough to annoy Burne-Jones. Ever since they had got on rather well. In 1955 Wilderness had married Judy. He had never been wholly sure of his acceptance, his "fit," but had recognised that the problem, if such it be, was probably of his own making. Burne-Jones was a toff. It was hard not to assume that toff and snob were the same thing. It meant examining, repressing, dismissing the accrued wisdom of an East End childhood and the ever-expanding knowledge gleaned in a life of crime. But he'd never have been any use to Burne-Jones without his criminal tendencies and talents. They were as valuable an asset as his German . . . or his Russian.

"Have you ever come across General Bogusnik?"

"Bogusnik? Are you sure you've got that right?"

Burne-Jones scribbled the name down in Russian and showed it to him: БОГУСНИК.

"Nothing wrong with my pronunciation is there? I may be bit rusty and I've never had the gift for languages you have . . . but . . ."

"But? But Bogusnik? The bogus bloke? You can't be serious. He might just as well call himself General Faker."

"Hmm," Burne-Jones mused. "Never occurred to me to look at it that way. Of course it would be pronounced Boggus rather than Bogus . . . and it hardly means the same thing does it?"

"It doesn't mean anything . . . it would be something like ПОДДЕЛНИК in Russian. The joke's in English, which is what makes me think it's fake. Pointedly aimed at us. In short, a trap."

"I doubt that."

"He's real?"

"So far as we can tell."

"Meaning?"

"He started showing up in reports from our men in Moscow in '56, just after Khrushchev's secret speech to the Twentieth Party Congress. No mention of him before that and no one has yet been able to get us anything more than a blurred snapshot. Could be any little fat bloke. God knows Russia seems to be full of little fat blokes. And this little fat bloke has been in charge of Geoffrey Masefield for the last three years."

"Oh hell, not that useless twat."

"Really, Joe? Let's have a little respect for one of our own currently residing at Comrade Brezhnev's pleasure."

"It's because he's a twat that he got nicked. Talk about cloak and dagger. Masefield swirled the cloak, brandished the dagger, and if he'd had a big black hat they'd have spotted him the split second he got off the bloody plane."

"We all make mistakes, and perhaps recruiting Geoffrey was one of mine. Nevertheless, we do not abandon our own, do we?"

There had been, Wilderness knew, many an occasion when the Service had done just that. The ethic in play here was not the public one but Burne-Jones's private one. In Berlin in '48 he could have left Wilderness to his uncertain fate. He had not. He had rescued him, promoted him, with "Fuck up one more time, Joe, and I'll let them have you."

"Am I to take it General Faker wants to do a deal?"

"Yeees. Not sure what. But old Geoffrey is the card he's slapping on the table. We give him what he wants and we get Geoffrey back."

"What have we got that he wants?"

"I'm assuming until Bogusnik says otherwise that it would be like for like."

"Comrade Liubimov?"

"Well, they're not getting George Blake."

"All the same, Liubimov's a much bigger fish than Masefield."

"When I said like for like, Joe, I wasn't expecting a quid pro kopeck."

"Liubimov got fifteen years, he's served nearly half. He'll be eligible for parole soon. Masefield got life. Who knows if they'd ever let him out?"

"Which is why I'm not playing big fish little fish. If the trade-off is Liubimov, so be it."

There had been trade-offs before. The British would meet the Russians at the Staaken checkpoint on a bleak, absurdly straight stretch of the seemingly infinite Heerstraße where the DDR met the British Sector of West Berlin with a concrete wall. The Americans would meet them at Potsdam where the Glienicke Bridge spanned the Havel, between a "free" American Sector and a communist East Germany. For the last couple of years both had served as a handy meeting points for the exchange of prisoners. In 1962, the Americans had received Gary Powers, pilot of the U-2 spy plane shot down over the USSR, in exchange for Rudolf Abel, a second generation Anglo-Russian busted as a spy in Texas in 1957. Only last year the British had had Greville Wynne, a spy Wilderness thought of as almost as hapless as Geoffrey Masefield, returned to them in exchange for Gordon Lonsdale, a "super-spy" serving twenty-five years in a British prison. A walk across a line had set them free. Wilderness had seen the Glienicke Bridge only from the Berlin side. It had redefined distance in a way the checkpoint at Staaken didn't. Short, and steely, it had looked to him like the longest, ugliest walk on earth. Stark, almost bare—no floodlights, no lookout towers. It put the "cold" in Cold War. Staaken would be at least quick. Liubimov would hop from one car to another and never feel the cold.

"Do you fancy a bit of a trip, Joe?"

"You mean a swap at the Staaken checkpoint?"

"I wasn't thinking of anything just yet. I was thinking we should get to know General Bogusnik and hear what he wants rather than over-anticipate. He's offering to meet."

Good bloody grief.

"You mean you want me in Moscow?"

"As you have made abundantly clear over the last year, you want to get back in the field. Does it actually matter where?"

Wilderness said nothing.

"And . . . off the record, you're wasted behind a desk . . . it was just a necessary precaution . . . for a while."

"So what you're saying is that having grounded me for more than two years because you couldn't have me flogged in public any more, you now want me to go to Moscow?"

"Oh no. Too risky. He'll meet us halfway. East Berlin, Joe. Your old stomping ground."

"He's in the Russian Compound?"

"No. I gather he's installed himself at the Adlon."

"Well . . . the compound probably doesn't have room service. But at least we know one thing about him now. General Faker is a hedonist."

In Berlin in '63 Burne-Jones could have left Wilderness to his uncertain fate. He had not. He had rescued him, declined to promote him a second time, but had reiterated the "Fuck up one more time, Joe, and I'll let them have you."

The thought of Staaken or Glienicke was grim, the outposts of nowhere, the ends of the earth . . . but Berlin . . . Berlin as a whole, Berlin in all its unwholesome sectors . . . he still had very mixed feelings about Berlin. But he had just heard "you're wasted behind a desk" and if Berlin was what got him out from behind a desk . . . well, Burne-Jones would never get him behind one again, and if crossing walls and bridges was the price of his freedom, then he'd pay readily. His own freedom was worth so much more than Masefield's. Geoffrey Masefield was incidental to the plot. For that matter so was Comrade Liubimov—Bernard Alleyn.

"Start with Alleyn."

"Eh?"

"Nip along to the Scrubs and talk to Alleyn. We never got what you might call a full confession out of him in '59. There's more he could tell us. There are names he could name. Particularly as we've just dangled freedom in front of him. The thought that we might bring him close to exchange and then change our minds might change his."

"But we won't change our minds, will we? We want our Geoffrey back."

"Of course we won't, but he doesn't know that."

"Alec, he was interrogated by Jim Westcott. If Westcott couldn't get him . . ."

"Westcott was Five's man. This is our op. Masefield is our man. As you say, getting our Geoffrey back is what matters. I'd rather Five handled none of it. Too many cooks and all that malarkey. Just spend a couple of days at the Scrubs. Have a bit of a chat. Get to know him. After all this could take quite some time. It would be as well to know the man. Masefield's life may well depend on him."

$104

Wilderness had been in prisons before. Many times in a capacity loosely similar to this, several times on the other side of the bars. Military glasshouses during his early days in the RAF, two nights in a Finnish jail after a slight misunderstanding with a traffic cop, a couple more in a police cell in West Berlin until Burne-Jones came riding to the rescue and a week in Spanish custody until threats of a "diplomatic incident" prevailed on General Franco's government. He'd left without his gun and with his passport stamped "*Deportado—indeseable.*"

The Scrubs was better than all the others, except perhaps Finland, but no less depressing. He had often wondered whether the preference for two glossy, but muted colours on the wall—dark brown in all its limited variations, an optional black stripe, lots of bottle green—was a matter of Victorian taste or a form of punishment in itself.

A prison officer escorted Alleyn into the room. Alleyn looked fit and healthy, as though the diet agreed with him even if the prison-blue uniform did not. He looked much as he had in the photographs published at the time of his trial. If there was such a thing as prison pallor, Alleyn had a touch of it. What he had had in abundance was six years of bed, board, and all found.

The officer stood by the door with his hands behind his back.

Wilderness turned to him.

"Was there something?"

"Standing orders, at all times the pris . . ."

Wilderness held out his warrant card.

"You know damn well who I am. So bugger off."

The man glared at Wilderness but left all the same. Locking Wilderness in with Alleyn. Then he stood on the other side of the glass observation panel, looking in. Rooms like this were most often assigned to meetings between prisoners and their solicitors, who could be seen but not heard.

Wilderness had anticipated this. He chewed gum for twenty seconds while Alleyn stared in silence, then he picked up the copy of the *Guardian* that was lying on the table, took the wet "spadge" from his mouth and glued the front page of the newspaper over the glass.

"He might think I am a danger to you," Alleyn said.

"Really, Mr. Alleyn? I doubt that somehow."

"I've sat here with countless men from MI5 over the years. You're . . . different. You're not the same . . . class."

"How do you know? I've not said half a dozen words."

"I learnt long ago that an Englishman betrays himself in his first sentence."

"Well," said Wilderness. "You'd know all about betrayal, wouldn't you?"

Alleyn was actually blushing—embarrassed.

"I'm sorry. I meant 'reveals' not 'betrays.' I really shouldn't—"

"Let's begin again, shall we? No, I'm not MI5 and you know why I'm here. Joe Holderness, MI6. I'm here to get you out."

Alleyn's cheeks lost their flush, his sangfroid resuming. He coughed into his right fist. Looked up at Wilderness.

"Am I worth it? Is one Alleyn worth a Masefield, Mr. Holderness?"

"That would appear to be the current rate of exchange."

"Have you ever met Mr. Masefield?"

"A couple of times."

"I wonder if he enjoyed Moscow as much as I enjoyed England?"

Wilderness had no real idea if a "debrief" should have a set pattern. It probably shouldn't ramble like this. He still thought Burne-Jones was wrong not to get in a professional interrogator . . . but if he wanted Five kept at arm's length, so be it. He would just have to follow where Alleyn seemed to be leading, and hope to seize the rudder occasionally.

"What have you enjoyed most, Mr. Alleyn?"

"I can answer that. But first a favour. In here I am Alleyn, if only because they can't pronounce Liubimov, followed by a number. Whilst I am grateful for the explicit courtesy of an almost forgotten title, would you mind if we got onto first-name terms? I would consider it a great kindness."

He was looking straight at Wilderness, blinking his blues eyes a little. Completely serious.

"After all, we may be here some time. And after that who knows? Perhaps a journey overseas, as fortune-tellers always say when they've read your tea leaves."

It wasn't outrageous, although Burne-Jones would probably have found it so; it was quirky and perhaps if there were ice to be broken, the man had broken it.

"All right. As I said, my name is Joe."

"Delighted to make your acquaintance, Joe."

Quirky was inadequate, this was parodic. They weren't in Wormwood Scrubs, they were in an early Noël Coward or using one of the pages Oscar Wilde had abandoned on the study floor.

"And to answer your question. My family. The greatest source of delight I have ever known. Kate, my wife. Our daughters Beatrice and Cordelia. Do you have children, Joe?"

What did the answer matter? What did it matter if Alleyn returned home and Liubimov told the KGB everything he knew? If the KGB didn't know everything worth knowing about Wilderness after more than fifteen years as an SIS agent then they were idiots.

"As it happens I also have two daughters."

"How old are they?"

"Year and a half or so. They're twins."

He might as well volunteer the names. Alleyn would only ask if he didn't.

"And they're called Joan and Molly."

"And you see them every day."

Wilderness probably did see his kids every day. Most days he was a commuter on the Northern Line, exactly like half a million other office workers. He kept a Browning .25 automatic in the wife's underwear drawer—that might be the only difference—but saw no point in betraying himself to Alleyn as just another desk jockey.

"No. You know the nature of my work. The demands."

"Of course, of course."

A pause, as they finally got to the point.

"I have not seen my girls for six years."

"I know."

"In fact, I don't even know where they live now."

It was a hostage to give to fortune. One Wilderness would not give. He knew where Kate Alleyn had taken her daughters, he knew what alias she was using, and he would not be the one to tell him.

§105

Wilderness's kids were at what he had dubbed the slug stage of growth. Crawling around on the floor, much tottering, some walking, and messy at both ends.

Judy had gone back to work less than a month ago. A reliable nanny and a reliable father, who made damn sure his son-in-law got no overseas postings—not so much as a wet weekend in Warsaw in over two years—and her life fell neatly back into place.

Wilderness watched from the bathroom doorway, a vodka and tonic in hand, as the nanny buffed them dry with a towel after their bath and they made noises which, if so disposed, he might interpret as giggles.

Alleyn's kids would be teenagers now. For all that Alleyn seemed to want to identify with him—grasping at any similarity in their lives as though he'd been thrown a line—he was a good ten years older than Wilderness, their lives at different stages from the start and Alleyn's suspended in the timeless skylessness of Wormwood Scrubs for the last six years. Wilderness could not imagine his own daughters as teenagers, though their personalities were clearly emerging, glimpses of the girls-teenagers-adults they might become. Joan was much like Judy, and Molly much the quieter—point a camera at them and Joan reacted instinctively as though she were in the spotlight and Molly stared at it with a quizzical expression on her face . . . "What is that thing and how does it work?" . . . the catwalk model and the quantum physicist.

He had not wanted children, if only because he never thought about having children, and already he could not imagine life without them. And with that he could not imagine what Alleyn was going through.

He might find it in himself to feel sorry for Alleyn but he'd rather not. He might find it in himself to tell Alleyn what he wanted to know, but he'd rather not.

Alleyn was his ticket out of England, and that was all . . . a ticket back to Berlin, the sooner the better . . . but Berlin was just the launchpad. He'd deliver Alleyn back to this Bogusnik bloke, and then . . .

$106

Wilderness got little out of Alleyn that Jim Westcott had not in 1959. Wilderness told Burne-Jones that he should get Westcott out of his (second) retirement and put him in with Alleyn one more time.

"He's clingy."

"Eh?"

"He talks to me as though I've been sent to him . . . I dunno . . . as some sort of therapist."

"You mean like a masseur?"

"No, like a fucking psychiatrist. And he identifies with me at every turn . . . the shrinks call it transference."

"Weeeeell . . . you're both spies . . . and you both went to Cambridge . . ."

This latter had not occurred to Wilderness, and to have it pointed out now was not helpful. Just one more topic to avoid.

"Alec, I'll get nothing out of him. He won't name names. Let's stop now."

Burne-Jones declined. Instead Wilderness went on playing audience/buddy/analyst as Alleyn veered directionless between revelation and reminiscence.

Revelation: He'd passed the battle plan for Suez to the Russians forty-eight hours ahead of the botched invasion. What Khrushchev knew

Nasser knew by the time the first British parachute blossomed over Sinai.

Revelation: Khrushchev had been told about the impending Bay of Pigs invasion before Kennedy. Although quite how Alleyn had known about this nearly two years before it took place served to shroud this revelation in yet more mystery.

Revelation: He had passed the entire tech specs of the UK Blue Streak missile programme to the Russians just before his arrest, which might have had something to do with it being cancelled the year after.

Reminiscence . . . on and on and on . . .

"Joe?"

His use of Wilderness's first name had become habitual. It made Wilderness wince inwardly—too pointed to be casual, too contrived. The effusive friendship of a friend who wasn't a friend.

"Did you take time for a honeymoon, Joe?"

Where the hell did that come from? He was bowling googlies.

"No," Wilderness replied. "And I blame your lot for that. I'd been married two days when you started playing silly buggers on the Finnish border."

Honesty and tone of voice were no deterrent.

"I did. Not immediately, of course. Whit Week 1948. A warm gust of spring after a long winter. We had saved enough for a journey. I would have loved to go abroad, to travel on the Continent, but that wasn't possible. Currency restrictions made it so awkward. And I was under orders not to leave England. I'd passed every check, every level of vetting imaginable, and still they panic at the thought of me facing Customs and Excise at Dover. No . . . we decided on the Isle of Man . . . almost like leaving England but not quite. A long train ride out of Euston, and a longer sea crossing from Liverpool to Douglas. Then a touch of unanticipated magic . . . a narrow-gauge steam railway down the east coast to Port St Mary."

Wilderness resisted the temptation to tell him to get on with it.

"It was the week I loved best. I have never felt more at peace. You will appreciate, peace is hard bought doing what I did . . . I have known so little peace. The Russians wanted me to meet with an agent while I was there . . . it was perfect, they told me . . . absolutely no chance we would be observed . . . I said no. Was I not entitled to some privacy?

Slightly to my amazement, they backed off. I think that was one of only three or four times in thirteen years that they did leave me alone when asked. Most of the time it was regular meetings to report nothing . . . the mere motions of spying . . . no substance . . . after all if I'd . . . where was I? . . . ah, yes, Port St Mary.

"Kate and I spent a week in a rented cottage overlooking the bay. Two rooms under a stone roof. No electricity . . . one cold tap . . . cooking on paraffin . . . Kate always slept until I brought her breakfast . . . I rose up with the lark in the morning . . . my God that's a quotation isn't it? and I've no idea from whom . . . and I sailed out with the lobstermen to haul in the pots."

Imagine, Wilderness thought, a travel piece from the *Sunday Times* magazine read out loud by a colossal bore.

"We ate fish caught with my own hands . . . we walked hand in hand around the crags at the southern tip of the island . . . watched puffins nesting on bare cliffs . . . I gathered wild flowers unknown anywhere else on earth . . . sandworts and hellebores . . . long since lost to the mainland. I pressed them into the flyleaf of the book I was reading, D. H. Lawrence's *Love Among the Haystacks*. Years later I used to open the book, and the colours of the petals had seeped into the paper so it was permanently stained red and yellow. I still had that book when your people came for me. I hate to think that it might be lost. That Kate might have sold it. Do you have something like that in your life?"

Wilderness didn't think he had. He had learnt to live without life's "souvenirs"—he found his mind needed no prompting by trinket and trivia. And he remembered hanging the key to the Berlin tunnel on a rusty nail in Erno Schreiber's apartment.

"My elder daughter was conceived in that cottage . . ."

Wilderness's daughters had been conceived in subterfuge and trickery and red rings on the calendar. He was not open to the romance of conception.

"In our first passion."

That was it. The last fucking straw. "Our passion"? Bollocks. He'd get Burne-Jones what he wanted even if it meant reducing this bastard to a puddle on the lino.

"Bernard, I am not insensitive to the tragedy that is your life."

"Tragedy, Joe?"

"You have dubbed it tragic. You may never have uttered the word, but that is how you see your life. Let us not argue over that. While I am not insensitive, do you know how many men have died as a result of information you passed to the KGB?"

Did Alleyn straighten his spine, sit a tad more upright in the face of the accusation? Did he feel the punch?

"Do you?" asked Alleyn.

"I could hazard a guess."

"I needn't."

The spine relaxed once more, the head dipped, and he spoke without looking at Wilderness.

"I know the facts. None. They have told me all along that it would be none."

He lifted his head to look at Wilderness. Not the firm stare of denial. A nervous gambler with a bluff hand.

"No one has died," he said.

His cheek twitched; there was uncertainty in the eyes that usually told only sadness. It was no time to spare the rod.

"Silesia?"

"What of it? They all returned, by ship out of Odessa as I recall."

"And the eleven RAF officers who never returned, who died in a gulag in Siberia and got buried in unmarked graves?"

Alleyn was staring again, blinking rapidly.

"The Courland operation in 1950?"

Not a word.

"Berlin in 1953. Budapest in 1956. Vienna in 1959. Probably the last man you killed."

"I . . . I . . ."

Wilderness waited, but the sentence had no ending.

§107

Judy crawled into bed at nearly midnight after a BBC late. Wilderness had relieved the nanny in time for tea, had bathed the girls and put them to bed.

"And how was Comrade Alleyn today?"

"Try asking about your daughters instead."

"No need, they are fed and bathed and snoring like drunken navvies. I peeked in to see for myself. You're good at this dad lark, but I draw the line at putting Guinness in the baby's bottle."

"Never been able to think of it as a lark."

"So bring me up to date . . . amuse me . . . I've spent all day with a French abstract painter who could bore for Europe. The man has an ego the size of the Eiffel Tower and could talk about himself till kingdom come. So . . . how is the prisoner? Anything we can flog to the *News of the World* yet?"

"You do realise that I am trying to get Alleyn to talk about himself, and while his ego clocks in at somewhat less than the Eiffel Tower . . ."

"Tell me . . . or I'll bite your ear off."

And feeling her teeth lock on to a lobe, Wilderness said, "He's much the same. Sad, sentimental, desperate for company and utterly oblivious to the nature of his crime."

"Aren't they all. The blindness of the fanatic."

"Oh, Bernard's far from being one of those."

"Then what does he think he is?"

Wilderness pondered this one.

"I think he thinks he's an Englishman . . . an unfortunate Englishman. He is . . . acculturated . . . did I just make up a word?"

"No, it's real enough."

"Acculturated to Englishness. To being English. He sends his compliments to you, by the by, for your programme on Tristram Cary."

"Good Lord. That's more than you did."

"It's electronic twaddle, not music."

"I shall bite you. Spare yourself and stick to the subject. In what way is the good comrade the unfortunate Englishman?"

"Well . . . he's in the Scrubs . . ."

"Get on with it, Wilderness."

"He has access to a daily paper, although it's chained to the wall and he can't cut out the coupons . . . He favours the *Daily Mail*, even reads Barry Norman's gossip column . . . He has a radio . . . listens to *The Archers* . . . loves Jimmy Clitheroe . . . cannot understand Ken Dodd . . . He has telly, a couple of nights a week . . . gets BBC2 . . . adores Joan Bakewell . . . but he misses going to the Wigmore Hall . . . the National Gallery . . . and above all he misses his lunches at the Garrick."

"Fucking hell. He's a member of the Garrick?"

"Yep. Pays by a bank order once a year. We did not confiscate his assets or cash and he is in regular correspondence with his bank manager at Holt's in Whitehall. I bank with Holt's. Your dad banks with Holt's. Comrade Liubimov is one of us. Alas, unlike them, I am not a member of the Garrick."

"And we . . . I mean you—the spooks—just let him?"

"Apparently so. It isn't illegal for a convict to have a bank account."

"Fuck me . . . I mean . . . they could have stood in the same queue at Holt's . . . he and Dad could have passed on the stairs at the Garrick . . . propped up the same bar . . ."

"Well . . . I won't be telling Alec that, will I?"

"I mean bloody hell . . . they won't let women in but they keep up the membership of a convicted traitor!"

"Spy. He's a spy."

"Oh no, sweetie . . . if he's *one of us*, if he's the unfortunate Englishman, then his misfortune is surely that he *is* a traitor?"

Wilderness pondered this one too. It informed, it qualified the tragedy that Alleyn had perceived, even if he would not so call it.

"Wilderness?"

"I'm listening."

"Do you actually like Alleyn?"

"I don't have to like him. I just have to deliver him. Think of him as less like a person and more like a commodity."

"Like those bags of coffee you used to smuggle in Berlin? Or like the diamond necklaces you nicked from people in Hampstead who are now our neighbours?"

"Do you want me to like him?"

"No. But I would find detachment on your part, indifference to the man or to his fate, a bit out of character."

"Judy, I am not going to involve myself in the troubles of Bernard Alleyn."

§108

Alleyn looked as though he had slept badly.

"I've thought about what you said yesterday. Suppose for one moment you are right—that men . . . that is British agents . . . died because of me . . ."

"Those eleven RAF officers weren't agents. They were liberated POWs with every expectation of freedom, not another prison camp and execution without trial. They were your allies."

"I didn't kill them, and I didn't betray them."

"They died because they'd shared a hut with the real Bernard Alleyn."

Alleyn drew breath loudly. He was finding none of this easy. If being Bernard Alleyn was wearing not one mask but a series of masks, layer upon layer, then they were beginning to slip.

"Which I did not know until you told me yesterday."

Wilderness said nothing to this. Just looked at Alleyn and waited.

"I was told the opposite. That after a decent . . . "

He winced, a facial twitch that said he'd just chosen the wrong word.

"Decent . . . Good Lord . . . is any of this decent? After . . . after a brief interval all the survivors of VIII-B would be shipped home. I may have passed some of them in the time I spent at the camp. I may have. But I spoke to none but Alleyn. I didn't know those men . . . I didn't betray them. Can one ever betray those whom one does not know?"

He bowed his head for a moment and scratched the back of his neck where the blue woollen blouse chafed. Looked up at Wilderness. Wilderness was not going to bail him out with a question or a comment.

"Suppose for a moment you are right. That British agents in . . . Berlin . . . in Budapest . . . in Vienna . . . God knows where . . . died as a result of my actions. Suppose that the KGB has lied to me all along."

It was hard not to be self-indulgent and let out a sigh laden with irony.

"Suppose all that has happened, just as you say. I didn't know those men either. But I know the men you are asking me to name. And that *would* be a betrayal. I would have their deaths on my conscience as surely as you think I have deaths of those eleven RAF officers. I can't do it. I would like to help you. I will cooperate with you as I cooperated with Mr. Westcott, but not in that way."

§109

Wilderness reported back to Burne-Jones.

"We're not going to get anything more out of him. We may as well exchange as soon as possible."

"Is he that steadfast?"

Odd choice of word, thought Wilderness, as odd as "decent."

"No. He's about as steadfast of one of Madge's blancmanges. But he's eaten up with guilt. He won't drop anyone else in it. It's as simple as that. His last words to me today were 'haven't there been enough deaths?'"

"We don't take Russian agents out behind the bike sheds and shoot them. As a rule, nine times out of ten, we deport them."

"Try telling Alleyn that. Why would he believe us?"

"Perhaps because we didn't shoot him? Merely banged him up in the Scrubs where he's suffered all the hardships of the prison library."

"This is going nowhere. I'm booking myself a flight to Berlin."

Wilderness was aware of the contradictions. Alleyn was enough the Englishman to grasp the truth of what Burne-Jones had just said. It ought to be perfectly possible to offer him the reassurance he sought, however much success might depend upon patience and repetition.

Wilderness would not be the one to say it again. The one who doubted it was Wilderness and with every repetition he doubted it more. He wondered how many men had met their end "behind the bike sheds," as Burne-Jones had so euphemistically rendered it, using the vocabulary of a prep school. And with it he wondered who played at being the Englishman better . . . himself or Leonid L'vovich Liubimov?

"There is one thing. Before I go."

"Eh, what?"

"Before I go . . . someone needs to do my job."

"Not following you here, old man."

"My desk fills up with paperwork, usually dumped there by you. If I'm handling the exchange of Masefield and Liubimov . . . who is going to deal with it? You said yourself this could take some time."

"Ah . . . what do you have in mind?"

"We get someone in to do the bloody paperwork."

"Oh, a new recruit, eh?"

"No. A rather old recruit."

§110

Wilderness had left messages for Swift Eddie at Scotland Yard. At one point he had even been put through to Eddie's boss, a Commander Wildeve, whom Wilderness had no recollection of ever meeting.

He got home shortly after seven, to hear the telephone ringing as he turned the key in the lock. No sign of Judy and the twins, most probably at her mother's in Campden Hill.

He picked up the phone.

"Joe?"

"Eddie? Been trying to reach you all day."

"Urgent, is it?"

"Fairly."

"Secret, is it?"

"Not particularly. I wouldn't discuss it on the top deck of a 38 bus, but . . ."

"Then come over. I'm around the corner."

"Around the corner?"

"Church Row. Number 17."

It took a second or two for the penny to drop, and when it did Wilderness felt stupid.

"Troy?"

"Both Troys as it happens, and if it's a spook thing I'm sure they'll give us a corner to ourselves."

It was not a situation he would have chosen—he had intended to get Eddie alone—but it seemed it had chosen him. He hoped Eddie could not hear him hesitate.

"No, no . . . that'll be fine. I'll be over in about fifteen minutes."

After all, if they couldn't talk spook in front of the Home Secretary, then where in London could they talk spook? And if all else failed, he could nab him as he left and have all the discretion of a Hampstead street corner.

Church Row was grand. The two sides of the street did not match, it was the work of half a dozen different architects, but still it was grand . . . in a way Perrin's Walk wasn't. Perrin's Walk was tarted-up garages, Church Row was fading beauty, beauty fading into greater beauty as time and age wrote themselves across it.

A beauty in her fifties, age and time writing well, answered the door.

"You must be Joe. Eddie talks about you so much I almost feel we've met. Dinner will be a little late, say half past eight, but you will stay, won't you?"

One thought, one line ran through Wilderness's mind: "I'm late, I'm late, I'm late." And if he'd had a pocket watch he would have consulted it before tumbling down the rabbit-hole.

"I'm Rod's wife," the beauty added, as though he were looking as dumb as he felt.

"Yes, I'm Joe Holderness, Lady Troy."

"Cid, please. Or the Women's Institute will have me opening bazaars. The blokes are all in what Rod laughingly calls the library."

She did not show him in so much as point him in the right direction.

He would not have laughed. This tight, sage-green and walnut room held more books than even Burne-Jones could muster.

Rod Troy was facing into the room, braces on his back, odd socks and slippers on his feet, and as he turned, a gin and It in one hand. The free hand was Wilderness's to shake.

"Joe. How nice to meet you after all this time. How nice to have a real spy in the house."

Wilderness glared at Eddie as he shook. Eddie was perched on the edge of an armchair, little legs just reaching the floor, a large scotch in his fist.

"It's not exactly a secret, Joe," he said. "And you're more real than I ever was."

Next to him, sprawled more languidly, but scarcely any taller, toes seeming to tap the carpet rather than rest upon it, was the younger Troy brother, Frederick—an ex-copper with an unenviable reputation.

Eddie stayed put, as though to move were more effort than a little fat bloke could aspire to. Frederick Troy sprang to his feet, small and dark and nimble.

"Rod's forgetting his manners, Joe. What can I get him to get you?"

"Oh . . . what Eddie's having will be fine."

Rod looked from the one to the other.

"You two know each other?"

"Fifty-nine, wasn't it?" Wilderness said.

"Fifty-eight," said Troy. "I was still a copper in those days."

"Yes . . . I heard you'd retired."

"Quit would be more the word. Eighteen months ago. Followed by a year in New York that damn near killed me."

"An accident?"

"Tuberculosis. I almost coughed myself to death like some poor bugger in a Dostoevsky novel."

"But you're OK now?"

"Touch wood."

"You won't be going back to the Yard?"

Wilderness hoped Troy would say no. If it was yes he'd never prise Eddie out.

"No, I won't."

Rod reappeared. Thrust a whisky and soda into Wilderness's hand.

"Ask him what he means to do now. Won't answer me when I ask. Fifty years old . . . "

"Forty-nine," said Troy.

"Forty-nine years old and he does bugger all."

Over dinner Wilderness found it hard to revel in Rod Troy's indiscretions, the ins and inners of the Labour cabinet, a government that had been in office less than a year, and at that by the skin of its teeth—it would surely go to the country any minute for a bigger majority.

It was Frederick Troy who interested him. The last time they met had been a knot of tensions—each of them in his professional mode. He had seen the task in hand more than he had seen the man.

He got a good look at him, and had Troy anything to say would have got a good listen, but the man was taciturn. Rod held forth, Cid did her best to draw them all into conversation, and Wilderness was surprised how forthright Eddie could be on things political. Left to their own devices the room would have dissolved around Rod and Eddie, as Eddie laid into the Wilson government with the righteousness of a convinced socialist—a word he would not apply to the prime minister.

Troy said nothing.

Wilderness looked on, appraising—a more than fleeting resemblance to the young James Mason of fifteen or so years ago, thick, unruly black hair not yet turning to grey . . . a small, dark elf of a man . . . something from a Diaghilev ballet . . . bespoke suit and shoes, a tailored shirt, worn, gold cuff links handed down the generations . . . it cost a lot to dress a Troy, he concluded . . . no rings on the manicured hands, a pianist's hands, as Eddie had said . . . and Wilderness realized that Troy was not listening to his brother, or to anyone at the table, that his left hand held a fork, but his right was forming chords on the tablecloth and in his head he was playing music, the fork would occasionally stab an airy nothing rather like a conductor's baton . . . and a moonsliver razor scar on the left cheek . . . and obsidian eyes . . . there was a Russian folk song he recalled from his training . . . "Dark Eyes," "Ochi Cherniye":

Очи чёрные, очи пламенны
И манят они в страны дальные,
Где царит любовь, где царит покой,
Где страданья нет, где вражды запрет

It ended something like

"Вы сгубили меня очи чёрные. "
You have ruined my life, dark eyes.

Well, his reputation preceded him. It was said Frederick Troy had ruined several lives. Eddie's had not been one of them. Wilderness had been the one who had almost ruined Eddie's life.

Troy broke the spell of his own hidden music and the spell of Wilderness's gaze. He got up from the table, uncorked another bottle of wine. Wine wasn't just red or white to Wilderness. He'd grown up beer and skittles but encountered good wines long ago, on the grounds that it paid to know what you were stealing.

Troy filled Wilderness's glass and seeing the look in his eye turned the bottle around to show him the label.

"Haut-Bailly '43," he said. "Rather a good year."

"The '45's better."

"Touché, Joe. Touché."

Wilderness and Eddie had smuggled plenty of wine in their Berlin days, including a couple of dozen cases of the Haut-Bailly '45, which they'd sampled far too young. And they'd had a brief, disappointing encounter with ten thousand bottles of first growth claret. Yes, Wilderness had been the one who had almost ruined Eddie's life.

Wilderness cornered him over coffee.

"Would you care to be real again?"

"Eh?"

"You said, not two hours ago, that I was more real than you'd ever been."

"I meant a real spy."

"So did I."

"Joe . . . what are you up to?"

"I have a very tricky mission coming up. I need someone to take over from me in London. For two years now I've been Burne-Jones's desk jockey. This is my chance to shuffle it all off onto someone who actually likes being in an office."

"Me?"

"You."

"Are you offering me a job?"

"I am so empowered."

"I'd be back in Intelligence?"

"Often a misnomer, but yes."

"And where would you be?"

"Back in the field. Back in the game. With any luck the old man will never get me behind a desk again."

"The field? Another bloody misnomer. Which field?"

"Berlin."

"Oh bloody Norah, not again."

"Oh yes."

"When was it? Sixty-one? Burne-Jones wanted you to run the Berlin station and you . . ."

"Eddie. To be fair he never actually asked."

"Only because you told him to stuff it before he could ask. And now you can't wait to get back?"

"It's different."

"In what way different? I'll tell you what's different. You're different. You've got a wife and two kids. And you're not nineteen any more. Berlin isn't different. It's still bloody Berlin. In '48 we got busted, you got shot, Frank buggered off, Yuri walked away with the cash and I damn near got nicked impersonating a cabinet minister! In '63 you did stuff I don't want to know about, but the rumours are still whizzing around two years later. Joe, Berlin has been a disaster area for you. It's marked on the map with a big black cross and a sign saying 'here be dragons.' Joe, you've had two good years. Your life has never been so stable. And whether you know it or not, you've looked happier than I've ever seen you. Do you want to end up like Troy when you're fifty? No wife, no kids, a string of ex-lovers he's cast off or who've cast him off, no significant relationship in his life whatsobloodyever? Berlin? Berlin? Why would you ever want to go back to bloody Berlin?"

"You want the job or not?"

"When do I start?"

"I fly out Tuesday. So, be there Monday morning."

"Don't I even have to give notice?"

"It's a transfer, Ed, not a resignation. Burne-Jones will have someone deal with the paperwork. He'll placate Commander Wildeve. You get a desk and a secretary. The delightful Alice Pettifer."

"Meaning she's anything but?"
"Meaning nothing of the sort."
Eddie mulled a moment.
"Can I bring me coffee machine?"

§111

Berlin

British Intelligence in West Berlin operated out of the back of a travel
agent's on Kantstraße. They even sold holidays and airline tickets and
turned a profit. This did not fool the Russians, but then again it was
not designed to fool the Russians, merely to tone down their own presence in the city to the point where the native Berliners did not think
that every other foreigner was a spy—to foster the illusion that Berlin
belonged to Berliners.

Berliners called in to book travel. Russians parked outside whenever
things were slack just to see what could be picked up in moments of
sheer idleness. It might have been easy to "lose" anyone among the
dozens of travellers who called in each day, but no agent not known to
be an agent, no agent whose identity was concealed, ever called there.
Wilderness was not such an agent.

The British also owned the lease on an apartment building in Bleibtreustraße, around the corner from the shop. "Our man in Berlin," lived in
one, his assistant in another, and all but one of the rest were let to ordinary
Berliners to maintain the illusion of ordinariness. The last apartment was
kept for agents such as Wilderness, for those passing through on business far from secret. The functioning policy was "do not try to conceal
the obvious." As for the far-from-obvious . . . Wilderness had thought
running Masefield out of Berlin a risk in the first place. It was little short
of a miracle he'd not been busted in Berlin rather than Moscow. That
they might get him back in Berlin was not ironic, it was merely practical.

As well as being handy for the shop, the apartments had reserved parking. Out front, as Wilderness arrived, was Dickie Delves's preposterous sports car in British racing green—flying the flag as he called it—and a rather tatty black 3-litre BMW 501. It was in this that Wilderness drove east, skirting the right-angled bulge in the wall that split the wasteland the Russians had made of Potsdamer Platz, over to Friedrichstraße and in through Checkpoint Charlie. There was nothing makeshift about Checkpoint Charlie any more.

The Adlon Hotel had and had not survived the war. The front half, which had faced Unter den Linden, had been blown to buggery. The back not only survived, it never closed. It simply cauterized itself from the ruins at the front with rough, unplastered brick walls and carried on. Some 70 or so of the original 325 rooms still functioned. A restaurant, of sorts, still functioned. The bells did not. Ringing for room service was pointless. When the Allies finally carved up Berlin, several weeks after the Russians had taken it in an orgy of looting and raping, the Adlon found itself a hundred or so yards inside the Soviet Sector, and as such Soviet property—the private fiefdom of the conquering army. Portraits of the Hohenzollern emperors which had graced the lobby burned on bonfires, to be replaced by photographs of Ulbricht and Stalin.

Bogusnik had taken a suite, several suites, on the fifth floor. No one raised an eyebrow when Wilderness asked for him by name. In a sector with no tourists, a KGB general might be a more typical guest than not—a sybarite too self-indulgent for the Russian Compound.

The lift strained all the way to fifth floor, and the gates opened with a screech of metallic pain.

A big Russian, as tall as Wilderness but more muscled, was waiting for him without pretence—shirtsleeves, shoulder holster—and the gun in his left hand.

"Mr. Holderness?"

"That's me."

"Arkady Vasilievich Anakin. I am General Bogusnik's man. Now, please excuse this, but hands against the wall while I pat you down."

Wilderness complied. The Russian pulled out the standard British-issue Baby Browning he'd carried for years now.

"You'd expect me to have a gun," Wilderness said.

"And you'd expect me to take it off you. I understand. I would feel the same. It would be like going out without your trousers."

"How aptly you put it, Arkady Vasilievich."

The Russian holstered his own gun, and with the Browning he waved Wilderness towards a door on the other side of the corridor. Two sharp knocks, and he thrust the door open.

"Please, I follow."

On the other side of the room a short, stout man in civvies stood with his back to them. He seemed to be rattling around at the drinks cabinet as though he hadn't heard them enter.

"Comrade General?"

Nothing.

"Comrade General?"

The general turned, a glass of vodka in each hand. Smiled at Wilderness.

"Arkady Vasilievich, give the man his gun and leave us alone. We'll be fine."

Arkady handed the Browning back without a flicker of expression and left. Wilderness stood holding it, watched Bogusnik ease his arse into an armchair.

"Eh, Joe. Put the gun away. Are we going to shoot one another after all this time?"

"I don't know, Yuri. It all depends. What's with this Bogusnik nonsense?"

"Sit, and I shall tell you."

Wilderness aimed the gun at Yuri's head, held the shot for a few seconds, then stuck the gun back inside his jacket. Yuri knocked back half a vodka and smiled serenely. A fat, vodka-fuelled Buddha.

"Take it, Joe. Join me in a drink for old times' sake."

Seated, with a glass in his hand, Wilderness asked again.

"What's with this Bogusnik nonsense?"

"It's my real name. Myshkin was a . . . nom de guerre . . . pinched from a Dostoevsky novel. As I recall, you remarked several times that I bore no resemblance either physically or morally to Prince Myshkin. In the years before the revolution another name was often a necessity. Bronstein becomes Trotsky, Ulyanov becomes Lenin, and so on."

"Why change back?"

"Oh . . . that was in '56. After the Twentieth Congress. Khrushchev had denounced Stalin, and Myshkin was the name I'd used throughout the Stalin years. I had few ways to disassociate myself from Stalin and Beria, but changing my name was the most obvious. I was never much under suspicion, but Bogusnik was my Dzhugashvili so . . ."

Yuri trailed off, one hand tracing waves in the air as though to finish a sentence he could not find words for. Wilderness studied him. He'd never had any real idea how old Yuri was when they'd met in 1947, perhaps forty, but now he looked more like seventy. He was still stout, fat even, but the flesh beneath his chin hung jowly like a turkey, his face a blotchy combination of grey and red, the skin on the backs of his hands dotted with liver spots. Even his eyebrows looked old—grey-white twists spiralling out into space like the whiskers on a mangy tomcat. However much he'd prospered, time had not been kind to Yuri Myshkin.

"Drink up, Joe. You would not leave an old friend to drink alone?"

"An old friend who left me with a bullet in my gut and waltzed off with all my money."

"Hmmm. Who told you that?"

"Well, I was there when you shot me!"

"I wasn't aiming at you, Joe. It was an accident. I knew you'd be OK. Larissa Tosca had a tail on me. Some clumsy kid, who made his presence all too obvious. He rescued you. If he hadn't been there, I would have done so."

Wilderness said nothing. It might be plausible. It might be an outright lie.

"No . . . I meant, who told you I took the money? Frank Spoleto?"

Wilderness said nothing.

"I thought as much. Joe, ask yourself this. Up until that night had I ever lied to you, robbed you or cheated you or proved unreliable? Since that night has Frank done anything else but lie to you, rob you, cheat you and prove himself unreliable?"

Wilderness said nothing. This was beyond just plausible, it was absolutely true.

"I kept an eye on you. Even in '63, when you and Frank cooked up that mad scheme here in Berlin, I kept an eye on you."

Wilderness had seen Yuri several times in West Berlin in '63, and with some reluctance had ascribed it to a surfeit of imagination.

He downed his vodka and held out the glass for a refill.

"Help yourself. Getting out of a chair feels like climbing Everest these days."

Wilderness topped them both up, said, "Let's drop it, Yuri. I'm here on other business, and if I never see Frank again it'll be too soon."

"Ah, at last, the unfortunate Mr. Masefield."

"Our Geoffrey. The perfect candidate for a honeytrap. You must have thought we'd sent you a Christmas present."

For a moment Wilderness did not know how to read the expression on Yuri's face, but it seemed to be genuine bafflement—he'd no idea what Wilderness meant.

"Honeytrap? What honeytrap? There was no honeytrap."

"The Tsitnikova sisters?"

"We didn't know about them until after we caught Masefield."

"Then how did you catch him?"

"A routine search of his room. We'd searched it every visit he made and he came up clean. The last time he got lazy or clumsy and we found a Minox and three rolls of film showing the specifications for Chelyabinsk. We arrested that bastard Matsekpolyev at once. We gave him an academic inch and he took an academic mile. And then we felt like idiots that we'd underestimated Masefield and so we went over everything we could about his Moscow visits. We arrested Tanya Dmitrievna. She broke down on the first day and we arrested her twin sister, and felt twin stupid. We had thought Mr. Masefield too . . . too hapless, too guileless to be a spy."

"Under the radar."

"Eh?"

"It's what Burne-Jones said when he recruited Masefield. He would slip below your radar. I told him it was nonsense."

"All the same, he had a good run."

"And the sisters?"

"Taken out to the forest and shot. A bullet to the back of the head. Buried where they fell. I would not have been so harsh, but it was not my case. I took over about a year later."

"No trial?"

Yuri shook his head.

"And Matsekpolyev?"

"Too important to shoot. We . . . shall I say . . . we treated him as the Catholic Church treated Galileo. All we had to do was show him the instruments of torture—a metaphor you will understand—to be certain of his recanting. He saw himself as some kind of honest broker—evening up the balance of power in the interest of world peace. What an arse. Just like Fuchs. Spare me these self-appointed saints."

"He kept his job?"

"Yes. No more travel, not even Poland or the DDR, no dacha, no medals . . . one foot out of line and his nuisance value will outweigh any importance he has in his field and he too might visit our forest."

"Is Masefield here?"

"Yes. He has his own suite. You will find him a little the worse for wear, slimmer, greyer . . . but he has not been mistreated, indeed for the last ten days he has been 'treated,' the flunkies that pass for room service in this place, clean sheets, decent food, wine with his evening meal . . . everything but hookers."

"Can I see him?"

"Of course. It's why we're here. Don't be too hard on him. He told us fuck all. The blandest of confessions. He's a lot tougher than he looks."

§112

Down the corridor Arkady Vasilievich thrust open a door for Wilderness.

"Not locked?"

"Where does he have to run to?"

And then the door closed, and Wilderness found himself in a room as big as Yuri's facing a small man who had his nose buried in a newspaper.

The man looked up, as though expecting nothing but the routine, nothing that would distract him from whatever he was reading.

He thrust the paper aside and was easing himself up off the sofa when Wilderness waved him back down.

"Good Lord . . . Mr. Brown?"

Wilderness took the armchair opposite Masefield.

"This lot know all there is to know about me, Geoffrey, so we can drop the alias. I'm Joe Holderness."

"What . . . what . . . brings you to Berlin? Oh God, that sounds unbelievably stupid, doesn't it?"

"You mean you don't know why you're here?"

"Haven't the foggiest."

"How long have you been here?"

"Two weeks, now. They look after me rather well. Food's a hell of a lot better than prison rations. Bogusnik even takes me out walking from time to time, although it's pretty obvious he'd shoot me if I so much as stepped off the kerb."

Wilderness doubted that.

"Got to know the old boy rather well, actually. Decent sort of chap."

Wilderness doubted both parts of that too.

"Geoffrey, I'm here to get you out."

"Out?"

"Out."

"Out . . . how, exactly?"

"A swap. Bogusnik wants to exchange you for a Russian."

"Good Lord . . . not George Blake?"

"No. Blake's a Dutchman and you're not worth a Blake. Leonid Liubimov. You probably remember him as Bernard Alleyn."

"Oh yes. I followed the trial in the papers. I felt rather sorry for Alleyn."

"Don't. I've got to know Alleyn rather well. He has an abundance of self-pity, enough to need none from anyone else. He's had six years in the prison library. He looks fit and healthy, which is more than I can say for you."

Masefield ran his hands down his torso, down to his thighs as though trying to assess the man Wilderness could see.

"I suppose I have lost weight."

Yuri's assessment had been wide of the mark, Wilderness thought. Masefield had lost about three stone, and wasn't just a bit greyer, he was almost white. Four years in Russian custody had put fifteen on him.

"Did they knock you about?"

"You mean torture? No. Bit of a slap from time to time if they thought I was taking the mickey. The regular punishment was to take all my clothes and leave me standing in the shrivelling cold in front of one of the interpreters—and they were usually women . . . highly amused at the sight of an English willie in sub-zero temperatures. But I don't think that was really a punishment so much as a routine. No . . . I think I can honestly say I was more badly abused at school. I never left the Lubyanka. It was as if they kept me in Moscow because they always meant to exchange me, although I find that hard to believe. And I suppose there are worse places."

"There are. Vladimir, out on the road to Siberia. Mordovia in the south. Not many prisoners survive either."

"And please don't worry. They asked lots of questions, of course they did. But they got no answers. I told them nothing they didn't know already."

"Water under the bridge, Geoffrey. None of that matters now. I have no mandate and no wish to debrief you. I'm just here to get you out."

"A swap, you say. Do you know where and when?"

"When? No. But unless something unforeseen crops up, about ten days. Where? Out at Staaken checkpoint, where the DDR meets the British Sector. Two cars pull up. Two doors open. That's all there is to it."

"Will I get to meet Alleyn?"

"In all probability you will pass like ships in the night. Why on earth would you want to meet Alleyn?"

"No reason I suppose. Tying up a loose end. Meeting the man who is, as it were, my alter ego."

"Now that really is gilding the lily."

"But . . . speaking of loose ends. There are one or two things I need to—"

Wilderness was shaking his head.

"No, no there aren't. Whatever it is, it's over. There are no loose ends."

"Please, just ask General Bogusnik. If there are another ten days . . . I'd like to say goodbye to Tanya Dmitrievna. I need to say goodbye to Tanya Dmitrievna. I know she was KGB, I know she betrayed me, but really . . . I must see her one last time."

Oh bloody hell. Tell him or not tell him?

"Geoffrey, she's dead."

"What?"

"The KGB had Tanya and her sister executed four years ago. They didn't betray you."

"Oh God."

"If anything you betrayed them."

"Oh God. No. No no no no no no no no no no."

§113

"Why the fuck didn't you tell him?"

"What? And have him hysterical for the last two weeks? No, the question is why did *you* tell him? There was no need to tell him. You could have got him back to England without him knowing! This shit storm could have burst over Burne-Jones's head not mine."

"You could have warned me."

"Joe, how was I to know you'd do something so stupid?"

A cough behind them. The discreet seizure of their attention.

Arkady Vasilievich said, "I gave him a small shot of morphine. Just enough. He's calmed down. Geoffrey weighs so little, it was easy to have Pavel sit on him while I put a needle in his arm."

"In England we'd have just given him a cup of sweet tea and a choco-late biscuit."

Arkady Vasilievich smiled.

Yuri waved the whole situation away with the palm of his hand above his head and sat down with a bump.

"Joe, Joe, Joe, I am weary of all this. I am too old for this racket. Give me men who know when to shut up."

And to Arkady Vasilievich, "Bring him in in five minutes. I think we both need to talk to Geoffrey."

Wilderness sat down too. For a while all he could hear was Yuri sighing.

Then Yuri said, "Tell me. Have you seen Liubimov?"

"Of course."

"And he is how?"

"He is . . . he is more English than I'll ever be."

He'd seen Yuri get the giggles before. Now he watched him slowly erupt like a long dormant volcano into a croaking laugh that set his jowls shaking.

"Joe, Joe, Joe . . . what are we doing to the poor bastard? Liubimov is going to hate Russia!"

A knock at the door. Arkady Vasilievich came in. Masefield stood passively between him and another outsize, shirt-sleeved, gun-toting Russian whom Wilderness took to be Pavel.

"Geoffrey, please sit. There are one or two things we should discuss."

Masefield sat down without a word. Yuri waved his men away.

As soon as he heard the door close behind them Masefield lunged forward and before Wilderness could so much as flinch he had his hands around Yuri's throat.

"Murderer! Murderer! Murderer!"

As the door burst open Wilderness had Masefield by the back of his collar. For a man who weighed next to nothing he felt like a pig of lead and seemed to have the tenacity of a tiger.

He swung him off Yuri and in one joint-wrenching motion spun him around to face Arkady and Pavel.

But the guns were already out.

He dropped Masefield to the floor, and opened his jacket to show the Browning neatly tucked into its holster.

"Put the guns away! We don't need guns. Do I have my gun out? Do I? Put the guns away!"

Nothing.

He stepped over Masefield, put himself between him and the guns.

"Shoot him and you have nothing to trade."

Pavel waved his gun slowly, tracking between Wilderness and the prone figure of Masefield on the floor behind him.

A groan from the sofa. Yuri had turned very red and was wheezing.

"Oh, fuck this," Arkady Vasilievich said, stuck his gun back in his shoulder holster and stepped past all of them to pick up a small silver tin from the side table.

"Open your mouth, Comrade General. Steady. Steady. There."

The pill slipped under Yuri's tongue. In seconds he seemed to be breathing more easily. In a minute or so his colour began to return to its normal, pasty, sun-starved Soviet grey.

"Geoffrey. You fucker," was all he said.

Wilderness hauled Masefield to his feet. Now weightless as feathers.

"It wasn't him. Understand? It wasn't him. He had nothing to do with Tanya's death."

Masefield was on the verge of tears. Wilderness had no sympathy and no wish to see his tears. He shoved him back towards Pavel and said, "Give him another shot. Make it bigger this time."

And Pavel led a passive, tearful Masefield back to his room. A hand upon his arm, showing a more gentle touch than Wilderness would have offered.

As he passed Wilderness, Arkady Vasilievich whispered, "This happens. Be warned, this happens."

§114

Yuri was on his feet now.

"Let us get some air. A stroll outside. Perhaps when we get back Mr. Masefield will have recovered his composure."

The Yuri Wilderness had met just after the war would not have known "metaphor" or "composure" in either language.

They rode down together in the lift, Wilderness looking at the top of Yuri's balding head, neither speaking.

Out in Pariser Platz Wilderness tried to remember when he'd last set foot there. Probably 1948. He'd looked through the first incarnation of the wall in 1961 when it was nothing more than coils of barbed wire, and he'd crossed Unter den Linden a few times in 1963 without ever turning into the square.

It was shocking.

They strolled at Yuri's pace out into the empty plain behind the Brandenburg Gate. The Russians had cleared away the rubble and the

wiry saplings of the post-war years, but that was it. Pariser Platz had
been smoothed out and abandoned. The phrase "sweeping it all under
the carpet" came to mind, as though he might lift a stone slab and find
all the dust and rubble brushed away. It resembled a very neat bomb-
site. Clean lines of utter nothingness.

They'd reached roughly the centre, the arches of the pockmarked
Brandenburg Gate off to the west, the jagged lines of bomb-blasted
buildings no one had yet seen fit to demolish off to the east. Wilderness
had watched newsreel footage in the cinemas of his thirties childhood,
the sleekly massed ranks of the Wehrmacht goose-stepping down Unter den Linden. And in 1947 he'd stood here as the ragged remnants
of Germany's final army—the hopeless and hapless Volkssturm—had
dragged themselves in from Russia and Poland to collapse on the spot—
Nell Burkhardt's father one of them—something else Yuri had arranged
behind the scenes.

"Yuri. I'm appalled. You lot have had this place to yourselves for
twenty years. Maybe it's cleaner, but apart from that it looks just the
same as it did in 1948."

"So?"

"You've built nothing. Bugger all."

"We held a competition. Did you not hear? Architects from all over
Europe, vying to redesign the centre of Berlin. Everyone except poor
old Albert Speer. Locked up in Spandau and so ineligible. A pity. We
could have got his plans for nothing."

"I heard the competition was all a fake. You had no intention to
build anything."

"Perhaps. Perhaps we have our reasons."

"I'm all ears."

"Perhaps we are saying to the Germans, 'you mess with us twice and
this is what we do to you. Mess with us a third time, and all Germany
will look like this.'"

Wilderness looked up at Viktoria and still wondered which way she
should be facing. As it was she gazed down upon nothing. A void.

"A punishment?"

"Of course it's a punishment."

"You don't think that Germany's been punished enough?"

"I don't know. Nor do I care. They're just fucking Germans."

"What do you care about apart from money, Yuri?"

"I say again, if it's the money that bothers you, you should be dealing with Frank."

There was a large stone. The height and size of a posh family tomb in an English churchyard. Wilderness had no idea whether it was an obelisk or just another chunk of wartime detritus. Yuri perched his backside on it, breathing deeply. Wilderness waited for him to speak again, turned over a fragment of rubble with the toe of his shoe. Cream tile, with streaks of red and yellow glaze, something that looked like a cherub's arse—a piece of an Adlon bathroom or lavatory, lying where it had fallen more than twenty years ago.

"But since we are talking of deals."

"We are?"

"We are. There is more to our deal."

"Strings?"

"No. Not strings. A . . . a condition."

Wilderness said nothing. Waited for the string to jerk.

"You get Masefield. I get . . . Liubimov."

So far so good, but Wilderness wasn't going to fill in any blanks however slowly Yuri spoke.

"I get Liubimov . . . and the ten thousand bottles of claret you stole in 1947."

Oh shit. How the fuck did he know about that?

V

Lawton Frères

The only advice I can give to aspiring writers is don't do it unless you're willing to give your whole life to it. Red wine and garlic also helps.

—Jim Harrison

§115

45 Schlüterstraße, West Berlin: October 1947

"Where the bloody hell have you been?"

"Does it matter? I'm here now."

"Here, but twenty minutes late. And may I point out, Corporal Holderness, that as this is your first appearance in the last ten days, to show up on time might be considered a courtesy."

Wilderness liked Rose Blair. An upper-class English beauty who had seen fit to serve her country in this bum-freezing Berlin winter. But there were limits.

"I don't answer to you, Rose."

"It's Miss Blair to you, you cocky little prick. And we both answer to Burne-Jones. I'm getting fed up covering your arse all the time."

"Then don't."

"You're here to denazify Nazis. You can't do that if you don't meet any, and I've had one of the bastards stuck in my office for the last fifteen minutes trying to chat me up in two languages. Now, get the slimy bugger in here, give him his Persilschein and get rid of him!"

She slapped the usual buff file on the desk in front of Wilderness. He looked down at the cover.

Wölk, Rüdiger Ludwig. b. Potsdam 27.9.09

Below the name was a box grid applied with a rubber stamp, red ink faded to pink, and the comments and initials of his two predecessors in the assessment process whereby Berliners were judged and given or denied their right to rejoin society, to have their ration status revised, to return to their pre-war job and in many cases to have their membership of the Nazi Party if not expunged then rendered harmless to them with a certificate of absolution—hence the derisory and accurate nickname for the scrap of paper, *Persilschein* . . . it washed whiter than white.

Box one read in spidery scrawl:

Party member. Declined 1.3.46. JBD.

Box two read, more legibly:

Hold over. Reassess in 12 mon. 19.12.46. PW.

"Hold over for what? New evidence? The twelve months aren't up yet. And who was PW?"

"I've no idea about any evidence new or old, Holderness. I just type. PW is Squadron Leader Wallis. I will say this for him. He made you look good. Just read the file, will you. I'll give you five minutes. Two if the bugger tries the verbal equivalent of a feel-up one more time."

Rüdiger Wölk was a Nazi and had never sought to deny it. Wilderness had met idiots who did, oblivious to the fact that the Allies possessed complete records of party membership. The only issues in dealing with Nazis were: youthful error, which allowed that the young could be virtually brainwashed; compulsory membership, which had applied to any city, state, and civil service occupation from town planners right down to kindergarten teachers; and, so difficult as to be absurd, the opinion of the assessor that the former Nazi might now be "worthy." Wilderness, a lowly RAF corporal, had the power to grant or deny a *Persilschein* to anyone.

He was on the last paragraph when the door was thrust open and Rose Blair barked out Wölk's name. Wilderness looked at his watch. Three minutes. Clearly he hadn't kept his words to himself.

If there was a stereotypical Nazi, Wilderness hadn't met him. It would help his job enormously if they fell into two simple categories . . .

Fat Bastard—e.g. the Göring type.

Skinny Bastard—e.g. the Heydrich type, or the one that had vanished after the war, what was it . . . Eichmann, or something very like that.

Wölk was neither. Five minutes after this one left Wilderness would be hard-pressed to describe him.

Rose Blair had not given him enough time. He had a gloss on the man now standing in front of him. He'd not studied the dossier. He'd not interpreted the simplicity of facts into a structure of understanding.

Wilderness glanced up at Herr Wölk, waved him into the chair and raced though the final half page.

When he'd finished he saw a man in his late-thirties, looking much the worse for wear . . . pasty, vitamin-deficient skin, bloodshot brown eyes, thinning, prematurely grey hair. The clothes said more than his features. Threadbare. Like so many other Berliners. His jacket shiny at the elbows and shot at the cuffs. So, what else was new? Another importuning middle-class German, who'd probably supported Hitler, been disappointed in defeat, who'd struggled to make his living ever since, and resentful to find the Allies unforgiving.

And the man saw him.

"You're just a boy."

"Good start, Herr Wölk. Get right up my nose, why don't you?"

"I'm sorry, it's just that I was expecting . . ."

"What?"

"Someone in authority."

"I *am* authority. Don't let the two stripes on my arm fool you. I work for British Intelligence and I have the same authority over you as a man with three pips or a crown on his shoulder."

"I'm sorry."

Wilderness doubted this.

"Herr Wölk, if you want your *Persilschein* why not just tell me what this folder doesn't? Tell me about yourself. Give me a reason to give you what you want."

"I have told all this to you people before."

"And you will tell it again, and, if I say so, again and again."

Wölk did not sigh or shrug. He looked straight back at Wilderness, not giving an inch.

"The file records my party membership. You will know that. You will also know that as an employee of the city of Berlin, membership was compulsory. Not joining would have put me out of work as surely as the British have put me out of work these last two years."

"But you do work."

"As a labourer. My wife too . . . she is what we call a *Trümmerfrau*. Before the . . . before . . ."

Quite, thought Wilderness. Before what? Everyone used the phrase "before the war," but Wölk had just stopped himself saying "before the peace" in the same nostalgic tone.

"My wife taught classics at a *Gymnasium*. I was a railway technician, an engineer. I rose to run the railway yards in the south and east of Berlin, the passenger stations, the freight yards and . . . the marshalling yards."

At last something that wasn't in the dossier. All Wilderness had read was the word "engineer." Wölk was trading with him. He was trading detail for hope. It was the first thing he'd given away. Wilderness wondered why there'd be an all but immeasurable hesitation before "marshalling yards."

§116

He called on Erno Schreiber on his way home. One floor below the flat he shared with Nell Burkhardt on Grünetümmlerstraße.

If the teapot was stuck on the landing and the door slightly ajar it meant he was "at 'ome," as the toffs back in England would put it, and certainly at home to anyone who, as Wilderness usually did, brought his own tea.

Erno didn't look up from whatever he was doing with a magnifying glass and a spotlight.

"Anything new, my boy? I do hope so. I've had enough of the Lady Londonderry Mixture to last a while."

"Of course. Lapsang souchong. A smoky little number all the way from China."

"And stolen from the PX?"

"Tastes just the same as if it weren't stolen, Erno."

"I'll put the kettle on."

"Although I will say this for Nell . . . she can pull a face that says 'this tea or this coffee tastes stolen.'"

Over tea, Wilderness asked, "Do you recall a Rüdiger Wölk?"

"Recall in what context?"

"City railways. Says he ran the railways in Berlin. East of the Lichtenberg Bahnhof, south of the Anhalter Bahnhof."

"And he wants his *Persilschein*?"

"Yep."

"And you haven't given it to him for what reason."

"He's an arrogant gobshite. He exudes Nazi arrogance."

"And you are trained in distinguishing Nazi arrogance from all the other forms of arrogance?"

"OK. You made your point. But I am trained to trust my instinctive reactions."

"If it smells wrong, it is wrong?"

"Something like that."

"No . . . the name rings no bells . . . but I have ever been a stay-at-home. Riding in trains gives me no pleasure and never did. But Nell might know. Her father was almost certain to have known him; they were both city engineers after all. Sewers, railways, all the same really."

§117

"Did you meet many of your father's colleagues?"

Wilderness had eggs. Yuri was as unreliable as the next *Schieber*, except where eggs were concerned. You asked for eggs, you got eggs. As long as you didn't ask where he got them. Wilderness also had a specimen of the ubiquitous German potato, a bulb of garlic, a couple of manky onions and half a pound of bland American cheese. Peas would have been nice, but fresh peas in October? In the city that had nothing? By the time Nell had got home he had the makings of a passable Spanish omelette.

"It's good," Nell said. "You're becoming quite the cook, aren't you?"

"Are you avoiding my question?"

"Yes. You've never asked about him before."

"I've never needed to."

"So I'm right."

"Right about what?"

"That you wouldn't ask about a man whose absence has torn at my heart every day for nearly three years unless you had an ulterior motive."

"I have a reason, not a motive. Will that do?"

"Ask."

"Wölk."

"Rüdiger Wölk?"

"Yes."

"So the bastard is still alive? And . . . let me guess . . . he has come to you for his *Persilschein*?"

"Why 'the bastard'?"

"Do you know what he did for the city?"

"I think so . . . he ran the railways . . . he had an office at the Anhalter Bahnhof, another at the Lichtenberg Bahnhof . . . and . . ."

"And what?"

"And what is it he's not telling me?"

She put down her fork, pushed her meal away, not half-eaten.

"I imagine he portrays himself to you as some sort of benign stationmaster . . . and innocent facilitator of the movement of goods and commuters on their way across Berlin?"

"Pretty much."

"And what were the Jews bound for Auschwitz that he penned up in the marshalling yards in the east? Commuters or goods? People or chattels? Joe, he was a Nazi. Not the token party member my father was, but a believer. He was a Nazi who willingly sent thousands to their deaths."

"Was this known at the time?"

"You know it wasn't. We were a city wearing blinkers. Even now when all the secrets have unravelled you can still hear people . . . you've heard them yourself . . . in the bars, in the cafés . . . 'the Führer was deceived' . . . 'it's all propaganda . . . the Jews weren't gassed they were resettled.'"

Wilderness gently pushed the plate back towards her.

"I didn't mean to ruin your meal."

"It's not your fault. I'll be a hundred years old before these Nazi bastards stop cropping up in my life. They are ghosts, Joe. Living ghosts. Berlin is a city of ghosts and Germany is a haunted country."

He covered her hand with his.

"I won't let him go. We've got this 'bastard.'"

"I didn't think you would."

§118

When Wilderness got to Schlüterstraße the following morning, intending to log in with Rose Blair and find a quick way to dismiss anything she had to say and get back to the serious business of black-marketeering, she simply held up a brown envelope and said, "Arrived half an hour ago by dispatch rider. An American dispatch rider."

Wilderness opened and read it.

Meet me at the Esplanade at 11. Urgent.
And keep shtum about this. Frank.

It was already 10:30.

"I have to go out."

"You've only just got here. And what about this lot?"

She held up a fistful of envelopes.

"Did any of them come by dispatch rider?"

She said nothing.

"Well," he said. "There you are."

§119

"Why are we meeting here? We could just as easily have met at the club, it's not fifty yards away."

Frank said, "I don't want to be overheard by any Tom, Dick, and Harry. Or I should say, every Tom, Dick, and Yuri. And certainly not by that bitch Larissa Tosca. This is between you and me."

"What is?"

"Rüdiger Wölk."

"How quickly word spreads."

"When are you due to meet him again?"

"Tomorrow."

"And what do you have it in mind to say to him."

"That he's not getting his *Persilschein* and he's damn lucky not to be on trial."

Frank was shaking his head.

"No. Joe, just give him the paper and have done."

"He's a Nazi. Not a run-of-mill, 'I was only doing my job' Nazi, a Nazi with blood on his hands."

"All the same, he walks. Kid, this isn't your old pal Frank talking to ya, this isn't even Captain Spoleto United States Army Intelligence, this comes straight from the top. The generals say he walks. The generals, capisce?"

"Why?"

"It looks like we need him. Need him back in his old job. Berlin's railways are a pile of crap. We need to reinstate him, and it's been decided at the top that that's what's gonna happen."

"So muggins here gets to whitewash him?"

"You're the right guy in the wrong place. Just so happened he registered in the British Sector in '45. So he's your pigeon. Just give him the paper and forget you ever saw him."

"I do a lot of crappy things, Frank. Teaming up with you being pretty high on my list of crimes, but I do not give *Persilschein*s to Nazis."

"Shit, kid. You're gonna have to."

"Or what?"

"Or my people talk to your people and Burne-Jones gets a phone call from General Robertson . . . do I need to say more?"

"You do. Who has decided to put Nazis back in their jobs?"

"Mostly us. An American decision. The British grumbled but accepted that a Germany that lets the talent fester is never gonna have schools, railways, or a civil service that works. The French? Sure, they were spitting feathers, but who cares what the French think? The Russians? We ain't gonna tell the Russians. They'll find out. I've no doubts about that. And they'll try for the high moral ground, say they denazify and we don't and blah blah blah. Joe, we've tried the pure version of Germany. It doesn't work, so we'll go with the grubby, shabby, guilty version."

"I had wondered why he came in ahead of his review. We didn't send for him. You sent him, didn't you?"

"Yep, and if I'd realised you'd be playing it by the book I'd have warned you and told you not to bother. He says you put him through hoops, same questions over and over, trying to trip him up."

"But you didn't warn me. You thought I'd just pass him."

"Yep."

"Fuck you, Frank."

Wilderness got up to leave. Frank put a hand on his arm.

"This could kill the whole operation, kid."

Wilderness looked down at him. The bright-eyed, bushy-tailed Spoleto swagger was missing. He sat down again.

"How do you mean? 'Kill'?"

"The team is you, me, Swift Eddie, and Yuri. Four of the finest hustlers Berlin has ever seen. We can agree the other guys don't count for much. But if one of us drops out, the whole operation falls to pieces. Any one us of gets posted out of Berlin and it's over. If you fuck this up, if you start playing your *Persilscheins* by the book, when we all know the goddamn book is made of India rubber . . . you'll get shipped home . . . but since Yuri will only deal with you, the sweetest little black-market scam this side of the Mississippi is history. Give him the paper, Joe. If you don't, the guy who replaces you will."

"If it's a fait accompli . . . why not just reappoint Wölk and forget the *Persilschein*?"

"It's absolution. It has to look kosher. Not just now, but in ten or twenty years' time. And who knows what Germany will be in ten or twenty years? He has to able to wave that scrap of paper and say he was absolved."

"And if I do this how many more Nazis will come to me with Uncle Sam's seal of approval wanting my blessing?"

"I don't know. I wish I could tell you it would be zero. But I can't. Now, can I tell him he can skip the meeting tomorrow, and you'll just mail him his *Persilschein*?"

Wilderness said nothing.

§120

He got in at ten, expecting Rose Blair to make a sarcastic comment, something about "three days in a row, my word." Instead she was on the phone. She cupped the mouthpiece with one hand and whispered to him.

"Spoleto for you. And Wölk is waiting in your office."

"Frank?"

"Hiya, kid. I couldn't get hold of Wölk last night. He may just show up anyway."

"It's OK, Frank. He's already here."

"So, we don't have a problem?"

He hadn't told Nell. He was not sure how he could ever tell Nell.

"No, we don't."

"Good. I owe you one."

No, Frank, you owe me everything.

"Miss Blair, pass me a blank *Persilschein*."

Wilderness signed, dated, and stamped it.

"Now type in Wölk's name."

"He's clean? I had him down for a right bastard."

"No, he's not clean at all, but he's free."

Wölk was standing by Wilderness's desk, hands clasped behind his back like the Duke of Windsor on inspection.

He unclasped his hands, put his right inside his overcoat and set a small brown package, bound in faded red twine, looking like foolscap pages folder over and over, on the desk between them.

"Please, take this."

Wilderness made no move to pick it up.

"Please, take this. Give me my papers, and no one will be any the wiser."

Wilderness sat down.

"See Miss Blair in the other office. She will give you what you want. Good day to you, Herr Wölk."

"And good day to you, Corporal Holderness."

Wilderness stared at the package.

Waited.

Foolscap, red twine, and black sealing wax.

Waited.

About five minutes later Rose Blair came in.

"He's gone. Have we seen the last of him?"

"I do hope so. The thing about absolution is it ought to be absolute."

As the door closed behind her, Wilderness stood up and was about to sweep the package into the waste-paper bin when it occurred to him that Wölk was not expecting to be so readily accommodated, that he had not talked to Frank and that the bribe, if such it was, was his idea and his alone.

Curious and curiouser.

He opened it. Flecks of sealing wax fell to his desktop. It was in French, and whilst Wilderness's French was passing good he had no idea what to make of the sheaf of papers in his hand.

§121

He met Eddie at the Marokkaner Club in Grolmanstraße.

"Why are we back here? We haven't been here in months."

"It's a Frank-free zone. I don't want Frank hearing any of this. Not now, possibly not ever."

He told Eddie of his encounters with Rüdiger Wölk and passed him the papers Wölk had given him.

"A bribe?"

"He thought it was a bribe. He'd no idea Frank had already told me to rubber-stamp him. He bribed me . . . after the act, shall we say."

Eddie leafed through the papers.

"I know bugger all about wine."

"Me neither, but I can count. Ten thousand and eighty bottles of pre-war vintage claret."

"But you're always lecturing Frank about wine."

"That's because the ignorant slob knows even less than me. The bugger couldn't tell champagne from Irn-Bru. If they don't make it in Milwaukee . . ."

"Ten thousand and eighty. Got to be worth something hasn't it?"

"Or not. Not all wine is the good stuff. Some of it's got to be rubbish. I dunno, bad harvest, poor harvest . . . all sorts of things could make a difference."

"But they're posh names, aren't they? Margaux. Lafite Rothschild. I mean Rothschilds do everything, don't they? They even have their own bank."

"Question is, Eddie, where did Wölk get this and what exactly is it?"

"You're asking the wrong person."

§122

"Boys, boys. This is . . . amazing."

Wilderness had rarely seen Erno so animated. Pacing up and down in front of the wood stove.

"All but one of these is first-growth claret, under the 1855 classification. Mouton Rothschild is second growth, but why be picky, they're some of the finest wines on earth. Château Margaux 1934? It's God's own tipple! Mouton Rothschild '29. Yiyiyi, boys, how did you come by this?"

"Half the time, Erno. First, tell me what it is."

"It's proof of ownership. Just like the deeds to a house. The man named here . . ."

He looked down at the first page again.

"Henri-Pierre Dukas . . . this man has eight hundred and forty cases stored with Lawton Frères in Bordeaux. Perhaps my analogy is wrong. Not the deeds to a house, but the bank book for a deposit account. Think of the wine brokers as a bank and the wine as money. Now, where did you get this?"

"Wölk."

"Wölk?"

"The bloke I was asking you about a couple of days ago. Director of Berlin's railways, or some of them. I did ask Nell. He wasn't one of those forced into the party just to keep his job; he was one of the faithful—a committed Nazi. And I am asking myself where he got these papers and I'm coming up with only one answer."

"Stolen?"

"More likely offered as a bribe by someone, and let's assume that was Monsieur Dukas, as he passed through the marshalling yards of Berlin to be herded into a cattle truck bound for Auschwitz or Treblinka or . . ."

Erno sat down with a bump.

"Of course, how could I be so stupid?"

He let the sheaf of papers float down to the floor.

"We'll never be free of it, will we? Germany has cursed itself."

"Yep."

Eddie said, "Typical. We get our hands on a fortune and it turns out to be dirty money."

"The dirtiest," said Erno.

§123

Wilderness drove out to the officers' mess at Gatow. He was looking for a regular customer of his, an RAF pilot—Flight Lieutenant George "Foxy" Brush.

A uniformed corporal would not normally be allowed into the mess, but there was scarcely anyone, the German waiters included, to whom he had not sold coffee, sugar, butter . . . and as long as he minded his p's and q's his rank was all but ignored.

He'd never flown with Foxy, but if Foxy flew planes as inebriated as he drove cars, what Wilderness was about to ask had risks.

"George. Are you still doing runs out to SHAPE HQ at Rocquencourt?"

"Yep. Twice a week. Fridays and Wednesdays. Why, do you fancy a few nights on the razzle in Paris? Those French tarts'd eat a boy like you alive."

"No. I need to get to Bordeaux. I was hoping you might get me as far as Orly and I could play it by ear from there."

"Consider it done. The price'll be twenty-five."

"Twenty-five what?"

"Twenty-five pounds of your best PX java. I don't know how you get away with it."

He twisted in his seat, yelled "Johnny!"

A waiter came over.

"Whisky soda. *Zweimal*, Johnny. Chop, chop."

Then to Wilderness.

"Fair offer, Joe, take it or leave it. But I can throw in something useful as well."

"What?"

"I'm meeting old Ginger Henshaw. Least I will if the bugger ever wakes up. Just got in from Blighty. Tells me he's on the diplomatic run next Wednesday. Paris to Lisbon."

"Via Bordeaux?"

"I doubt it, but while you savour the delicious single malt I just bought you, you work out what it's worth to you if old Ginger can be persuaded to develop a little engine trouble somewhere near Mérignac."

"Where's that?"

"French airfield, just outside Bordeaux. Civil and military just like Orly. But a bit of a mess. I touched down there once or twice meself. You'd think the Krauts had been gone less than five minutes from the look of it."

"Diplomatic? Wouldn't that mean some sort of government official on board?"

"King's Messengers—the silver greyhound chappies. I've flown a few in my time. They don't want anyone asking too many questions, so they tend not to ask any themselves. Look, here's old Ginger now."

Squadron Leader Henshaw heard Wilderness out, stroked at a caricature waxed, ginger moustache and said, "I think we can manage that. But I can't pull the same stunt twice. You'll have to find your own way back to Orly. There's a train service. Bit slow, but it'll get you there. What are you offering?"

"Twenty-five pounds of coffee."

Henshaw looked at Foxy. Foxy nodded.

"Then we have a deal, Corporal Holderness."

"I won't be a corporal on Wednesday."

"Oh?"

"I'll be a lieutenant in the Welsh Guards."

Henshaw looked baffled. Wilderness hoped he hadn't dropped a brick in front of a man who'd take "impersonating an officer" seriously.

Foxy sniggered into his scotch. He'd seen Wilderness's officer "act" before.

"Keep promoting yourself, Joe, and you'll soon outrank me."

§124

There was a pip missing. First rule of a faker? You have to look right. No officer in a regiment as classy as the Welsh Guards would be seen dead with two pips on one shoulder and only one on the other.

Where had he lost it?

The uniform hung in the wardrobe at the "official" apartment he nominally shared with Eddie in Fasanenstraße. Eddie had gone out only minutes after Wilderness arrived, muttering about something of nothing.

The pip wasn't lying in the bottom of the wardrobe with the fluff and the mothballs. Only one thing for it. He's have to go back to Grünetümmlerstraße and ask Erno to go through his collection of buttons and pips and studs until he found a match.

§125

At Grünetümmlerstraße he found a committee waiting for him.

Erno, Eddie, and Nell.

He put the duffel bag down on the floor, one sleeve of the uniform trailing conspicuously.

"I'd no idea I was so popular."

"We would like to talk to you," Nell said.

Nell—hard as nails. Erno inscrutably blank. Eddie—sheepish, as though wanting nothing to do with this, and everything.

"You're getting ready to go to Bordeaux, aren't you? And I assume from the fact that you're carrying that uniform that you mean to do so representing yourself as a British officer."

"Just spit it out, Nell."

Much to his surprise it was Eddie who answered.

"You can't just con the French out of the wine, Joe."

Wilderness sat down on the spare chair, so obviously set out for him, facing the three of them—"prisoner at the bar."

"I never said anything about a con."

"Whenever you wear that uniform, there's summat dodgy going down, Joe."

"Eddie. I'm just going to ask about the wine. Is it still there? To whom does it belong? Do you think I stand a better chance of getting answers dressed as an RAF corporal or a lieutenant of the Welsh Guards?"

Nell said, "Why ask? Why not let be?"

"It's a loose end."

"Europe is a loose end, France is a very loose end, Germany is the raggedyest end of all. You cannot gather up every thread. And you would not be gathering up these if you did not think there was profit in it."

"Do you think so little of me, Nell?"

"You took a bribe to let a Nazi go."

"No, that is simply not true. Wölk bribed me after the Americans had told me I had to give him his soddin' *Persilschein*. I almost binned it. I opened it out of curiosity . . . Pandora's box . . . and once I did that . . . well, the wine became ownerless."

"The Americans?" she said. "Or just one American?"

"Fine. It was Frank. Frank in his official capacity. Frank told me the Kommandatura had decided on Wölk's reinstatement—Wölk and hundreds of others."

Erno said, "It's true, Nell. I have heard this from half a dozen people. The Americans are putting the Nazis back in their old jobs. All is forgiven in the interests of efficiency."

"Forgiven but not forgotten. And it says nothing of what Joe is about to do."

"You think I will steal the wine?"

"If you get the chance, I know you will."

"Nell, what would you have me do?"

"It's pointless asking you not to go . . . instead I would ask this of you. If you are serious about gathering up loose ends then . . . find the heirs of the man Wölk robbed. Where you can create justice, create it."

Wilderness said, "Eddie, Erno? Do you agree with Nell?"

Erno nodded.

Eddie said, "Yes. She's right. We can't work this con. It's wrong."

"Then we won't."

§126

Upstairs, back in their own room, Nell slapped Wilderness across the face as hard as she could.

"Why did I have to be your conscience, Wilderness?"

Wilderness said nothing. Tasted blood. Looked back at her without flinching. If she was going to hit him again, so be it.

"Without me would you even have a conscience?"

In bed they lay awake, back to back, a no-man's-land of vacant sheet between them.

Hours passed. He could hear her breathing, and surely she could hear him? They each knew the other was not sleeping.

Then Nell said, "What did you mean by 'Pandora's box'?"

"It's a Greek myth—"

"I know that."

"Then its meaning should be obvious. Once you open the box, whatever comes out can never be put back in."

"The wine? The Frenchman? The matter of ownership?"

"Yes."

"I regret to say you are right."

"Perhaps I should never have opened it."

"But you did. And now you cannot walk away from this."

§127

Lawton Frères Wine Merchants,
Quai de Bacalan, Bordeaux

Wilderness would have put Auguste Lawton at about seventy-five. Short, bald with wisps, watery blues eyes paled into transparency, bespectacled, dapper—a sophisticated, upper-class Frenchman, who for unfathomable reasons spoke English with a faint Irish accent.

He heard Wilderness out, nodding patiently once in a while.

"Forgive me, Lieutenant Tatten-Brown, but you are just a boy . . . "

Exactly what Wölk had said to him.

Wilderness bit his tongue.

"Your war was spent where . . . school . . . university?"

"Yes. I've never been in combat. I was called up after the war ended."

"Combat isn't quite the issue. I too have never fired a shot in anger. Too old for both world wars, and a babe in arms during the War of 1870. No, I meant the experience of war. Battle might be unimaginable, and we prize the artists who recall it or imagine it for us, do we not . . . Homer, Goya, Tolstoy. Can you imagine occupation? Do you know what we went through here in Bordeaux, keeping the semblance of normality?

"The first phase might have been the worst. The first three months after Dunkirk. Being regarded as the defeated and everything we owned the spoils of war. Theft, looting, wanton destruction.

"Some of our finest vintages disappeared down the throats of men who would not know Château Margaux from Château Wicklow . . . even more went on the backs of lorries to be shipped back to the Reich. I have it on good authority that Göring stole eighty thousand bottles from a single *cave* in Paris.

"But . . . we had a month or more before the Germans arrived, knowing all the time that they most certainly would arrive. Our bricklayers had never been so gainfully employed. Every merchant and *négociant* in Bordeaux bricked up some part of their *caves* . . . some even moved wine out of the city and sealed it up in caves, not *caves* but caves . . . another sank two thousand bottles in his pond . . . and one of my oldest friends picked out his best two hundred bottles and vowed he would drink every single one before the Boche banged on his door . . . he got through less than a hundred and fifty but one has to admire the effort.

"Then, the chateaux were taken over. Do you know how Haut-Brion spent the war? As a rest and recreation home for Luftwaffe officers. In Mouton Rothschild the Wehrmacht used priceless paintings for target practice, and at Cos d'Estournel they pinged bullets off the bells in the towers, just to hear them ring.

"But, things settled down. The Germans appointed *Weinführer*s to every region. Men who knew their job. Ours was a decent man. But from then on he was our only buyer, there was only one market, one customer, for French wine . . . and as they shipped more and more, so wine production fell . . . no men to prune the vines, no horses to work the land . . . a shortage of bottles, a shortage of copper sulphate . . . by 1942 wine production was barely half of what it had been in 1939 and they took more and more of less and less.

"We resisted, of course we resisted. Silently. We hid our fine wines and shipped the *pisse de cheval* to Germany. It didn't always work, but many a good bottle stayed home while someone in Germany drank our worst wine from a bottle with a fake label. We have a phrase for that—*vin de trois hommes*, two men to hold down a third as he will only drink it if forced.

"Things changed. That brief if ambivalent stability was spent by 1943. Two things changed drastically—the Germans began shipping Bordeaux Jews east, and the Maquis had become organised and ubiquitous, and there were reprisals.

"This brings me to my old friend Henri-Pierre Dukas. He was not a Jew, nor was he in the Maquis . . . but all his sons were. Dominic, Jean-Jacques, and Régis.

"Knowing that he was at risk, Henri-Pierre decided to . . . consolidate, I choose that word carefully . . . to consolidate his wine. He was nothing to do with the wine trade—he was a publisher of crime novels . . . in the trashy American style of private eyes, hoodlums and fast women . . . but they had sold in the millions and Henri-Pierre became wealthy, and he put some of his wealth into wine. He'd been a regular buyer, but in 1934 he bought four vintages en primeur—Lafite-Rothschild, Latour, Margaux, and Haut-Brion. We have always received an allocation from the four 'first growth' chateaux, and Henri-Pierre had bought two hundred cases of each, a total of nine thousand six hundred bottles.

"He asked us to set them aside, a hole in our *caves* where the Boche would never find them. At the last minute he added forty cases of Mouton Rothschild '29 which had been in the cellar of his own home. Hence the figure you have in front of you. Ten thousand and eighty.

We redrew the certificate of ownership that May—that is the document you now have. Henri-Pierre was insistent on paying for storage for twenty-five years, until 1968. An odd thing to do, but it shows you how apprehensive, if not fatalistic, he was.

"Two months later a train destined for Germany was derailed east of Mérignac. The Maquis killed very single German on the train, and the Jews being transported fled into the countryside. It was common knowledge that the Dukas brothers led the local Maquis. The Boche arrested Henri-Pierre, and announced that they would shoot him unless his sons surrendered themselves. What they did not know, what no one knew, was that two of the brothers had been killed in the raid on the train, and the third badly wounded. There could be no surrender.

"Of course, they did not shoot Henri-Pierre. Once the track was repaired, they put him on the next train east.

"Three weeks later, this arrived."

All the time Auguste had been talking, two documents had sat on the desk between him and Wilderness. The folded foolscap certificate of ownership and a small brown envelope of wartime economy paper. He slid the envelope across.

Wilderness opened it. Read the single page.

"May I ask what this means?"

"It is a deed of transfer, whereby Henri-Pierre Dukas transferred ownership of the wine to one Rüdiger Wölk. It is signed, witnessed, and dated."

"But hardly legal?"

"The problem is it is. The signature is Henri-Pierre's."

"But it was done under duress."

"I know that. You know that. But what proof do we have? And I think at this point, Lieutenant Tatten-Brown, you know more than I do and that I have talked quite enough. Who is Rüdiger Wölk?"

"He was an official of the Berlin railways. In innocence, he ran passenger trains through Berlin's stations. In guilt, he oversaw the marshalling yards in the east where people were herded into cattle trucks and shipped to death camps."

"A Nazi?"

"Yes. He dispatched thousands to Auschwitz."

"Am I to assume that was Henri-Pierre's fate?"

"Treblinka is more likely. The journey from Bordeaux to Auschwitz would be unlikely to have taken him through Berlin. The Nazis tried not to draw any more attention to what they were doing than was necessary. A train to Treblinka would have passed through Berlin. They might have chosen that point to turn their prisoners off one train and onto another. It's not unheard of. That's when Monsieur Dukas met Wölk. He bribed Wölk, and Wölk cheated him."

Auguste removed his glasses, tilted his head back slightly, and pinched the top of his nose as though fighting back tears.

"How odd to still be shocked by what one has always known."

"I'm sorry to have to be the one to tell you."

"Is this man Wölk in British custody?"

"No. I'm afraid not."

"But you confiscated the certificate of ownership?"

Being Tatten-Brown was in itself a lie, but if he could get through this meeting and utter just one lie, Wilderness would be relieved.

"Yes," he lied.

"Then perhaps you should be its custodian, as I see no proper resolution to this matter."

Auguste slid the certificate back to Wilderness.

"I was thinking," Wilderness replied. "Of Monsieur Dukas's heirs. The boy who was wounded in '43 . . ."

"Was dead by '44. No, there are no heirs. Henri-Pierre was an only child. There are no cousins, no nephews. The Dukas family was originally German. From the Hamburg area I believe. But after the War of 1870 no one ever mentioned their origins again. There might be distant relatives in Germany. Who knows. Europe has lost its link with much of its own history. Every church—bombed by one side or the other, it really doesn't matter which—was a repository of record. Many of them are gone now. We may never get back the Europe we knew."

"But . . . supposing someone were to turn up . . . supposing someone were to present themselves as the owner of Monsieur Dukas's wine?"

"Clutching the document you have?"

"Yes."

"Then I would feel obliged to call the police. The wine is . . . what would be the word? . . . the wine is the *object* of a war crime. A crime

I cannot prove, and nor, I fear, can you . . . but we both know it happened. I would not set myself up as judge. I would leave that to others. And in order to do that my first recourse would be to call the police."

He drew the brown envelope back to his side of the desk, opened one of the drawers and dropped it in.

"It's past noon, Lieutenant. I have been preoccupied, but my manners have not yet deserted me. Would you care for a glass? Nineteen forty-five was our best vintage ever. A small harvest but a rich one. A gift from God, as though peace and freedom were not their own rewards. Far too young to drink now, of course, but I believe I can find a '34 that might convince you your journey was not entirely wasted."

VI

Walls & Bridges

Где говорят деньги, там молчит совесть.
Where money speaks, conscience is silent.

(Russian proverb)

§128

Pariser Platz, East Berlin: November 1965

"I didn't steal ten thousand bottles of claret, Yuri. I don't have ten thousand bottles of claret."

"Split hairs. You have the certificate of ownership—the one that Nazi gave you back in '47—and don't tell me you haven't. To have lost it or thrown it away would be stupid, and you're not stupid."

"Did you set this up just to get your hands on the booze?"

"No. But I knew Masefield was Burne-Jones's man. Just as you are Burne-Jones's man. If I offered to trade Masefield, who else would he have sent but you. And as you're here . . . let's talk wine."

"I'm giving you Liubimov. A far bigger fish than Masefield. Why on earth would I give you ten thousand bottles of claret?"

"Give? Did I say 'give'?"

"You're losing me here, Yuri."

"Find out the current market price of the wine and I will top it by ten per cent. And I pay cash. Dollars."

"Ten per cent?"

"I can sell on at better than that."

"Back home?"

Yuri nodded.

"You'll sell on to all your old cronies in Moscow? Every apparatchik in every rural dacha gets to drink first growth vintage claret?"

Yuri nodded.

"I take your point, even though you state it silently. Pearls, swine, Russians. And no, not perhaps every old crony. And not every apparatchik. I wouldn't waste a drop on Khrushchev. But it's enough to give me a more comfortable old age than I can expect as a hero of the Soviet Union. You can't eat medals. And I am looking to my old age, Joe. Think of it as my pension."

Wilderness wondered for a moment if Yuri was joking, and could find nothing in that walnut of a face to make him think he was.

Yuri eased his backside off the stone he'd been sitting on for the last five minutes.

"Now, let us walk a while. My arse has gone to sleep and we would appear to have Unter den Linden to ourselves."

"You mean you've had it closed off."

"If you got it, baby, flaunt it."

"Yuri. It's not going to be as straightforward as you think. Rüdiger Wölk—the Nazi—is still the owner of the wine. The Frenchman made it over to him. Under duress, but actually the paperwork was legal. The French acknowledged this, but say they regard Wölk as a war criminal and would call the cops if there were any attempt to claim or remove the wine."

"Hmm . . . as you English say, they sent you away with flea in your ear."

"Pretty much."

"And where is this Herr Wölk now?"

"I don't know. He'd only be in his mid-fifties, he may still be in his job, he might even be respectable or prosperous. I haven't given him a lot of thought over the last fifteen years."

"I have. Not the last fifteen years, but the last fifteen days. He left the Berlin railways in '61. We had, after all, made his job all but impossible. We chopped the railways up like yesterday's spaghetti. He went into private haulage, air freight and such, and, as you have suggested, prospered. He is a wealthy man. He has a villa out in Dahlem, an apartment in Charlottenburg, a summer home in the South of France, a Mercedes, a Maserati, one of your British mini-cars . . . and a chauffeur. I know. I asked Nell."

"Nell?"

"You think I would come to Berlin and not get in touch? Her mother was . . . the love of my life."

Wilderness let this go. He had no wish to discuss Nell's mother—a woman he'd never met—and had a temptation to ask about Nell that he would resist.

"So, Joe . . . who would you like the papers transferred to?"

"What?"

"We can snatch Wölk any time. Dahlem to the Glienicke . . . what? . . . fifteen minutes, twenty? A pleasant holiday in the DDR . . . just what he needs. And his signature on a transfer of ownership."

"You want me to sanction a kidnapping?"

"Do you really care what happens to Herr Wölk?"

"Yes."

"Then tell me what you want."

"If you snatch Wölk . . . it has to be seamless . . . no cock-ups . . ."

"We've done this before, Joe."

"And once he's signed . . . he vanishes without trace . . . no dumping him back on our side . . . no gulag . . . no shallow grave . . . dig it deep."

The brief silence that followed wasn't enough for thought, deep or shallow, it was simple acceptance.

Their walking had slowed down to a stop. Yuri looked at his watch.

"Come, let us lunch."

"You must be kidding. Lunch in East Berlin? I'd sooner have sex in Murmansk."

"Of course not. You think I eat the pig swill these fuckers call food? We go West. And by the way I have had sex in Murmansk. Pays to keep your socks on is all I will say.

"Pavel can bring the car round. You can drive, I don't drive any more."

§129

The car was a massive 3.5 litre ZIM-12.

"You know what I'd really like?"

"Yuri, I couldn't begin to guess."

"I too would like one of your British Minis. But I doubt I'd fit in one these days."

"OK. Where to?"

"The French restaurant on the Tegeler See. The Pavillon. I think the occasion calls for claret."

§130

Slow-roasted shin of pork that slipped gently off the bone. Mashed potatoes with garlic and parsley. Onions that swam in butter. A bottle of Château Mouton Rothschild '29.

Was Yuri toying with him? Asking for a bottle from the same chateau and year as those they had horse-traded for? Or had he merely ordered what he knew and liked?

Wilderness had never had Mouton Rothschild before. He'd never tasted anything like it. Dusty, dry, granular on the tongue.

"What do you think?"

Yes, he was toying with him.

"'S'OK."

Yuri smiled. An old man's uncontentious smile.

"Just OK? And we have ten thousand and eighty bottles?"

"Yep."

Where had he got the precise figure? He hadn't told him that.

"I am not a greedy man, Joe. Keep the eighty. You might get to like it a little better than OK."

Yes, he was definitely toying with him.

"Twenty per cent and you're on."

"Twenty per cent? Hmmmm . . . to think I knew you when you'd swap half a pound of coffee for a dozen eggs. Twenty per cent? Okey-dokey. Done."

§131

When Wilderness got back to the Adlon Masefield was sleeping. Wilderness let him.

He sat and picked up one of Masefield's magazines. A two-year-old copy of *Encounter*. Good bloody grief. Did Yuri have no idea who funded *Encounter* or was the CIA "house mag" just a random choice? He leafed through the bundle. *Newsweek*, the *Listener*, the *Economist*, the *Sunday Times* magazine. Ah, so it was just random. All these had in common was that they were in English and rather out of date. He settled on *Private Eye* instead—a magazine with a delightful capacity to ruin Burne-Jones's breakfast.

Half an hour passed. The sheer malice of Lord Gnome and the anarchic antics of Spiggy Topes had begun to pall. Wilderness stood over Masefield and took a second look. That he had aged was a given, but now he revised his opinion. Masefield looked ground down, and Wilderness wondered if that metaphor might not have a literal quality to it. It seemed as though bits of him had been worn away, that any second now raw bone might burst through parchment skin and he would resemble one of those partially unwrapped mummies they kept in the British Museum.

The eyes opened.

"That was . . . nice. I could get to like morphine."

"Don't. On the pension Her Majesty has lined up for you you won't be able to afford it."

Masefield swung his legs off the couch, shook his head like a wet dog.

"Have you been here long?"

"No."

"I think I owe you an apology."

"No. Just don't do that again. I don't mind you getting yourself shot, but I was in the line of fire too."

"All the same. I'm sorry. Is Bogusnik telling the truth?"

"About the Tsitnikova sisters? Oh yes. He wasn't in charge of the case."

"So he's not a killer?"

Such an odd remark . . . and a flashback so vivid it was unnerving. Yuri opening up with a Sten gun on a bunch of neo-Nazi teenagers—not one of whom survived.

"Oh, he can kill. I've seen him do it. All I'm saying is that he didn't kill the Tsitnikova sisters. He had nothing to do with what happened to them. If he had he would hardly feel the need to deny it.

"Now . . . listen to me, Geoffrey. All this is going to take a little longer than I told you."

"How long?"

"Dunno, but more than ten days."

Masefield pondered.

"I can handle that. After the Lubyanka I can probably handle anything. But I've read every damn magazine in this place. I know what colours are trendy in Hampstead, I've read reviews of concerts on the Third Programme I've never even heard, I understand that Albert Finney could be the biggest thing on the English stage since Laurence Olivier and I know what the *Economist* is predicting for 1959. In the Lubyanka I got so bored I even read the scraps of *Pravda* they gave us to wipe our arses on."

Wilderness couldn't help smiling at this.

"Point taken. Yuri isn't trying deprive you of anything. Just a limited imagination on his part. I'll be in London, tomorrow or the day after. I'll see you're sent books."

§132

It crossed Wilderness's mind to call Eddie from Delves's office on Kantstraße. And it also crossed his mind not to.

He wanted no record whatsoever of what happened next. No flapping ears, no hidden recorders. It could wait till he got home.

The following morning he sat quietly in the travel agent's, outside Delves's office—the same office in which the whole Masefield mess had splashed down four years ago.

About 11:00 a.m. Gretchen brought an envelope through from the front desk.

"This came for you. Big man, driving a ZIM."

She raised an eyebrow, almost mockingly.

Wilderness opened the envelope.

The deed with Wölk's signature, a witness named Ullmann, who had signed as a "Civil Law Notary Public of the DDR"—Wilderness had no idea whether Ullmann was real or not, nor did he care—and the assignee "John Wilfrid Holderness," described as "Representative of Her Britannic Majesty's Government."

The deed—done.

"Gretchen. Would you get me on a flight to London? This afternoon. Anything after two."

Delves emerged from his office.

"Joe. Didn't know you were here."

Wilderness could not warm to Delves, and knew it was just class prejudice.

"I'm not, Dickie. I am gone."

"London? I do envy you. I haven't had a London run yet this year." And aiming to overcome prejudice . . .

"Anything I can bring you, Dickie?"

"Tea bags, old man. Indian Prince. Get 'em at any branch of the Co-Op. And a jar of Marmite, if you'd be so kind."

§133

London

Wilderness called in at Queen Anne's Gate. The door to his office was ajar. It was his office. He was sure it was his office. It just didn't look like his office. It was neat, it was ordered. And a glass and stainless steel contraption sat on one of the bookshelves dripping hot coffee at the speed of glaciation.

"Touch nothing."

He turned. It was Alice Pettifer.

"This man is a saint. Edwin, patron saint of tidiness. I may never work for you again, Joe Holderness. If it turns out that he's also a dab hand at the ironing board I may marry him. I have met the superior being. All other men are *Untermenschen.*"

"And where is our Übermensch?"

"In with Burne-Jones."

"Does Alec know I'm back?"

"No. I'd sneak out now if I were you."

"I need to see Eddie."

"Then you may wait in here."

"What? It's still my bloody office."

"No it's not. You're a field agent again. We don't provide offices for field agents—we provide fields."

Wilderness sat in the visitor's chair, musing on the possibility that Alice and Rose Blair might be related. It felt oddly pleasing. To be sitting on the wrong side of the desk, and to know it was the right side.

A short, fat figure in the doorway.

"Don't even think about sloping off. He knows you're here."

"Good morning, Übermensch."

"Eh?"

"Never mind. It's you I need to see, Ed. Can you call by Perrin's Walk in the morning? We'll have breakfast and talk."

"We can talk now."

Wilderness looked around the room, making sure Eddie took in the gesture.

"Not in here we can't."

"Oh bloody 'eck. When?"

"Nine, nine thirty. Judy's usually out of the house by then."

"Burne-Jones wants to see you."

"OK."

Wilderness stood in Burne-Jones's doorway, pointedly not crossing the threshold. Burne-Jones had his head down scribbling in the margins. He glanced up and straight back down again.

"Everything go OK in Berlin?"

"Yep. We get our Geoffrey back as soon as I can get my ducks in a row."

"You saw Masefield?"

"Yes. A bit frayed at the edges. Perhaps a bit guilty about having confessed. He told me he told them nothing they didn't know already. I believe him. In his position I'd have given them Tom Radley in 3-D and stereo."

"Jolly good. And what did you make of General Bogusnik?"

Truth or dare?

"Just as you said. Another fat little Russian bloke. Put him in a homburg and a mac on top of Lenin's tomb on May Day and you wouldn't be able to tell him from the other half dozen fat little Russian blokes."

"Jolly good."

§134

Perrin's Walk, *London* NW3

"Bogusnik is Yuri."

"What?"

"Turns out it's his real name. Myshkin was his nom de guerre for the Stalin years."

"Amazing. I'd have put him down for dead or purged by now."

"Me too, but he's not. If I invoke cliché and say he's very much alive, it would be an exaggeration. He's very much half-alive. He's in poor health. Heart trouble, from the look of it. And he wants to retire."

"And swapping Masefield for Alleyn is his swan song?"

"Almost. He also wants the claret you and I stumbled across in '47."

"What? As part of the deal?"

"Yep. No booze, no Geoffrey."

"How did he find out? You never told him, I never told him."

"That was the first question that ran through my mind."

"But you asked him?"

"No. I didn't need to. It was Nell. Yuri knew how many bottles there were, even teased me by serving up a Mouton Rothschild '29 at lunch. It was Nell."

"Could have been Erno."

"No it couldn't. It was Nell. Yuri has kept in touch with Nell, and only Nell, having a memory like an elephant, could have readily told him how many bottles, even down to the chateaux and the vintage."

"Might she have told Frank?"

"Nell wouldn't give Frank Spoleto the time of day. Frank knew nothing; Frank knows nothing. He got Wölk reinstated and that was an end of it.

"I still have the certificate of ownership. I dug it out last night. You're not the only one who can file things in an orderly manner. The merchants in Bordeaux have a transfer in Wölk's name dated 1943. And I have a transfer in my name dated 1965. Wölk signed it over. And once he did, what Yuri is asking for became doable. It'll take a bit of fixing . . . I'll need French cooperation . . . but it's doable."

"How did you get Wölk's signature?"

"I left that to Yuri."

"And what does Burne-Jones say to all this?"

"Nothing. I haven't told him. He doesn't need to know. And he won't know. It's why we're meeting here."

"What you said about Wölk . . . you know getting his signature on the transfer . . . you couldn't have faked that? You didn't need to involve Yuri. Find a signature in records. Erno copies it . . . Bob's your uncle."

"My way is better."

"Why alert Wölk to what we're doing? He could be trouble."

"Oh no. Herr Wölk will never trouble anyone again."

Eddie let this one sink in.

"You're letting Yuri have him."

"No, I'm letting Yuri bury him."

"You had Wölk killed? God, Joe. There are times I think I don't know you at all."

"Me neither."

Judy had appeared at the foot of the staircase. A staring, silent baby on her arm.

"The nanny's running late. Eddie, you take Molly. Joe, if you'd bring the prima donna down."

She thrust the child at Eddie. He grasped Molly with unease and reluctance.

"Don't worry, she's just been on the potty. She'll be dry and odour-free for a while now. Joe!"

As soon as Wilderness had gone up to the nursery, Judy sat opposite Eddie and said, "I'm due at work in less than an hour, so I'll be quick. How long have we known each other, Eddie?"

"Since I came down from Birmingham in '56."

"And I like to think that in all that time you have never lied to me."

"I haven't. I was just an ordinary copper until last week. There was nowt to lie about."

"Good. Now . . . are you and my husband up to anything illegal?"

"Judy, he'll be down in a soddin' second!"

"No he won't. I left him to put a nappy on Joan. He's utterly cack-handed at it. He'll be five minutes at least. So . . . tell me."

"I don't bloody know. I wish to God I did."

§135

Wilderness sat with Joan on his knee.

She burbled, slipped in the odd, comprehensible word from time to time.

Eddie sat with Molly on his knee.

She farted, stared across the table at her father with unrestrained malice.

"Joe, what's my part in all this?"

"Easy. Remember that French bloke who was with their Intelligence when we were in Berlin—Didier Pascaud?"

"I cleaned him out at pontoon more times that I can count. Lousy card player."

"Let's hope he doesn't bear a grudge. He's with the Sûreté now, the national cops. If this is to work we need a copper on our side. If anyone threatens to call the cops . . . well, we'll have our own."

"Like having a Special Branch copper with us?"

"A bit like that, but mostly not."

"Good, 'cos we both know what a bunch of wankers they are."

"I've dealt with Didier a few times over the last couple of years. So, first . . . you get him on the phone and make a formal MI6 request for assistance."

"How much can I tell him?"

"Everything."

"Except that you killed Wölk."

"Drop it, Ed."

"I love the way you prefaced all this with the word 'easy.'"

"Second . . . you buy a truck."

"A truck? What with?"

"Petty cash. Give the receipt to Alice."

"How big a truck?"

"Big enough for ten thousand bottles of wine."

"About thirty-two cubic yards, then."

"Did you just do that in your head?"

"I may be cabbage-looking, but . . . it's a biggish truck. Ten thousand bottles of wine, that's . . . about eight tons. Biggish, but not too big."

"We'll take it in turns to drive."

"What?"

"I told you. I can't do this on my own."

"When did you tell me that?"

"I'm telling you now."

"I'm a desk jockey, Joe. Not a field agent. You got me in so you didn't have to do the bloody paperwork."

"Speaking of which. Third . . . get the truck listed as a diplomatic bag. All the right papers, all the right rubber stamps. We have two . . . or is it three . . . frontiers to cross."

"Joe . . . I'm lost. What the fuck are we up to?"

"We're driving ten thousand bottles of wine from Bordeaux to East Berlin, under diplomatic immunity. I checked—a diplomatic bag is whatever a diplomat says it is . . . brown envelope, sack of dirty laundry . . . truck full of wine. All the same thing. They may not search; they may not confiscate."

A louder than usual baby-fart punctuated their conversation.

"Your daughter and you—you both just crapped on me."

§136

"What next?"

"Who me? It appears I'm on nanny duty today. I'll go down to the Scrubs tomorrow morning and get Alleyn out. Masefield is in what passes for the lap of luxury in East Berlin. He's at the Adlon. I don't see why they shouldn't have parity. Let's see if we can't make his last few days in England a little more comfortable. Then he can go back to Mother Russia and tell her what a decent set of chaps we are."

"Y'know . . . that sentence was so loaded with sarcasm I can't tell whether you feel sorry for Alleyn or not."

"'Not' would be the answer. Can you let the Scrubs know we're springing him and let me have whatever piece of paper I'll need?"

§137

Under the illusion that she might thus have his attention, Judy was in the habit of saving important matters until the post-coital moment.

"What are you and Eddie up to?"

"The job. Just doing what your old man pays us to do."

"Then why do I get the feeling there's something a bit dodgy going down?"

"Because you're a nosy, posh tart who's never satisfied."

"This posh tart could rat this cockney oik out to her dad."

"But she won't."

Up on one elbow now, all semblance that it was just sticky-time word-fun evaporating as she met him eye to eye.

"Seriously, Wilderness. You slipped back into the field. I took my eye off your balls and you slipped back into the field. That's not what I wanted. Ever. We have two daughters. We have no money problems.

We should be happy as a pair of nesting squirrels, cocooned in fur, surrounded by hazelnuts . . . happy in the hollow tree of marriage, sensuous and satisfied in the sunlit meadow known as the rest of our fucking lives."

Wilderness said nothing. Admired her turn of phrase, but said nothing.

§138

Wilderness met Alleyn at the main gate of Wormwood Scrubs with a black Civil Service Humber Snipe driven by Nerk from Special Branch, who also doubled as guard. Combining the two jobs seemed to put him out of sorts as though one task or the other were beneath him. Wilderness tried to speak to him as little as possible. He hated the Branch. There seemed to be only two qualifications for joining—size of feet and lack of imagination.

Alleyn emerged, a brown paper parcel bound up with white string tucked under his arm. A moth-eaten suit clinging to his body.

Neither spoke until the gates clanged shut.

"You don't know how good that sounds, Joe."

"Believe me, Bernard, I do. What's that awful smell?"

"Mothballs, I believe. Rather ineffective mothballs."

In the back of the Humber, Wilderness wound down a window.

Alleyn said, "I do have a better suit."

"You do?"

"At my tailors. Foulkes and Fransham in Savile Row. They've been holding it for me since 1959."

"Won't that stink too?"

"Good Lord no. No mothballs. It'll be in one of their camphor-lined rooms."

Wilderness spoke to Nerk.

"Take us through the West End, would you. Savile Row."

"Thank you."

"Why am I not surprised?"

"Surprised at what?"

"That you have a Savile Row tailor and that they didn't shut your account when you got nicked."

"Oh, they wouldn't, would they? I mean to say . . . as long as the bills are paid . . ."

"Don't worry, Bernard. Guy Burgess's tailor only closed his account when the bugger died. I have every confidence they'll ship anything you want to Moscow."

"I was hoping it might be ready now. I mean . . . they've had six years."

$139

"I am told I have lost weight."

"Once again, I'm not surprised."

"No . . . I mean they'd like an hour or so to take in the waist."

"Then we'll grab a coffee somewhere."

"No . . . I'm needed here."

"OK. Then I'll grab a coffee and Nerk from Special Branch can stay on the door."

"I won't run, you know."

"Bernard, you have nowhere to run to."

"But if you're going out, perhaps one last favour . . . there's a book I'd like . . . if you're going anywhere near Hatchards."

"That's not a favour, that's a cheek."

"Just something I read in the prison library. A memory I'd like to keep. A souvenir of England, I suppose."

"What?"

"I'm sorry?"

"What's the book?"

"Oh . . . Betjeman's autobiography, *Summoned by Bells.*"

"That's how you want to remember England? An England neither you nor I have ever known."

"Indulge me, Joe. And don't worry about the money. I have an account there too."

In Hatchards Wilderness picked out half a dozen Penguin and Pan paperbacks, not quite at random—Graham Greene, Kingsley Amis, Alan Sillitoe, John le Carré—charged them to Alleyn's account and had them mailed to Masefield. Feeling wicked he signed the card, "Happy days. Your old pal, Leonid."

Then he sat in a caff in Swallow Street. *Summoned by Bells* was a quick read. By the time he got back to Foulkes and Fransham he'd read most of it. This wasn't an England he'd want as his "souvenir." For all the beauty recalled, for all the musical measure of his blank verse it seemed to Wilderness that it was an England, a childhood, that Betjeman had hated, a portrait of a nation rooted in cruelty—not the savage cruelty to be found in Tolstoy or Dostoevsky . . . a very English petty cruelty. It was Betjeman's "Damn You England," a title John Osborne had given to an open letter in the *Tribune* a few years back. Burne-Jones had all but boiled over in anger when Judy had read it out to him over breakfast.

But Alleyn beamed with delight as Wilderness handed him the book, folded back the dust jacket and traced out the bells stamped in the boards with his fingertips.

"You don't know what this means to me," he said.

"You're quite right," Wilderness replied. "I don't."

$140

The suit fitted beautifully. Alleyn looked svelte. Looked younger. Smiling at his own reflection in the full-length mirror.

Wilderness had bespoke suits. But he'd never been able to afford Savile Row. He had his made by Jakobson and Hummel in the Mile End Road—cheaper than Savile Row. Better than Savile Row.

"A million dollars. That's the cliché isn't it?"

"Eh?"

"I feel like a million dollars."

"I wouldn't know, Bernard. When I get my hands on my first million I'll let you know."

Special Branch Nerk ground out his cigarette on the York paving and made a passable attempt at standing up straight.

Wilderness sat in the back of the car with Alleyn once more, leaned over the seat and told Nerk, "The Belsize Park house."

Alleyn looked puzzled, turned his head as Wilderness sank back in his seat.

"Not Heathrow, then?"

"Sorry, Bernard. Not just yet."

Only when the Humber climbed up Haverstock Hill did the words "Belsize" and "Park" seem to register fully with Alleyn.

"Oh," he said. "Just another prison."

"No. A better prison. No goons. Your own lavatory. A morning paper. Decent food."

Standing on the pavement Alleyn said, "You know MI5 held me here in '59?"

"No. Does it matter? We just borrowed it from Five. They won't be troubling you."

"Then why not simply leave me in the Scrubs?"

"Because I choose not to. You can go back to the Scrubs if you wish. I'm not looking for gratitude."

"It wasn't a complaint, Joe. I was just curious."

It was the same room. Redecorated in the interim, a tasteful, mute magnolia, and the boarded-up windows unboarded, if still locked, southern sunlight pouring in. More light than he'd seen in years, as though saved up and released in a torrent. Just for him.

"You choose?"

"I'm not going to debate this with you, Bernard. You'll be here until I can get you to Berlin."

"How long?"

"A couple of weeks. No more, I would hope, but certainly no less. There are things I have to do."

"Such as."

"Don't ask."

"Then perhaps a last favour."

"Betjeman was your last favour."

"But I shall have read the book by nightfall."

"What is it you want?"

"We passed a library on the hill, perhaps you would be so kind as to enrol me."

Alone. Wilderness gone. Nerk bumbling with a teapot in the kitchen below. Alleyn sat on the bed and watched the sunlight play across the toes of his shiny black beetle-crushers.

It was just another prison. It was a prison with a double bed. A bedside radio-cum-teasmaid. It was just another prison. And it felt so oddly like coming home.

He kicked off his shoes, swung his legs up on to the bed. His bedroom—their bedroom—in Cholmondeley Road had faced south, southeast. One of the delights, perhaps the greatest delight, of a Saturday summer morning was to draw back the curtains and watch the sunbeams dancing in Kate's hair while she slept. A Titian red that age seemed not to dim. He'd stare as long as he wished, or as long as he could, until the next greatest delight, his two daughters, burst in to wake her.

Now he slept.

Alone.

Dreamt.

Not of Moscow.

But of Highgate.

Of Titian hair and sunbeams.

From the kitchen a waft of PG tips penetrated his reverie.

But failed to wake him.

§141

Alice Pettifer called Wilderness.

"Are you ever showing up for work?"

"As you said, Alice, I don't have an office, so I am working at the kitchen table. I have Joan and Molly in high chairs, so I believe we have enough for a quorum and in the event of an international crisis Molly can push the nuclear button."

"Ha bloody ha. Joe, I am looking at a chit for five hundred quid from Saint Edwin. He wants to buy a 1960 Mercedes truck out of petty cash!"

"Give him the money, Alice."

"I can't do that unless Burne-Jones signs off on it."

"He won't thank you for telling him, you know that. He's not interested in process or strategy; he's interested in results. The last thing he wants is a field agent bringing him queries about petty cash. Just stick it in front of him and let him sign it. He won't even bother to read it."

"Will I ever see the five hundred pounds again?"

"If all goes well, Ed can sell the truck when the job's done."

"Is this *really* necessary?"

"Do we *really* want Masefield back? If it were up to me . . ."

"OK, OK."

§142

Swift Eddie called Wilderness.

"Got the truck."

"Good man."

"I have a bit of a problem."

"Which is?"

"Didier Pascaud insists on talking to you in person."

"I'll give him a call."

"No. I mean in person. Face-to-face."

"Then I'll get on a ferry later today. Pay, pack, and follow."

"Eh?"

"Sir Richard Burton, our man in Damascus in God knows when. Left that message for his wife, the redoubtable Isabel, when he was recalled to London."

"What does that make me? The redoubtable Eddie?"

§143

Rue Perrée, Paris

Wilderness met Didier Pascaud in a bar in the Third Arrondissement.

"I assume that you want anything you say off the record?"

"And so do you. Joe . . . I have done some strange things for you over the years . . ."

"And I like to think I have been able to return the favour from time to time."

"But this is the strangest."

"I'm listening, Didier."

"Eddie assures me all this is legal."

"It is. I would not ask you to present yourself in your official capacity if it weren't."

"But . . ."

"But?"

"I don't know how to phrase this precisely in any language. There is honour at stake."

Wilderness just about had a handle on honour. The English version. The French version was close to unfathomable. It ran so deep, so deep.

"The scars of war are still visible in my country. The English may trumpet Dunkirk and D-Day as great victories . . ."

"Actually, Didier, Dunkirk was a great defeat."

"Bear with me . . . but they do not have to contend with pervasive notions like occupation and collaboration. To the English, war crimes happened on another continent—this one. We do not fight the Germans any longer, but we are still fighting ourselves."

"OK. I'm with you now. The wine . . . Dukas . . . Wölk . . . Treblinka."

"Yes. All of those things. And there's something about the fact that it all revolves around wine—my country's greatest asset . . . the soul of France is in her wine—that makes it all so . . . so questionable."

"Questionable? So what's the question?"

"Eddie clammed up on me when I asked about this Nazi, this man Wölk."

"He's being discreet. Possibly too discreet. What do you want to know?"

"That there is a possibility of some kind of justice in all this. That in giving the Russians ten thousand bottles of claret to get your man Masefield back we are not compounding an ancient crime of the occupation but bringing it to some sort of resolution."

"Dukas is dead. We can't do a damn thing for him. And he has no family."

"Wölk."

"Wölk got justice."

"He's dead?"

"Oh yes."

"No trial, no public remorse?"

"And no beating chests, no hair pulled out, no wailing women, no Greek chorus. He's dead, Didier. I insisted on that. I wouldn't be surprised if Yuri Myshkin pulled the trigger personally."

A pause. Didier cradling his untouched glass of claret. Warming on the palm of his hand.

"Then, let's drink to that. One less Nazi in the world. And let's drink to Yuri . . . an old friend, an old bastard I had not thought of in almost twenty years."

A drink, another drink, and a third.

Then Wilderness said, "I'm expected in Bordeaux the day after tomorrow. I've briefed them, but there are bound to be questions."

"Don't worry," Didier replied. "I'll be there."

§144

Paris to Bordeaux was an arduous drive.

Six hundred kilometres.

A truck with a top speed of sixty miles per hour and roads with a top speed of less.

They took it in turns.

Half an hour out of Bordeaux, Wilderness was at the wheel.

"You know," Eddie said, seemingly apropos of nothing. "I'm surprised there was no room to bargain."

"Not quite with you there, Ed."

"I mean . . . no deal to be done. OK, we get Masefield, but Yuri gets everything he wants. He gets Alleyn and we give him ten thousand bottles of wine."

In for a penny . . .

"Not give. He's paying us a hundred and fifty thousand dollars."

"What?"

"Current market value of the wine is just under a hundred and fifty thousand dollars. I know. I checked with Christie's. An average of £5 7s 6d a bottle. That's roughly fifteen dollars. More than a tenfold increase on the 1934 price. Yuri will pay us the market price plus twenty per cent. Call it a hundred and seventy thousand dollars. That's eighty-five thousand each."

"Stop the truck!"

"Eh?"

"Pull over. Pull over right now!"

Wilderness braked and swung the truck into a lay-by with a screech and a spurt of gravel.

Eddie leapt a little fat bloke's leap to the ground, plumping down.

Wilderness had little choice but to follow.

"You wait till we're ten miles from Bordeaux to tell me it's all a fuckin' scam? And then you let rip with your statistics, to dazzle me. Your missis was right. It's in the things you don't say . . . it's in the fuckin' spaces between what you do say . . . It's a scam!"

"No. It's not."

"Is this why Burne-Jones isn't supposed to know?"

"Don't be stupid, Ed."

"Does Didier know?"

"No. Didier would not understand. It's not a scam. But Didier would not understand. He's a policeman."

"Why didn't you tell me all this back in England?"

"Because you might not have set foot outside England. Ed, it's not a scam. The beauty of it is it's all legit. Wölk was the legal owner. He made the certificate over to me."

"Only because you had Yuri put a gun to his head."

"You think he'd have signed any other way?"

"Put a gun to his head and pulled the bloody trigger!"

"Telling me that won't make me care, Ed. I told you. He had it coming. Rough justice, but justice all the same."

"Vengeance, more like."

"Vengeance and justice are not always the same thing, but they can be . . . sometimes."

"And the French bloke? Henri whatsisname. Where's the justice for him?"

"There is none. No more than there was in 1947. He was murdered. We just took out his killer. I cannot pretend that is justice for Henri-Pierre. Justice might have been coming home to find his sons alive and his cache intact. We can't give him that. No heirs. No living relatives. We've known that for nearly twenty years. But that's no reason to give his wine to the French government or to our government. Where's the justice in that? They're just taxmen. Little grey men in suits. And without the wine we can't give justice to our little grey man—Geoffrey Masefield. That there's profit in it is a pleasing coincidence. Ed, it's seventy-five grand. Seventy-five grand that belongs to no one. If it's a scam, it is the sweetest scam ever. No one gets hurt, no one gets robbed. And we walk away with eighty-five grand each. Are you really going to turn that down?"

If Ed could have squirmed like a schoolboy caught scrumping he would have. His face, so plump, so amiable, was twisted into something Wilderness took for grief—grief at the death of his conscience.

"I can't bloody afford to," he said softly. "You really are the Satan I should put behind me, aren't you? Unlike you I spent the entire war in the army—not shinning up drainpipes and nicking women's jewellery. Then a tour of duty in Intelligence in Berlin, from there to the Birmingham Police. I'd still be there; I'd still be a bloody constable in hobnail boots if Troy hadn't rescued me. I'd never have made sergeant. And other ranks' pay is bugger all."

"And now you're paid on par with a Chief Inspector. And that's not down to Troy. That was me. Ed, when will we ever get our hands on a pot like this again?"

"Dunno. Every time we got close to it in the old days it seemed to slip though our fingers."

"Not this time."

"What's different? It's you, me, and Yuri . . . again!"

"What's different? No Frank. That's what's different. Ed, do what Yuri does. Look upon it as your pension."

"Pension?"

"That's what he's calling it. He said, 'you can't eat medals.'"

"We haven't got any fuckin' medals! If medals were grub we'd still be starving.

"Joe, I've had nearly twenty years of living within the law. Nine of them as a Scotland Yard copper. Since 1956 the dodgiest thing I've done is place the odd bet with a kerbside bookie. Now . . . it feels too much like the old days. We're *Schieber*s again. You say we're operating within the law, we have diplomatic passports and the biggest diplomatic bag in history . . . so why do I feel like a *Schieber*?"

"Get back in the truck and drive, Ed. You need to take your mind off things."

§145

Lawton Frères Wine Merchants, Quai de Bacalan, Bordeaux

Alexandre Lawton was, at first sight, nothing like his grandfather, Auguste. Thirty at most, as tall as Wilderness, with thick black hair combed back from his forehead and deep blue eyes. But his voice was the same, a voice that Wilderness could never imagine raised in anger—and his clothes were as elegant and as expensive. Just one of his cuff links would cost Wilderness a month's pay.

Pascaud made the introductions and he and Wilderness held up their identity cards. Wilderness handed him the certificate of ownership and the deed of transfer.

Alexandre barely glanced at their ID. Instead he read the documents, and spread them out on his desk—the same desk Wilderness had sat at before in 1947. He placed the original deed of transfer bearing Henri-Pierre Dukas's signature next them—like three cards dealt from the shoe in a baccarat game.

Unlike his grandfather he chose to speak in French.

"This appears to be all in order. But you will understand if I say I am baffled. You will understand if I say I am disturbed. The war is back. There are ghosts in the room. The war was my childhood. And to a child growing up in the war the war was total; it was everything. And just when I thought I might have escaped it . . . abroad in the sixties, an unimaginable decade . . . a new France . . . a new Europe . . . a new man when I look in the mirror rather than a frightened child . . . you gentlemen unearth it on my own doorstep. Burrow like rabbits into the depths of our *caves*. I say again, there are ghosts in the room. And one of them is Henri-Pierre Dukas. A man I scarcely knew. A man who vanished into *nuit et brouillard* when I was seven."

Wilderness thought he understood the musing, and he couldn't hear a question. Hadn't Nell said something almost the same twenty years ago? That Berlin was a city of ghosts? He wasn't sure Pascaud had understood, but they'd agreed—he would stick to statements of fact, and if the arrangement did not proceed to a simple, quick compliance . . . Wilderness would do the talking.

"I can't pretend that this does anything for Monsieur Dukas or his family. Monsieur Dukas was a victim of the war. You should look upon Geoffrey Masefield as a victim of another war. A hapless victim who got caught in the crossfire, in a country he should never have set foot in, doing a job he was poorly equipped to do. We can save Masefield. It would be nice to be able to tell you that we're all doing this for France but we're not. We're not even doing it for the West or the Allies or NATO. We're doing it for one man. And if we don't he'll become a living ghost. The Lubyanka is full of ghosts."

Alexandre wasn't looking at Wilderness as he spoke. He was twirling the certificate of ownership around on the leather top of his desk like a slow Catherine wheel.

He stopped. Looked from Pascaud to Wilderness.

"Had you said *'pour la patrie,'* Mr. Holderness, there might have been a grain of poetry in it. 'For NATO' would have had none—none whatsoever. For the man? Well . . . I hope he's worth it. Let us lay this ghost to rest."

So saying, he placed both hands on the desk, spread his fingers and gently slid all three documents towards Wilderness.

"Shall we say nine thirty tomorrow morning? I am ready."

§146

At 7:30 a waiter in the Hotel Arouet showed Wilderness and Eddie to their table.

A large man was already seated, messily eating a large breakfast and scattering croissant crumbs across the tablecloth with the self-confidence of one who considers himself beyond reproach.

"Sit down, boys, the coffee's getting cold."

"Oh bloody Norah," said Eddie.

"Good morning to you too, shortstuff."

Wilderness said nothing.

"Whassamatter, kid? Cat gotcha tongue?"

Wilderness slid into the banquette.

"What are you doing here, Frank?"

"What am I doing here? Jeez but that is rich. Do you honestly think you guys could pull a stunt like this and me not get to hear about it?"

Eddie turned his back and started to walk away.

Wilderness said, "Ed! Half a mo. Just take a seat."

Eddie froze.

"Ed. Please. Just sit down."

Eddie pulled out the spare chair and sat—silent in red rage. Frank was stabbing the air with his fork now, globs of scrambled egg launching into space.

"Did you think you could call the Sûreté and me not get to hear about it? Do you think you can strike a bargain with Yuri Myshkin and me not get to hear about it? Do you think you can set up a hundred-seventy-thousand-dollar scam and not fucking include me? You pair of cocksuckers!"

The briefest hiatus—as though Frank had finally arrived at the insult he had intended all along. His punch line. He shovelled in more eggs, striving to combine his own indulgence with a gaze of unflagging reprimand for Wilderness.

Eddie reached out. Put his thumb under the saucer of Frank's café au lait and flipped it into his lap.

Frank spat egg.

"Jeezus H. Christ!"

"You want to walk back into Joe's life, that's his problem, but I'll be fucked if you're walking back into mine after eighteen Frank-free years."

And he was gone.

"What the fuck . . . the little momzer damn near scalded my balls!"

Wilderness beckoned to a hovering waiter.

"Deux cafés au lait, s'il vous plait."

Tossed Frank a napkin.

"You asked for that. Now, mop up and tell me what you want."

"Jeez, jeez, jeez . . . who would ever have thought that worm would turn."

"Less of the worm. Are you done? Are you dry?"

"No, you dumb fuck. I'm soggy."

"Just be grateful it wasn't me."

"What's that supposed to mean?"

"Just tell me what you want."

Another pause for discretion as the waiter set coffee in front of them. When he asked if Frank needed any help, Frank thrust the sodden napkin at him and waved him away.

"What do I want? I want the old deal. Full partnership. Fifty-five grand. Not a penny more, not a—"

"OK. We both know where that cliché leads. What makes you think I'd give you so much as a nickel?"

"Because I can think of a couple of ways I could really fuck this up for you if you don't."

Wilderness could think of half a dozen ways Frank could fuck this up.

"All right. But you'll have to earn it."

§147

Frank was still belching up his breakfast when Eddie backed the truck up to the Lawton Frères warehouse.

It didn't surprise him in the least not to see Alexandre—he'd said his piece. Instead two men in brown warehouse coats, one clutching a clipboard with a receipt for Wilderness to sign: "Her Britannic Majesty's Representative"—he'd never be able to see himself as such. And a third at the wheel of a forklift—one hundred and twenty-five cases to a pallet.

"Frank. Up top."

"What?"

"Get up inside and stack. There are nine hundred cases and they're not going to stack themselves."

"Are you kidding?"

"In Berlin you never lifted a thing. You never got your hands dirty. You want a full partnership? You get your hands dirty. So stack or fuck up the deal in whatever way your twisted imagination can come up with. There are no passengers on this trip."

"I don't fucking believe this."

"Believe!"

"OK. OK. I can muck in with the rest of the guys. Just fuckin' watch me."

He slipped off his jacket, tossed it at Eddie, who let it fall to the ground. Then he got a knee above the tailgate . . . and then he got stuck.

"Would it be beyond the two of you to give a guy a shove here?"

Wilderness thrust at Frank's backside and sent him flying into the truck head first, to roll on his back.

"Sheeit!"

"You ready up there, Frank?"

Wilderness could not see Frank's face. From inside the truck his voice sounded both angry and plaintive.

"You gonna make me eat shit, Joe? Is that it?"

"If at all possible, Frank, at every turn."

§148

"OK, Joe. You've had your fun. You've twisted Frank's balls. He's so keen to get a cut right now you could roll him in dog shit and he'd come up smiling. But it's not going to last, is it? Frank hefting wine, Frank hefting anything is a one-off novelty. Any minute now he'll revert to being the Frank we all know and hate."

"I've other uses for him."

"Like what?"

"We're in a truck, a fully laden truck. He's in a Citroën DS. He can move much faster than we can. He can be at the Helmstedt border crossing hours ahead of us."

"So?"

"Do you know how many vehicles use that crossing every day? Do you have any idea how many levels of inspection there are?"

"I'm just a simple copper, Joe. Or I was till two weeks ago, and right now I wish I was again. No, of course I don't bloody know!"

"Four thousand eight hundred vehicles a day go down the autobahn. In order to do that, they have to pass West German Customs, West German Police, the Frontier Defence Force, the British Army and the British Frontier Service. That's just our side. On the DDR side—"

"OK. OK. I get it. What's Frank's part in all that?"

"To have them all prepared, briefed by a smooth-talking CIA con artist may save a lot of explanations. I don't want to get stuck in a queue while our own side argues the toss about our diplomatic immunity. Look at it this way. He's an unscrupulous bastard, but right now he's our unscrupulous bastard. An unscrupulous bastard with CIA credentials. Cuts a hell of a lot more mustard with the Germans than we do."

"And when he's smoothed the way for us, charmed the German sparrows off the German trees . . . can I kill him?"

"Only if you have a complete character bypass."

Eddie sighed, one last burst of defiance surfacing.

"Can I go home, now?"

"Knock it off, Ed."

"No Frank, you said. It was music to my ears. Yet here he is. How did he find out?"

"I don't know. Does it matter?"

$149

It was twelve hours to Wiesbaden.

Eddie was close to silent the whole way, taking the driving over from Wilderness at two-hour intervals with scarcely a comment.

Wilderness began to wish he'd specified "a truck with a radio."

On long bus rides when he was a boy his grandfather had played a time-wasting game with him, usually rendered pointless by the old man's inability to spell—"I spy with my little eye, something beginning with . . . "

He could not think of a pastime less appropriate to the occasion. And if he made a joke of it, penny-to-a-quid Eddie would not find it funny. He began to wonder whether the sole result of the venture so far had not been the death of Eddie's sense of humour. That and the loss of twenty-five thousand dollars each to the deeply undeserving cause that was Frank Spoleto.

$150

Hotel Dannoritzer, Wiesbaden

Frank did not appear at dinner.

Wilderness walked around the car park. There were three Citroën DSs, none of them Frank's. If he'd had enough and buggered off Wilderness wasn't going to look for him and he wasn't going to care.

But he was there at breakfast—just like the day before, sat at the table ahead of them, at least one course and a messy tablecloth ahead of them.

"Ed—you get clumsy with the coffee, so help me I will knock your bloody block off."

Frank loved English slang. Occasionally he got it right.

Eddie blew him a raspberry.

Wilderness said, "Where were you?"

"I had business. You two clowns are not the only irons I have in the pot."

"By all means. Mix your metaphors."

"What?"

"So you're working another scam. I don't care. Just get to Helmstedt before we do."

"Don't worry. I'll be there. Gimme an hour before you set off. I have to nip into Bonn."

"Nip?"

"Sure. As in 'nippy.' It's not much more than an hour from here. I have a couple of things to take care of and then I'll scoot on over to Helmstedt and I'll be all yours."

"Company things or Madison Avenue things?"

Frank grinned, munched on his toast, and grinned.

"What makes you think they're not the same thing?"

When he'd knocked back another cup of coffee and left, Eddie said, "Nip . . . scoot . . . ?"

"What's your point, Ed?"

"It's the vocabulary of the nursery. They're words designed to convey innocence, to fool us into thinking he's not chock-a-block with dodgy schemes and ulterior motives."

"I don't care. He can be robbing the Federal Bank, assassinating Adenauer. If he shows up at Helmstedt he shows up and that's all there is to it.

"And if he double-crosses us this time, you won't have to worry about shooting him. I'll shoot him myself."

"I was joking."

"I wasn't."

§151

Helmstedt was beginning to sprawl as Checkpoint Charlie had sprawled, but in a different way.

Everything on the British side looked as temporary as it had in the forties—a deliberate avoidance of steel and concrete, of anything that might suggest that this crossing—Grenzübergang Helmstedt–Marienborn—and the division of Germany might be permanent. Hence a string of wooden huts offering the illusion that the most heavily guarded frontier in the world was no more substantial than a World War II RAF base abandoned to the grass and weeds of the home counties.

The merest glance across the border gave the lie to that: minefields, tank traps, concrete posts, barbed wire, the denaturised Death Strip, watchtowers to watch—and watchtowers to watch the watchers.

Eddie slowed the truck at the first sign.

ALLIED CHECKPOINT
ALPHA
POSTE DE CONTRÔLE ALLIÉ

"I've got one question. Where is he?"

"Count your blessings and swing left, Ed. Swing left. Military and diplomatic lane. Or we'll be stuck in a German visitors' queue for hours."

As they drove past a motionless line of Volkswagens, BMWs—every make the Bundesrepublik had to offer—a British Land Rover was speeding towards them. It swung sideways across them. Leaving rubber stripes across the tarmac.

A man in what looked like Royal Navy uniform leapt out. Naval uniform, but not quite—something odd about it. An officer of the British Frontier Service, rank indeterminate.

He took in the UK number plate and appeared to be reading whatever was written on the front of the truck. Wilderness had no idea what that might be. He hadn't even noticed. And if he'd noticed he hadn't remembered. It was just an anonymous second-hand truck.

He opened the door and leapt down.

"Are you blind? Military and diplomatic only. Not bloody plumbers!"
The officer pointed to the script above the windscreen.

N°⁵· Fountain & Sons
Plumbers' Merchants
Guildford, Surrey

Oh shit.
"We're not plumbers."
"I don't care if you're Thomas Crapper himself. Get back in line."
"We're . . ."
Wilderness handed him his identity card and the four pages of government guff covering the diplomatic bag.
The officer shifted away slightly, read it with his back to Wilderness and, still turning pages, said, "Oh God. I hate it when you bastards turn up."
A Citroën DS roared past the truck and screeched to a halt next to the Land Rover.
"Then here's a bigger bastard for you."
Frank stepped out of the car. All suit and smiles.
"Hi there. Good to meet you."
Good manners led the officer into a trap. Once gripped in a handshake, Frank would not let him go and steered him gently away from the truck into the pretence of shared confidences. He flashed his ID so quickly it was back in his pocket before the man could even react.
"We'd greatly appreciate your cooperation here. Joint operation and we'd like to expedite. You understand? Expedite."
"Joint with whom?"
"Your people, my people . . . no names, no pack drill, no cops, no customs."
The officer flourished the paperwork.
"It says 'diplomatic bag.' Where is it?"
Frank pointed to the truck, an open palm, an inclusive sweep of the arm.
"You're looking at it."
"What? The plumber's truck?"
"Sure . . . now if we could just move along—"

"The truck? You can't stand there and tell me that that truck is a diplomatic bag?"

Frank gestured at Wilderness.

"Joe?"

"I'm the diplomat. It's a diplomatic bag. I could bring the *Queen Mary* through here on a low-loader and declare it a diplomatic bag if I so chose."

"What's in it?"

"Can't tell you that."

"Where's it going?"

"Can't tell you that either."

"You do realise that whatever I do or say to 'expedite,' that lot . . . "

He pointed over his shoulder to the East.

"That lot will ask you the same bloody questions and won't be fobbed off by the answers you're giving me! Try telling them 'no cops, no customs'!"

Frank said, "We'll take our chances. And we are, most sincerely, very grateful for your cooperation."

"OK. Don't say I didn't warn you."

The officer got back into his Land Rover and drove down to the barrier.

Wilderness said, "What kept you?"

Frank said, "Does it matter? I'm here now. Hands gladdened. Babies kissed."

§152

Wilderness and Eddie sat in the truck in the no-man's-land between the Western and Eastern barriers. Helmstedt behind them, Marienborn ahead of them.

Through the windscreen they could see Frank talking to the DDR border guards. They couldn't hear him, and Frank's big gestures seemed all the louder perceived in silence.

"Y'know," said Eddie. "Making him earn his keep might be a good thing, but his German was always crap. Right now he could be racking up ten years in a gulag for all three of us or selling his mother into slavery."

Frank was heading back to the truck.

Wilderness got out to meet him.

"They . . . they need to see inside. Just a formality."

"Nothing doing, Frank."

"It's completely kosher. They check the load, then they seal the truck with one of those clip-on tags they have . . . which guarantees no one else will mess with us between here and Berlin. After all, we both know how many times these guys can pull you over on the autobahn and ask for bribes."

"Are you sure you got that right?"

"Sure I'm sure."

"If they get to open the truck, they'll just help themselves. Do they know what's in it?"

"Not yet, but—"

"But nothing. If they get the truck open they'll rob us blind."

"So, what's a few cases of wine? We kiss a few babies, we lick a couple of asses . . . we give away a case or two."

"You are, against the very grain of your infinitely cynical nature, being naïve. They'll steal half of it and call it a tax. And every VoPo, every Stasi between here and Berlin will be pissed on vintage claret before we even get there."

"So what do you want me to do? You're leaving me fuck all options here, kid."

"I want you to earn your keep."

"You tell me that more often than Bob Hope sings 'Thanks for the Memory.'"

"Get me a phone line to Yuri."

"What? Jeezus H. Christ, Joe. There've been no phone lines from here to the East since . . . since . . . "

"Since 1952. I know. Find a way. Turn the car around. Get back to Helmstedt. Find a hotel for us . . . and find Yuri."

§153

Hotel Öde, Helmstedt

It was early evening the next day before anything changed.

Frank came into the bar, grinning—he grinned a lot—as though it was all an adventure, something to make the years roll away.

"I found him. He'll call you in five minutes. There's a phone booth in the lobby just off to the right. It's a lousy line, but what can you expect? If it had a horse this place might just qualify as a one-horse town. The call's routed through our embassy in Switzerland . . . then Belgrade and finally reaches our little Russian chum in Berlin. It could be quicker just to stand in the street and yell."

Yuri's first words were, "So, Frank is back. I can imagine how happy that makes you."

"I don't have to live with him for long."

"You don't have to live with him at all. Say the word and he can join Herr Wölk."

"No. There's a queue of people wanting to murder Frank. Let's not jump it. Besides, we shoot a CIA officer, someone's bound to come looking for him."

"As you wish. I cannot budge those bastards at Marienborn. They're Germans, after all . . . just a bunch of bandits. No ideology but theft. I could draft Russians in, but it's very public. It would attract far too much attention. So, I want to move you to another checkpoint. Ellrich."

Ellrich was further south, two or three hours away.

"There's no road crossing at Ellrich, Yuri. It's a railway line."

"Exactly. Let's see the Germans argue with an armour-plated Red Army train. Be there at midnight. I'll have everything in place."

§154

Ellrich

They'd passed through Bad Harzburg, skirted the Brocken, with dreams of witches in flight. The temperature had plummeted and it was darker than was imaginable. The headlights picked out a solitary British Frontier Service officer, buttoned up in his navy blue greatcoat, waving a lantern at them, less the guardian of an international frontier than a signalman on a branch line in Dorset.

"Mr. Holderness?"

Wilderness reached for his ID, but the officer said, "You're expected," and waved them on.

"Expected where?" said Eddie. "Even on full beam I can't see a sodding thing. There's nothing out there but a thousand miles of barbed bloody wire. *Mehr Licht, mehr Licht!*"

The magic of the word—no sooner had he said it than a bang cut the silence and the darkness lit up with a dozen arc lights, night become day, an island of brilliance in a sea of nothingness, and they found themselves facing a massive steam engine, recumbent on the tracks, purring like a giant cat . . . a gleaming red star on the smokebox door, a chain of armoured coaches coupled behind it, a gun turret at the end of the chain . . . and a miasma of steam curling off it to settle in silky ribbons around the steel wheels.

"Bloody Norah," said Eddie. "I reckon we've stumbled into the plot of *Doctor Zhivago.*"

The British officer waved his lantern again, on into no-man's-land. As the truck bumped over the railway lines Russian soldiers sprang out of darkness to surround it.

A uniformed captain leapt onto the running board.

"We're transferring everything to the train. Pull up by the second coach, and my men will unload for you. The general is waiting on the other side. Who's the idiot in the yellow Citroën?"

§155

They went through the inner gates into the DDR, walking on the railway sleepers. The watchtowers passed a roving searchlight beam across them. There was little to see. Not so much a place as the remains of a place. Almost everything levelled to dust. The one surviving building, a single-storey brick blockhouse missing its doors and windows, had been sliced in two by the inner frontier fence—and the half in no-man's-land bulldozed. It stood at the edge of the East, a jagged line of broken brick, presenting its scars to the West. If Wilderness had not known where they were he would never have guessed from looking at the scene around him. It was a ruin. And Germany was still peppered with so many ruins.

The Russian captain pointed to the gap in the wall where the door had been.

"The general will see you now."

Frank muttered, "Airs and fuckin' graces. He's a KGB spook, not my fuckin' dentist."

Yuri was standing, hands outstretched, in front of a roaring pot-bellied stove, wrapped in a winter overcoat, sable collar drawn up to his chin. The door of the stove was open—yellow flames catching them all in a flickering ribbon of light.

Frank said, "For Chrissake, Yuri, this place is fucking freezing. Why do we have to meet in here? It may not be my idea of the Chattanooga choo choo, but that looks like a nice, warm train you have out there."

Yuri turned to look at them, expressionless, then back to the fire.

"Do you have any idea where we are?"

"Yeah—the middle of fuckin' nowhere."

Wilderness said, "We're in Juliushütte, you idiot. What's left of it."

"So?"

"It was a concentration camp, Frank. Liberated by the US Army in 1945 . . . or were you looking the other way at the time?"

"Sure. Fine. Whatever. Is there a point being made here that I'm missing?"

Yuri moved away from the fire, pulled on his gloves slowly, spoke slowly.

"The next time one of your politicians decides to call the Berlin Wall a demonstration of the failures of the communist system, the next time he wonders out loud why we call it an anti-fascist barrier, remember this. Twenty thousand people died here. Many of them Russian POWs. Otto Brinkmann, the commandant, was captured by your troops in 1945. In 1947 you sentenced him to life in Landsberg Prison. And in 1958 you freed him. Who knows where he is now? A man in his fifties . . . an executive of Krupp or VW? A man prospering under the new regime in the West? Or perhaps he has gone even further west, to Madison Avenue, to sell us shit for toothpaste?"

"War's over, Yuri. The USA stopped fighting it in 1945. As for the 'new regime' as you call it. If it had been left to us, we'd've put Germany back together long ago. You fucked that up in '48. I don't care that a handful of old Nazis are still out there somewhere. If we'd shot them all the West would be in as big a mess as the East. Nothing would work. And thanks for the dig at Madison Avenue—really snide."

It was as though Yuri had not heard him.

"This man, Brinkmann . . . one day, not long before his capture, came across a prisoner so desperate for food he had taken a knife to a corpse. Brinkmann's response was not to stop him, or to feed him . . . it was to have salt and pepper brought out to the cannibal . . . and he watched as the beast ate the testicles of the dead man.

"The next time you want to reinstate a Nazi, just remember this."

"Oh. I get it. Is this all about Wölk? Is that it? That was twenty years ago."

Wilderness said nothing.

Yuri said, "Let us go now. Too many ghosts among the ashes."

§156

Two o'clock in the morning.

The train crawled across the DDR. A roar of steam and smoke, steel wheels rattling on steel rails. And, Wilderness guessed, an average speed of less than twenty miles an hour.

He relished the anachronistic luxury—a 1913 private coach, built, Yuri said, for one grand duke or another, but never used. Plush upholstery in crimson and royal-blue velvet . . . its own dining room . . . its own kitchen . . . its own cook.

Yuri had served dinner.

Excused himself with, "I am old boys, I need sleep far more than I need food. Enjoy. Order whatever you wish."

Roast chicken. Parsnips. A bottle or two of Château Smith Haut Lafitte '45.

"Has he opened the stash already?" Frank asked.

"Wrong chateau, wrong year."

"Thank God for that. I mean . . . Château Smith. Got to be fake."

"Frank if you can't say anything intelligent, try saying nothing."

"OK. Check this out for smarts. The man is a hypocrite. They're all hypocrites. He takes potshots at capitalism . . . and he wines and dines like a fat cat. All the goddamn perks. His own private train? Let me say that again for emphasis. His own *private* train. Back home only the president has a setup like this. And no one's used it since Roosevelt."

"Perhaps it's Russian hospitality. And he isn't wining and dining. We are."

"Perhaps it's Russian greed. Don't kid yourself. He won't be donating ten thousand bottles of claret to charity."

As the waiter brought dessert, Eddie got up and walked to the back of the coach.

Wilderness found him on the open-air platform, in front of the gun turret, watching Germany crawl by.

"What are you doing?"

"Wishing I smoked."

A pause. A deep breath. A portent.

"You know. I was actually relieved when you and Frank left Berlin in '48. When you finally got back to England I was happy to know you. When I moved to London in '56 happy to be friends again. But I tell you, Joe, this is straining our friendship. I'm not sure how much more of life I can take with Mr. Larger-Than-Life."

"It's almost over. When we get to Berlin . . ."

"At this speed will we ever get to Berlin?"

"When we get to Berlin. I call London. Tomorrow, they stick Alleyn on a plane. I meet him off it at Gatow. We wait till it's dark, drive to Staaken, do the swap. And it's over. Frank takes his fifty grand and buggers off back to America."

"I'd like to believe you. Joe. Really I would. But he's the bad penny. He'll always turn up just when you don't want him to."

Wilderness weighed up Yuri's offer to kill Frank. Silently. Momentarily. And rejected it again.

§157

Wilderness persuaded Eddie to sleep, but shunned sleep himself. He watched the train turn south through Weimar, and around dawn it swung north again to pass Leipzig. And there it sat for four hours. It was two in the afternoon before the train was skirting south Berlin and close to four and by the time it pulled into the old Ost-Güterbahnhof—another semi-derelict site, sprawling between the tracks that led into the Ostbahnhof and the east bank of the Spree.

Frank looked at his watch.

"Fourteen hours to travel a hundred and twenty miles. What does that average at?"

"I don't care, and nor should you. You didn't get your hands dirty. As ever someone did the hump and carry for you."

"Is he going to pay us now?"

"That wasn't the deal. We hand over Liubimov, he hands over Masefield . . . then we get paid."

"Meanwhile he gets to keep the stash?"

"Y'know, Frank. There are times I think you don't trust Yuri."

§158

RAF Gatow, Berlin

Wilderness spotted his mistake almost at once. When Nerk from Special Branch led Alleyn down the steps from the Lockheed Hercules handcuffed.

Three o'clock in the afternoon. A bright, clear winter's day. Enough light for any paparazzo with a long lens to photograph the two of them arriving "in chains."

"Did you board at Brize Norton like this?"

"Standard procedure, sir."

"Bugger procedure. Did it ever occur to you as the shoe leather and knuckle dusters of the Secret Intelligence Service, that this might be a secret? Get the cuffs off now!"

Alleyn rubbed at his wrist, politely thanked Nerk for his freedom.

"Please explain the problem, Joe."

"Photographers, Bernard. If they spotted the two of you at Brize Norton or if they spotted you here . . . then two and two will readily make four and Staaken will be crawling with the buggers when we hand you back. Not what I want. Not what Bogusnik wants. Not what anyone wants. Come on. Back into Berlin. We've taken a suite at the Kempinski. You may have to cool your heels for a bit while I think up Plan B."

§159

"I need the bridge."

"What?"

"Staaken is compromised. The silly sods back in London shipped Alleyn out in handcuffs, in the middle of the day. God knows how many people have worked out what we're about to do, but most of them will be waiting for us."

"So . . . you're saying I have to 'earn my keep' yet again? Don't mince words, Joe, just spit it out."

"OK, Frank, earn your keep. Get on to your people. Tell them we want to do the exchange from the American Sector to Potsdam. Across the bridge, tonight. Minimum military presence. You can tell them who I am, but Alleyn's name stays secret and so does Masefield's."

"There. Wasn't so hard was it? All you have to do is ask your Uncle Frank. Consider it done."

"Fuck you, Frank."

"And you'll handle General Gutbucket?"

"I'll have to go East. Could take a couple of hours. It's not as if I can just pick up a phone and call him, any more than I could at Helmstedt."

"Well, who cut the phone lines? Us or them?"

"Just do it, Frank."

$160

It was after six when Wilderness left the Kempinski to drive into the Russian Sector. Delves's assistant Gretchen was coming in as he was going out. They met on the pavement.

"Ah, glad I caught you. You didn't come into the office today and I think you might want to see this."

She handed him a decode.

"It came for you last night. I'm not allowed to sit on triple *p* messages."

XXXPettiferLON to HoldernessBER.PPP/4772XXX

YOUR WIFE CALLED. I TRANSCRIBE WITH ALL
EXPLETIVES AND PUNCTUATION AS INSTRUCTED.
ALICE.

WHERE THE FUCKING HELL ARE YOU? FOUR DAYS YOU
SAID! FOUR FUCKING DAYS! IT'S BEEN TEN FUCKING
DAYS ALREADY! I'M BRINGING THE GIRLS UP ON MY
OWN! YOU'RE NEVER BLOODY HERE! YOU COMPLETE
AND UTTER FUCKING BASTARD, WILDERNESS!

"Will there be any reply?"

§161

Yuri said, "It makes no difference. A shorter trip for me. But it's over
water. I suggest you wrap up well, Joe."

"I'd like to see Masefield. Explain the change of plan to him."

"Of course. He's still where you left him. He's been reading all day
every day since your box of books arrived."

Out in the corridor Pavel was stuck on a straight-backed dining
chair, reading, lips moving.

"Что значит *paraphernalia*?" he asked Wilderness.

What does "paraphernalia" mean? Wilderness tilted the book up
to see the cover. *Our Man in Havana* by Graham Greene. One of the
books he had shipped out to Masefield. Not perhaps his first choice
as an English primer.

"Stuff, clutter, things. Although I think it originally had something
to do with a dowry. It would be something like принадлежности in
Russian."

"Ah. 'Stooff.' Such a good word. So much simpler than принадлежности.
'Stooff.' I may get to like English after all. You want Geoffrey? He's in
there with all his *stooff*."

Masefield was staring at the wall. A half-finished jigsaw on the rug at
his feet—the Tower of London, complete with Beefeaters and ravens.

"Almost time, Geoffrey. Alleyn's in West Berlin."

Masefield's head jerked as though Wilderness had snapped him out
of reverie.

"You've seen Bernard Alleyn?"

Wilderness sat opposite him. Caught what he saw as a hint of nutti-ness in his eyes. Dismissed it as nerves. After all, why would Masefield not be nervous?

"Yes. I picked him up at Gatow a couple of hours ago."

"How is he?"

The question was gently startling. Masefield was asking a question it had not occurred to Wilderness to ask. How was Bernard Alleyn?

"He looks a lot better than he did when I got him out of the Scrubs a while back. I suppose you'd say he's lost his prison pallor."

"And of course, I haven't."

"Not yet, no. But you'll be free soon . . ."

"How soon?"

"It would have been just about now, but I'm afraid there's been a delay. It'll be more like eleven o'clock. And it'll be on the Glienicke Bridge. Bogusnik will drive you out. We'll exchange in the middle. It's . . . traditional."

"You couldn't just take me back with you now?"

"There are rules, Geoffrey."

"You've never struck me as being the kind of man who gave much thought to rules."

"There's too much at stake not to in this instance. I suggest you pack."

"Pack what? I own nothing. I've read all the books you sent. The chap outside is working his way through them now. I have nothing, and the really odd thing is that having nothing seems a bit like being free."

"No . . . 'stuff'?"

"Quite. No 'stuff.'"

Wilderness got up to leave.

"Then I'll see you in Potsdam. There's only one rule. Do exactly what you're told. Say nothing, do nothing unless I or Bogusnik tell you."

"Will there be guns?"

Wilderness pondered the question. Remembered his first conversa-tion with Masefield. "A spy is not a spy without his gun."

"Of course there'll be guns."

"Ah . . . as if I wasn't a bundle of nerves already."

§162

The bridge across the Havel at Glienicke had a more formal name—the Bridge of Unity, but few would ever call it by that optimistic title, and certainly no Berliner would.

Under moonlight it looked grimmer than ever, a chiaroscuro of light and dark, everything starkly monochrome, black rather than its daylight dirty green, a couple of Bismarck-era guardian statues reminiscent of Berlin's taste for the pompous, a striped, cantilevered barrier and a sign in four languages warning that the American Sector ended at the middle of the bridge. As if anyone could forget. As if anyone could make that mistake.

Two West Berlin coppers and three US military, a captain and two grunts, were waiting for them at the barrier. Wilderness approached, Frank just behind him, Eddie and Alleyn standing by the car, keeping distance.

"I was expecting Mr. Delves," the captain said to Wilderness.

"You got me, Holderness, MI6."

"We liaise with Mr. Delves. He should be here."

"He had to stay home and wash his ego."

"I'm sorry?"

Frank whipped out his identity card and said, "Shine your flashlight on this, kid, and then just do as the man says."

The captain took a moment.

"All right. Colonel McKenna? Which one's the prisoner?"

Alleyn raised his hand, like a child in school.

"OK. I'm not happy about this. I mean, we got very little notice. But OK. Now, am I to expect any trouble?"

Wilderness shook his head.

"If there's trouble I'll handle it. You don't set foot on the bridge, whatever happens."

"And how many of you are going up to the line?"

"Just me and the prisoner. Now can we get on with it?"

The captain turned to the two privates, made an upwards gesture with his right hand, and the barrier rose.

"McKenna?" Wilderness said to Frank sotto voce. "You look about as Scottish as spaghetti vongole. And how long have you been a colonel?"

"Who cares. Just do it, Joe. And watch the sarcasm. He doesn't get it. Not all Americans are like me."

"Thank God for that."

Wilderness turned to Alleyn.

"Bernard? You ready?"

Alleyn came forward, stood next to Wilderness.

"Would it matter if I weren't?" he said.

"Not a damn, Bernard, not a damn."

The wind off the water was icy. Icy but appropriate.

Yuri stood a foot or so inside the DDR. Whoever was backing him up, Germans or Russians, he'd left at the far gates. Wilderness could just make them out, perhaps five, perhaps six of them. Masefield was about fifteen feet behind Yuri, away to the left, a small suitcase at his feet—the "stuff" he said he didn't have. He was wrapped up fit for Shackleton in Antarctica, a rabbit fur Russian hat on his head and thick mittens on his fingers.

Wilderness wished he had a sable hat like Yuri's, so much classier than rabbit, wished he was wearing mittens or gloves—his fingertips would turn blue the second he took his hands from his pockets. But Yuri wasn't wearing gloves either—his left hand sunk in his overcoat pocket, his right toying with a button. Gloves and guns were a recipe for a blunder. How to shoot yourself in the foot in one easy move.

Wilderness showed his hands, the open gesture, and felt the sting of frost at once. He stood opposite Yuri, less than three feet away. The four men on the bridge in perfect symmetry. Two knights and a two rooks upon a chessboard.

"We can't go on meeting like this, Yuri."

"Joe, Joe, always the jokes."

"Let's do it, then."

Yuri beckoned to Masefield, Wilderness to Alleyn.

Masefield took five steps forward and then stopped, staring straight at Alleyn. Wilderness turned. Alleyn had not moved.

"Bernard, for fuck's sake."

Still, Alleyn did not move.

Yuri said, "I thought you were ready?"

"Gimme a moment, Yuri."

Wilderness walked up to Alleyn, put himself between Alleyn and Yuri, back turned, voice subdued.

"For fuck's sake, Bernard. What is the bloody problem? We've been preparing for this for months. Don't give me first-night nerves and don't come the prima donna on me."

"I'm not sure I understood a word of that. But . . . I'm not going."

"What?"

"I won't cross. You can't make me. You don't have the authority."

"Bernard, I have the authority to blow your bloody head off if I so choose!"

"But you won't."

He was almost smiling as he said it, and Wilderness knew in his bones it had been a mistake to get to "know" Bernard Alleyn.

"Probably not. But Yuri will, and he doesn't need any authority. He *is* authority."

"Joe, take me back to England, lock me up and throw away the key. I'm not going back to Russia."

"Why tell me now? Why not this afternoon? Why not last month?"

"Perhaps it has something to do with my first sight of a real Russian in God knows how long?"

"Jesus Christ. Stay put. Do not take so much as single step backwards, or so help me, Bernard, if Yuri doesn't shoot you I bloody well will."

Wilderness walked back to the line. Yuri's eyes reading his face.

"So?"

"I can't get him any closer, Yuri."

Yuri stopped playing with his buttons, flipped one loose, parted his coat and unclipped the flap of the holster at his waist, where, in better days, he had kept his pipe. Now he drew out a Makarov 9mm and pointed it at Alleyn.

"Cross. I order you, cross!"

Alleyn sunk his hands deep in his overcoat pockets and stared back at him in silence.

"No man, no deal!"

"What do you mean, no bloody deal?" Wilderness said. "Yuri, I can't make him cross. He's your bloke. I agreed to bring him to the border.

That's all I can do. You can shoot him. I can't fuckin' shoot him. I'd get bleedin' well court-martialled!"

"No man, no deal, no money!"

"Money?" Wilderness heard Masefield say—he'd almost forgotten about Masefield—"What money?"

"No money!"

"Yuri. Where's the fuckin' money?"

"Your man has the money. But unless Comrade Liubimov crosses over, you get nothing. Ничего не получите."

"I have the money?" Masefield said.

"That wasn't the deal, Yuri."

And Wilderness watched as Masefield knelt down, cast off his mittens and opened the brown suitcase he had carried to the line with him, and saw the wind catch a dozen hundred-dollar bills and toss them in the air like dead leaves.

Then he saw as through a windowpane of streaked glass Masefield hefting the case, and with a swing of his arm he had hurled it high over the side of the bridge. The case spun like a bowled cricket ball, scattered its contents into the air, and all around them green snow fell as a hundred and fifty thousand dollars blew into the night. Then the splash as the empty case landed in the lake. Then the silence, broken only by the bird-like fluttering of falling money, wings against the windowpane. It had looked unreal. It felt unbelievable. He had done it. He hadn't done it. He had done it.

Yuri turned slowly, took his gun off Alleyn, and pointed it at Masefield.

"I don't care. Shoot me," was all Masefield said.

Wilderness drew his Browning and levelled it at Yuri.

Slowly Yuri swung his arm around until they faced each other, eye to eye and gun to gun.

Behind them a clatter of boots as soldiers from each side began to run across the bridge. With his gun in his right hand pointed squarely at Yuri's forehead Wilderness gently patted air with his left, waving the soldiers back. Yuri did the same, and neither side advanced any further. Wilderness and Yuri stood motionless, the tall man and the short man . . . looking into each other's eyes.

"Well, Joe?"

"Well, Yuri. Another fine mess."

A few feet away Masefield and Alleyn, the short man and the tall man, also looked into each other's eyes, and there they could see themselves.

And the men holding guns could not.

§163

They left Eddie at the Kempinski, to "guard" the silent, unthreatening Bernard Alleyn. Wilderness wondered if he'd ever speak again. All the way back from Potsdam he'd sighed the sighs of a maiden in the throes of poetic *Sehnsucht* but said nothing. But then neither had anyone else. Eddie drove. Frank sat next to Eddie and stared through the windscreen. All Wilderness could see was the back of Frank's head, and if the back of any head could convey expression this one would surely say "seething rage."

Then, the remaining *Schieber*s gathered at Erno's apartment on Grünetümmlerstraße.

Once inside, little or nothing would make Frank shut up.

"Tell me, Joe. Do you wax your fingertips every fucking morning just so money won't stick to them? What is it with you? Every chance you get you blow. It's like money was your Kryptonite. I give you fifty thousand dollars for Marte Mayerling. You blow it. You have fifty thousand coming to you for this caper. You blow it—and worse you blow my fifty thousand along with it. I never thought I'd say this about you. You impressed from the start way back in '47 . . . you were the Cockney kid who thought big, you were the guy who was going to make us all rich—but kid, let's face it, you are a loser! A two-time fucking loser. I am not hanging around to see us go under a third time, because nobody floats third time around. Consider me gone."

But he wasn't gone. He was still standing there. Puffed up with his own anger. A fat, lazy slob of a man in a Saks Fifth Avenue suit. Wilderness caught him under the chin with a right hook and decked him.

"Проиграем мы все."

Frank stayed down, sat on his backside rubbing his jaw.

"What's that supposed to mean, you cocksucker?"

Wilderness knelt down. Face-to-face. Frank wasn't going to hit him back. Frank knew damn well he'd never win a fistfight or a gun fight with Wilderness.

"Проиграем мы все. Everybody loses. Get this through your thick head, Frank. This isn't about you. *Everybody* loses. Eddie loses fifty fuckin' grand. I lose fifty fuckin' grand. Alleyn goes back to the fuckin' Scrubs . . . and what in God's name becomes of Masefield?"

"Should I care? The little bastard just tossed our money in the Havel."

§164

"Erno. I need another gun and another passport."

"I still have your Walther."

"The one I shot Marte Mayerling with? No. Something traceless. Something that's never shot anyone."

Erno disappeared into the back room and emerged clutching a Smith & Wesson.

Wilderness laid his Baby Browning on the mantelpiece. The key to the Monbijou–Tiergarten tunnel was still hanging on its nail, where he'd left it two years ago.

"You're going east?"

"Thinking about it, Erno."

He took the key off the wall. It weighed more than his pistol. It weighed more than memory. He put it back.

"No. Why would I ever want to go down there again? What have you got for me?'

"Smith and Wesson 52. Untraceable, as you requested."

Wilderness turned it over in his hand.

"Silencer?"

"Sorry, Joe. No can do. The magazine is full, but holds only five cartridges. .38 Specials. Much more stopping power than your Browning, and five is all I have, so . . ."

"'S'OK, Erno. I wasn't planning on shooting anyone, let alone five times. If I fire it once I reckon I'm dead. It's just . . ."

"I know. A precaution."

"More than that. Not having a gun would be like . . . like going out without trousers."

"The passport's another matter . . . I need time. If you're going east tonight or tomorrow, forget it."

"I've made my mind up. I'm going tonight. I'll go legit, through Checkpoint Charlie on my own passport. A fake's too risky after all the times I've been through this year. And they can't refuse a diplomatic. I'll take my chances, as I doubt Yuri has been coherent enough the last few hours to tip them off. No, the passport's not urgent. I'll give you the details."

"If I work through the night, perhaps . . ."

"Like I said. Not urgent."

§165

In the stairwell a dark figure was waiting for him. Even wrapped up for winter, a heavy overcoat and a headscarf, he knew her at once. She turned as she heard the stairs creak.

"Joe?"

"Nell."

"I was just at the Kempinski."

"Then you don't need me to say anything. Eddie never could keep a secret. It's why he makes a lousy spy."

"If it weren't for your friends, would I ever know what you were up to? In 1963 did you ask for me? No—if it wasn't for Erno I would have known nothing. And if it wasn't for Eddie I would know nothing now."

"You never want to see me, Nell, so what is it you think you need to know?"

"You can't walk way from this."

"That's exactly what you told me in 1947. Remember? Rüdiger Wölk? I couldn't walk away from that either. You sit on my shoulder like Jiminy bleedin' Cricket."

"You cannot leave Geoffrey Masefield to the Russians. No more *Hinterbliebenen.*"

The word gave him pause. So deliberately chosen, so complex in its meaning, invoking loss, bereavement, abandonment . . . those left behind The first time he'd hear the word, Erno had mumbled it after half a bottle of Polish vodka, and Wilderness had not heard the 'b,' and had found himself musing on a word that did not exist but was ripe with meaning, *Hinterliebenen...* those behind love... heartbreak added to abandonment. But, then, Frank and Eddie's old nickname for Nell had always been "Breakheart."

"At last, you get to the point. Nell, I've no intention of leaving our Geoffrey behind, and certainly not to Yuri's tender mercy. But . . . let me ask you . . . who am I talking to, Nell Burkhardt or a member of Brandt's staff? You want Geoffrey out; does the mayor's chief of staff want a diplomatic incident? If I get him out will you be celebrating or just handling another diplomatic incident?"

Nell did not even blink at this. A thorough refusal to be chastised.

"Do what you have to do, Joe. Whatever the fallout, I will deal with it."

"How pleasant to have your blessing."

"It gives me no pleasure to be your conscience. It never has."

"Right now my conscience doesn't need you, because my mind was made up half an hour ago. Nell, you can be so fuckin' po-faced. And if there's any *Hinterbliebenen* it's us not Masefield. We're the *Hinterbliebenen,* Nell. You and me, and we have been since 1948."

He stepped past her into the street.

He did not look back.

He'd been unnecessarily cruel and he knew it.

He did not look back.

He kicked himself all the way to Bleibtreustraße, but he did not look back. If he lived though the night he would have a lifetime in which to look back, a lifetime for Nell Burkhardt to tumble into his dreams.

§166

Wilderness got Dickie Delves out of bed.

"I need the car."

"Eh? What? I thought Gretchen gave you keys to the BMW?"

"It's your car I need. The Austin-Healey."

Delves looked flummoxed.

"Not quite with you here, old man."

"I'm going east. I need something with a bit more oomph."

It was pleasing to know he had guessed right—that "oomph" would be the word Delves would understand, and that it probably answered all the questions Delves might now not bother to ask.

Still in his pyjamas, Delves gave him the keys and followed him down to the street, where the preposterous toy in British Racing Green was parked next to the sedate, anonymous BMW.

"There's a couple of things you need to know. First off, only three gears, with overdrive on second and top, but you can manually—"

"Just tell me how fast it goes, Dick."

"Factory specs will tell you 106, but I've tweaked it here and there and had 114 out of her on the autobahns, and nought to sixty in eight seconds. Look, Joe, you're not planning anything . . . well . . . foolish, are you? I mean . . . you will bring the old girl back in one piece, won't—"

To slam the car into gear and roar away seemed to Wilderness to be the only way to stop Delves talking.

By the time he got to the zoo, the rain that had loomed since dusk had burst upon the city, hammering down on the canvas roof of the car. This was good, rain was good, rain was what he wanted.

At Checkpoint Charlie the border guards were nonchalant. They'd seen him before; they'd seen the car before, just not in this combination. It was obvious nothing of what had happened on the Glienicke Bridge had got out yet. Yuri was telling no one, and that meant the game was still in play.

§167

There was no guard outside the Adlon, just a doorman sheltering from the storm who paid no attention to him. Wilderness took the stairs. He'd have the element of surprise, he told himself, as they would not be expecting him or any hostile force inside the safety of the Adlon, but there would be no element of surprise in stepping out of a stuttering, creaking lift. He'd expected Pavel or Arkady to be by the lift door on the fifth floor, but the corridor was empty.

Wilderness could hear nothing from inside Yuri's room. Gun in his right hand, he turned the doorknob as gently as he could with his left. Surprise had no part in it. Yuri was alone in the room, perched on the edge of an armchair, and didn't even look up. Wilderness aimed his gun at Yuri, uncertain whether he would ever be able to pull the trigger.

Softly, "Yuri."

Yuri did not look up.

Wilderness walked up to him, knelt down. The glassy blue eyes seemed to be focussed on his left hand. A small pill nestling in the palm, the tin open on the side table, half a dozen pills scattered. And Yuri dead.

He set his gun down on the table. Felt for a pulse in Yuri's neck. Looked into his eyes. Yuri dead.

He thought back to the bridge. How Yuri had turned red in the face, had tried to keep his gun on Wilderness but had surrendered to the pain and clumsily clapped his right hand, still holding the pistol, to his left arm. He had groaned, he had sworn.

"Черт возьми! Еще раз . . . "

Oh fucking hell. Not again.

And he had wilted.

Wilderness had holstered his gun, crossed the line, but before he could reach Yuri, Masefield had caught the little man, one hand supporting his shoulders, the other tossing the pistol aside. Then he had reached into the pocket of Yuri's overcoat for the tin of pills. He held it out to Wilderness.

"It's nitroglycerin, and I don't have enough hands."

Wilderness had slipped a nitro pill under Yuri's tongue.

Yuri had breathed, sighed, cursed again.

"Другой прекрасный беспорядок, Стэнли."

Another fine mess, Stanley.

Wilderness had said, "Я же вам сказал."

I told you so.

Masefield had beckoned on the Russian soldiers at the southern end of the bridge, who had been rooted to the spot, and had turned Yuri to face them. Then he had steered him step by slow step in their direction. A man with a giant toddler learning how to walk. Wilderness thought he heard Yuri muttering his name, "Joe, Joe, Joe." Or it could just have been monosyllabic sighs and curses. Or it could have been angels in the winter wind . . . "Joe, Joe, Joe."

He had looked behind him. Alleyn was ten or twelve feet away. Hands still sunk in his overcoat pockets, eyes on Yuri's retreating back.

Wilderness had walked past him, muttered, "What the hell are you waiting for, Bernard?" and walked on, back into the American Sector, back into West Berlin.

It was entirely up to Alleyn whether he followed or not . . .

"Joe, Joe, Joe," whispered on the wind, and hundred-dollar bills carpeted his stepping westward.

Now a voice behind him said, "Он умер?"

Is he dead?

"Yes. Died reaching for his pills."

Arkady Vasilievich drew level, standing over him. He had a Makarov in his hand, but it dangled at the end of his arm pointing at nothing.

Wilderness said, "I'm going to move my right hand. I'm not reaching for the gun. I'm going to close his eyes."

The Russian squatted down next to him, looked into Yuri's eyes much as he had done himself.

"Then do it. You were his friend. I just worked for him."

Wilderness reached out and with the thumb and largest finger of his right hand closed Yuri's window on the world.

They stood up. The Russian was in shirtsleeves, a soft chamois leather holster strap twining itself around his shoulders—he slipped the gun back in.

"Perhaps this is timely. It pays to know when to die."

"Will you or I be that lucky?"

"Who knows? I doubt you would have been the one to shoot him anyway."

"Probably not."

"And you have come for your Mr. Masefield?"

"Of course."

"Then you had better take him. I'm afraid I have my hands full just now. I have to get the general's body back to Moscow, which cannot be a secret—died in the line of duty after all—a state funeral to follow, no doubt. But I also have ten thousand bottles of claret which must be a secret. I haven't room or time for Mr. Masefield."

"You're keeping the wine?"

A wry smile from the Russian.

"You have a plan for getting it back to the West?"

"'Fraid not . . . the plan includes just me and Masefield."

"Then I say again, take him. He's yours."

The Russian called out to his partner.

"Pavel. Tell Masefield to get ready!"

Pavel's head appeared through the open door connecting the rooms.

"Что?" What?

"The general is dead. Tell Masefield he's got two minutes."

Again, "Что?"

Wilderness stepped aside. Let Pavel get a look at Yuri.

"Только добро погибает юным."

Only the good die young.

"Just do it, Pavel."

Wilderness pointed at his gun.

"OK?"

"Yes. OK. Just try not to shoot anyone between here and the West. I don't want any dead border guards. Even if they are only fucking Germans. We already have a diplomatic incident on our hands just explaining what happened on the bridge."

"Or," said Wilderness. "What didn't happen."

"Liubimov? You're welcome to him. If he doesn't want to come home . . . fukkim. No Order of Lenin, no dacha, no state pension. Fukkim."

"Masefield will take some explaining too."

Arkady Vasilievich looked at Yuri, looked back to Wilderness, a plot cohering at the tip of his tongue.

"Well . . . you stormed in here, waving your gun around, scared the general to death and abducted our prisoner, didn't you?"

"Yes," said Wilderness. "I'm sure that must have been it."

§168

Wilderness had left Delves's car further down Wilhelmstraße, close to the corner of Französische Straße.

"Get in."

"Where are we going?"

"North, over the Marschall Bridge and out through the Invalidenstraße checkpoint. The Russians will have to report your escape simply to cover their own arses. The Germans will expect us to go south to Checkpoint Charlie. So we'll go north. I reckon we have about ten minutes before the balloon goes up."

"Can we get there in ten minutes?"

"Trust me, Geoffrey. Get in and trust me."

Three blocks along Französische Straße Wilderness turned left into Friedrichstraße about four hundred yards north of Checkpoint Charlie. There was no traffic. The rain was getting heavier and the streetlights began their flickering dance, which seemed so characteristic of life in the East. Everything worked some of the time. Nothing worked all of the time.

Wilderness floored the accelerator. Under the railway tracks at the Friedrichstraße Bahnhof, across the Spree, to bring the car to a halt a few feet from the turning into Invalidenstraße.

"Why have we stopped?"

"Geoffrey, you're all questions and no answers. Get out. We're folding the roof back."

A strange, if not pointless, feature of the Austin-Healey 100M was that the windscreen folded down onto the bonnet, level with the top of the wooden steering wheel. It was the kind of car that an upper-class English prat would drive wearing goggles and a scarf, rather in the manner of Mr. Toad in *The Wind in the Willows*—but, then, as far as Wilderness was concerned Dickie Delves needed only a few warts to be Mr. Toad.

With the roof tucked away, the windscreen flat, Wilderness walked all around the car, as though weighing it up. Then he let air out of each tyre in turn and Masefield watched the car drop by about an inch.

"Every little helps," Wilderness said. "Now, get behind the seats and keep your head down. As low as you can go. And don't budge until it's all over."

"Until what's all over?"

"Just shut up and do as I say."

"I can't. I'm scared."

"Geoffrey. It's me. Holderness. There's nothing to be scared of."

"I know it's you. And there's everything to be scared of. This scares me. You scare me. You've always scared me."

"Geoffrey. It's not four hours since you dared a KGB general to shoot you."

"That was in another lifetime."

Wilderness said nothing. Got back into the driver's seat, swung the car onto Invalidenstraße, and let it sit, idling.

Checkpoint Charlie had grown hugely in four years. Had spread out to the size of Clapham Junction, as the Russians added traffic filters and barriers so close together that they created a chicane no car could take at speed.

Invalidenstraße was simpler. Constrained by the river ahead of it and the old Army Medical School on the right, which either the Germans or the Russians seemed loth to demolish, there was no way to spread out. It remained a narrow crossing point, perhaps the narrowest, with two simple swing barriers about eighty yards apart, the furthest right on the Sandkrug Bridge itself, where the British Sector began. If they made it, he'd feel far happier explaining to the British than to the French or the Americans. Not that he thought any explanation was required. Not that he had any intention of ever explaining.

A year or two back, a bunch of students had tried to crash through in a bus in broad daylight. They almost made it, but by the time they hit the border barrier the bus was riddled with bullets and veering off course. The walking and wounded had disembarked within two feet of freedom, and the Russians had demanded better precautions. The trees in front of the medical school had been thinned, a second inner barrier had been erected, and something resembling a provincial British bus station had been built between the two, with high, angled, concrete shelters and glaringly hideous sodium lights. It was still the better bet—practically straight, a slight wiggle before the first barrier, but no filtered lanes and no chicane. All he wanted was for the lights to go off. To stop their dance and just give up for a couple of minutes.

The Invalidenstraße checkpoint was "Germans only." At this time of night the guards would be expecting a bit of peace and quiet. The international traffic would be through Checkpoint Charlie, whose motto might as well be "we never close." But, if Invalidenstraße also never closed it certainly slept. They'd be expecting nothing, they'd be dozy and lazy, and on a night like this they'd be sheltering from the storm and whoever drew the short straw would be the lone poor bastard standing out in the rain.

The street lamp above him was already out. The line of lamps ahead of him, trailing away to the checkpoint a quarter of a mile off, were flickering. All he wanted was for them to stop dancing.

There was a crack of lightning bright enough for Wilderness to catch a glimpse of the lone bastard on duty, then all the lamps went out at once.

"Head down. Don't move. Shut up."

He had the car up to sixty in less than eight seconds and at sixty-five he flicked the headlights on. Lone Bastard was caught in the beam like a dopey rabbit. Self-preservation proved the better part of valour, and as the car shot towards the barrier he jumped aside, not even attempting to hoist his sub-machine gun. Wilderness ducked, blind for a second as the car shot under the barrier. Head up. Pushed it to seventy before the second, ducked again and heard the windscreen shatter as the steel arm of the second barrier scraped along it, felt shards and splinters pepper his forehead, found himself blinded by the blood streaming into his eyes . . . and lost control.

The car hit the kerb on the passenger side, spun one hundred and eighty, burst a back tyre on the kerb, spun twice more and came to rest against the railings of the Sandkrug Bridge, facing back into East Berlin.

He sat a moment, tasting blood and silence. Rested his forehead on the broken steering wheel. Wiped the blood from his eyes. Climbed out into the road. Saw figures moving inside a goldfish bowl. West Berlin coppers in their bucket helmets . . . and handful of Tommies . . . and a lieutenant in British Army uniform, mouthing at him—lips moving without sound. Then suddenly he could hear again, a bang inside his head, and realised that the man was calling him a "stupid twat" in German—"*Dumme Fotze, du dumme Fotze!*"

The border guards were squaring off to each other, East to West, West to East, rifle to rifle, across the barrier, but no one fired.

"Yeah," said Wilderness. "I'm sure you're right."

And handed the man his diplomatic identity card. He'd always thought of it as something off a Monopoly board—Get Out Of Jail Free.

The lieutenant wiped the blood from it and shone a torch at the card and then at Wilderness.

"Diplomatic! As in diplomatic bloody incident?"

"Do you know of any other kind?"

"You flash bastards."

"Fuck off."

He turned his back on Wilderness, walked to the barrier waving his arms at the border guards saying, "It's all over. Stop. Stop. Everybody stop!"

Wilderness heard a noise behind him. The sound of a man vomiting. Masefield was on the tarmac behind the car. Wilderness offered him a hand up. He was shaky, trembling, lost.

"Oh God," Masefield said. "You're covered in blood."

"And you're covered in puke, but am I complaining?"

Masefield looked around him, back at the border, at the waving arms and brandished guns, listened for a moment to all the shouting.

"Nothing to be scared of, you said."

"They won't shoot now. Shooting into no-man's-land is one thing, so's shooting *Flüchtling*s in the river. Firing right across the border at British troops . . . they don't want to start World War Three. Give 'em a minute and they'll bugger off."

"What . . . what now?"

"We bugger off as well."

"Where? I mean . . . where can I possibly go now?"

"I don't know where you should go, Geoffrey. It's entirely up to you. The world may not be your oyster but it's sure as hell your pint of whelks."

Wilderness walked away, off the bridge, down Invalidenstraße. A hundred yards on, vision blurred once more by the blood running into his eyes, he knelt down and washed his face in a puddle of rainwater. Once down, the effort of getting up again seemed beyond him. He did not want to linger, he did not want to give Masefield the chance to call out to him while he was still within earshot, he did not want to hear so much as a thank you. He did not want to attract the attention of the West Berlin Police. Telling border guards to fuck off was one thing, tackling regular coppers another. Out past midnight. Covered in blood. Armed. It would take some explaining. The diplomatic identity was both protection and process—a process to be avoided. He dragged himself to his feet and set off in the direction of the Lehrter Stadtbahnhof. It looked like he felt. Once as busy as Waterloo but a ghost of a station since the division of Berlin, caked in grime, its empty spaces sprouting weeds and birch saplings among the broken beer bottles, a no-man's-land entire unto itself . . . but one train still stopped there—the S-Bahn. He paid his thirty pfennigs, rode the S-Bahn, high above dark and drowned Berlin, past the skeletal ruins of the Reichstag, along the edge of the Tiergarten, to Savignyplatz and walked from there back to Erno's.

§169

At Grünetümmlerstraße Erno was still awake. Still at work. He glanced up as Wilderness came in. Looked at the mess he was in, but asked no questions. Flipped his eyepiece back down and hunched over his desk.

"You look as though you might need stitches, Joe."

"I'll live, Erno. Where is everybody?"

"Frank has not been back since you threw him out. Who knows, if we are lucky he may never come back. Eddie phoned from the Kempinski a while ago. No one can get any sleep, so Alleyn has taken Eddie on at chess. I wish him luck. I was never able to beat Eddie at chess. And Nell left you this."

Wilderness turned the envelope over in his hands.

"And this is what exactly?"

"I believe it is her address, the one she has always made me promise never to give you. I wonder what you said to change her mind, but I shall not ask."

Wilderness looked at the three letters on the envelope as though they were written in Linear B . . . J-O-E. Quite incomprehensible. He stuffed it in his pocket, kicked off his shoes, slewed off his mac, and fell onto the sofa.

"And Mr. Masefield, Joe?"

"At large. That's as much as I know and right now as much as I care."

"So . . . Yuri saw sense?"

"Yuri saw nothing. He was dead when I got there."

This made Erno pause. The pen went down, the eyepiece hinged to his spectacles went up.

"Natural causes I hope?"

"Yep. His heart gave out."

"I wonder . . . is this sadness I feel at the passing of a total bastard? And is bastardy ever total?"

"He had his good points. They'll be interred with his bones."

"You know how I met him? At the end of the war. May '45. He was the lover of Nell's mother, and when she died he was Nell's protector. One of us will have to tell her he's dead."

"Yeah. One of us. One day."

"He never asked for anything in return, never laid a hand on her. At a time when everything had its price and the price of everything was sky-high. That was rare."

"Yeah. Well . . . could we save the total bastard's wake till morning? I am *totally* knackered. Erno, I am the walking dead. I have to sleep."

"Take the bed, Joe. I will be up most of the night finishing your passport."

"You got everything you need. Photo and so on? Stuff . . . ?"

"Yes. I have stuff. But you set me a task with all the names. Why so many?"

"Just a whim."

He lurched into the bedroom. Felt the onset of dream or delirium, asleep and awake at the same time. Numbed desire as a muttered mantra

. . .

    I

        need

            sleep.

                I

                    need

                        sleep.

                            I

                                need . . .

                                    . . .

Wilderness slept.

Nell Burkhardt tumbled through his dreams.

An age rolled over.

He woke to find himself clutching the unopened envelope.

And clutching the photograph of Joan and Molly that he kept in his wallet. He'd no memory of taking it out. He propped the envelope and the photograph up side by side on the bedside table. Joan was grinning like an idiot, Molly staring quizzically down the lens with a po-face worthy of Nell Burkhardt.

There was no rush to do anything today . . . if today was the day after and he had not slept two days or a week. There was no rush . . . he might open the envelope later.

After breakfast.

There was no rush . . . he might never open it.

§170

The Irish Sea: December 23

On the ship, *Deirdre of the Sorrows*, crammed with people going home for Christmas, an hour or so out of Liverpool, Alleyn looked at his passport again. It wasn't hard to guess why Joe Holderness had "made" him Irish—he must have rambled on far too much, told Holderness far too much . . . all those visits to his wife's family among the protestant ascendancy, the kith and kin that ran south from Killiney bay all the way to Cork. It was a simple cover and simple covers were to be relished. But why so many names? James Vincent O'Flaherty de Lanier Wilde? Was this Holderness's joke? The plain English of James, the pure Irish of Vincent O'Flaherty, the touch of Norman French in de Lanier . . . the utter outrageousness of Wilde.

Try as he might he could not seem to remember them in the right order.

He tried a mantra—penetrating repetition . . .

James
    Vincent
        O'Flaherty
            de Lanier
                Wilde

And back again . . .

                Wilde
            de Lanier
        O'Flaherty
    Vincent
James

Much as he had done twenty years ago with

Bernard
    Forbes
        Campbell
           Alleyn
           Alleyn
        Campbell
    Forbes
Bernard.

Now, on a whim, he was Wilde.

The moment he was dreading never came. He passed silently and swiftly through customs, to find there was still no passport control. No need at all to recite his list of names.

He stepped out into the Dublin streets, sheathed in all the anonymity of a fake passport and a gabardine mackintosh. A new identity, another identity to add to those he already had.

It was coming on to rain, a grim sky overhead.

"Taxi, sorr?"

He found himself facing a cabbie. Why not?

He climbed in.

The cabbie slung his suitcase in the front rack, and as he slipped into the driving seat leaned over to ask, "Now, sorr, where to?"

Alleyn looked back at the roughly pleasant, smiling face, felt the whiff of whiskey on his breath.

All he knew was what Holderness had told him, that when Kate had finally walked out on him after the trial she had done as she had promised, and taken the girls back to Ireland with her. Holderness had written her address down on a piece of paper for him. Alleyn had not asked how he had obtained such information. Nor had he read what was on the paper. He kept it tightly folded in his wallet. A Pandora's box. All he knew was what Holderness had *told* him, that Kate and his girls were somewhere in Ireland.

"Where to, sorr?"

"I don't know," Alleyn said. "I really don't know."

Tomorrow.

He'd read the address tomorrow.

Pandora's box.

He'd face her wrath tomorrow.

The cabbie stared at Alleyn.

Alleyn stared at the envelope.

"Are you lost, sorr?"

"Yes," said Alleyn. "I do believe I am."

There was no rush . . . he might never open it.

$171

London: December 24

Wilderness answered the doorbell not long after breakfast. A bloke he'd never seen before—Aquascutum overcoat, cashmere scarf, pigskin gloves, not a hair on his young head out of place—was standing by a black cab. The engine was still running, a plume of exhaust trailing in the Christmas cold, a grumpy-looking cabbie stacking cardboard boxes on the doorstep.

"Mr. Holderness? I am Anatoly Ruslanovich Dobrynin. Soviet embassy. Would you sign here please?"

"What is it?"

"I believe it is eighty bottles of Mouton Rothschild '29. There is a note. Here."

Wilderness opened the note.

> Shall we consider this account settled?
> Arkady Vasilievich Anakin

The cabbie gave out one of those contrived London cabman's theatrical sighs that implies that the tip cannot possibly be big enough. The last box was torn at the corner. Wilderness signed the receipt, bent down and pulled out two bottles of claret. Gave one to each of them.

"Please convey my thanks to Arkady Vasilievich, and report that my answer to his question is 'yes.'"

The cabbie hefted his bottle.

"Mowt . . . mowt . . . wot is it?"

"Russian beer, best drunk by the pint. Knock it back as quick as you can and don't let it touch the sides on the way down. It's traditional."

"Right you are, guv'nor, very kind I must say. A merry Christmas to you."

As the cab disappeared at the end of the lane the postman wheeled his bike to Wilderness's door.

"Mornin', Joe. Half a dozen for the missis and just the one for you."

"Has Judy given you your Christmas box?"

"Nah. Not yet."

"Then help yourself to a Russian beer."

"Russian beer, eh? Funny-shaped bottle. What's it taste like?"

"Brown ale."

Wilderness opened the one letter addressed to him.

A Christmas card depicting a wintry scene in Pennsylvania.

Just done my annual week in the shelter to find out if everything works. Claustrophobic and depressing as sin, but I'm ready. Oh boy, am I ready. Armageddon? Bring it on!
Jack Dash

On the mantelpiece stood a clock that had not ticked in years. It still served a purpose. Wilderness stuck letters, postcards and the odd unpaid bill behind it—things he was ignoring yet not quite ignoring. Judy never looked there. She was physically incapable of not opening and answering at once anything addressed to her. It was his mail that sat for days.

Jack Dash's postcard joined a growing stack. He picked up the one right at the back. Plain and brown. His name in Nell's writing. Plain and brown and unopened.

He picked it up. It crossed his mind to open it. Was there ever a time to poke around in the dark recesses of the heart or the dark recesses of Berlin?

He put it back.

Unopened.

A domani.

YOU ARE LEAVING
THE AMERICAN SECTOR
ВЫ ВЫЕЗЖАЕТЕ ИЗ
АМЕРИКАНСКОГО СЕКТОРА
VOUS SORTEZ
DU SECTEUR AMERICAIN
SIE VERLASSEN DEN AMERIKANISCHEN SEKTOR

Stuff

Khrushchev
Not for one minute do I think Nikita Sergeyevich was present when Frieda Schulze jumped on September 25, 1961 . . . but he does say in the second volume of his memoirs (published in the seventies) that curiosity got the better of him and he took a secret tour of West Berlin at about that time. He isn't precise about the date. He concludes, "I did not get out of the car." Yeah, right.

Sillamäe
I've bent the chronology but not by much. It was another twenty years before the plant produced reactor-grade enriched uranium, but it had been producing uranium oxide since the end of the war and by 1950 was a major source of U_3O_8 and by the time of perestroika, and the independence of Estonia, had produced almost 100,000 tonnes of the stuff.

Chelyabinsk
It was a closed area at that time. Nuclear cock-up in the late fifties. It has been termed "the most polluted place on earth." No sooner had I started looking into Chelyabinsk than it was struck by a meteorite. As if they didn't have enough problems. It was, and may still be, a major site for the production of zinc and in the sixties was at the heart of an atomic weapons complex that stretched for miles.

LBJ
I'm deliberately vague with the timetable here. He did visit Berlin just after the wall went up. Robert Caro, a biographer at work on what must be the biggest biography ever written of an American president, doesn't mention the visit . . . hence I felt free to improvise. Chroniclers of the Wall give differing versions; some say he did get to Potsdamer Platz,

some say he didn't . . . and one really does have the line about him skipping out on the US Army's parade to go shopping . . . so I improvise.

U-2

The USA began to fly U-2 spy planes over the USSR in 1956. Ike managed to keep that a secret for four years before one was shot down. The USA keeps its secrets well . . . er . . . not as well as the UK. For two months over 1959–1960 the flights were out of Turkey and piloted by the RAF. We managed to keep this under wraps until 1997. My heart swells with national pride . . . we can keep a secret, we're still on top . . . zzz . . . zzz . . . Britannia Rules the . . . whatever . . . Last Night of the Proms . . . zzz . . . zzz . . . yawn.

Wine

I could not have got the wine remotely right without the assistance of someone who knows a damn sight more about the subject than I do—Tim Hailstone, whose knowledge of vintage claret is only exceeded by his knowledge of Bob Dylan and the Who.

Austin-Healey Incident

This actually happened—twice. Not at Invalidenstraße, but at Checkpoint Charlie. And in an Austin-Healey Frogeye Sprite rather than the model I deploy . . . already forgotten which . . . as I know absolutely nothing about cars and have not attempted to drive one since 1966 . . . all those knobs and pedals . . . so confusing . . .

Indium

Eventually a use was found for indium. It's what makes touch screens possible. At the time of writing there is thought to be between two and five years' supply left, mostly in China. At 0.052 parts per million it is number 16 on the British Geological Survey's 2012 risk list. Prices fluctuate, but, again, at time of writing, I reckon Geoffrey's stash of indium to be worth about $36,300,000.

Acknowledgements

Gordon Chaplin
Sam Redman
Marcia Gamble Hadley
Nick Lockett
Allison Malecha
Tim Hailstone
Elizabeth Graham-Yooll
Sarah Burkinshaw
Peter Blackstock
Elizabeth Cochrane
Morgan Entrekin
Cristina Zadi
Amy Hundley
Claus Litterscheid
Clare Alexander
Joaquim Fernandez
Matias Lopez-Portillo
Stanley Moon
Lesley Thorne
Sarah Teale

Gianluca Monaci
Deb Seager
Cosima Dannoritzer
George Spigot
Sue Freathy
Daphne Meacham
Angela & Tim Tyack
Antonella Piredda
Briony Everroad
Fran Owen
Sue Freathy
Ivo Bufalini
Zoë Sharp
&
Ion Trewin
1943–2015—my editor for over twenty years, who plucked me off the scrap heap, and who died just as I finished this book.